T0150352

# Praise for *Courting Pandemonium*

"You find yourself rooting for the people in this book, and there are some surprising twists. And an ending you can't be prepared for."
— *The Baton Rouge Morning Advocate*

"*Courting Pandemonium* is an extremely funny book."
— *New Orleans City Business*
— *New Orleans Magazine*

"In this zany new novel with more twists than a centipede has legs, Barton keeps readers mesmerized until the final page and demonstrates once again his skill at depicting our crazy world."
— *Library Journal*

"In a basketball setting peopled with feminists and fundamentalists, Barton handles the developing situation with compassion, insight and wisdom. Through his inimitable style, the author shows the reader that not only can victory take on many forms but it also can come when one least expects it."
— *The Abilene Reporter News*

"A funny tale."
— *The Indianapolis News*

"Barton is an original, a novelist who has not delivered what some expected, but has delivered nonetheless."
— *The Atlanta Journal and Constitution*

"*Courting Pandemonium* will appeal to anyone who enjoys a good tale well told. Barton's colorful characters, wit and iconoclastic view of society make this battle of the sexes believable and thoroughly entertaining."
— *The Saint Charles and Geneva Chronicle*

"Thought-provoking and yet refreshingly entertaining, there is not a dull moment in this entire book. *Courting Pandemonium* is heart-warming, insightful, funny and exhibits much wisdom and sensitivity."
— *The Macon Telegraph and News*

# About the Author

In addition to *Courting Pandemonium*, Fredrick Barton is the author of the novels *The El Cholo Feeling Passes*, *Black and White on the Rocks*, and *A House Divided*, which won the William Faulkner Prize in fiction. He is also the author of the collection of essays *Rowing to Sweden* and the jazz opera *Ash Wednesday*. From 1980-2008, he served as the film critic for the New Orleans weekly, *Gambit*. His many awards include a Louisiana Arts Prize; the New Orleans Press Club's annual criticism prize 11 times and its highest honor, the Alex Waller Memorial Award; the Stephen T. Victory Award, the Louisiana Bar Association's prize for writing about legal issues; and the Award of Excellence from the Associated Church Press for his feature essay "Breaches of Faith" about recovery efforts in New Orleans after Hurricane Katrina. Rick received his B.A. from Valparaiso University and earned graduate degrees at UCLA and the Writers Workshop at the University of Iowa. Valparaiso honored his lifetime achievements with an honorary Ph.D. in Humane Letters. Rick has been on the English faculty of the University of New Orleans since 1979 where he has served as Dean of Liberal Arts and as Provost and Vice Chancellor for Academic and Student Affairs. He currently serves as Director of the Creative Writing Workshop, UNO's MFA program in imaginative writing, which, with his colleagues, he founded in 1990.

# Courting Pandemonium

Also by Fredrick Barton

*The El Cholo Feeling Passes*

*Black and White on the Rocks (With Extreme Prejudice)*

*Ash Wednesday*

*A House Divided*

*Rowing to Sweden*

# Courting Pandemonium

Fredrick Barton

With Illustrations Either Hand-Drawn
Or Carefully Traced by the Author

**UNO PRESS**

Printed in the USA.

ISBN: 9781608011018

Copyright © 2013 by Fredrick Barton.

Book and cover design: Lauren Capone

**UNO PRESS**

University of New Orleans Press

unopress.org

For

Joyce Markrid Dombourian, of course

Proofreader, Companion, Fellow Traveler, Friend

and

In Loving Memory of

Peter Mampreh Dombourian, 19201992

Joyce Boyle Dombourian, 1919-2004

V. Wayne Barton, 1925-1997

# Acknowledgments

I am indebted to my administrative co-workers at UNO, Libby Arceneaux, Rebeca Antoine, Judy Scott, Tricia Adams, Bob Cashner, Merrill Johnson, Peter Schock, Dennis McSeveney and Scott Whittenburg, for their daily support over many years; to esteemed UNO creative writing colleagues, Joanna Leake, Joseph Boyden, Amanda Boyden, Barbara Johnson, Neal Walsh, Randy Bates, Richard Goodman, Kay Murphy, Carolyn Hembree, John Gery, Justin Maxwell, Henry Griffin, and Erik Hansen; to my treasured Valparaiso friends for their years of encouragement, Mark Schwehn, Dorothy Bass, Peter Lutze, David Nord, Martha Nord, Ed Uehling, Marilynn Uehling, John Feaster, Sue Feaster, Buzz Berg, Arlin Meyer, Sharon Meyer, Renu Juneja, Mel Piehl, Eileen Piehl, John Ruff, Gloria Ruff, Al Trost, Ann Trost, Lenore Hoffman, Joe Otis, Allison Schuette, and Margaret Franson; to my sister Dana, my mother Joeddie and my father Wayne; to Will Campbell; to the UNO Press under its capable new leadership of Abram Himelstein and its capable staff, editor G.K. Darby, and assistants, Kara Breithaupt, Allison Reu, Alex Dimeff, Jen Hanks, and especially Lauren Capone for her dedicated and talented design work; and to Joyce Markrid Dombourian, my partner of 36 years.

I also want to acknowledge the central role in my life of a long list of beloved students a partial contingent of which includes: Lindsay Allen, Jamie Amos, Denise Dirks, Kevin Kisch, Sue Louvier, Jessica Viada, April Blevins, Peter Keith-Slack, Danielle Gilyot, Erin Grauel, Nick Mainieri, Stephen Leonard, Mark Babin, Amanda Pedersen, Corina Calsing, Casey Lefante, Barb Johnson, David Parker, Kristin Van de Biesonbos Gresham, Chrys Darkwater, Arin Black, Matthew Peters, Jessica Emerson, A.C. Lambeth, Bill Loehfelm, Missy Wilkinson, Abram Himelstein, Rebeca Antoine, John Pusateri, Matt

Baldwin, Nancy Rowe, Kelly Wilson, Robert Ficociello, Brian Olzewski, Lucas Diaz-Medina, Kyle Mox, Robert Bell, Glenn Joshua, Stephen Walden, Amanda Anderson, Jennifer Spence, James Fenton, Allison McNeill, Jocelyn Paxton, Glenn Adams, Neil Thornton, Shana-Tara Regon, Paula Hilton, Andrew Moore, Jonathan Leavitt, J.G. Martinez, Paula Martin, Carr Kizzier, Linda Treash, Joe Longo, Jennifer Kuchta, Leo Dubray, Joyce Tsai, Jason Altman, Craig McWhorter, Michael Mahoney, John Tait, Anna Hunter, Neil Fears, Robert Brown, Ken Berke, Maxine Conant, Marisa Rubinow, Joseph Boyden, Amanda Buege, Richard Schmitt, Elizabeth Rosen, Melanie Christensen, Katheryn Laborde, Mark Whitaker, Johnny Townsend, Darren Smith, Sheryl Kohlert, Kathleen Rief, Kevin McDermott, Cooley Windsor, Tom Kizcula, Maurice Ruffin, Daniel Morales, Hannah Choi, Carolyn Mikulencak, Matthew Bains, Cara Cotter, and Larry Wormington.

"The answers to all the important questions of life are
two: sex and death."
—Woody Allen


"What about basketball?"
—Sheila McIntire


"We are all terminal cases."
—John Irving


"I'd like him to case my terminal."
—Sheila McIntire

# BOOK ONE:

## Before  Barbara  Jeanne  Bordelon

# CHAPTER ONE

As I was given this story, now two decades ago, Marshall McCall "Mac" McIntire was born in the eye of a storm. And all of his life he never seemed to get out of it. Which was unfortunate since he grew up to be the mildest mannered of men. But controversy seemed to hound him all of his days. Mac was born at New Orleans Baptist Hospital at just about the very moment that Hurricane Charlene sat on top of the city and scared the daylights out of everyone but Mac's mom, who was busy bringing Mac into the world.

Baptist Hospital isn't really run by the Baptists anymore, but in those days it was, and most of the hospital personnel were kind of religious at that time. Not that the religious inclinations of the male staff were particularly relevant. The exclusively male doctors weren't *at* the hospital when Mac was born. They had sense enough to know that Baptist Hospital was located in an area of the city prone to flooding and that hurricanes were prone to cause floods. Likewise, the black male orderlies knew that a hurricane was no time to be working at a hospital that only treated a bunch of sick white people. So on the day that Mac McIntire was born, Baptist Hospital was staffed entirely by female nurses. (This was an omen, of course, since the rest of Mac's life would find him singularly surrounded by women.) And the nurses' religious inclinations *were* important because, just as Sheila McIntire was going into the final stages of her labor, they were all crowded into the small first floor chapel praying that they wouldn't be blown down Napoleon Avenue and into the Mississippi River and that Lake Pontchartrain wouldn't be washed over its teeny levee and drown them before they could marry doctors and live happily and affluently ever after.

Nurses had rather more limited ambitions for themselves in the 1950's than they do today.

The only male at Baptist Hospital at the time of Mac's birth, other than Mac himself, of course, was Mac's father, Elmer. A man of the cloth, Elmer Kanter was leading the prayer meeting in the hospital chapel. It was the grandest day of his life. But not because his son was about to come into the world. For Elmer Kanter would play little direct part in his son's life. It was the grandest day in Elmer's life because he was surrounded by about forty terrified women, absolutely most of whom were under the impression he might be influential in saving their lives.

But as Sheila McIntire would observe about sundry beliefs she encountered in her long life: "Boy, were they wrong." In fact, there was some sad metaphorical truth to Sheila's contention about her husband's behavior in the last moments of her pregnancy: "That son of bitch wasn't even prayin'. He just got that bunch of husband-hunting, medical do-gooders to kneel and close their eyes so he could sneak around the pews and peek up their starched white knickers." Sheila McCall McIntire was always a woman of vividly expressed opinions.

She was also a woman who habitually did things alone. She was practically alone when she'd married Elmer. Only a Vancleave, Mississippi, justice of the peace and his wife were in attendance at the wedding. "And I damn well sure wish Elmer hadn't been there," Sheila would later tell Mac. "It was bad enough to be knocked up by the little Bible-spouting peckerhead. Having to marry him was nothing short of humiliating."

So it was fitting that Sheila was alone when she gave birth to her only child. She sweated, and she groaned, and she screamed (she would never admit to the screaming, of course), and she pushed her son out of her. And by the time the eye of Charlene had finally pushed northwest out of the city and on toward Baton Rouge and the head maternity nurse remembered her patient, Sheila had located some obstetrical instruments, cut the umbilical cord and sponged Mac to a fine rosy pink.

Sheila's nurse was chagrined and profusely apologetic when she burst into the delivery room to find the whole process of the birth completed and the infant snuggled to her patient's bosom. But Sheila dismissed her *mea culpas* with a characteristic, off-handed generosity. "I'm sure you had more important things to attend to," she remarked without taking her eyes from the baby. Only later when Sheila learned that the nurse had been in a prayer meeting did she wax angry, and even then only at Elmer against whom she bore a seemingly primordial grudge.

Sheila's union with Elmer was, to say the least, unorthodox. Sheila was 5'11" tall, wide of hip and thick of waist. She was stocky rather than fat, though, and not at all badly proportioned. It was just that she was so distinctly *large*. All through high school in her central Louisiana hometown, Sheila McIntire had been one of those good old girls who was involved in every activity from the drama club to the yearbook staff. She was very popular with her female classmates and, in a robust, palsy sort of way, numbered many boys among her friends as well. But she was not the sort of girl who ever got asked out. Her girlfriends occasionally talked someone into taking her to a party or a school dance, but he seldom came back for seconds. And in the end, she even had to suffer a blind date to her senior prom. Her male classmates' reluctance to date her is probably best captured in the explanation of the school's football captain who observed, "It's not that ya think Sheila could probably start for us at linebacker; it's that ya think she might make All League."

When Sheila graduated from high school, her family had little money and less inclination to send her on to college. To another young woman this might have proven a bitter disappointment. But Sheila, though bright and widely curious, had never been an enthusiastic scholar. She believed that educational institutions were bastions of requirements, very few of which actually related to real learning.

So at age eighteen, with no regrets, Sheila set off to begin her adult life. Her family presumed she'd find some kind of work near them and continue to live at home, but Sheila was determined to move to New Orleans where she could be on her own. She rented a small apartment on Maple Street and after a few days of searching the want ads found a job as a sewing instructor at the municipal home for unwed mothers on Broad Avenue.

Sheila quickly proved popular with her sewing pupils who were inevitably dispirited products of New Orleans' lower middle- and working-class homes because, unlike the home's administrators and other teachers, she didn't constantly talk to them in a whisper as if they were seriously diseased and hovering on the brink of death instead of just social ruin. She also didn't bombard them with a lot of pious utterings about how the ways of God are mysterious and the love of Jesus boundless. In her own way Sheila was a religious woman, but as she later explained to Mac about his unchurched rearing, "I've just never been able to escape the impression that most churchgoers are jerks."

Sheila's attitude toward institutional religion made highly ironic, both her eventual involvement, and even the circumstances of her initial acquaintance, with Elmer Kanter. She met him at a First Baptist Church social. Sheila had taken to attending the church's young adult gatherings in order to have a social life that didn't involve hanging around bars. Nice women didn't hang around bars in the 1950's. And though it's a term Sheila would have resisted in applying to herself, she really was nice. Aside from church socials,

Sheila's only other outlet for human interaction in her first months in New Orleans was limited to her sewing pupils who weren't normally allowed to leave the municipal home and who, because of their maternal condition, tended to be morose.

So Sheila began frequenting the Baptist church socials, soaking up a lot of fruit punch and almond cake and genuinely enjoying many of the young people who gathered there, many of whom were not nearly so pious as to make Sheila sick. Most were relatively new to New Orleans, most, like Sheila, hungry for the opportunity to meet and be with people their own age.

Among the group, of course, was Elmer. He was six years older than Sheila, a graduate of Louisiana College, a veteran of the Korean War, a first-year Baptist seminary student, and in most every way imaginable, a Mutt to Sheila's Jeff. He was barely 5'9" in his elevator shoes and thin and wiry and seemingly as tough as beef jerky. As is true of all infatuations, it's hard to pinpoint exactly what attracted them to each other. Aside from their striking physical differences, Sheila was painfully frank and openly humble while Elmer was a yarn-spinner and a shameless boaster. He was good looking, though, and probably the most popular member of the Baptist social crowd. Though Sheila later liked to deny it, secretly she always remembered the breathless wonder she felt when he first began to flirt with her. Outside the church's Fellowship Hall, Sheila found her attraction to Elmer increased by his habit of peppering his speech with an occasional curse word and his fondness for dropping by her apartment with a six pack of beer. As Sheila would later explain to her son, "In those days I didn't understand the difference between the terms *liberated* and *libertine.*"

In sum, there was something faintly risqué about Elmer, and Sheila was drawn to it. He wasn't run of the mill. He wasn't predictable. He liked to have a good time. But then one night at Sheila's apartment after they'd *each* put away a six pack of Jax, Elmer had the good time he'd been angling for for weeks, and a son was conceived. "Hell, it was just as much my fault," Sheila later explained to her son when Mac mouthed some teenage mutterings about hating his father. "I made the little bastard do it to me twice. After the first time, I was just barely getting started."

When Sheila confronted Elmer with the news of her pregnancy, he was not exactly enthusiastic, a fact that Sheila not only recognized, but resented. "How do you know it's mine?" he asked her with a distinct tone of defiance.

"Take my word for it," Sheila suggested.

Elmer bristled and said, "I don't know that I see it in my interest to do that."

"Look at it this way," Sheila advised. "You could take my word for it, and then I won't tie your peter up in a knot so tight you'll need Alexander's sword before you can manage your next piss."

Though short in formal education, Sheila could wax very literary when she wanted to. But it's doubtful that Elmer got the allusion.

What he did get, though, was the point. And they were married that same week.

# CHAPTER TWO

The union of Elmer Kanter and Sheila McIntire, I might needlessly observe, was not exactly a marriage made in heaven. Elmer expected that Sheila would shortly mold herself to fit the fifties profile of a Baptist preacher's wife. That is, he expected she would become a soft-spoken house slave who referred to herself only in the first person plural, as in: "God has graced *us* with an interim pastorate in Amite and *we* have accepted with joy and thanksgiving."

Elmer had another *expect* coming.

He had neglected to inform Sheila that being a pastor's wife was a full-time job. He had neglected, for instance, to inform her that henceforth she could look down the long road of her life and see endless duty as a Sunday School teacher, which she probably could have abided, even though the lesson planning was guaranteed to ruin her Saturday nights forever. And he had neglected to inform her that she would have to be a Training Union leader, which would ruin her Sunday afternoons in preparation and Sunday evenings in execution (an apt term for Training Union as far as Sheila was concerned).

Elmer had furthermore neglected to inform her that she could scratch every subsequent Wednesday night from her calendar so as to attend an abbreviated mid-week church service known as Prayer Meeting. But most important, he had neglected to inform her that she would become an obligatory member of the Women's Missionary Union, an absolutely bizarre congregation of the church's devoutest females with whom she'd be expected to meet every Tuesday night and pray as if possessed for poor, starving African children whom they wouldn't even let through the doors of their sanctuary should the little black buggers dare to survive their most recent famine and make their way to New Orleans or whatever Southern location Elmer might find himself lucky enough to be pastor in. In addition, Elmer had neglected to inform Sheila that she could not conceivably have a job of her own. And that her job at the home for unwed mothers was most certainly *not* the kind of work a pastor's wife would *ever* undertake since it was more than a little unseemly for a religious woman to be associating with fallen women.

To all of which, when Elmer *did* inform her, Sheila replied, "My ass."

Elmer responded that Sheila would also have to curb her occasionally earthy manner of expressing herself.

Sheila considered answering this last instance of husbandly correction by remarking, "My ass*hole*," but while she was still only contemplating doing so, she felt the little fetal Mac give a kick, and she quickly reconsidered. She felt about coarse language much as she did about the consumption of alcoholic beverages. It was an activity perfectly suited for adults, but one which those under eighteen lacked the maturity to engage in. She acknowledged that her Mac-to-be was unlikely to be influenced toward negative behavior while still in the womb, but she didn't ever want to set bad examples for him, and so in preparation for her maternal duties to come, she took a different tack. Instead of pestering Elmer with another vulgarity, Sheila merely said, "We'll see," which Elmer naturally took to indicate the hesitant beginning of his wife's lifelong acquiescence to his authority.

But Elmer also had another *take* coming, too.

For what Sheila really meant when she said, "We'll see," was not, "Oh, I'll give your proposition greater consideration," but rather, "Since my mind is made up, there's no use in our arguing about it further." Sheila said, "We'll see," not in an effort to postpone the moment of issue's reckoning, but out of a kind of courtesy once an issue was settled. She was the last person to shy away from a necessary confrontation, but she had extraordinary compassion for those who suffered defeat. And Elmer was most definitely defeated in his desire for Sheila to become his servile second banana. "We'll see," was her way of not rubbing it in.

By all accounts then, this marriage lasted longer than it might have been expected to. Though, of course, it didn't last very long at all. Elmer would probably have had the marriage annulled had Sheila not been so immediately in the family way. He knew within moments of beginning their life together that she was the confoundedest woman he'd ever met, and he knew he was in trouble. Elmer was a rather long ways from being the brightest guy around. As Sheila later put it: "He was a friggin' Baptist preacher, wasn't he?" But at the same time, he was blessed with a country boy's sure savvy for what was right in terms of appearances. And what wasn't.

Sheila wasn't.

Sheila didn't even look right, being bigger than he was, and she certainly didn't act right. She *did* mind her manners when around his seminary colleagues, foregoing pronouncements of "bullshit" or "donkey balls," both of which she declared at appropriate moments when with her own friends. But she just never managed to seem very devout. She didn't pepper her conversation with a lot of religious expressions like, "We've sought *His* guidance in this matter," or "We've asked the Lord to show us the light of *His* will." As a matter of fact, she just could not bring herself to refer to couplehood with Elmer in the first person plural at all.

But wish for it as he might (and frequently did), Elmer's getting rid of Sheila was no easy matter. Baptist ministerial candidates were not supposed to diddle sweet young things they picked up at church socials. And they certainly weren't supposed to knock them up. But those were the mistakes of Elmer's immediate past, mistakes which he had obscured by the act of matrimony. Now he had significantly greater problems. Because even if Baptist ministerial candidates were married to paganistic shrews, they simply did *not* divorce them. Divorce was to a ministerial career what turpentine was to paint. A divorced preacher didn't get called into the pastorate; he was lucky to find work with a social agency. So as much as the notion was occasionally galling to Elmer, he considered himself stuck to Sheila like glue.

But as Sheila rejoined when Elmer shared this little conviction with her: "Elmer's glue don't stick shit." And in the end, when their marriage *was* terminated, it was at Sheila's instigation. Little Mac was just a year old and Sheila wasn't sure he'd quite understand, so she tried to explain her decision to him in the simplest possible terms. "Your old man's a dick," she said, holding him aloft so she could stare intently into his pale blue eyes. She mopped his fine blond hair back across his head. "Most men, in my experience, are dicks," she continued. "But that doesn't mean you have to grow up with one for a daddy. Because I love you. And if I let your daddy's habits rub off on you and make you into just another male stinker, I could never forgive myself."

Mac replied with a particularly astute gurgle at that moment, and Sheila presumed she'd provided an adequate explanation, for why her son was to grow up with a mother for a father. But in case this initial explanation was not sufficient, Sheila repeated it to Mac throughout his childhood whenever the youngster thought to implore, "Why don't I have a daddy like other kids?"

Among Sheila's many admirable qualities was her consistency.

The demise of Sheila and Elmer's union was no great loss to the history of matrimony, of course. They had never gotten along terribly well, and Elmer had cheated on her almost from the very start.

It was the practice in those days for seminarians to support their theological studies by maintaining so-called weekend pastorates whereby they studied during the week and drove to usually rural church fields, somewhere within a two-hundred-mile radius of New Orleans where the parishioners were so poor they couldn't support full-time ministers. On their weekend flocks, the seminarians perpetrated various pastorly acts such as housing themselves and their families in the church's parsonage, visiting appropriate ailing parishioners, and always preaching Sunday mornings and evenings and eating big fried chicken dinners Sunday noon with some deacon or other. For their services they were paid about enough to keep a wife and child in married student housing and retire most of their tuition requirements.

Elmer, unfortunately, in the year and a half he was married to Sheila never managed to land one of these sinecures. So he had to support his family by doing what was called "supply preaching" which meant filling in for some pastor who was sick or on vacation. This activity brought in a tidier sum of cash than might be expected. But it also required that Elmer journey out of town to different locations almost every weekend. Normally he left on Saturday afternoons and spent the night somewhere within an hour's drive of his Sunday preaching obligation. It was thus in small-town cafes, truckstops, and bars all over southern Louisiana that bull-slinging Elmer warmed the heart cockles of various waitresses and barmaids with whom he committed adultery just as frequently as he could talk them into it.

You'd think, being as careful as he was to fornicate only when out of town, that he could have kept it up for years. But Sheila knew. She knew from the beginning. And it pissed her off, of course. But she bided her time because she could detect no particular purpose in making accusations that she knew Elmer would only deny. And she lacked anything in the way of proof.

Years later, when he was just entering his teens, Mac asked his mom just how it was that she knew his daddy had been unfaithful. "I could smell it on him," Sheila snapped with the irritation that leapt into her voice whenever the subject was her former husband.

"Smell it on him?" thirteen-year-old Mac queried with a grimace of confusion.

"Sex has a mighty distinctive fragrance," Sheila explained to her reddening son, who never failed to be embarrassed by his mother's incredible frankness.

The climactic episode in Elmer and Sheila's brief marriage came when Elmer inadvertently brought home a souvenir of his ecstatic romp with a saucy little blonde named Bonnie. Bonnie Spencer was a nineteen-year-old hash slinger at a road-side diner in Bogalusa whom Elmer had sparked one

Saturday evening while leaning on his elbows across a damp counter. She was one of those wide-eyed, small-town girls who thought that New Orleans was a million miles and several cultures away. She'd encountered men from the city before, of course, but none had tarried to put the hustle on her. Elmer wangled permission to escort her home when the diner closed at eight o'clock and figured his luck was running solid sevens when she revealed that her parents were in Alexandria for a state convention of druggists. Bonnie showed reluctance at first to invite him into the neat, two-story cape cod, but she finally relented with a near squeal of hospitality and parked him in a comfortable, if slightly formal, living room while she went to the kitchen to get Cokes.

Elmer rhapsodized in her absence about what he was certain were the delights of her girl's pink bedroom. But the fact is he never got to see another single part of her house. He did get a bursting eyeful of Bonnie, however, after he coaxed her out of her white cook's uniform. The key to Elmer's success was his unrelenting barrage of flattery. But lest Bonnie get sold short, she was hardly a victim in these undertakings. She was a decent, reputable girl of average intelligence and negligible possibilities, who was condemned beyond hope to an eternal life in a safe but absolutely boring little town. So one Saturday night she just grabbed for what gusto she could get.

Now Elmer was indisputably a sexual predator, but he was not an altogether thoughtless one. When he had bountiful Bonnie naked and genuinely passionate in what Erica Jong would later term a "zipless fuck" kind of way, he momentarily worried that they would leave some telltale stain or other piece of evidence which might get Bonnie in trouble when her parents returned. So he placed her orlon uniform between the beige shag carpet and her creamy white hips. And he tucked her silky white panties into the back pocket of his trousers just before he stepped out of them.

Imagine Bonnie's enduring panic the next day when Elmer was already a receding memory and she had managed carefully to gather a uniform dress, a half slip, a garter belt, and two nylon stockings which were scattered in sundry locations and across various pieces of furniture in her parents' living room. But under no cushion or chair or table or sofa could be found her once deliciously damp panties.

Well, though Bonnie Spencer remained sure for heart-pounding days that to indict her for diminished virginity those criminal underpants would soon reappear just as magically as they had vanished, her panic was nothing beside Elmer's when those adulterous step-ins materialized on his dinner plate later that week in New Orleans.

As Mac would later tell Barbara Jeanne Bordelon with fine, wry understatement, among Sheila's many other qualities was a flair for the dramatic.

---

Discovered in the course of Sheila's habitual, pocket-emptying laundry preparations, those smoking pistol panties were the conclusive evidence Sheila had been looking for. Elmer was caught so off-guard by their sudden appearance in place of the slab of roast beef he'd been expecting that it took him agonizing moments to think of something to say. Finally he managed: "Why are these panties here on the dinner table?" He thought that a) a facade of bewilderment was his best chance for survival and that b) his pretense that the panties were "on the table" rather than "on his plate" was the least incriminating way of stating that bewilderment.

As mentioned previously, Elmer did not lack for savvy. He did, however, lack even a modicum of hope.

"Those panties ain't 'on the table,'" Sheila pointed out, about the moment that baby Mac, his mother's most devoted fan, gurgled some infant's observation and banged his hands together as if clapping. "And they also ain't on the scrawny ass of whoever they came off of." Sheila had this notion that violating known grammar rules was a way of emphasizing one's annoyance. "Which *is* why they find themselves at the moment on your plate in the place of the dinner that might have been located there otherwise."

"What do you mean?" Elmer asked, clearing his throat. He was stalling, and Sheila knew it. She spooned some over-cooked English peas onto her own plate beside the meat she'd placed there earlier and sat down to eat. She didn't speak again until she'd cut herself a piece of roast, forked it into her mouth, chewed, swallowed and taken a sip of milk.

This momentary silence seemed interminable to Elmer who felt that he must now know the hopeless terror of someone whose head has been placed in the guillotine and lies waiting for the brief sing of metal as the blade begins to drop. He felt as if his own body belonged to some other. He was rigid. All natural, fluid movements suddenly became alien. He hoped that his face registered befuddlement. But he was sure that his eyes showed the wildness of an animal cornered.

Finally Sheila said with a misleading calmness, "Just whose little behind did you sweet talk out of those things, *Elmer*?" There was a nasty derisiveness to the way she pronounced his name.

"What do you mean?" Elmer tried again. Redundancy harbored little hope of escape, he realized, but he could think of nothing better.

Sheila rewarded him with a viciously patronizing smile. "*Darling,*" she said, the sarcasm splashing all over Elmer and burning him in a thousand places as if he'd been sloshed with acid, "just whom do these dainty little items belong to?" She fetched the panties up off the plate between forefinger and thumb as if they were dirty.

"Well, uh, you . . . I presume," Elmer said. It was his best move in the game. Which is only further evidence of how much out of the game he was.

"Oh *really*?" Sheila cooed. She looked at Mac and said to him, "That's the sweetest compliment Daddy ever paid Mommie, don't you think so, Mac?" Mac didn't offer an opinion one way or the other. Sheila stood up and held the briefs stretched open in front of her. "Notice anything unusual," she said to Elmer who opted for no comment. "You see, honey, I haven't been able to slide my big old ass inside a piece of elastic this small since I started counting my age on two hands."

And so divorce proceedings were begun.

All in all, Sheila and Elmer managed to conduct their dissolution with remarkable civility. Elmer must be credited with a spirit of cooperation. But Sheila was thoroughly sensitive to his special needs. She arranged to move Mac and her belongings out of the seminary housing and to take the third-floor staff apartment at the home for unwed mothers. She demanded sole custody of baby Mac but in exchange asked for neither alimony nor child support. In fact, she allowed Elmer to sue *her* on the grounds of abandonment. As she explained to a friend, "Just because the little fart is a fucking weasel doesn't mean I want to ruin him for life. The way I figure it, Elmer can do a lot less damage in this world as a Baptist preacher than he might if I forced him into something like used car sales." She might have been wrong about that judgment, but to protect Elmer's profession, she made no claims about his adultery. And she even suggested that he tell people that when she left him, she did so with the intention of becoming a Catholic. Sheila knew well enough that if anything could save his career, it would be that.

And as a matter of fact it worked. By most all the Baptists Elmer was forgiven his sin of divorce and was regarded as somewhat of a martyr, a dedicated Christian whose devoted love had been spurned by a papist. Shortly before he graduated from the seminary and received his call to a small pastorate in Newman, Alabama, he married again, this time a shy twenty-year-old virgin who regarded as a divine blessing her future life as a pastor's wife.

For a brief time Elmer regarded himself as divinely blessed, too. He'd managed to wiggle out of his marriage to Sheila without lasting complications, and he'd found in Betty Huber, his second bride, a woman who would never prove the professional embarrassment that Sheila proved constantly. Betty played the piano in their new church and embraced her wifely duties with dedication and enthusiasm. In three years she bore Elmer three daughters and in so many ways aided him in becoming the picture of a promising and prosperous young pastor.

Unfortunately Betty also gained forty-five pounds and in the process developed a kind of self-satisfied and self-righteous demeanor that turned

Elmer's stomach. Soon, his eyes began to wander again, but he now lacked the opportunity to woo all the waitresses and barmaids of his past. As Betty grew increasingly repulsive to him, he found himself thinking ever more frequently of Sheila, who was, of course, a substantially large woman herself, but in a robust, healthy, athletic way that stood in distinct contrast to Betty's burgeoning slovenliness. But even though some years later Elmer and Sheila would again have a "relationship," after he had founded his Soldiers for Jesus organization and had become by way of his syndicated TV religious hour a national figure, it can hardly be said that Sheila was ever again, even momentarily, beguiled by Elmer Kanter's charms.

# CHAPTER THREE

Life after Elmer for Sheila McIntire (she instantly resumed use of her maiden name) and her infant son (whose last name she quickly arranged to be her own) thoroughly disproved society's notion that a child needs parents of both sexes in order to grow up well-adjusted and happy. Of course, in Sheila, Mac had a most unusual mother.

Many courageous people today are designated "survivors," and I am naturally tempted to employ such a term in describing Sheila. But so often "survivor" depicts a person who fights through life's ceaseless trials with a grim defiance that precludes an unaggressive posture, genuinely carefree moments, or the experience of joy. In this way Sheila was not a "survivor" at all. She'd made a girlish mistake with Elmer, she'd learned her lesson, she'd corrected her error, and now she forged forward without bitterness or even regret. Had there been no Elmer, there'd have been no Mac, and the last thing in her life Sheila would regret was her son.

It's true that Sheila's life was meager in material terms. But even though she earned only $100 a week at the home for unwed mothers, she never for an instant felt deprived. Her habits were frugal but didn't feel imposed, and it seemed to Sheila that she had possessed at least enough money to do anything she desired.

Before her separation from Elmer, Sheila had left Mac days at the seminary nursery, a day-care center available free to students and to faculty for a nominal fee. After her divorce, of course, such a service was no longer available. So Sheila just hauled little Mac right downstairs to her duties at the home for unwed mothers. Sheila was popular enough with her superiors that they were reluctant at first to confront her with their disapproval. And then, much to their surprise, they discovered that far from being a nuisance, Mac actually proved useful in accomplishing certain aspects of the home's mission.

Most of the women in the home planned upon arrival to give their babies up for adoption, and a majority even went through with those plans. A sizeable minority, however, decided at the last minute to keep their children, whatever hardship they had to endure to do so. Yet, sad, even terrifying as it is to note, many of these women knew practically nothing about babies. (They obviously didn't know some important essentials about sex either.) So Mac became their living model.

He didn't long remain a "baby," of course. Soon he had teeth and began to walk in a stumbling, awkward career that sent him as frequently sideways and backways as it did forward. But he was still in diapers and several times a day provided the unwed mothers with opportunities to practice the necessary art of changing. He was such a cooperative child, giggling and flinging his feet upward toward his head while rolling gently back and forth on his back, that he made this lesson in parenting considerably less unpleasant than it might have been.

While Mac was still being bottle fed, the unwed mothers also rehearsed mixing formula, heating it to just the right temperature, and testing it by squeezing drops on the inside of their forearms. They particularly enjoyed practicing this last step, and often mild bickering would break out about whether or not the formula had been prepared to the correct temperature. The bottle would be passed around, and the milk dropped onto so many forearms that Sheila would worry that Mac wasn't getting enough nourishment. At night, when she got him upstairs, she repeatedly asked him, "Hungry, baby?" until that phrase became a staple in his limited vocabulary. At the unwed mother's home he'd lurch about the sewing room parroting, "Hungry baby, hungry baby" until some worried goodheart would lead him off to the kitchen and fix him another bottle.

These multiple feedings may have had something to do with the incredible rate at which Mac grew, although his mother's genes probably mattered rather more. At any rate, by the time Mac was three years old, he was as tall as most first-graders and considerably huskier. Like his mom, though, Mac managed to be bulky without being fat. His large head was full-faced, but there was no hint of the double chin that many well-fed little children have.

Mac's weight and size, however, were not the most important developments during his early years as a resident at the unwed mothers' home. That distinction belongs to the surely unparalleled amount of loving attention

Mac enjoyed. His experience was the opposite of what he had encountered at the day-care center where one adult supervised the activities of twenty-five children. At the home for unwed mothers, Mac found *his* activities supervised by twenty-five young women. If he fell and someone wasn't there to catch him before he hurt himself, then he was smothered with a dozen kisses to make it better even before he'd managed to decide whether the pain was great enough to warrant crying.

One might worry that such unabated supervision would prove stifling or that Mac would be spoiled by all the attention. But Sheila's influence on the unwed mother precluded any such occurrence. She forbade them to coddle Mac when he was bad or to tolerate the slightest fit of temper when he was grouchy. "If it's my job to teach y'all how to raise these kids you've got no business being about to have," she counseled, "the last thing I should be doing is letting you turn my kid into a brat. I don't want a brat. And neither do any of you."

As a result of Sheila's guidance for the unwed mothers' seemingly boundless affection, Mac grew up a child who, without possessing a shred of arrogance, never suffered a moment for want of self-confidence. He was blessed with that special security that comes from the certain knowledge of being loved. This security would serve him very well many years later when his fundamental human principles were put to the severest test.

One might suspect, growing up as he did surrounded by women, that Mac would become what was then called a sissy, a little male child afraid of boys' rough and tumble games, one who'd develop interests in such "female" activities as sewing and cooking and playing with dolls.

Far from it.

Or rather, it was much more complicated than that. The fact was that Mac did grow up with an interest in sewing. His mother, after all, earned her living as a sewing instructor. So it was only natural that he should take an interest in his mother's livelihood. By the time Mac was nine he had become quite skilled at a sewing machine, both as a repairman, and as a practitioner. "Better my son the seamster than my son the teamster," Sheila used to recite to her brothers when they worriedly found Mac bent over the old White she'd been given as a graduation present from high school. Mac never developed a flair for design. But he could follow a pattern with as much care as anyone. And by the time he entered junior high school, he regularly made all his own shirts (which, as might be expected, saved Sheila a great deal of wardrobe money through the years) and often made birthday and Christmas presents for friends and family.

It was also true that Mac acquired a devoted interest in the culinary arts. This last was not the result of his mother's tutelage, however, but of self-defense. For Sheila was a rotten cook. She was not a patient person and never mastered the moderation that good cooking requires. In Sheila's skillet, for example, bacon always progressed directly from cold to burnt. An impolite relative characterized her kitchen skills this way: "Sheila McIntire is the best friend indigestion ever had." Mac was eleven years old and eating at a school friend's house when he discovered that lima beans didn't have a natural charred and toasty taste. So just as early as he could, Mac took up cooking.

As was true in his sewing, Mac was a lifelong functionalist rather than artist. He worked with the basics: beef, pork, chicken, fish, shrimp, crabs, and oysters. And he made meals that were always tasty and nutritious even if they were never mistaken for fancy. By the time Mac reached high school, Sheila had surrendered nearly all the cooking responsibilities to her son, confining herself to the making of her dark-roast coffee which Mac could never make strong enough to suit her. Sheila probably would have marveled at her son's cooking ability had she noticed a particular difference between what he made and what she had prepared in the past. When Mac occasionally teased her about her habitual burning of such simple items as toast, Sheila showed her sportswomanship with a hearty laugh at her own expense. But she really never knew what Mac was talking about and mildly suspected that he was making the whole thing up.

"My mom," Mac would confide many years later to Barbara Jeanne Bordelon, "could never be accused of having good taste."

But despite Mac's acquisition of skills most frequently associated with the female of the species, he hardly grew up a pantywaist. His being surrounded by women proved no obstacle to manliness. Mac got so much successful mothering while Sheila was at work that she was freed up once the workday was done to devote her energies to proper fathering. And like any father, Sheila introduced Mac to the joy of sports just as soon as he was old enought to hold a ball.

Sheila had always resented the fact that public schools had provided so few female sports when she was in school. She felt gypped that there was no football for women and that women's basketball and softball were intramural, rather than interscholastic, sports. Sheila was a competitor, but she'd never had the opportunity to get her fill of the kind of competition that was so widely available for males.

Nonetheless, Sheila didn't push Mac into sports. She instructed him about how to throw and catch a football. She showed him how to position his fingers on the strings so as to throw a spiral, how to cup his hands around the ball so as to catch a ball on the run. Sheila hoped Mac might like football, but when he didn't, that was fine. In the yellow glow of many a New Orleans afternoon, she also tossed a baseball with her son, and on the cracked asphalt court behind the unwed mothers' home, she taught him to shoot a basketball. And when he did show an interest in playing those sports, Sheila was thrilled, all the more so because the choices were wholly his own.

# CHAPTER FOUR

Mac's early career as an athlete centered around his relationship with his mother. After her day's work with the unwed mothers, the two of them would adjourn to the tiny, fenced yard behind the home and fill up the waning hours before nightfall with games. At first it was merely catch, Mac wearing an oversized glove Sheila had bought him with the economical plan of his being able to use it for some years to come, and Sheila using an undersized first baseman's mitt she had carted through life since girlhood. As Mac got older, Sheila engaged in some preliminary coaching, teaching how to let his glove give when catching a straight pitch to avoid stinging his hand, or how to shade his eyes when positioning himself under a fly, or how to drop to one knee when fielding a grounder.

When Mac was about eleven, Sheila bought him a basketball and they began to utilize the sad remnant of a basketball court that occupied one corner of the cramped yard behind the unwed mothers' home. Like an isolated gargoyle, a weathered gray backboard hovered on its corroded pole over a cracked, grass-sprouting slab of asphalt onto which, years ago, someone had painted yellow facsimiles of a three-second lane, foul circle and free-throw line. Into the brisk orange of a New Orleans fall afternoon, Mac hauled the ball of his destiny, occasionally bouncing it with both hands against the gritty blacktop. Sheila lugged a pine kitchen stool on which she stood to attach to the rusting metal rim a nylon net, which, to prevent its being stolen, she'd climb back up to remove at each practice's end. Though he later believed that his mom's insistence on using a net helped make him into the deadly shooter he would become by junior high school, at the time he thought it mysteriously pointless. But when he complained that they could have just as much fun shooting at a bare rim, she answered him with a bit of doggerel:

A snatch should be virgin

If it's without fur, yet.

The same as a basket,

Which is lacking a net.

Sheila loved dirty limericks and other kinds of naughty verse and was forever concocting her own. But she refused to tell her son what a "snatch" was or what she meant by "fur." All she would say was, "Neither is all it's cracked up to be." And then she enjoyed a delicious laugh at her witticism.

From the beginning of their basketball training, Sheila and Mac would never limit themselves to merely shooting around; they would always engage in a game of H-O-R-S-E or some other competition. Sometimes, mother and son would be joined in their play by more mobile representatives of the unwed mothers. Sides would be chosen and actual games would be played, though obviously not with consummate skill. The games were spirited, though, Sheila refusing to let them be otherwise. Years later, Sheila supposed that Mac's amazing grace while driving to the basket dated to those days in which he'd had to learn to propel himself among opponents with bellies as round and ponderous as the ball he dribbled, opponents whom he not only needed to avoid but into whom he dared not charge.

On the days when unwed mothers didn't join them, when he was still very young, Mac liked a game called Poison which demanded little real basketball skill but gave him the opportunity to fling the ball against the backboard with all his might. Sheila played Poison with him because he liked it. But she could never understand the sense of the game which put only a minor premium on the ability to make baskets. Sheila's favorite game when they played alone was Twenty-One, a game of free throws and lay-ups. She enjoyed the discipline of a foul shot, and the game gave Mac an opportunity to compete since he was strong enough to be accurate when close to the goal.

At the outset of their competition, Sheila always won, of course. She was stronger and her mature body was more skilled. Her total mastery of her son lasted more than two years. They played several times a week, and it never occurred to her to let Mac win. They played; they had fun. And Sheila won because she was better.

Later, when Mac's strength increased to match and surpass his mother's, they continued to play. And Sheila remained competitive longer than one might imagine. She was well-coordinated and a determined competitor. They even continued to play long after Mac was able to dominate her thoroughly, long after he was an All-State selection in high school, long after he led the University of New Orleans on a miraculous trip to the NCAA's final four. But in all those years after Mac entered his thirteenth year, Sheila never won a single game, of Twenty-One or any other shooting game they played.

Once, however, when Mac was fourteen, Sheila suspected him of deliberately trying to let her win. She questioned him about it, knowing that if she confronted him he would not lie to her. "I just didn't want you to feel bad, Mom," he explained. "Because I don't think you're ever gonna be able to beat me anymore."

Sheila wanted to hug him because she recognized compassion in what he was doing, more compassion than she could hope for in a son. But instead of embracing him, she addressed him sternly. "Marshall McCall," she said—she inevitably used his formal names when she was trying to impart something important—"all of the fun of sports is in *playing* to win. If I *play* to win, even if I lose, I have the fun that sports intend. On the other hand, if you allow me to win, even from the best intentions, you do me no favor at all, and you deny yourself the fun you deserve. Do you understand?"

Mac nodded uncertainly.

"Promise me that you won't ever do this again."

Though he didn't wholly understand Sheila's point at the time, Mac promised. And he kept the promise all his life, even when he was called the most heinous names for doing so.

This was probably the most crucial lesson to emanate from their hours of playing basketball together, though there were certainly other lessons which transpired as well. In the early days, when Mac was on the losing end of the daily score, for instance, he developed the sportsmanship that would remain one of his becoming characteristics for the rest of his life. And in the purely physical arena, it was on that black-top court behind the unwed mothers' home that Mac developed the somewhat unusual shooting style that he would maintain throughout his days as a player.

For the observant fan of professional and UCLA basketball, Mac's was a style similar to that of Jamaal (nee Keith) Wilkes. It involved starting the shot, not in front of and above the head, but rather below and behind it. In Mac's case this shooting style stemmed from his earliest days with his mom when the ball was heavy and awkward for his eleven-year-old arms. Starting the shot back and low allowed him to generate greater momentum in lofting it toward the basket. By the time he was strong enough that such a starting position was no longer necessary, he had become so accustomed to shooting that way that it never occurred to him to tamper with his "natural" style. Sheila was not student enough of the game to notice that Mac's shot was unorthodox. But if she had, she wouldn't have cared. He was accurate. That was all that mattered.

Or it was all that mattered until he reached high school and a well-meaning coach insisted that he learn to shoot the "correct" way. By that time, Mac was a husky 6'4" and had just led his Capdau Junior High teammates to the city's championship game. Capdau lost that game but through no fault of Mac's shooting as the big Capdau center made eight of nine from the field and five of seven from the free-throw line.

Warren Easton High School basketball coach Johnny Ronalds was delighted to have Mac join his squad the following year. The youngster arrived at Easton with an excellent reputation as an earnest, if not overly-gifted student, and as a talented, "coachable" ball player. But Ronalds agonized about the "awkwardness" of Mac's shot and just as soon as he was legally allowed to do so showed Mac how to shoot "properly." He insisted that Mac begin devoting his practice energies to learning this new style. Mac was perplexed, but, as always, did as he was told, even shooting in the new manner in his weekend contests against Sheila. Sheila didn't notice at first that her son was shooting the ball differently—she wasn't yet the student of the game that she would become—but she did notice that Mac was shooting poorly and finally asked him the reason. When he explained that he was practicing the shot his new coach had taught him, Sheila instantly directed that he take ten jump shots in his old fashion. Mac did so and made them all.

Sheila made an appointment to speak with coach Ronalds.

"Why are you trying to fuck up my boy?" she demanded of the coach when admitted to his office that next week.

"Ma'am?" the coach said, thinking he must have misheard her infinitive.

"Why are you trying to muck up the way my son shoots?" Sheila said, remembering a more benign consonant.

The coach explained that Mac was a player of tremendous potential and that he, as coach, was only requiring what he deemed necessary to improve Mac's game.

Sheila suspected that the coach was only doing what was necessary to establish his authority. But Ronalds argued that Mac's style of shooting was probably less accurate in the long run and certainly involved a "slower release." To illustrate the advantages of the new style of shooting, the coach drew Sheila some stick figures on the blackboard screwed into the chipped plaster wall of his office. The first figure showed a player shooting as the coach desired. It looked like this:

Under the figure he wrote the word, *standard*.

The second figure showed a player shooting in Mac's unorthodox manner. It looked like this:

Under this figure the coach wrote *Mac*.

Pointing to the two figures, he then attempted to convince Sheila that since the distance between the first stick man's "release position" and the position of the ball at the point of "dribble termination" was much shorter, employing the coach's method would enable Mac to get his shots off much more quickly. "And as Mac meets stiffer competition as he progresses to higher levels of the game," Coach Ronalds urged, "he's going to need that quicker release to continue the success he's enjoyed in the past."

Sheila studied the coach's drawing and considered the merits of his argument. There seemed genuine power to the coach's position, but she somehow couldn't shake her suspicion of sophistry. Like a politician's argument for more nuclear weapons, the movement from point to point seemed sound enough, but she knew nonetheless that it was desperately insane.

Then Sheila remembered something Mac had been taught by his junior high coach: "There's no need to dribble before you shoot," Coach King had repeated over and over until Mac had broken the fidgety habit of giving the ball an obligatory bounce just before shooting it. With this idea in mind, Sheila studied the coach's drawing more intently, wondering why, if you needn't dribble before you shoot, the relationship between the point of "dribble termination" and "release position" was so goddamned important.

She was getting sweaty just thinking about how she was almost fooled by the coach's stupid drawings and supporting hot air. She asked if she could borrow Coach Ronalds' chalk. He wrinkled his brow but handed her a broken stick. In front of the coach's first figure Sheila sketched in one of her own. The two together looked like this:

Under the second figure Sheila wrote the word *defender*. She was pleased she'd thought to equip her player with a determined, tenacious frown.

"Now it would seem to me," Sheila said, addressing the blackboard rather than the coach, "that a player attempting to shoot the ball in the 'standard' way would run a greater risk of having his shot blocked because the ball is released in a position so close to the opposing player's waving hands."

"Whereas," she stopped to chalk in a player to guard the one Coach Ronalds had drawn to represent her son. These two figures together looked like this:

"Whereas," she began again, "it should seem to me that a player shooting as Mac does would have a much greater chance of lofting his shot over the defender's arms."

Leaving her legs still planted toward the blackboard—she was prepared to draw pictures all day if need be to win her argument—Sheila pivoted on her hips to face the coach who seemed to have turned the pale green shade of a properly prepared margarita. The coach harumphed and adjusted the mesh baseball cap he wore squeezed onto his head.

"At this level, Mrs. McIntire," he croaked, "ninety percent of the shots a player takes are called jump shots. The shooter simply leaps out of the range of the defender's arms."

"I watch a lot of basketball, Mr. Ronalds," Sheila pointed out. "And it has always been my impression that there was no restriction on the defending player's right to jump as well."

The coach's greenness had advanced to the shade of the dark side of a dollar bill. "Missus," he rasped, "I feel I should remind you that I'm the coach of this team, that Mac has got to play for me, that I probably know more about the game of basketball than you do, and that I'll have to require your son, like any other player, to follow my instructions."

Sheila nodded brusquely and made her way out of Coach Ronalds' office. On the bus ride home she hatched a plan to appeal her case to the revered Adolf Rupp, head basketball coach at the University of Kentucky. She took a note pad out of her purse and then in a letter to Rupp reproduced the four stick figures she and the coach had drawn on his blackboard and composed a brief summary of the positions she and her antagonist had adopted. Before putting her note pad away, she flipped to a clean page and wrote the words "Coach Ronalds" at the top. Under this she drew the following picture:

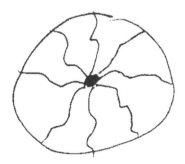

Under this picture she wrote the word *asshole*.

# CHAPTER FIVE

Coach Rupp did not answer Sheila's letter, and ever after that, she rooted for John Wooden to break Rupp's record for career victories. As Mac would later tell Barbara Jeanne Bordelon, "On matters of little importance, my mother can carry a grudge for a long time."

But as things developed, Sheila didn't need Rupp's adjudication. Coach Ronalds was not exactly persuaded by Sheila's argument, but he did take her position under serious consideration. Ultimately he decided that perhaps Mac McIntire had been shooting *his* way for so long that forcing him to change would harm rather than help. The coach remembered the funny batting stance that Stan Musial had used on his way to baseball's Hall of Fame. No one should ever be taught to bat that way. But how could Stan the Man ever have hit any better?

So at the next practice session, Coach Ronalds called Mac aside and told him to cease practicing the new shooting form. "We're going to give your way a year," the coach said, "and if at the end of this season we find that there are problems, we'll make a change at that time."

At the end of that season, though only a sophomore, Mac had led his team in shooting percentage. He also led them in rebounding and probably in assists, though Coach Ronalds, like most high school coaches of the era, was not progressive enough to keep that vital statistic. What Mac didn't manage that sophomore season was leading his team to enough victories. The Easton Eagles finished 13-12 and out of the post-season playoffs. So even though he was the only sophomore player honored on the ten-man All City team, Mac felt disappointed.

In the two seasons that followed, he and his team improved significantly. In his junior year, Easton went undefeated through the regular schedule and lost only in the quarter-finals of the state tournament to a clearly superior Baton Rouge Istrouma High squad that went on to capture the state title.

Mac's senior year was a cake-walk for an Eagle squad ranked first in the state polls from pre-season on. It seemed nothing could stop their steamroll to a state championship. Mac had now reached his full physical maturity at 6'6" and 220 pounds, and his fellow Louisiana highschoolers were practically powerless when he decided to muscle the ball to the basket. When defensed in the standard man-to-man, Mac was just devastating with his inside game. And when opponents went to a zone he just bombed them to death with his high arching jumpers from the corner.

Late in the year, asked what he thought could stop Mac, one rival coach thoughtfully replied, "Nothing."

But sadly, there was something that could stop Mac and his high-flying teammates. And it was discovered by Bunkie High School coach Jimmie Beamon just in time for their meeting in the state championship final. The strategy was a double team with three of the Bunkie players in a triangular zone and the other two following Mac wherever he went. The ploy totally confused Coach Ronalds' team, and they failed to adjust as the title they'd presumed theirs for the taking simply slipped out of their grasp.

In the first half the Eagles kept trying to force the ball in to their blanketed star and in the process kept throwing it away. In the second half, Ronalds had Mac withdraw to an extreme outside position in order to leave his four teammates an advantage in attacking the three-man zone left against them. If they'd had an offensive strategy for this attack, they would probably have been successful. But Ronalds lacked the time or the quickness of insight to devise one. For all practical purposes, Mac was removed from offensive participation. He finished the night with only eight points, six coming on free throws. And the Eagles were shocked out of their championship by fifteen points.

Like his teammates, coach and entire school, Mac was disconsolate. It was beginning to seem that life had designed a role as bridesmaid for him. But he was also fascinated by what had happened to him and the Eagles. Without a smidgen of vain pride involved, Mac remained convinced that Easton was a better ballclub than Bunkie. But Bunkie had beaten them with a superior coaching strategy. Mac recognized the value of this sad lesson, and he resolved to benefit from it in the days to come.

Sheila, on the other hand, was not nearly so ready to forgo the sweet pain of savage fury. She denounced Jimmie Beamon's cerebral victory as "unsportsmanlike." And she fashioned a scathing triple limerick in his dishonor that went like this:

There once was a young coach in Bunkie,

Addicted to winning: a junkie.

His name: Jimmie Beamon,

His game: double teamin'

His morals just those of a monkey.


For proof just ask the wife of the coach

Whose genes, all knew, were above reproach.

Then her snatch was steamin',

And coach in it was creamin',

And the eggs in her skillet were poached.


Yes, for proof just ask Mrs. Beamon

Who once had eyes that were gleamin'

Till she opened her gape

And bore Jimmie an ape

The man's spunk was simian semen.


As Mac would later explain to Barbara Jeanne Bordelon, "My mom could gross out guys in a fraternity."

# CHAPTER SIX

It would be wrong for me to leave the impression that Mac marched through high school with no more problems than the loss of an occasional athletic contest. For despite Mac's success on the basketball court (and on the baseball field where he was a power-hitting first baseman), he never developed a lot of grace in his social life. His large, strong body, so remarkably agile when writhing through harassing opponents on a drive to the basket, seemed an awkward stranger when in the presence of female schoolmates. His long arms and hamlike hands seemed to hang off him like somebody else's drapes. They were useful, but he just didn't know what to do with them.

Sheila was probably to blame for her son's social discomfort. She never put much stock in social graces and so trained Mac in few. She saw to it that he was polite, considerate and respectful of those who properly exercised authority. Beyond that, Sheila didn't give a fig. The result was that Mac reached high school age without a scintilla of that coveted quality called cool.

Part of his uncoolness derived from his attire. Sheila bought him the underwear and pants that he needed but was delighted that he continued to make his own shirts. Unfortunately, they looked as homemade as they were, not because they suffered from poor workmanship, but because they were so plain and so plainly different from what all the other guys his age were wearing. Mac noticed a bit—he wasn't blind—but he didn't know how to solve this aspect of his social problem. Homemade shirts just weren't ever going to approximate fashionable manufactured brands. But it never really occurred to him that he should ask Sheila for money to buy clothes.

Sheila didn't even notice. She knew nothing about style. She had become an adult in the 1950s and all the rest of her life would dress and wear her hair in the manner she had when she first moved to New Orleans. The result was that she looked middle-aged from the time she was in her early twenties.

Still, as the resident school hero, Mac could have overcome his storied frumpishness had he possessed other social skills. But he lacked them all. His idea of small talk was embarrassed silence. When Mac was around the unwed mothers at the home, he could relax and talk earnestly and sympathetically to them about their considerable problems. Or he could banter in a way that didn't even hesitate as it approached the frontiers of the risqué. But when he was around girls from his school, girls in whom he might develop romantic interests, all his words seemed to dry up like an abandoned ball glove.

So while in high school, Mac managed very few dates. He took a girl to the homecoming dance his sophomore year, but it turned out to be a colossal mistake. He wasn't a school hero yet, and the girl thus felt no obligation to be nice to him when she found out that he was too shy to fast dance. Mac was so big and strong that he secretly feared he might fling his arms about in a Mick Jagger jerk and send someone to the hospital. He agreed to slow dance with the girl, but he didn't begin to know how. When he stepped on her foot the second time, she contracted a splitting headache and demanded to be taken straight home. A couple of years later, the same girl began to let on that she'd been Mac's first girlfriend. But everyone knew that Mac McIntire had never had a girlfriend.

To celebrate their stellar junior season, Mac's basketball teammates rented a row of rooms for a Saturday night at the Alamo Plaza in Gulfport, Mississippi. Everybody had a date, and there was lots of preliminary talk about "bare tit," "stinky finger," and even "going all the way." Mac's teammates fixed him up with a senior named Holly Jackson, "Hand Job Holly" as she was scandalously known by one and all at Warren Easton High. There was scarcely a boy at the school Holly hadn't serviced at some time or another. Or at least there was scarcely a boy who didn't *claim* having enjoyed Holly's attentions. Mac was both excited about and ashamed of agreeing to Holly as his date.

One of the girls had brought her stereo along to the motel, and a couple of the guys had acquired enough whisky and beer to threaten serious trouble. Everybody danced for a while, but pretty soon they got down to the serious business of making out. Some couples sat on the floor; others stretched out on the beds. Mac filled an oversized and dusty easy chair with Holly curled in his lap like a giant kitten. Within an hour, his lips and cheeks ached from non-stop kissing. Mac was enjoying all this, but he couldn't shake the aggravating wish that he and Holly knew each other somewhat better. When she whispered a suggestion that the two of them go outside to sit in a teammate's car, Mac knew exactly what she had in mind, but only a part of him wanted to do it.

"The part most men do all their thinking with," is how Sheila put it.

In the back seat of the car, Holly was on him with a renewed intensity. They hadn't been there long when another couple climbed in up front with a greeting of, "Don't mind us." Almost immediately short gasps and muffled moans spilled over from the front seat like runaway ivy. Mac endeavored to concentrate on his kissing, but he couldn't help but hear the rip of zippers being manipulated and the rustle of clothes being rearranged. Then suddenly, Holly reached up under her pleated skirt and yanked off her panties.

On the basketball court, Mac was the kind of player who inevitably took advantage of an opening. But in the backseat of some parent's Impala, Mac couldn't imagine his next move. Holly Jackson was a one-girl version of Bunkie's double team. She looped a leg over one of Mac's massive thighs and sat up facing him astraddle his knee, then she slowly unbuttoned her blouse and pushed her bra up over her breasts. Mac thought he was going to die.

And soon, *le petit*, Holly's hand inside his khakis, he did just that.

At school in the days to come, though he repeatedly employed circuitous routes to class, Mac seemed to run into Holly at every turn. She'd toss her short golden hair and say, "Hi Mac," with an expectancy that was heartbreaking. Mac felt awful. He hated the fact that he didn't like Holly very much and could not forgive himself the first tingle of arousal he felt every time he saw her.

Mac felt enormously sorry for Holly Jackson. She was a fairly bright kid who did better in school than most anyone realized. She had a freckled, perky, pleasing face and a thin, lithe body she didn't mind showing off to a boy willing to look. She was Hand Job Holly, and she never failed to deliver. She had no trouble getting dates. But no guy ever went out with her more than a couple of times. Holly Jackson managed to graduate from high school with her virginity intact, an achievement not matched by numerous other girls in her class.

Mac thought about asking Holly out again. But Mac knew that if he took Holly out again she'd feel duty bound before the evening's end to slip her hand inside his pants again and that he wouldn't do a thing in the world to stop her. And he knew he wouldn't respect either one of them in the morning.

Somehow, Sheila had managed to raise a kid with an unusually stubborn moral streak. It was a streak that couldn't help, somewhere down the road, but get him into trouble.

Because Mac went through most of his senior year dateless, rumors began to circulate about school that he was gay. In addition to his infrequent dates, accusers offered as evidence his fondness for sewing and cooking which he flaunted by taking a home economics class and pulling down an A. No one really believed these rumors, of course, because in those days no one actually believed anyone was gay. But Mac heard the rumors, and they hurt his feelings. Sheila did her best to console him. She told him to just forget it, that there was something sinfully perverse about a society eager to worship heroes in our midst and just as eager to see its heroes humiliated.

Whatever the truth of Sheila's observation, it didn't help Mac. So then she suggested that there was no big deal, really, about being gay. "A fag is just a person with a slightly different taste in sexual activity," she said. "And though I'm confident there are lots of different ways to do it, I bet it all feels just about the same when you get there."

"Mom!" Mac said, indicating that she was embarrassing him.

"Well for Chrissake, Mac. If you're gonna let this fairy shit bother you, why don't you get some girl and plug her on the corner of Canal and Gayoso just about the time everybody's arriving for school. That should put an end to it. And I doubt you'd have to look too hard to find a girl to lie down for you."

"Be serious, Mom," Mac said, realizing that Sheila was trying to elevate his mood with outrageousness.

Rejecting public, heterosexual fornication, Mac and Sheila finally settled on the less controversial plan of getting Mac a date for the senior prom. Mac wanted to go. But his shyness and social clumsiness had deterred him from asking anyone out. Now, every girl Mac could think of already had an escort. Even the homely girls who never went out had long since manipulated every connection in their power so as not to be left sitting home on prom night.

That's when Sheila came up with the idea of Mac's taking one of the unwed mothers. It was the perfect solution, a notion as wonderful as chocolate. Abandoned, unwanted, for the most part unloved, and most assuredly without prom plans, there were currently twenty-three unwed mothers that Mac could choose from.

Mac agreed and proposed asking Edith Jenkins, a nineteen-year-old graduate of Nicholls High School from New Orleans' working-class Ninth Ward. Edith was the prettiest girl at the home, but that was only part of the reason. When she'd first arrived, Mac got to know her instantly because she was so determined to keep herself in shape. The girls who availed themselves of the home's largess had to agree to abide by its strict regulations, one of which was never to leave the home's grounds except with express permission. This permission was not routinely provided for such things as jogging. So Edith did her running around and around the home's tiny back yard, twenty restricted laps to the mile. Mac, who was dedicated to physical fitness, found Edith's determination inspiring and further found their common interest in exercise a natural reason for getting to know her.

In the evening, when Mac would return to the unwed mothers' home after basketball or baseball practice, he would usually find Edith, attired in her baggy gray sweatsuit, pounding out laps in a yard too tiny for her ever really to lengthen out to a comfortable stride. At first, he merely uttered some passing words of encouragement. Later he lingered to make conversation as Edith whizzed repeatedly past the yard's chain-link side fence.

What Mac found most attractive about Edith, however, was neither her physical pulchritude nor her commitment to conditioning. It was her buoyant spirit which refused to give in to the depression which was the pervasive state all around her at the home. Like most of the girls who had to resort to the home for unwed mothers, Edith had arrived with few possessions. One of these, however, was a transistor radio which she kept tuned to local popular music station WTIX. Perhaps her daily transfusion of rock 'n' roll enabled Edith to face her destiny with a contagious black-humored defiance that never strayed into the self-indulgence of bitterness.

Edith had had to resort to the refuge of the home when her Catholic family disowned her upon learning of her pregnancy. Actually, it was only Edith's father, a piece-worker at the aluminum plant in Chalmette, who had totally disowned her. Her oppressed mother still sent her pilfered dollar bills in envelopes that bore no return addresses. "Mom probably thinks I have no idea where the dough's coming from," Edith told Sheila and Mac. "It never occurs to her that I might recognize her handwriting. But even if she were smart enough to disguise that, I'd still recognize the special smell of the money, which is a combination of aluminum dust, cheap cigar smoke, Woolworth's discount table plastic, and asshole. And that can only mean that it's been lifted from Daddy's wallet."

The final reason Mac wanted to ask Edith to be his prom date, and in some ways the most important reason, was that she was only five months pregnant. And whereas she had already started to "show," she hadn't started to "show" enough so that the casual viewer would likely think: "That girl's been knocked up."

Sheila was as fond of Edith as Mac was, but she nonetheless endeavored to convince her son to ask Helen Donalds to his prom. Helen was an unattractive and overweight sixteen-year-old whose ailing ego was in dire need of a booster shot.

Mac was not exactly enthusiastic when Sheila broached the idea to him.

"No," he said.

Sheila tried the humorous approach. "Her name's Helen, son. Just think of her as Helen Ahoy, the face that launched a thousand chips."

Mac smiled in spite of himself. "That's awful, Mom," he said. "And it's ugly."

Sheila appealed to her son's bleeding heart.

Mac employed a powerful coagulant. "Helen's over eight months pregnant," he pointed out.

"Yes," Sheila argued. "But she's so fat nobody would notice. Her parents didn't even know until her mother discovered she hadn't used a Kotex in six months. Poor kid was too dumb to just throw them away. Kept them stored under sweaters in the bottom drawer of her dresser where her mother found them one day, figured out the truth and kicked her out of the house."

"That's a horrible story, Mom." Sheila was getting to him, but his will to resist was fierce. To crack him she had to resort to the only strategy she knew of which could get to Mac McIntire; she double-teamed him. She got Edith Jenkins to lobby on Helen Donalds' behalf. Edith pointed out that she got pregnant after graduating from high school and had gone to her prom. Helen, on the other hand, would never even finish high school. Mac represented the only opportunity for a prom date she'd ever have.

So finally he relented, comforting himself for a time that at least this act of generosity would work to his benefit by putting an end to the fag rumor. But then with dawning alarm he worried that despite her family way, Helen Donalds was so utterly sexless that being with her might not really designate him a certified heterosexual.

Sheila, Edith and Mac all agreed that it would make no sense and do no good to have Mac ask Helen to the prom as if he were secretly enamored of her. As Edith observed, "Helen is pregnant, but that's not the same as stupid." So they settled on a straightforward, if diplomatic approach. Mac asked Helen if she'd like to attend the prom as his date, explaining that he didn't have one and that he reckoned Helen might not be going to get to go to a prom of her own and so, well, he figured that they could each do the other a favor. Helen's chubby face creased into a mask of joy and she accepted immediately. Sheila quickly set about making the necessary arrangements with the home's administrators, who, yielding to Sheila's influence, had begun to liberalize a whole host of their Victorian regulations.

In the two weeks before the big occasion, Sheila directed all the lessons in sewing class toward the making of formal gowns. This gave Helen the opportunity she needed to outfit herself with a proper dress and gave all the other unwed mothers, who were almost as excited as Helen herself, the chance to contribute oohs, aahs, and design suggestions.

By the time prom night arrived, Mac was feeling pretty good about his plans. He was well aware of Helen's rapture and rightly figured that almost any high school student could go to a prom but few had the opportunity to do so while providing someone else a genuinely special memory. Mac was guilty of a bit of self-congratulation on this occasion, but I suggest that you join your narrator in forgiving him this minor vanity.

Mac bought Helen an orchid wrist corsage, and, at the appointed hour, dressed in a handsome white dinner jacket with black satin lapels, came downstairs from the third-floor apartment he still shared with his mother. Waiting there to meet him were not only Helen and Sheila, but all the unwed mothers who had each played some part in getting Helen dressed. As Mac made his way from the central hall in the home's massive but shabbily furnished living room, he saw on Helen's beaming face that this night was as special to her as the wedding she'd never have.

She was damp with bittersweet expectation, and as pretty as she would ever be, her moist face a glowing pink. One of the unwed mothers with eventual plans to go to beauty school had done Helen's brown hair up in a high bun into which she'd braided a spray of artificial white flowers. Her dress was oyster white, gathered with elastic across her armpits and underneath her bust. From the elastic to the floor, the dress hung loose but hardly loose enough to conceal Helen's bulging abdomen. The neckline was scooped daringly low, but the student seamstresses had added a pale mesh material to cover Helen's cleavage. Into the dress's bosom they had thought to attach an absorbent, terry layer to protect against massive breasts which had already started whimsically to lactate.

Mac greeted Helen with a kiss on the cheek and helped her attach the corsage to her right wrist, then helped her reattach it to her left wrist after someone pointed out that it would be less likely to get knocked about there since she was right-handed. Then Mac stooped slightly as Helen attached the red boutonniere she'd purchased for him with some of the fetid money Edith Jenkins had received from her mother in envelopes bearing no return addresses. Sheila took a couple of snapshots. Everybody clapped. The other unwed mothers crowded around Helen as if she'd just won first prize in a beauty contest. And they were off.

But they never got to the prom. Helen went into labor about two blocks from the unwed mothers' home. So instead of driving down to the Jung Hotel where the prom festivities were about to start, Mac drove directly to Charity Hospital and checked Helen into obstetrics.

There was quite a bit of confusion about the registration. Since Helen was whisked directly away, Mac was left to oversee the filling out of forms.

Problems began almost immediately after "Mother's name?" when the brisk and starchy admitting nurse asked Mac, "Your name?"

"Why do you want to know that?" Mac responded. He wasn't being difficult, but he just wanted to make sure that the nurse wasn't guilty of unwarranted assumptions.

But the nurse, who possessed a patience that was lethal, just peeled back her eyelids with the calmness of cannon being raised to a target and said while looking at him starkly over her glasses, "We normally list the names of both mother *and* father."

Mac wagged an index finger back and forth saying, "No, no, no. You must misunderstand. Helen is an unwed mother."

Nurse Starchy fixed him a smile acid enough to dissolve concrete. "We list fathers, if known, whether married or not."

"Well, I'm not the father," Mac said, laughing nervously, wishing he hadn't.

"I see," said the nurse. "And just who *might* you be?"

"I'm her prom date," Mac said.

The woman finally lifted her head to look at him more naturally. She let her translucent, gray-rimmed reading glasses slip from her nose to dangle by a chain against her white-encased bosom. She looked at Mac in his tuxedo and flower-adorned lapel and surely thought him an escapee from a shot-gun wedding. "Okay," she said with just the faintest weariness slipping into her voice. "Let me cross out here where it says 'father' and pencil in 'prom date.'"

Mac thought of how much less humiliating it would have been just to let everybody go on thinking he was gay.

To aid in getting things straightened out, Mac called Sheila who came down as a representative of the unwed mothers' home bringing Edith along with her, all comely in a pale blue party dress that scarcely revealed her rounding tummy. Sheila's plan was to substitute Edith as a last-minute, though improperly dressed, prom date for Mac. But by the time they unraveled the mess at Charity it was nearly eleven-thirty and the prom had less than forty-five minutes to run. So, Sheila suggested that the two teenagers enjoy the remainder of the evening with a private party in the top-floor apartment at the unwed mothers' home.

Sheila drank a couple of beers with the youngsters before retiring so they could be alone. What exactly she thought they needed privacy for was not even clear in her own mind. But if they had slipped out of their nice clothes and fornicated right there on the living room rug, that would have been all right with her. Sheila approved of sex, wanted Mac to have fun on his prom night and liked Edith. And she was confident that Edith couldn't get pregnant. Again.

But Mac and Edith spent the night on the living room couch just talking. They talked about whether Edith was going to go through with her ostensible commitment to give up her child for adoption once it quit being a fetus and started being a baby. They talked about whether she would go back to being a secretary afterwards or whether she'd be able to find a way to go to college. And they talked about Mac's coming years at UNO and about what he planned to do afterwards.

Worried about the impact of alcohol on her fetus, Edith left the drinking to Mac who made his way slowly through a six pack before falling asleep with his head nestled in Edith's hair. At some point she had relaxed inside the long arm he'd thrown across the sofa back and she finally dozed off with her head against his chest.

Sheila found them thus intertwined when she awoke early the next morning to a jangling phone and forged her way into the living room to announce to the slumberers the news she'd just received: Helen Donalds had have given birth to a mammoth baby boy, had refused to honor her commitment to surrender the child for adoption, and had rapturously named him after her prom date.

With considerable bewilderment and to predictable derision, young Marshall McIntire "Mac" Donalds marched through the first decade of his life a half step behind his zealous and crusading mother who first became a Soldier of Jesus and then alternated between outspoken support for and castigating opposition to the man for whom her son was named.

Mac and Helen would not exactly be friends in later years. But she would never forget him. She kept the corsage he gave her pressed between the dittoed pages of the National Directory of the Soldiers for Jesus. And she inadvertently did Mac one aggravating favor. She helped squelch the rumor that he was gay by constantly referring to her prom date as the father of her son.

# CHAPTER SEVEN

I am happy to say that with Edith Jenkins, his *other* prom date, Mac would stay in closer and more pleasurable touch through the years to come. With Mac on a full-ride scholarship at the University of New Orleans, Sheila had extra money and used it to help Edith with the part-time education she also undertook at UNO. In turn, Edith became Sheila's usual companion for Mac's home games at the Lakefront Fieldhouse opponents began to call "the Chamber of Horrors" once Mac started leading his Privateers to unexpected victories. Whenever possible, Edith and Sheila also attended Mac's away games whenever they could get there. They were in center court seats together the night at the LSU Assembly Center in Baton Rouge that Mac and his UNO teammates upset a heavily favored UCLA team in the days when John Wooden was still coach and the Bruins often went whole seasons without tasting defeat.

And together Edith and Sheila made the journey to Atlanta's Omni at the end of Mac's senior season to watch the Privateers make a valiant bid before bowing by ten to those same UCLA Bruins in the NCAA semi-finals. Two days later they were present again in the Omni when Mac's teammates repeatedly passed him the ball and practically refused to shoot themselves as they assisted their star in pouring in fifty-eight points while leading UNO to a victory in the consolation game and a third place finish overall.

By the time Mac graduated from college, Edith was not yet quite through. Despite attending school year round, her progress was slowed not only by the parenting she had to provide for the daughter, Carrie, she had decided to keep, but also by her developing involvement in student political activities. From the beginning of her college education, Edith experienced a profound awakening. She discovered writers who put voice to her unexpressed frustrations. She became an outspoken feminist, an activist at UNO for a greater female participation in campus affairs, for a more determined effort on the university's part to hire women faculty members and give women a greater presence in its administration.

For a time, Edith's feminism took a viciously anti-male form. She had good reason to fault men for the problems in her own life. Her father was the typical, tyrannical male chauvinist of her generation. And it was a man, after all, who had gotten her pregnant and then threatened to get his friends to testify that they had all had sex with her in order to frighten her out of thoughts of a paternity suit. Unfortunately, Edith's negative attitudes toward men came along at just the right time to head off any possibility of a romantic relationship with Mac. During the years that Mac was at UNO, Edith was, for the most part, aggressively celibate. For a brief time, however, she did have a relationship with one of her fellow campus feminists.

Dot Brodie was a bright young New Orleans woman, a graduate of Benjamin Franklin High School for the gifted. The college success she should have found as a result of her intellectual endowments, however, was tarnished by a debilitating speech impediment which made it almost impossible for her to participate in class discussions. But Dot had a burning desire to express herself, and in Edith's athletic, articulate charisma, she found the spokeswoman for her ideas. Together they made an impressive and effective team on the UNO campus, struggling for, and achieving, several important changes at their school, including the establishment of a women's center and a fledgling women's studies program. In the process of their endless hours of working together—Dot sitting at a typewriter, often pounding out the rush of words her tongue refused to speak—the two became deeply committed to each other.

Gradually their friendship developed a sexual aspect. Dot was an avowed lesbian. And Edith was both angry at the world of males and in a period of life very open to experimentation. Mostly, though, Edith succumbed to Dot's hesitant, painfully expressed entreaties out of a reluctance to be the agent of further rejection for a person she cherished and who had known in her life so little acceptance. Such an affair, born largely of sympathy, was doomed from the very start, of course, and the time came when Edith had to tell Dot that they couldn't be lovers any more. Having to do so was one of the enduring heartaches of Edith Jenkins' life.

Ironically, it was during the very period of her relationship with Dot that Edith developed a friendship with Mac more solid and inviolable even than they had enjoyed before. Sustaining their mutual dedication to fitness, they worked out together, lifting weights in the UNO gym and running together along the lakefront levees. As they sweated and gasped, Edith habitually lectured Mac about "what innate asses men are." As was his way, Mac listened. And through his listening, he learned an immense amount about the difficulties women face in our society and world.

Only occasionally would he tire of her ranting and remind her, "Hey, Edith, I'm a man too, you know."

To which she'd always respond, "Yeah, but you don't count."

Mac was never sure why he didn't count, but he liked Edith a lot, and since she was willing to forgive his unavoidable gender, he was willing to forgive her little inconsistencies.

One day when they were out on a five-mile run, while Edith was in one of her particularly radical phases, Mac interrupted a harangue he'd heard frequently before to quietly remind her again of his unfortunate sexual equipment. As usual, she replied, "Yeah, but you don't count." They ran another fifty yards before she added, "You and I could even fuck, and it wouldn't be at all like a man and a woman doing it."

Invoking his mother's sense of humor and referring to a certain ample appendage, Mac grinned and said, "Yeah, it'd actually be more like a woman and a horse doing it."

Edith laughed. But as if she needed to prove something to herself, she insisted after they finished their workout that they return to her apartment and make love.

The experience was a disaster. Mac sat on her sofa reading a news magazine and drinking a soft drink while she showered. He didn't really think she was serious until she marched out of the bathroom totally naked and reported that she'd be waiting for him in the bedroom.

As Mac showered, he felt a pervasive discomfort. Edith was his *friend*. He didn't want to sleep with her as an experiment in *dis*passion. On the other hand, Mac was decidedly attracted to the idea of sleeping with her as an act of *passion*. Edith Jenkins was a powerfully attractive woman, her lithe, muscular body precisely the kind he fantasized about. Who was he kidding? Edith was the very person he usually fantasized about. So you can imagine now with what sweet anxiousness he showered before climbing into bed with her.

The coupling that followed, however, was performed with none of the mystery and spontaneity which makes human lovemaking so special. Edith was very forthright in telling him how and where to touch her. This was guidance Mac appreciated and benefitted from. But she delivered her instructions in such a clipped, almost military manner that Mac felt less a lover than a student mechanic. And when Edith finally came she did so without the languorous build-up which would have proved pleasurable to Mac, which would have allowed him evidence of the success of his ministrations. Instead she just caught her breath twice and threw back her head and squeezed her thighs vice-like over his dutiful hand.

"Your turn now," she said when she finished.

Mac wasn't sure he really wanted a turn. But Edith had fetched her diaphragm from its bedside drawer and set about smearing it and filling it with spermicide. She then inserted it, and, grabbing hold of Mac, inserted him with the same blank proficiency. Once he was inside of her, she was very energetic in her efforts to please him. As he plunged into her, she caressed his back and whispered softly, "Oh, Mac," and later "Would it be better for you if I got on top?" But by that time the encounter had proceeded so far without the proper naturalness and tenderness that Mac was operating with less than maximum rigidity, and he feared he might wither into a boiled Oscar Meyer if he stopped to arrange a new position. So he pounded on to a most dissatisfactory end.

It remained unclear whether Edith felt she'd proved whatever point she'd set out to make. She never mentioned the initial circumstances of their mating again. But the experience clearly encouraged both Edith and Mac to keep themselves out of each other's bodies.

Through even this experience, though, they remained friends. Mac was like an uncle to little Carrie, and he continued to listen and watch with sympathy as Edith exorcized the demons of male chauvinism from her life. With time Edith would become a feminist who numbered many men other than Mac McIntire among her friends. She would become a feminist who was not anti-male in the slightest way, a special woman who could communicate even with hostile men and sometimes even make them see the error of their ways. With Mac's enthusiastic support and admiration, Edith would finish her studies at UNO, attend law school at Loyola, become an attorney on the local ACLU staff and ultimately New Orleans' first City Councilwoman.

But all of that lay in the future. For now Edith and Mac continued to work out together while debating the issues of the day. Mac confined his dating to other women. Unfortunately, none of the other women was the proper combination of Susan B. Anthony, Billie Jean King, Lily Tomlin, and Catherine Deneuve that he was looking for.

So Mac left college still looking for Ms. Right.

# CHAPTER EIGHT

Mac also left college looking for a way to invest the half million dollar signing bonus and $250,000 salary he was paid by the Boston Celtics to join their basketball team. Compared to what top draftees get nowadays, Mac's financial package sounds paltry, but he got what was a lot of money back then. Doesn't sound bad to me, even now.

Mac arrived at the Boston camp touted as the next Bill Bradley—a consummate team player, a tenacious defender, and a gritty position rebounder. Like Bradley, Mac suffered from that notorious "white man's disease" of being unable to jump with the soaring acrobatic grace of such black stars as Julius Erving or Elgin Baylor. But like Bradley, too, Mac had an uncanny gift to be around the basketball, to make up with incredible timing what he lacked in vertical leaping ability, and to collect through the course of an average game an astonishing number of what players like to call "garbage points." And with his unorthodox but deadly release on his jump shot, Mac was able to score over taller players, even those who could jump half an arm's length higher than he could.

Unfortunately, Mac's potential for professional stardom was never really put to the test. During a training camp scrimmage, he went up for a rebound and came down on Dave Cowens' giant right sneaker. Mac's left foot rolled over with the crunching sound of Godzilla stepping on a potato chip the size of Houston, and he was out for the season with severed ligaments in his ankle and a ruptured Achilles tendon. An operation ostensibly repaired all the damage. But it left his ankle so stiff, and he tended to favor it so much when he worked out, that he developed tendonitis in his right knee.

Mac had never really been fast. But his great instinctual court sense and all-out hustle had allowed him to make up in savvy what he lacked in speed. Now with two bad wheels, he was downright slow. He was reduced to only knowing where he ought to be but could no longer quite get.

With considerable regret, the Celts cut him before the start of what should have been only his second pro season.

But as Mac always maintained, he was incredibly lucky. He never played a single game of professional basketball but, due to the nature of his original contract agreement, was paid exactly one million dollars for not doing it.

He was also lucky because, when he got back to New Orleans only fifteen months after having graduated from UNO, he was still such a local celebrity that he was able to land a job in the field he wanted to enter in the long run anyway. On short notice he was hired by the Orleans Parish School Board to teach and coach basketball at Felix Broussard High School.

Another of Mac's recent stardom might have chafed that he was only hired to coach the junior varsity. But Mac was more than satisfied. He had incredible financial security, and if he ultimately wanted to coach on the varsity level, he was content to learn his trade at a lower level. He figured he had time on his side.

A long column by the sports editor of the New Orleans *States-Tribune* noted Mac's move into the coaching ranks. The article was basically sympathetic to Mac and the challenges of his life's sudden new direction. It detailed his many basketball exploits beginning in junior high school and moving through his glory years at Easton and then the University of New Orleans to his "brief and tragic professional career." But at the column's end, the writer wondered pointedly whether Mac could become that rare star player with enough "patience and empathy" to succeed as a coach.

This was an utterly counter-prophetic piece of speculation. For it was as a high school basketball coach that Mac would find greater notoriety than he would ever have achieved as a professional basketball player. As Sheila paraphrased some less profane pundit: "God sure works in fucking mysterious ways."

So it was that on a typically warm and humid September morn that twenty-three-year-old Mac McIntire went off to begin his new duties as a teacher and coach at Broussard High School. There he would soon make the acquaintance of Barbara Jeanne Bordelon.

And there he would keep his date with destiny.

# BOOK TWO:

Barbara Jeanne Bordelon's
Sophomore Season In High School

# CHAPTER NINE

As a first-year teacher, Mac had to put in his time as a "floater." This meant that he was obligated to change rooms every hour, occupying space vacated by other teachers who were enjoying their free periods. (In a distinctly different context, Virginia Woolf captured Mac's first-year obsession with someday having a room of his own.)

As a first-year teacher Mac also had to endure the agony of three preparations. He was given one class of U.S. Government, which was his college major and about which he knew plenty enough to teach high school seniors who weren't thinking about school anyway. He was surprisingly but pleasantly given the overflow class of home economics in which he was to teach cooking in the fall and sewing in the spring. Unfortunately, he had to devote most of his energies to three crushing classes of World Geography, which was his worst subject in college and about which he knew not enough to teach earthworms to slime. He had taken only one geography course while at UNO, and it had proved a disaster. In it, he received the only D of his college career. Mac had several memories of that geography course. All of them bad.

His professor, a disorderly and testy old pedant named Robert Tuttle (or Uncle Bob to Mac and Sheila who developed a whole routine on the man) was one of those sad teachers utterly terrified by his students. He would fidget and sweat if students tried to speak with him before or after class or visit with him in his office. He practically disallowed questions. And he possessed regrettable grooming habits. He always seemed to have a spot of lunch about his mouth, a smear of breakfast on his shirt or coat. Every day before he met Mac's one-thirty class, he stopped off in the men's room on the way from eating a solitary lunch in the campus cafeteria. Many felt he did this just to delay the required confrontation with his students. But there could be no doubt that he actually utilized the facilities because by the time he stepped up on the low wooden platform to address the class, his trousers bore an inevitable wet stain at the base of his pants' zipper. Thus ever after that lone geography course, whenever one of them would find the other guilty of some slovenliness, Mac and Sheila would employ the term "pulling an Uncle Bob," or later just "Bobbing it." As time passed, each could send the other into a frenzy of face wiping or clothes checking just by uttering the dreaded word: "Bob!"

But Mac's most bitter memory about Professor Tuttle's course derived, ironically, from the one special talent Mac could credit Uncle Bob with: his incredible ability to produce accurate, free-hand drawings of geographical shapes from any of the four cardinal directions. This was the skill Robert Tuttle employed to administer pop quizzes. On spontaneous occasions, when he'd arrive in class with freshly dampened trousers, he'd march immediately to the vast blackboard behind his lectern and begin to draw. Early in the semester he sketched a figure which looked like this:

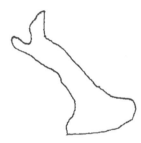

Under this figure he placed a large ?.

He then turned to the class and announced, "I want you to take a sheet of notebook paper and identify this shape. It's quite easy, so I'm sure you won't have any trouble with it. Subsequent shape identification quizzes will be rather more difficult."

Uncle Bob had a way with understatement. But like most of his classmates, Mac quickly recognized this first shape. On his paper he wrote "Italy." Just before he passed the paper up to the teacher, he added "Upside down."

The next class session Mac received this quiz paper back with the number seventy written in a smear of red ink near the top. From the podium Uncle Bob explained that full credit was available only to those who expressed in a complete sentence that the shape represented the nation of Italy as seen from either Austria or Switzerland.

This was when Mac began to suspect that World Geography was going to be hard. It was also when he really began to dislike Uncle Bob.

Later in the semester, Professor Tuttle dripped into class and put another figure on the board. The second one looked like this:

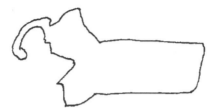

Under this figure he again placed a ?.

And once again he asked the class to make an identification. Mac was at a loss. Finally, with time elapsing he wrote: "Dumboland. As seen while feeding behind Tableland."

This answer did not endear Mac to Uncle Bob who posited that any serious geography student would have realized that the figure was Massachusetts as seen from Vermont or New Hampshire. Mac's paper was returned with a large red zero on top. Beside the number, Uncle Bob had written: "I'd like to introduce you to the complete sentence, Mr. McIntire, but in order to do so I fear I shall have to rely on you to provide the complete thought."

When Mac showed the paper to Sheila, she suggested Professor Tuttle try finishing his piss before putting his pecker back in his pants.

Near the end of the semester, Uncle Bob put one last figure on the board. Mac's last chance for a successful quiz performance looked like this:

As always, under the figure he placed a large ?.

Forlorn, Mac stared at the figure for a while. He had absolutely no idea what it represented. Finally he just wrote: "The figure appears to be Frankenstein, as seen from the neck up."

The paper was returned with its expected red zero. And Professor Tuttle again added a scrawled note. This one read: "Mr. McIntire, you are a lousy geography student. You are not a very good comedian either."

Uncle Bob had tricked him. He had spent hours studying an upside down Atlas. And now when the professor decided to sketch a picture of Chad, he'd done so right side up. Mac consoled himself with the admission that he probably could not have identified the drawing even if it had been produced in the usual topsy turvy manner. Chad was not exactly high on his priority list of places to know the shapes of.

When Mac explained the circumstances of still another poor geography performance to Sheila, however, she was not as easily consoled. "Uncle Bob," she said, snorting. "What a snob." She could feel herself about to break into verse. "What a brainless glob. What a blob."

"Mom," Mac said, laughing. "It's bad enough to be getting a D in geography.  Please don't make me listen while you rhyme, too."

But Sheila could not restrain herself and said:

There was a professor named Tuttle

Whose lectures allowed no rebuttal.

He sketched on the board.

He was out of his gourd.

And the front of his pants was a puddle.

There were clearly worse things in the world than having Sheila McIntire for a mother. Who better to teach Mac how to deal with adversity? And he certainly felt it adverse that the bulk of his first-year teaching had to be done in geography. So he made two pledges to himself from the very beginning. First, he promised that he would never sketch figures on the board and force his students to identify them. Second, he vowed never ever to pee in his pants before class.

# CHAPTER TEN

What Mac *did* try to do with his geography students that first year of his teaching career was to elicit a wonder from them at the vastness of human experience on this Earth. Always he tried to impart an understanding of the analogues other cultures bore to our own.

In short, I take note that long before the term became a political football, Mac seemed one of those secular humanists whom certain groups found responsible for most of the nation's moral ills. In fact, though he wasn't a churchgoer, Mac was a Christian. But he was humble in his own religious beliefs and presented the ideas of other world religions without prejudicial comment. He believed God had manifested himself to humankind in sundry ways and that most religions were legitimate ways to know the divine. Thus he was forever presenting the beliefs of Hindus or Buddhists or Bahais with all the enthusiasm he might have been expected to reserve for his own Christian tenets. He hardly managed to convert his students to his own ecumenism, but the benignity of his attitude was contagious, and students left his class somewhat more open-minded than when they arrived.

I must concede, however, that despite Mac's persistent effort and willed fervor, his success as a geography teacher was limited. His sympathetic, accessible personality made him popular, but his classes learned more about hard work than the issues that trained geography teachers would pursue. So he was relieved when he became a full-time home economics instructor after his first year at Broussard.

Like most things in his life, however, Mac remembered his experience as a geography teacher with some fondness. And well he should. For it was in his world geography class that he first met Barbara Jeanne Bordelon.

Actually, Mac and Barbara Jeanne "met" on Mac's very first day at Broussard when Mac called the roll in his post-lunch, fourth-period world geography class. But Barbara Jeanne, whom Mac subsequently discovered sat in the middle of the third row, was at that point nothing more than another "Here." On an especially muggy day some three weeks later, however, Barbara Jeanne's thin, freckled face forged its way into Mac's consciousness forever.

Mac had just floated into his third-story classroom from his duty as a lunch-room monitor when he spied a green-faced Harold Braxton leaning against the teacher's desk with one hand and waving desperately at Mac with the other. Wrinkle-browed, Mac started to speak to the student when the young man doubled over and vomited on the square-tiled floor, splattering his lunch with such force that it splashed backwards up against the desk and forward over Mac's shoes. Mac did his best to step around the vile orange mess on the floor in the hopes of reaching the student and steering him out of the room. But before Mac could manage, Harold vomited again, and Mac, who was not blessed with a particularly strong stomach, retreated into the far more pleasant air of the hall.

In the corridor, Mac blocked other students from entering the room and called to Harold that if he was going to throw up again, to please do it in a restroom. Then Mac gathered his other students about him and directed them to the cafeteria to wait for him. When he turned to take care of the sick boy, though, he discovered that lanky, brown-haired Barbara Jeanne Bordelon had entered the room and was now leading her distressed classmate toward the doorway. As she steered the boy into the hall, she said to Mac in passing, "You go on to the cafeteria, Mr. McIntire. I'll take care of Harry." Holding the boy's arm, Barbara Jeanne then guided Harold down the hall toward the restrooms.

In the lunch room that same delayed fourth period, Mac learned two unbecoming facts about his new place of employment: It had some genuinely bone-headed regulations, and it had an administration that was awfully quick to embrace outrageous decisions. In the process of trying to settle the class down for some sort of lesson, Mac asked them why in the world they thought Harold had just stood in their classroom and puked instead of going to a restroom.

Mac didn't really expect an answer to this question any more than someone expects an answer when he asks the sky, "Why is the world so screwed up?" But one of his world geography students nonetheless raised her hand and answered him. "I don't think Harry had a pass," she said. Mac shook himself like a boxer trying to clear his head. The student recognized that as her cue to explain. "Mr. Larrett," she said, referring to Vice-Principal Arnold Larrett, "told us during orientation week that except for the four minutes between classes that we were never to be in the hall without a pass. He said no matter what the reason we were to get a pass. He said even if we had to throw up, we had to get a pass."

Harold Braxton had evidently taken Mr. Larrett literally.

The second unbecoming fact that Mac learned that day began to come to light near the end of that same fourth period. Barbara Jeanne had come into the lunch room some twenty minutes after Mac had finally launched into a lesson on Malaysian yam harvests and had taken a seat silently among her peers. But as the hour was about to draw to a close, a student named Judy Trascio came into the cafeteria with a note that Mr. Larrett wanted to see Barbara Jeanne. Judy was an office courier—that is, a student willing to sacrifice the drudgery of a study hall for the pleasures of being a lackey.

Mac thought little enough of the note Judy handed him that he simply tucked it into the front pocket of his homemade shirt and looked down at his lecture materials to regather his thoughts, intending to continue on with his comments to the class. He intended to give the note to Barbara Jeanne at the end of the hour.

But when he looked up to address the class again, he found Judy Trascio still standing in front of him. "Thank you," Mac said with a smile of dismissal.

But Judy stood her ground and said, "Excuse me, but Mr. Larrett wants to see Barbara Jeanne immediately."

Mac looked at her quizzically but not really expecting her to know the reason for such urgency. Recognizing that look, Judy said triumphantly and with ill-disguised self-righteous glee, "Barbara Jeanne was seen going into the boys' third floor bathroom."

"I had to get Harry to a toilet before he ralphed again," Barbara Jeanne said from her seat in the middle of the room.

So Mac gave his class a reading assignment and asked them to behave, be quiet, and limit any necessary barfing to the bathroom, where they were invited to retreat without a pass the first moment they felt the need. He then accompanied Barbara Jeanne to the vice principal's office. The two of them, teacher and pupil, walked down the hall together like condemned men on the way to the gallows. Ahead of them, Judy Trascio strode with erect bearing and long deliberate strides as if she were a drum majorette. This was perhaps because she was a drum majorette. This was also because she was one of life's little rats' asses who delighted in others' misfortunes.

In the vice principal's office, Mac instantly interceded for Barbara Jeanne and explained the precise circumstances by which she had ventured into the boys' restroom. Mac presumed his explanation would more than suffice.

"Ahem," Mr. Larrett said when Mac had finished. I have noticed the frequency with which vice-principals say "ahem" just before they screw people. "It's very admirable, Mr. McIntire," Mr. Larrett continued, "for you to stick up for your student." He smiled with all the warmth of a moray eel. "I'd always heard you were a team player." (It really irritated Mac when people dropped references to his athletic accomplishments in situations where they were hardly relevant.) "But you have a class, I believe, and I think Barbara Jeanne and I need to have a little chat about lady-like behavior."

Mac didn't budge.

"Miss Bordelon," the vice-principal went on anyway, as if Mac had departed, "I have a report that several boys were in the act of urinating when you burst in upon them."

"I didn't notice," Barbara Jeanne said with a coolness that worried the edges of impertinence.

Mr. Larrett pursed his lips and said nothing. Barbara Jeanne waited. Mr. Larrett waited longer.

Finally, after a look at Mac, Barbara Jeanne explained, "I was just trying to get Harry to a toilet before he ralphed on the floor again."

"Well, did you give the boys utilizing the facilities any notice that you were coming in?"

Barbara Jeanne shrugged her shoulders almost as if she felt a sudden pain in the upper part of her back. "I didn't have time to say much," she said. "Harry was awfully sick. I had to put my arm around him to get him down the hall. And I could feel his stomach heaving. A couple of times he coughed a little, almost like a gag. I didn't even think he was going to make it."

"But weren't you embarrassed to be entering a boys' bathroom?" Larrett asked.

Barbara Jeanne looked at Mac again. "No," she said. "Why should I be? I've got two brothers."

"Ahem," Mr. Larrett said. "Miss Bordelon, you seem totally unaware of the gravity of your act. We just cannot have young ladies barging into the men's facilities whenever they take a mind to. It isn't decent. Two brothers indeed."

"She was just trying to help somebody, Arnold," Mac said. He wasn't sure whether he was supposed to address the vice-principal by his first name or not, but he didn't care a whole lot right then, either.

Mr. Larrett turned his head to Mac as if only just noticing that he was still, unfortunately, in the room. He showed his teeth in an absolutely poisonous smile. "I'm perfectly aware of the circumstances, McIntire. But rules are rules."

That was the tautological lesson Mac was going to have to confront throughout his relationship with Barbara Jeanne. In this case, the rules which were the rules said that any person of one sex entering a restroom designated for use by persons of another sex would be punished by detention or suspension dependent upon the judgment of the vice-principal. In this case, Mr. Larrett judged that Barbara Jeanne would have to serve five, one-hour detentions.

When Mac related this whole sordid tale that evening to Sheila, she chided him for not standing up for his student more effectively, or at least more vociferously.

"What more could I have done, Mom?" The question was forlorn but not defensive.

Sheila stewed about an answer for some minutes and then finally burst out, "You should have told that supercilious fart that he could jump up your ass and yell Bob."

This choice expression was one Sheila invented on the spot. Unfortunately, she was able to discover almost daily occasions for its invocation in the future.

# CHAPTER ELEVEN

Barbara Jeanne Bordelon came to Broussard High School with a set of athletic credentials much like the ones Mac had brought to Warren Easton nine years before. She was a middle distance runner who had not only won the city junior high championships in the 440, 660, and 880, but had also competed at the national Junior Olympics meet that summer in Chicago where she'd won a gold medal in the half mile.

In addition, Barbara Jeanne was an excellent swimmer who had placed in the one-hundred-meter freestyle and anchored her junior high team's 4 by 400 relay to a blue ribbon finish. She was ranked fifth in the state among fourteen-year-old female tennis players. And she numbered among her other athletic interests volleyball, softball, and basketball.

Mac, of course, knew none of this. As he was to remark just a short time later, Barbara Jeanne Bordelon's athletic accomplishments were among the best kept secrets in the city of New Orleans. So at the outset, Mac was drawn to Barbara Jeanne for reasons other than her physical talents. He admired her evident courage, and he was touched by her obvious kindness.

Barbara Jeanne acquired both of these qualities from her loving, devoutly Roman Catholic family. Her daddy, Henry Bordelon, came from an old Cajun family long since thoroughly Anglicized. Her mother, Marie, was old New Orleans Italian. The Bordelons took their religious beliefs seriously and raised their three children, Barbara Jeanne and two younger sons, in the faith, a faith they were forced to rely upon during Barbara Jeanne's tempestuous teenage years.

The Bordelons resided in Gentilly, a middle-class section of New Orleans that was perhaps the city's most fashionable for more than a decade after World War II, especially for young couples with families. By the time Barbara Jeanne reached high school, however, years of middle-class flight to the suburbs had left the area in decline. Henry Bordelon was a master carpenter who had gradually built his own small contracting firm. With his business centered so extensively near his Gentilly home, Henry resisted the rush to the suburbs even though he could have afforded to make the move. The summer after Barbara Jeanne's seventh-grade year at Capdau Junior High school, it was a move Henry desperately wished he'd made, even though no evidence ever came to light that tied the horror of one muggy August night to the Bordelon neighborhood. The perpetrators were never identified, never apprehended.

Barbara Jeanne had just pitched her teammates to another victory in their Ponytail Softball League at Harris Playground in Gentilly Woods. She was supposed to have gotten a ride home with a teammate's parents after the game, but for reasons which were never made clear, she was left behind and forced to walk. That needn't have been a problem. Her house was less than six blocks away. But on the way home, she was jumped and gang raped by a group of boys little older than herself.

Barbara Jeanne never knew for sure whether she had been a mere random victim of teenaged misogyny or whether the act of violence the rapists committed upon her virginal, boyish body was designed as a warning to all young women who dared to display athletic prowess. Barbara Jeanne thought that the felons were among a group of young males who had watched her pitch a no-hitter earlier that evening and who had derided her accomplishments with such jibes as "lesbo woman," "dyke lady" and "thimble titties." But she was never able to provide a positive identification of any of several youngsters the police singled out as suspects.

So in the end, the Bordelons followed the police department's suggestion and reluctantly let the matter drop. The police offered little likelihood even of making an arrest much less of gettng a conviction. Had Barbara Jeanne been able to say for certain who the rapists were, Henry thought he might have beaten them to death with his own hands. But with such an identification impossible, Barbara Jeanne's parents opted to protect their daughter's anonymity. In this regard, the police department had been very solicitous. And remarkably, though the Gentilly community was well aware that a teenaged girl had been raped in the neighborhood, not even Barbara Jeanne's friends seemed to know the identity of the victim.

At the outset, sustaining Barbara Jeanne's anonymity was made somewhat easier because of the limited nature of her injuries, which she passed off as the result of a backyard football game with her brothers. An instinctive fighter, she had struggled fiercely against her attackers, but they outnumbered her and overwhelmed her. They blackened an eye and bruised a pubescent breast. But Barbara Jeanne escaped otherwise unharmed.

Aside from the fact that she was impregnated.

Who knows how a person's character is formed? Perhaps certain humans are just born with extra measures of the will to endure. But perhaps again such traits are forged, rather than inherited. Whatever, Barbara Jeanne Bordelon's character was revealed in the aftermath of her rape. She was thirteen years old and barely aware that sexuality existed. But she was impregnated by one of a gang of faceless punks who knew not even the beginnings of what they did.

Someone more fragile than Barbara Jeanne Bordelon might well have capitulated to the horrors of existence at that point. But Barbara Jeanne was made of stuff too stern for surrender. And she was backed by parents too loving to tolerate self-pity. In other circumstances, of course, abortion might have been the answer. (I know without hesitation that I would have insisted upon such a course for a child of my own.) But the Bordelons were devout Catholics, and their religious convictions would not permit such an option. So they opted for the best strategy that *was* available. Barbara Jeanne was sent away for a year. Purportedly she had been invited to an institution that identified and trained potential female Olympic athletes. Everyone who knew Barbara Jeanne's athletic skills could believe she'd be someone selected for such training.

In reality Barbara Jeanne lived that year with her grandmother in the small south Louisiana town of Thibodaux. Meanwhile, in New Orleans, Marie Bordelon spread the word that she was pregnant, took to wearing maternity clothes and going out with padding underneath her smocks. In May, two months before Barbara Jeanne came home from "Olympic camp," Marie began to push a young "daughter" about the streets of Gentilly in a decade-old stroller.

The Bordelons took care of the attendant psychological perils of this plan by making it clear to Barbara Jeanne that she was in no way held responsible for what had happened to her, that she wasn't being sent away because they were ashamed of her. And to that end, both mother and father made frequent weekend trips to Thibodaux throughout the confinement of the year she turned fourteen, gave birth, and gave her child to her parents to be raised as her sister.

The logistics of allaying the suspicions of their friends and neighbors was another problem altogether. Barbara Jeanne's sudden disappearance had to be explained to her schoolmates. Her failure to return home for Christmas and other vacations had to be finessed. The charade of Marie's "pregnancy" had to be brought off. And the fact was that several among the Bordelons' closer associates were mystified by developments in Barbara Jeanne's life that year. But to a truly remarkable extent, the Bordelons learned that year most people will believe anything you tell them if you do so frequently and off-handedly enough.

I musn't leave the impression that the Bordelons manipulated this tragedy without abiding heartache, of course. Henry and Marie suffered enduring sadness that their daughter's innocence was snatched away so suddenly and so pointlessly. Barbara Jeanne lost a year of school and suffered a bout of depression after her child was born that was extenuated by the necessity that the baby, a girl she named Laura, had to be whisked away from her to New Orleans immediately after birth. Nights in the months before she would return home herself, Barbara Jeanne would lie awake in her grandmother's tiny guest bedroom, touch anguished adolescent fingers to her tiny, swollen breasts and start an easing flow of abandoned milk that mingled with the endless tears which dripped from her cheeks into a sticky, salty stain that covered the front of her pink nightgown.

Gradually, though, they all recovered. And they did so with a sense of determination far more fierce than any that had been present before. They all felt in an unspoken way that they had satisfied their lifetime requirement for victimization. Henceforth they planned to insist on justice with a greater urgency. The Bordelons were not exactly a liberal family, though their Catholicism had been influenced by the public careers of John and particularly Robert Kennedy. Certainly neither Henry nor Marie would have thought to identify with the women's movement. But their view of the world was altered by their experience with Barbara Jeanne's unwed motherhood. And it was that experience, known to practically no one save themselves, that was inextricably linked to their motivation to proceed as they did in the controversy that came to be called The Barbara Jeanne Bordelon Affair.

Mac McIntire, who had grown up with a mother for a father, could well have sympathized with Barbara Jeanne who grew up with a daughter for a sister. But, of course, he didn't know it for a long time. Nonetheless, the careers of Mac McIntire and Barbara Jeanne Bordelon were quickly intertwined by the tumultuous events that swirled around them both for all of Barbara Jeanne's three years at Broussard High School.

# CHAPTER TWELVE

The Barbara Jeanne Bordelon Affair probably began the morning in October when Mac tacked up announcements on various Broussard bulletin boards that he would begin holding tryouts the next week for the junior varsity basketball team. After school that day, Barbara Jeanne stopped by the home economics room where Mac taught his sixth-period class and asked if she could talk to him.

"Sure," he said.

"I'd like to talk to you about pronouncing my name," she said.

"Okay," Mac said. "Am I not supposed to say the N in Bordelon?" Mac made an attempt at giving her last name a more Frenchified pronunciation.

"Well, you're really not," Barbara Jeanne smiled. "But I don't mind so much as your calling me Barbara Jean." She pronounced her *Jeanne*, Mac's way, to rhyme with *green*.

"It's French," Barbara Jeanne said and then pronounced it correctly. It's my Grandmother Bordelon's name. It sort of rhymes with Don or Warren Spahn."

"Jeanne," Mac said, rhyming it more with *shun*. "Is that it?"

"Well, not exactly," Barbara Jeanne admitted. "Not too many people can say it correctly. Most of my friends just call me B.J."

Actually, a lot of Barbara Jeanne's friends called her "Cake," which was a nickname she'd picked up playing softball in the Ponytail League the very summer she was attacked. An enthusiastic coach encouraged his players by remarking that with B.J. pitching the opposition was a "piece of cake." As inning after inning passed without Barbara Jeanne's giving up a base runner, her teammates took up the chant, "Piece of Cake," gradually shortening it to a clenched-fist-punctuated "Cake!" every time B.J. retired another batter. And from that day forward Barbara Jeanne was "Cake" for some of her pals as often as she was "B.J."

But Barbara Jeanne didn't tell Mac all this at the time.

"Well, what if I call you B.J.? Would that be OK—B.J.?" Mac said, smiling, acting cute.

"That would be fine," she said.

"All right then, B.J. you are."

That settled, Mac was surprised when Barbara Jeanne didn't turn to leave. Instead she said, "But that's not really what I came to talk to you about."

"OK, B.J.," Mac said, still with the cute, "what did you really come to talk to me about?"

"I wanted to know if it'd be all right with you if I tried out for the junior varsity team."

Mac was surprised at this request—remember, he'd not an inkling of Barbara Jeanne's athletic credentials. But he didn't hesitate before he told her, "Sure, why not?" Then he paused before inquiring matter-of-factly, "Are you any good?"

"I think I could be," Barbara Jeanne said. She stood a second, as if something hadn't yet been said. "Are you really gonna let me try out?" she asked, her voice soft, but steady.

"Why wouldn't I? Is there a rule against it?"

"I think there may be," B.J. admitted. "I've never heard of a girl on a boys' team before."

"Well, neither have I," Mac agreed. "But why don't we worry about the rules after we see if you can make the team."

"Great!" B.J. said.

"See you next Monday," Mac said. After B.J. left, Mac gave her request little more thought. It never occurred to him that if Barbara Jeanne was actually good enough to earn a spot on his squad that whatever rules might prohibit her playing with boys couldn't be altered to accommodate her ability. But he frankly harbored few hopes that Barbara Jeanne's talents would be sufficient. Even had he been aware of what a superior athlete she was, he'd have had little cause to suspect that she could compete successfully against boys. For Mac knew an awful lot about athletics in general and an awful lot more about basketball in particular. He knew that women already held most of the records in long distance swimming, and he knew that they were expected soon to hold most of the records in running over fifty miles. He knew that even in sprint swimming, women were swimming faster times than men did only a decade ago.

But Mac also knew that women were at a significant disadvantage in sports like basketball that placed premiums on size and strength. He had known a lot of women, like his mother and Edith, who loved basketball and played it well. But he had never known a woman who could compete on equal terms with skilled men.

On the first day of practice, though, Mac realized he had perhaps finally met one. Forty-eight tenth and eleventh graders showed up for the first day of tryouts for the squad's fifteen positions. Most of them couldn't dribble, couldn't shoot, couldn't even catch the ball with any grace; some couldn't even run up and down the floor with adequate body control. Nonetheless, Mac regretted dismissing these hopeful players from the tryouts. In fact, he'd always speculated about a system of sports where all who desired to compete would be allowed to, a system where "team play" meant the obligation to utilize all the members of a team. But that was not the system he was operating under. Nor was it the system best suited for all sports organizations. And so, as gently as possible, Coach Mac informed the immediate rejects that their winter sporting activity this year would not be basketball.

Among the nineteen players Mac included for a second round of tryouts was Barbara Jeanne Bordelon. At 5'4", Barbara Jeanne was the shortest player still in the hunt to make the squad. She had only average jumping ability (in male terms). But she had more than adequate speed. Her best asset was her quickness, which, spurred by her determination, made her a tenacious ball hawk on defense. She was the kind of swarming defender that other players detested—forever slapping at the ball and thus hounding her opponent out of his natural rhythm. Her jump shot needed work, but Mac noticed that she possessed excellent control of her set shot. With practice, he thought, she should turn into a superb free-throw shooter.

Still, her making the team was by no means assured. Mac had six players who were at least six feet tall, including two gangly tenth graders who were pushing 6'6". Since Mac had never competed on the junior varsity, he was not exactly sure about how his team measured up. But he liked the looks of them. They were enthusiastic. And they appeared coachable.

Several factors finally led to Barbara Jeanne's inclusion. First was her hustle. Though Mac noticed that it at first irritated some of the boys, B.J. had the habit of running all the while she was on the floor. Instead of just jogging back to the end of the line after performing a drill, she always sprinted. Mac liked that. And he liked that the other players were perceptive enough to notice that he liked it. Soon they were all sprinting whenever they moved from one place to another.

Second, Barbara Jeanne made astonishingly rapid development with her jump shot. Mac had a little drill he used to teach this crucial shot. He had each player take a ball and jump straight up while simply lifting the ball over his or her head. The purpose of the drill was to make them realize that the first element of the jump shot was the jump. All too many young players, Mac had noticed, shot the ball *as* they jumped instead of holding it to release at the peak of their jump. It was a good drill. But benefitting from it was no guaranteed matter. Some players could perform the drill perfectly well and would instantly lapse back into a fatally early release just as soon as Mac instructed them to begin shooting again.

Barbara Jeanne, though, made impressively swift progress. Within a matter of days, she had basically mastered the process. And Mac noted with an almost nostalgic satisfaction that, probably because of inadequate arm strength, B.J. released her shot, much as he did his own, from behind and below her head.

But the third factor was the decisive one. Though she was so small that she could certainly play only at a guard position, Barbara Jeanne was probably the team's best defensive player. Or at least she was the team's defensive player most likely to produce a steal in a frantic situation. Her harrowing tactics would inevitably result in an excess of personal fouls. But Mac could imagine her being perhaps decisively effective if the team ever found itself trailing late in a game in which their opponents had gone into a stall. There would be no harm then if she were to foul. And she could perhaps save a game with a steal.

Shortly after Mac performed the unpleasant task of cutting the four remaining players who would not make the team, he called his other players out to the gym and sat down with them on the wrestling mats which were haphazardly stacked in a corner between the collapsible bleachers and the concrete-block wall. There he quietly gave them the speech which summarized his whole approach to basketball.

"Basketball is a game of love," he told his team. "And that means it's a game of shared joy. Others speak of the game as one of sacrifice, as one in which one player has to give himself up for another. But I don't think that's right. I see no sacrifice in passing the ball to a teammate who's open. I see only the shared delight of watching him score and bringing us all closer to winning. If we are to be a team, then we must love one another. We must love the player who doesn't even get in the game as much as we love the one who scores the most points. It is only through the testing our substitutes provide in practice that our starters can improve."

Mac smiled and looked his players over. Some stared at him intently; others cast their eyes down or away. Some let immature, self-conscious giggles tug at their lips for which Mac had to forgive them. "We must love the player who throws a pass out of bounds and costs us a game," he continued, "as much as we love the one who makes a free throw after the buzzer and snatches us a victory." He paused to make solemn eye contact with every player and smiled again. "And we must love a coach who sometimes gets frustrated with us and speaks to us sharply, who sometimes makes a decision that hurts our chances of victory. Because the coach is a part of our team too. And we must be confident of how much he loves us."

It was an embarrassing speech.

And Mac would never have delivered it in a truly public forum. But that didn't mean that the sentiments he uttered weren't deeply felt. And it was finally these very sentiments, embarrassing or not, that allowed Mac to find such success through all his years of coaching. He was one of those all too rare people in the field who built teams that were greater than the sums of their individual parts.

Characteristically, Mac's first team was a city-wide surprise. Or at least it surprised those in the city who thought they knew anything about junior varsity basketball squads. Nothing in particular was expected of the Broussard J.V. Bruins that year. But they managed to go a cool 23-2 losing both times to Jesuit, once in the regular season, once in the city championship game. The team had better personnel than anyone other than Mac had realized. String-bean forwards Donnie Start and Whitt McSeveney were erratic and too easily outmuscled. But they were both 6'6" and dominated many opponents by sheer size alone. Painton Richard and particularly Danny Waddell gave the Bruins an unusually solid backcourt. And best of all, chunky, gutsy Gary Cashner held down the middle in Mac's high-post offense and two-one-two zone defense and played every game with a fervor that was breathtaking. But the quality of the J.V. Bruin players that year only partially accounted for the team's success, for there were other schools with personnel at least as good. The Broussard tenth graders won so many games that year because they took their coach's counsel, learned to love each other, and really became a team.

The single player excluded from that special network of love was Barbara Jeanne Bordelon, who wasn't allowed to remain a member of the J.V. Bruins.

When word reached the Broussard principal that Mac had included a female on his squad, the first-year coach was summoned to a meeting with his boss. Dr. Samuel P. Riggs seemed born for administration. He was the essence of dignified. He looked like paintings of Robert E. Lee, gray and handsome, erect and almost regal.

Looks, of course, can be deceiving. For Sam Riggs had allowed himself to become little more than a figurehead and had surrendered day-to-day administration of his school to Vice Principal Arnold Larrett, whom you have met previously. It was, in fact, Larrett who brought to Riggs' attention that Mac had included Barbara Jeanne on his junior varsity squad. And it was Larrett who did most of the talking when Mac was told that B.J. could not play for him.

"New Orleans interscholastic athletic regulations," Larrett informed Mac, "expressly forbid males and females from competing against one another." With a wicked glance at Dr. Riggs, Larrett flashed his venomous smile at Mac and said, "Rules are rules, Mr. McIntire. Think back to your own playing days; you remember."

Mac resisted the impulse to invite Larrett to jump up his ass and yell, "Bob." Instead he tried to argue the issues involved. "First, there's the issue of whether Barbara Jeanne should have the *right* to play on this team. She's certainly good enough or I wouldn't have kept her. She beat out thirty-three other students for the right to be on my team. And she did it fair and square, no quarter asked, none given."

"Miss Bordelon's *rights*, as you put it," Larrett replied, "are not for us to decide. For us is to follow the rules." Dr. Riggs nodded his agreement.

"But we could be instrumental in changing rules that are unfair," Mac asserted.

"I think we lack a consensus here that these rules *are* bad, Mr. McIntire," Larrett laughed with feigned jocularity. Dr. Riggs shook his head in agreement. "Letting Miss Bordelon play with the boys could establish a disastrous precedent. For how could we then prohibit boys who desired to do so from demanding to play on the girls' team. And let me hasten to remind you, Mr. McIntire, there *is* a girls' team for Miss Bordelon to play on. Title IX has been quite clear about our obligation in that regard, and we have been in the strictest compliance."

There was much that Mac might have contested about Broussard's compliance with the spirit of Title IX, though he had little doubt that the letter of the law had been observed. But he reserved that approach for a later moment and took up instead the fear of boys invading girls' teams. "Nonsense," he said.

Dr. Riggs scratched his head and looked at Vice-Principal Larrett who cleared his throat. "Ahem," Larrett said.

"As I see it, the situation is precisely analogous to boxing," Mac pointed out. Dr. Riggs scratched his head on the other side, and Larrett emitted a cough of disbelief. "Precisely," Mac said, with arctic articulation. "A middle-weight boxer, if he's good enough, is fully entitled to challenge for the heavy-weight crown. While the converse, of course, is not true."

"Perhaps, to use your own terms, Mr. McIntire, if Miss Bordelon were a proven middle-weight champion, your case would possess more merit than it does," Larrett said, proving that he got to be vice-principal through moral turpitude rather than pure stupidity. "Now tell me truly; do you really see Miss Bordelon starting for your team this year?"

"No," Mac admitted.

"Well, then," Larrett chuckled.

"She'd play," Mac said. "She'd contribute."

"And don't you think she'd contribute more to our girls' team?" Larrett observed, his tongue darting between bared teeth.

"Of course she would," Mac said. "She'd eat a women's league alive."

"Well, then, don't you think we should provide her that opportunity?" Again Larrett flashed his strychnine smile.

Mac really didn't know the answer to this last question. But he suspected that Barbara Jeanne would be better off playing a limited role on his team than starting and starring for the girls' squad. The boys' junior varsity played a twenty-four game schedule. The girls' team (there was no junior varsity for women) played only twelve games. And Mac frankly had no confidence that the women's coach could offer Barbara Jeanne the kind of training that he could. But most of all, Mac thought the system ought to let Barbara Jeanne make up her own mind, not force its bureaucratic will upon her.

What Mac also thought, by the end of the season, was that losing Barbara Jeanne as a team member very well could have cost his team a city championship. In the final game of a season, still years before the shot clock, Jesuit beat the Bruins 52-51 and successfully froze the ball for the last minute and twenty-two seconds. In that time, a swarming B.J. might very well have come up with a steal that could have turned a crushing loss into victory.

Still, when Barbara Jeanne's sophomore season was history, Mac was not sure that playing for the Lady Bruins had been altogether bad for her. To the cheers of her teammates chanting "Cake, Cake, Cake," she did mature as a player during the year. In the process of leading the Lady Bruins to an undefeated season, she obviously got the playing time that she likely wouldn't have on the boys' J.V. And as Mac had predicted, she ate the girls' league alive. If anyone had kept such statistics, there's little doubt that B.J. would have headed almost every offensive category.

But Mac harbored certain reservations as well. B.J. played her sophomore season against competition she thoroughly dominated. And given the peculiarities of women's six-person, double half-court basketball, Barbara Jeanne's great defensive strength was utterly wasted. As a forward, she wasn't even allowed on the defensive end of the floor.

In the aftermath of the J.V. Bruins championship loss to Jesuit, Mac, his mom and Edith Jenkins sat over pizza and beer and analyzed the defeat. Just as was true when he was a player, Sheila and Edith seldom missed one of Mac's games. Inevitably, the talk turned to the absence of Barbara Jeanne Bordelon and the difference her presence might have made in the final.

"When they kicked her off the team," Sheila said, "you should have told them to eat a bag of shit and die."

"No," Edith said. "If you're really dedicated to women's athletic rights, as I think you are, you should have told them that you wanted to coach the women's team. Women deserve the best athletic training they can get. And there's little question that you're a more qualified coach than that ninny who directed the Lady Bruins this year. She's so incompetent, she almost managed to lose a game or two even with Barbara Jeanne in the line-up."

As fate would have it, before school ended that spring, the incompetent ninny filed for a maternity leave for the next year. And at Edith's vigorous urging, Mac applied for the opening, and, over the strenuous objections of one of the girls' team's mothers, who argued that a man coaching women was "dangerous, indecent, and probably immoral," he got it. The incident of objection was covered in the papers but never quite developed into a controversy. As a closing note to a column on an entirely different topic, the sports editor of the *States-Tribune* wondered in print, "Why would former UNO great Mac McIntire, off to such an auspicious start to a coaching career, want to take a step down to direct the women's team at Broussard?"

In a frenzy of dedicated activity through the remaining days of the school year, Mac set out to prove to the *States-Tribune* sports editor and all other basically disinterested parties that his taking the women's team was not a "step down." A self-appointed, one-person campaign committee, he instantly sought to upgrade the quality and commitment of New Orleans high schools to women's basketball. In many areas he found success because no one cared enough to resist him. His first objective was to ensure the participation of area schools in the women's state basketball tournament which had been running for years but had never included participation by Orleans Parish high schools. When he achieved that, he then set about guaranteeing that the women could play a schedule that included the same number of regular season games as the men. He met plenty of resistance on this point, even from other women's coaches. But continued reference to Title IX language convinced the School Board's athletic council that they'd be best advised to go along before they faced a lawsuit over the issue.

Sundry other deficiencies in the women's basketball program needed addressing, but with the above two major objectives accomplished, Mac really began to look forward to Barbara Jeanne's junior season. With a star of such magnitude in his starting line-up, he felt certain his Lady Bruins would dominate New Orleans area schools and might very well compete for the state title. What Mac had never accomplished as a player, he had every intention of accomplishing as a coach.

Then fate flipped its finger at Mac's destiny once more.

Barbara Jeanne Bordelon filed suit in federal court to be allowed to play with the boys.

# CHAPTER THIRTEEN

It is, of course, hotly debatable whether or not American justice grinds exceedingly fine. But Justice Holmes was indisputably correct in observing that it grinds slowly. There was, hence, worry from the outset of Barbara Jeanne Bordelon's suit that the courts would malinger so long in reaching a decision that she would graduate from high school and thereby render the case moot. The trial was not even set to begin until the middle of the summer before sixteen-year-old Barbara Jeanne entered her junior year in high school.

Basically, Barbara Jeanne's suit contended that she was discriminated against on two grounds. By not being able to compete against male athletes, the suit argued, she was denied exposure to the best possible competition, competition she deemed necessary to prepare her most successfully for her dream of earning a spot on the U.S. Olympic basketball team.

Second, she claimed discrimination by being offered competition only in so-called "women's basketball." Based upon the absolutely counter-scientific position that women athletes lacked the necessary endurance to play a full-court, five-on-five game, "women's basketball" restricted offensive and defensive players from passing across the mid-court line. This, Barbara Jeanne's suit maintained, not only failed to allow a player to exercise *all* her basketball talents, but directly inhibited the development of ball-handling skills and experience in the non-existent fast break.

In nearly every way conceivable, the suit concluded, "women's basketball" put Barbara Jeanne at a disadvantage in preparing herself to win a college scholarship and compete at the university level where the game of "women's basketball" had long since been consigned to the scrapheap for historical curiosities.

As defendants in the suit, Barbara Jeanne named the Orleans Parish School Board and its Interscholastic Athletic Council, Broussard Principal Dr. Samuel P. Riggs, Broussard varsity basketball coach Wayne Dawson, and former Broussard junior varsity basketball coach Marshall McCall McIntire.

As Edith Jenkins later explained to Mac, it was standard procedure in such a court action to sue everyone conceivably connected to the case to ensure that the justice sought was not wiggled out by those it was sought against.

But Mac was hurt nonetheless. And before he was hurt, he was angered by a small article on the suit that ran one June Saturday morning in the *States-Tribune*. It was from this article that he learned about the suit in the first place, learned even that he was named as defendant. The paper referred to him as "the coach who cut Miss Bordelon from his junior varsity squad. Without the services of Miss Bordelon," the article continued, "the 'baby' Bruins went on to capture the runner-up spot in the chase for the city J.V. crown last year."

Mac was astonished and even more hurt when he learned in that article of Edith Jenkins' involvement in the case. Edith, it seems, was the suit's instigator. She was in her first year of Law School at Loyola when she became acquainted with Barbara Jeanne's situation through her relationship with Mac and Sheila. Edith had originally contacted Barbara Jeanne just to put together a hypothetical action for a project in her trial advocacy course, but the more she worked with the materials, the more she became convinced that B.J.'s suit really ought to be litigated. So she contacted the firm of Lutze, Piehl, Nord, Schwehn, Uehling and Feaster, a partnership of six female attorneys who were particularly interested in cases concerning women. Edith had met Karen Lutze at the ERA rally, and through Karen, had become friendly with the other members of the firm.

Ordinarily, Edith would have confided all of this to Mac and Sheila from the very outset. They were her best friends. Sheila (and now Mac indirectly, of course) was still helping Edith shoulder the financial burden of her education. And with Edith caught up in the grind of law school, Mac and Sheila, either singly or together, provided most of the baby-sitting for Edith's daughter Carrie.

But Edith had delayed informing them of her project at the beginning because she wanted to complete it and deliver it to them as a kind of surprise. She was shocked and dismayed then, when Karen Lutze insisted that Mac be named as a defendant. Edith felt like a cross between Susan B. Anthony and Benedict Arnold. She was proud of what her ideas and initiative had wrought, but she was so sick about its implications for her relationships with Mac and

Sheila that she could just never bring herself to inform them beforehand of what was about to happen. I can't emphasize her distress enough, when, at just about the same time that Mac sat reading his Saturday paper, she sat reading hers and found herself referred to in the Barbara Jeanne Bordelon article as a "family adviser and legal consultant."

Imagine her dread only moments later when she answered the ringing phone and heard Mac's voice bark from the receiver, "Get your fucking pussy ass over here. I want to ask you some questions. And you better have some goddamned answers."

Feminists of other ilks might have been incensed at such a solicitation. But Edith's jockish earthiness saved her from offense at genital references. Besides, she expected Mac to be upset and granted his right to be. What concerned her now was how to find a way to save their friendship. In a bind, she opted for impish flippancy.

"You'll have to be more specific," Edith said. "My pussy and my ass are entirely separate orifices."

"Cut the crap, Jenkins. I . . ."

"Ah, I guess it's my ass you're after, then," Edith interjected.

"That's disgusting," Mac replied but with less edge in his voice. "Just get over here," he ordered her. "And stow the cute at your place."

When Edith arrived at the apartment on the top floor of the unwed mothers' home where Sheila and Mac still resided, she found Mac with a day's growth of stubble on his chin and a half-empty cup of cold coffee in his massive right hand. He was pacing around the cluttered living room in a long-sleeved, homemade shirt, a pair of tattered gym shorts and sandals.

He was not happy.

"Reporting as ordered, *sir*," Edith said as she entered the cramped apartment, as usual without knocking. She stopped on the other side of the coffee table from where Mac had suddenly sat down on the sofa and drew herself up into the sort of still salute that Shirley Temple executed in her childhood movies.

Mac let her hold her exaggerated position in a pointed silence for a long moment before he finally relented and said, "What's appropriate?"

Edith slumped into an easy chair. "I don't know," she said, her voice small.

"Should I try 'fuck you?'" Mac said. "I'm sure Mom would in this situation."

"Sheila has never tried to fuck me," Edith rallied. "You did once, though. An awfully long time ago."

Mac didn't smile. He pointed at the newspaper on the sofa. "I understand you're a consultant now. Care to consult with me?"

Edith shrugged. She was ready to take her medicine.

"A legal consultant and family adviser, I believe, is your new vocation." Mac picked up a sheaf of legal papers off the coffee table and waved them at Edith. "Maybe you'd like to look these over for me, consult with me and then perhaps offer some advice."

Edith bent forward in her chair to take the papers, but Mac refused to hand them to her. "What are they?" she asked, sitting back again.

"Oh, they're just the various documents associated with a piece of property I just bought with some of the money the Celtics paid me for not playing basketball in the NBA. It's a big place, a giant place, in fact. It isn't even a house really, though I'm planning on turning it into one. And you know what I've been planning on doing once I got it fixed up?"

Edith shook her head. She didn't know what this was all about. She had thought the papers were those notifying him that he was a defendant in the Barbara Jeanne Bordelon Case.

Mac set the papers back down on the coffee table, swung his legs up onto the couch and lay back against the arm. He twined his fingers behind his head and spoke to the ceiling. "I was gonna ask you and Carrie to come and live with us until you finished law school. I know you've been struggling to make ends meet. And I thought eliminating rent might help out some. In the new place you could have a whole side of the house to yourself. But now I'm thinking maybe I shouldn't do that." He turned and looked at Edith whose fine fair skin had turned chalky and gone taut over her face. "What do you think?" Mac said.

Edith could feel tears well up in her eyes. "I think you should listen to what I have to say."

"Okay," Mac said quietly.

As Edith explained, and Mac came to realize how inadvertent most of the developments had been, he softened and ultimately even apologized for having been angry. "But what I still don't understand," he protested to Edith after she'd related the whole of her story, "is why you convinced me to go for the girls' coaching position only to turn around and try to take my star player away from me."

Edith assured him that the second development came months after the first, that she'd only recently realized that Barbara Jeanne's case was really litigable, and that at any rate she still felt Mac ought to want to coach the women's team, Barbara Jeanne or not. "The point I made about your coaching the girls," she stressed, "was that varsity women should get better coaching than junior varsity boys. You're a better coach than the incompetent ninny, so you should have been moved into that position. That whole argument seems to me to make sense regardless of what happens to Barbara Jeanne."

Mac took a deep breath and rubbed at his lidded eyes with his finger tips. "I hate it when you make sense," he said. "I've always hated it. Especially when it means I'm required to do something for which I can no longer feel sorry for myself."

Edith smiled, got up and moved to sit beside Mac on the tattered old sofa. She put his arm around her shoulders, and she put both arms around his waist. "Does that mean I might still get an invitation to share your new house?" she asked.

"It's not exactly a house," he said.

"What exactly is it?" They were still holding each other like two fond siblings.

"It's more of an abandoned railroad station," Mac said. "You know, the one on the river-side corner of Oak and Leake."

Edith pulled back away from him and stared up at his rugged face. "You bought the old Carrollton Railroad Terminal?"

Mac raised his eyebrows and nodded.

"And you plan on living in it?"

Mac nodded again.

"And you want me and Carrie to live in it, too?"

"Well, first I want you to work on it with me," Mac said. "It's just one huge room now. That, the small ticket office and the two bathrooms are the whole thing."

"Uh huh," Edith said, rolling her eyes. "But what are its disadvantages?"

"Finding a place to utilize the old wooden benches. You know, the kind with the thick back and the seats on either side."

"Mac," Edith said seriously. "Why in the world do you want to make that old thing your house?"

To explain, he stood up and casually rested the palms of his hands against the textured ceiling. "Kiddo," he said, "I've lived in this four-room apartment with its eight-foot ceilings my entire life. Or at least all that I can remember of it. In my new place, I won't bump my head into the light fixtures and my elbows into the walls. Want to hear my plans?"

Mac sketched a crude blueprint of the renovations he was planning as he talked. "I want two separate living spaces," he explained, "one for me and Mom, and one for you and Carrie, each with two levels of rooms—there's plenty enough height; the roof peaks at nearly thirty feet. Downstairs, I want to put in a study for me and sewing room for Mom. On your side, another study and a playroom. In between these two areas, I'll have a dining room, a kitchen and a central living room which rises all the way up to a skylight at the top. We'll have four bedrooms upstairs and a big den over the kitchen and dining room that looks down into the living room. And we'll have enough bathrooms so that we can all shower at the same time if we want to." Mac concluded his drawings and looked up at Edith. "What do you think?" he asked

"It sounds fabulous," she said. "But what do you need me for?"

"Good taste," Mac said. "You know I don't have much. And Mom doesn't have any. You can advise me about colors and carpets and drapes. That sort of thing."

Edith was touched. "Mac, baby," she told him softly. "You don't have to give me half your house to get me to help you with it."

"I know that, dumbass," he said. "I'm getting you to live there for Mom's sake."

"Sheila?" Edith said, falling for his trap.

"Sure. She's lived with unwed mothers for so long I don't think she knows how to live without them. So I have to get her one to make sure she'll be comfortable.

"How did you get to be such a colossal asshole?" Edith asked.

"Practice," Mac said. "Good genes. But mostly practice."

In the excitement over the purchase and renovation of his fantasy home, Mac kept his mind off Barbara Jeanne and her lawsuit. Since the situation was completely beyond his control, he was determined to avoid worrying about it. If B.J. played for him in the fall, that would be wonderful because his Lady Bruins would be a powerhouse. On the other hand, if the suit got settled in time and B.J. played with the boys' team, then that would probably be good for her.

As the beginning of the trial slowly approached, Mac devoted his concerns to other things. In the process he sometimes forgot that he was even a defendant in the proceeding.

Unfortunately, his involvement wasn't forgotten by others. And they were already beginning the process that would eventually make Mac into their most unwitting hero.

# CHAPTER FOURTEEN

Mac spent most of his summer hanging around the work site on his new home, watching the progress of the renovations and redesign, more often than not picking up a hammer or saw or later a paint brush to help out as he jawed with the workmen. Somewhere during that time of sweet anticipation, of consultation with Edith and debate with Sheila about decorating and furnishing plans, the new abode developed a nickname, a shorthand that stuck. First Sheila, and shortly Mac and Edith with her, began to refer to the place as "the Terminal." Eventually, when remodeling was complete, the structure looked more like a home than it did a railroad station. But even long after the edifice had become thoroughly domesticated, it always remained "the Terminal." Mac thought the name fit perfectly since it was the last house he ever planned to own.

When he wasn't at the Terminal, Mac could usually be found downstairs at the unwed mothers' home. Physical exercise had grown much more popular for pregnant women, and Mac adopted the habit of drifting into the home's lounge during the unwed mothers' ten to eleven free hour and leading those who were in the mood in a round of calisthenics or, if the weather was nice, rousting the energetic out to the backyard blacktop for a game of basketball. Afterwards, he would often follow them to the sewing room where he would meander among the unwed mothers at their humming machines and offer words of advice and encouragement. During this summer, Mac grew closer to the unwed mothers than he had been since his high school days, and they were as fond of him as they would have been of a devoted brother.

Summer evenings, Mac divided between two other activities. He was engaged in a massive sewing project trying to make all the drapes for his new house. This undertaking would have been significant enough had the home been the standard suburban tract house. But the window space in the Terminal included one stretch at the back of the living room that ran twenty-eight feet wide by twenty-six feet high. Watching Mac labor over the light-weight material she'd helped him selected, Edith commented, "You might have an easier time draping a mountain gap."

When he wasn't sewing, Mac spent his summer evenings dating a variety of new women in his life. Even he marveled at this. Mac was not normally a very introspective man, in part because, other than socially, he was not a self-conscious man. But he recognized that his burst of dating presented a sharp change from the past. He wondered if this meant he was getting old. He didn't feel old, and of course, he wasn't. So he decided that his newfound desire to date resulted from a vacuum in his life. Until now, Mac had been driven by the need to prepare for the next season, a future he could actually influence through the discipline of physical conditioning and repetitious drill. But he was a player no more. And though he still worked out, it was no longer with the sweet jab of expectation goading him to execute one more sit-up or shoot one more jump shot. In the absence of that anticipation, in a summer of waiting to learn if the player he had wanted to keep would be successful in escaping from the team he had embraced in order to coach her, Mac turned to dating.

"I wonder if that means romance is born of a vaguely anxious boredom?" he asked Sheila one night.

"I'd say more of indigestion," Sheila replied without looking up from the mammoth spread she was hand-quilting for the king-sized bed Mac was planning to purchase for his room at the Terminal.

"Come on, Mom, you must have had some romantic urges in your time."

"In my time?" Sheila snorted. She adjusted the half-lensed reading glasses she had taken to wearing when doing needle-work. "What do you think I am? Some relic from another historical period? This *is* my fucking time."

"Yeah, but to my knowledge, you haven't been doing a whole lot of fucking, your time or not." Mac watched as Sheila gave an almost imperceptible jerk. He knew it always surprised her when he talked like she did. And there was an occasional puckish side of him that enjoyed shocking her.

"I been doing my share," Sheila growled.

Mac was momentarily slackjawed. "Come on," he said.

Sheila adjusted the quilt over her lap to lay a patch on the next section. "You're not home every night. How do you know what I do when you're not around?"

"Who've you been doing it with?"

"I thought you wanted to talk about romance," Sheila said.

"I thought that's what we were talking about."

"No, it seems we've slipped off into talking about fucking. Fucking and romance are altogether different. They sometimes coincide, but not often. Romance usually comes before fucking and is commonly killed off by it. Lots of people can manage to be romantic on the way to bed. But a damn sight fewer can manage to sustain it through to waking up the next morning."

Mac shook his head slowly and then knelt at his mother's feet and helped her spread the finished section of the quilt away from where it was gathered in her lap. After a moment he said, "So you figure romance is better, huh?"

Sheila looked over the tops of her half-lensed reading glasses at Mac before returning her attention to her sewing. "On the contrary," she said. "Fucking is unquestionably better. Romance is bullshit. It's not real. It makes people act stupid. Fucking, on the other hand, is good for you. It releases tension. It improves your attitude toward one person in particular and the world in general. It's fun. It's not fattening. And it doesn't leave you with a hangover."

Mac looked hard at his mom before he said, "You're an ornery old bitch, aren't you?"

Sheila adjusted the quilt again. "So I've been told," she said. She sewed a stitch or two and then thrust the needle straight down into the material. She took off her glasses, laid them in her lap and looked over at her son who was sitting on the floor, his back against the couch, his long, splayed legs seeming to stretch across the entire cramped living room. "What are you trying to talk to me about, Mac?"

"Why I'm so horny all of a sudden."

"You've never been horny before?"

"Of course, I've been horny before. I've just never been horny all of the time before."

"You've always been busy before."

"Then sex *is* born of boredom."

"It can be, yes. But that's not what you said at the outset. You said romance was born of boredom. Romance is born of stupidity."

Mac laughed as he was supposed to. Sheila started back at her sewing, and a comforting little silence settled over them like a cool sheet on a warm summer night. Finally, Mac said, "Do you believe in love, Mom? Love between a man and a woman?"

"Of course," Sheila replied without looking up from her work. "It doesn't happen very often. People frequently mistake romance for love. But there can be love between a man and a woman if the circumstances are right."

"And what are those circumstances?" Mac asked.

"Well, everybody these days talks about equality. And I'd lend my vote for equality, too. But I don't think that equality is measured in evenly parcelled tasks, obligations, responsibilities or whatever. Not any more than on a basketball team where all players are certainly equal but one is expected to handle the ball, another to rebound, a third to score. The kind of equality I'm talking about is measured in terms of commitment. It's a complementary kind of thing far more often than it's a precise one-for-one . And I think it's got to be based on companionability. If you're gonna love somebody, you're gonna need to like doing the same things—things other than fucking, I might add, though fucking is certainly right in there."

"So I should marry someone like Edith, huh?"

"You should marry Edith or someone like her, yes."

Mac didn't pause to acknowledge the distinction in Sheila's affirmation, but speaking more toward the ceiling than his mother, he said, "The problem is that there aren't too many like Edith, as far as I can tell. And Edith isn't interested in men. Or at least she isn't interested in me. We're more like brother and sister."

"You could get over that."

"I'm not so sure."

"Then you should marry someone *like* Edith. If you marry. There's no law which says you've got to marry at all. Some of us have managed to find very companionable lives without marrying."

"Yeah, but you had me, Mom," Mac teased.

"You and the unwed mothers," she reminded him.

"And some occasional, mysterious fucking, it seems."

"I didn't say anything about its being occasional."

Mac laughed again. "So you think it's okay to be fucking someone you're not in love with?"

"I'm afraid there'd be a world-wide sex shortage otherwise."

"You're not serious."

Sheila chuckled and shook her head. "Not entirely. Look, Mac, you're a grown man. You know as much about this as I do." Mac started to interject that he wasn't so sure, but Sheila waved him off and continued. "You know that although you don't have to be in love with somebody to fuck them, it'll only be any good if you've got a damned good liking for them. And you've got to be sure that the other person's feelings are the same."

"That's not so easy, Mom."

"Of course not. That's the other reason, in addition to being bored for the first time in your life, that you're so horny this summer."

Mac looked at his mom with a devilish gleam in his eye. "Maybe the main reason I'm so horny this summer is that my appeal to women strays too frequently to the paternal-fraternal and too seldom to the vaginal-oral."

"Don't leave out anal," Sheila said, never to be outdone.

"That always was your best orifice, Mom," Mac said, growing as agile on the court of coarse as he was on a basketball court.

# CHAPTER FIFTEEN

Mac paid lots of attention to his courting that summer. He went out with a young teacher from his school, with a law student Edith had introduced him to, and with a woman coach he'd met from another high school. But he didn't find the woman with whom he could engage in some comfortable, all-court sexual gymnastics until mid-July when he met Stephanie Williams, a Tulane graduate student in English.

Mac met Stephanie in a Loyola University classroom at a rally for Barbara Jeanne Bordelon. A group of New Orleans feminists were organizing a march to the Camp Street courthouse where Barbara Jeanne's trial was to be heard beginning the next week. The preliminary rally was held to make plans and assign such chores as making picket signs and serving as marshals. Mac went along because he was a supporter of Barbara Jeanne and because Edith was one of the organizers. Furthermore, he thought it would be nice for some men to show up and perhaps illustrate by their presence that fairness, not gender, was the issue in Barbara Jeanne's suit.

The number of men who showed up, however, was limited to Mac himself. Typically embarrassed, he squeezed into the room's last row of seats and tried to appear invisible. But he was spotted by Stephanie Williams who was sitting next to him. She leaned over and whispered to him, "Are you a spy for the opposition or just not feeling well?"

Mac laughed self-consciously. "I guess I *am* feeling a little uncomfortable," he conceded.

"Feeling sort of like a banana at a fig convention?" Stephanie asked.

"Something like that," Mac said, puzzling over the implications of her fruit metaphor.

When the meeting ended and Mac was picking his way among the crowded desks toward the exit behind Stephanie, she commented to him over her shoulder that from the looks of him, he might know something of the basketball side of this dispute.

"How so?" Mac asked.

"You're tall. You probably played basketball at some time or another."

"A little," Mac admitted.

Outside, they paused and chatted about the merits of Barbara Jeanne's case. Stephanie was ignorant of most of the particulars but was excited that New Orleans feminists finally had a rallying point. Stephanie was bright and witty, and Mac was attracted to her immediately. She had shoulder-length black hair, a trim physique and an open, teasing smile. A milkspot flaw on one of her front teeth added a girlishness to her allure.

When they had been talking outside Bobet Hall for about fifteen minutes in the smothering July heat, Mac boldly suggested that they continue their conversation somewhere that operated an air-conditioner. Stephanie accepted this proposal, and they agreed to meet at Mother's Tavern, a bar located in the River Bend. She took a half-step away from him before turning back, extending her hand, and introducing herself. "I'm Stephanie Williams," she said, coming clean with him from the start.

"Mac McIntire," Mac said, pumping her hand. She did not recognize his name which surprised, half-relieved and at the same time half-worried him.

After several hours of talk in the dark smoky recesses of Mother's, when his belly was full of Dixie Beer and hers of the house white, Stephanie offered to fix Mac dinner. At her apartment, she grilled a couple of steaks and tore up lettuce for a salad. Somewhere amidst these preparations, Stephanie adjourned to her bedroom long enough to slip into something more comfortable. She didn't employ this particular cliché, but the calf-length, sleeveless caftan she put on was doubtless more comfortable than the jeans and T-shirt she had been wearing earlier—especially since, as Mac was to discover, she had neglected to don so much as one stitch underneath it.

Mac became aware of her underwearlessness when he failed to resist peeking through the billowing arm holes in her smock. And he spent the rest of the evening ashamedly maneuvering for even better glances down the garment's low-cut flowing front. Yes, even basically decent men are relentless voyeurs. And at the moment Stephanie bent forward to remove the dinner plates and he was able to look from the hollow at the base of her throat all the way down to paradise, he decided that he had absolutely met his mother's requirement of liking Stephanie enough to enjoy sleeping with her. But alas, Mac was not the kind of man who could maneuver a young lady into the bedroom on a first date. So he and Stephanie finished a bottle of red wine, and then Mac made his thickened and unsober way home.

He asked her out again soon, of course, taking her to the movies. But it was not until their third date, one instigated by Stephanie, that they finally slept together. Stephanie took Mac to a dinner party with a group of her friends from graduate school, all of whom regarded Mac as a kind of curiosity piece. They made little effort to conceal the superiority they felt toward him, a mere secondary school teacher. But they were fascinated by his involvement in the Barbara Jeanne Bordelon Affair which was drawing an increasing amount of media attention, and they thus engaged him in conversation that was almost affable.

Mac began to suspect the possibility of sex when, after several glasses of wine, Stephanie began to rest her hand under the table on the tree trunk of his thigh. His suspicions were heightened when she invited him back to her house afer the party even though it was nearly two a.m. and they had already imbibed enough alcohol that a "nightcap" was neither needed nor even appealing. But Stephanie fixed them concoctions of grapefruit juice and gin nonetheless. "The juice will put back some of the vitamins we've used up tonight," she explained.

That made enough sense to Mac for him to accept the tumbler she handed him. But nearly full glasses were to greet them the next morning. That's because when Stephanie sat down next to him on the couch even he could imagine no reason for not immediately kissing her, wondering as he did so whether he was following the proper program for seduction or whether more modern sorts just advanced directly to cunnilingus.

Finally, Mac confessed that he'd actually like to sleep with her. And when he did, Stephanie whispered breathlessly into his ear, "I thought you'd never say so." She took him by the hand and led him to her bedroom where she untied her wrap-around skirt to reveal that her lack of underwear was habitual.

Somehow Mac managed to overcome his inevitable clumsiness about getting himself undressed, and the lovemaking that followed was long and languorous. Stephanie encouraged him not to worry about whether or not she came, explaining that she often didn't the first time she slept with a man. And then she came anyway, which made Mac feel all the more successful.

In the days that followed, Mac and Stephanie sprouted a relationship that involved a lot in the way of sex. The game had changed, but Mac approached it in his old manner: practice, practice, practice. Stephanie seemed like a fantasy girlfriend. She wanted to do it everywhere and in every way. If they were driving across town, she wanted to fellate him in the car on the way. If they were at a party, she wanted to sneak into a bathroom together for a stand-up quickie, her dress hiked up above her inevitably bare bottom, one leg splayed wide on a bathtub ledge or toilet. Half the time when he went to pick her up, she greeted him at the door totally naked, fabricating the most baldly ridiculous excuses for just why it was that she hadn't on so much as a piece of lint when he arrived. "I just got out the shower, but I didn't want to keep you waiting," she might say. "My towel snagged on the sofa coming to the door." Or, "I forgot what time you were coming, and all my clothes are still in the dryer."

The sexual chemistry between them was so potent that even when they weren't just about to have sex or even when they'd just finished, Mac kept his hands on her. When they were doing things as mundane as straightening up a cluttered room, Mac would seize whatever momentary opportunity to twine his fingers around a quickly stiffening nipple. When they prepared a meal or washed dishes, Mac would stand against her, one gigantic paw slipped inside her skirt or shorts, forever gently kneading at the swell of her buttocks.

But Sheila was not nearly so smitten by the new woman in Mac's life. "She's a cunt," Sheila complained.

Mac objected that it was most unmodern to characterize a person purely by reference to a sexual organ. "Besides," he pointed out, "Stephanie is one of the most cerebral women I've ever gone out with."

"So she's got a brain," Sheila replied. "How often does she employ that end of her body when she's around you?"

Mac laughed and shook his head. "You worried I might be getting in as much fucking as you these days?" She didn't even bother to reproach him with a look. "Come on, Mom, you're the one who told me that an active sex life was good . . . if you were having it with someone you like a lot."

"I never said fucking should be the sole activity of a relationship," Sheila asserted.

"It's not, Mom."

"Yeah," Sheila challenged. "What else do you two do?"

"We . . ." Mac said. "Why, we talk a lot. We go out to dinner. We go to the movies." Mac didn't say it, but he had to admit that most all of their activities merely supplemented the greater urgency of sex.

"She ever work out with you?"

"She's not very athletic, Mom. She's in good shape and all, but she's just not very interested in sports."

"As I said, she's a cunt," Sheila concluded.

Well, no, Stephanie Williams was not a cunt, though she had one which she made available to Mac, along with a couple of other orifices, during the torrid days of New Orleans' long summer. And during the early and most intense period of their frequent coupling, Mac thought that he had perhaps found an activity to rival basketball.

Which just goes to show you how orgasmic euphoria can seriously cloud your faculties of judgment.

# CHAPTER SIXTEEN

While Stephanie and Mac were still in their white hot stage, Barbara Jeanne Bordelon's trial began in federal district court. The proceeding turned out to be long and complicated. The judge ruled during pre-trial motions that the plaintiff was obligated to prove *both* that she had been unfairly denied a place on the boys' team *and* that the girls' team did not provide her an adequate opportunity to exploit her athletic skills.

This meant that Mac would ultimately be called as both a plaintiff's and a defense witness. Along with members of the Interscholastic Athletic Council (who testified to the rule prohibiting males and females from competing against each other), a referee and a women's coach (who tried to explain the differences in the rules governing the men's and women's games at the high school level), and a local university coach (who testified that female graduates of Louisiana high schools were at a distinct disadvantage when they suddenly had to play by men's rules at the college level), Mac was summoned to establish that he had indeed judged Barbara Jeanne one of the fifteen best junior varsity basketball players at Broussard High School.

By the time Mac actually took the witness stand, the intense glare of media attention, which had greeted the trial's opening, had softened considerably. And the one column report which ran in the *States-Tribune* second section utterly failed to capture the sympathetic nature of Mac's testimony. The newspaper account identified Mac as "the former UNO and Boston Celtic forward and the coach who dismissed the Broussard school girl from his boys' basketball squad. Under cross examination by defense attorneys," the article went on, "McIntire testified that he had not seen Miss Bordelon as a potential starter and that she would have only seen limited action as a member of the boys' team."

In fact, it had been the defense attorney and not Mac who had employed the phrase "would have seen only limited action," and Mac had been summarily cut off when he had tried to explain his belief that Barbara Jeanne could have proved invaluable in late game situations and might even have been the one missing element that cost his team a championship. This point might well have been established on re-direct, of course, but B.J.'s attorneys were not in possession of the information. Despite repeated encouragement by Edith Jenkins, Karen Lutze, who was trying the plaintiff's case, refused to interview Mac. "It's because of men like him that women like Barbara Jeanne Bordelon can't get an even shake in the world," was the way Lutze dismissed Edith's suggestion.

And when Edith persisted that, "Not all men in this world are enemies, and Mac McIntire *certainly* isn't an enemy," Lutze just fixed her with a stare one part gelid incredulity and one part flaccid resignation.

"Answer one question," Lutze said. "If your Mr. McIntire is one of the good guys, why did he dismiss Barbara Jeanne from his team, and if he had no choice, why didn't he resign?"

Edith tried to explain that Mac did what he did because, "He doesn't believe in futile gestures."

But Karen quickly retorted, "Yeah, and maybe he doesn't believe in equality of the sexes either."

To which Mac responded when Edith reported the conversation to him, "Fuck her."

Edith didn't pass Mac's imperative along, but the breach between Mac and B.J.'s counsel was never bridged, and the damage this caused to her case was incalculable. Swallowing both his pride and his irritation, Mac left messages at the Lutze, Piehl, Nord, Schwehn, Uehling and Feaster office expressing a desire to consult about Barbara Jeanne's case. But Karen Lutze never returned his calls.

Then, to Mac's outraged dismay, his performance on the witness stand was so widely misunderstood that even Stephanie, who followed developments closely in the paper, accosted him at the house-warming party he threw to celebrate moving into the Terminal. "I thought you were on her side," Stephanie remarked caustically on that stormy night just before school began.

"I am on her side, goddamnit," Mac insisted, instantly irritated. A thunder crack sounded outside as if to register God's agitation too.

Wide-eyed, Stephanie nodded her head disbelievingly. "Yeah," she said.

"Just what would make you think otherwise?" Edith wanted to know.

Edith hadn't really been a part of their conversation, but had been hovering nearby eavesdropping.

Stephanie shifted her attention to Edith with an undisguised air of haughty annoyance. "Well, he certainly didn't do her case any good on the stand, now did he?"

"Were you there?" Edith asked, her tone that of an interrogating barrister.

"No," Stephanie said with one breathy burst of contemptuous laughter. "But I can read." She licked her lips. "Can you?"

"I can do better than read," Edith said, leaning forward from the waist a little like an umpire getting in position to call balls and strikes. "I can think."

Stephanie took a swallow from the drink she was holding and said to Mac, "You haven't introduced me to your guest."

"Stephanie Williams," Mac said, "Edith Jenkins."

Already turning to walk away, Edith said, "If you really knew Mac, Stephanie, you wouldn't have any doubt that he was on B.J.'s side."

When Edith was out of earshot, Stephanie said to Mac, "Well just who is Miss Edith Jenkins?"

"My best friend," Mac said. "And as of today, in a manner of speaking, my roommate."

Stephanie's head swivelled ever so slightly to the left. "Your roommate?" she asked.

Mac then explained in some detail the long-term and complicated nature of his relationship with Edith Jenkins. At the end Stephanie laid her hand flat against her bosom and said with a dry laugh, "Well that's a relief."

But the evening of Mac's house-warming party for the Terminal marked a turning point in his relationship with Stephanie all the same. They had never before exchanged sharp words, and the biting conversation that Edith interrupted perhaps awakened them both from a summer of sensual somnolence. When Mac took Stephanie home, for the first time since the night of her friend's party, they did not make love.

In the weeks that followed, they began to see each other less often. In large part this was due to the beginning of both their school years. But the misunderstanding over the Barbara Jeanne Bordelon Affair was an ominous blip on the climatic radar screen on their relationship.

In mid-September, several weeks after the night of his party, Mac was called as a defense witness. Defense attorneys primarily wanted him to establish the approximate parity between the girls' and boys' basketball programs, in terms of number of games and the opportunity for participation in post-season play-offs. The irony was that such parity as existed at Broussard did so because of Mac's frantic efforts that spring. Of course, this was hardly relevant, and thus another factor was chalked up against Barbara Jeanne's suit. Again the plaintiff's attorneys missed a significant chance by not questioning Mac on other elements to be considered in weighing parity: uniform quality and age, travel budgets, access to the school gymnasium for practice time, the scheduling of women's games either immediately after school, or sometimes *after* the completion of the boys' teams' practice sessions rather than as a part, say, of men's and women's varsity basketball doubleheaders on Friday and Saturday nights. But Karen Lutze was not a sports fan, and by the time Mac concluded his second testimony, she had lost the services of Edith Jenkins, who, like Mac and Stephanie, had started back to school.

Still, Barbara Jeanne and her supporters arrived at the courthouse in early October with considerable optimism to hear the judge's verdict, delivered only weeks before the start of the year's basketball practice. The plaintiff had won a fair share of the trial's points, and, despite her earlier failings, Lutze concluded with an emotional closing statement calling on the judge to enter *Bordelon v. Orleans Parish Schools* in the legal lexicons alongside *Brown v. The Board of Education*.

Fortunately, Barbara Jeanne and her parents arrived early and missed most of the madness that was developing on the courthouse steps. All three of New Orleans' national network television stations had camera crews on location and were going about the process of interviewing members of the crowd, which was also gathering for the first time since the trial's opening day. Louisiana's chapter of the National Organization for Women had encouraged its members and sympathizers to turn out to demonstrate their support for Barbara Jeanne's cause. Some of these sensible and committed women had brought along signs and banners with up-beat slogans like:

### Foul Sexism Out of New Orleans High Schools

or

### Slam Dunk 'Em Barbara Jeanne

But by the time Mac and Sheila and Edith arrived, a more hostile group of women from the radical Feminist Organization of Louisiana had also gathered with placards expressing rather more provocative sentiments like:

### Cut the Balls Off Men's Basketball

Because he was recognized only as he passed through the exterior revolving door into the courthouse, Mac managed to slip through the crowd without incident. He would not be so lucky coming out. For inside the courtroom, the judge ruled in favor of the school system. In a brief statement, he argued that Title IX guaranteed female students an equal opportunity to participate in athletics, but nowhere did he find that such equality could arise only out of access to the same programs. Furthermore, he contended that the proceedings of the trial had served to convince him that, though the games of men's and women's basketball were played by slightly different rules in Louisiana high schools, women's basketball was an "equal" athletic activity so far as the law was concerned.

Barbara Jeanne's attorneys and family were obviously disappointed but promised to fight on in the court of appeals. Barbara Jeanne's supporters outside the courthouse took the news somewhat less calmly. Violent oaths were uttered in sundry quarters of the crowd. Scuffles broke out, and several were arrested. But the crowd turned most vicious when Mac appeared at the top of the courthouse steps. He was the only one of the principals originally named in the suit who had shown up for the verdict. And in the eyes of the radical members of the crowd, he was the enemy. As he made his descent, flanked by Edith on one side and Sheila on the other, he was cursed at and spit upon. Someone from the Feminist Organization of Louisiana had even come prepared with eggs. And by the time Mac, his mom, and best friend reached their car, they were bespattered from head to toe.

There were many in the crowd, of course, even among that angry number who assumed Mac their bitter enemy, who opposed this attack upon Mac as pointless and conceivably counter-productive.

But one among the crowd saw in Mac's humiliation a vast potential. This was the conservative clergyman who had recently launched a regional radio ministry and was looking for an issue he might be able to climb astride and ride into the bright lights of a television campaign. The attempt of a young woman to invade the sacred locker rooms of men's athletics might be just the issue. If so, none other than Elmer Kanter, Mac's long missing dad, figured that he was just the man to mount it and gallop onto the national stage.

# CHAPTER SEVENTEEN

Mac had more immediate problems, however, than the ones that would be caused by his renascent father. First, he had to figure out how to get the dried egg out of his one suit. Then, he and Edith had to figure out a way to keep Sheila from committing multiple acts of homicide. Sheila was not at all happy to have served as a target for mishomonistic women bearing chicken ovi. And for days afterwards, she engaged in idle but deliciously violent reveries.

"Edith and I could probably infiltrate their organization," she reported to the breakfast gathering at the Terminal one morning. The eggs they were eating probably prompted her thoughts of sweet revenge. "Then when they're not looking, we could jump up and machine gun them to death."

"Mom!" Mac chastised.

"OK, so we probably shouldn't machine gun them to *death*. Everybody deserves at least a chance for repentance. We could practice at a shooting range first. Then, when they weren't looking, we could jump up and shoot off their toes. That'd probably make them sorry."

Mac shook his head. "What would the loss of their toes have to do with the fact that they threw eggs at us?" Edith asked.

"OK, goddamnit," Sheila grouched. "We'd shoot the fingers off their throwing hands. How does that grab you, Ms. Technicality Monger?"

Mac ate his breakfast and sipped his coffee. Edith picked up her plates and Carrie's and took them to the sink to wash. With a snort, Sheila got up from the table and scraped her nearly full plate into the garbage sack. Every little movement she made around the kitchen was punctuated with a little explosion, an extra-heavy step or a piece of silverware placed down in the sink with too much force. Finally, Sheila said, "We could shoot their titties off and spread rumors that they were really men. That would fix 'em." Mac and Edith burst out laughing at that and Sheila had to join in. And so this particular rage passed.

But from time to time in subsequent days, Sheila would still announce her vengeful fantasies. "I'd like to throw them all in a giant pot and hard boil them," she remarked while banging some pots around.

To which Mac replied, "I think they're already pretty hard-boiled, Mom."

"Then I'd like to trap them in the world's largest skillet and scramble them to death," she confided conspiratorially.

"Remember, you're only supposed to scramble their tits off, Sheila," Edith said.

As Sheila's daydreams of violent retribution grew ever more metaphoric, she began to develop genuine plans for an actual political response. Using Edith's contacts at the local chapter of the National Organization for Women, she proposed the printing of a pamphlet of denunciation of the violent actions of certain members of the Feminist Organization of Louisiana.

Leaders at N.O.W. expressed interest but explained that they would prefer discovering ways to bring their radical sisters back into the fold rather than alienating them further from the responsible mainstream of progressive feminism. Mac and Edith urged upon Sheila the basic wisdom of N.O.W.'s approach, and so Sheila dropped her outward pushing of the project. Inwardly, however, the wheels of scandalous verse began to turn. Scathing rhymes were formed and secretly recorded. Sheila felt sure they would ultimately be needed.

But for now she bided her time.

# CHAPTER EIGHTEEN

Mac, on the other hand, had no time to bide. The time for the beginning of basketball practice was upon him. And with Barbara Jeanne consigned to his team, at least until the U.S. Fifth Circuit Court of Appeals could reach a determination in her case, Mac felt constrained to develop an offense to capitalize on his star's extraordinary skills, yet flexible enough to be used successfully by his other players should Barbara Jeanne suddenly be granted her wish to move to the boys' squad.

Devising such an offense, though, was by no means a simple task, particularly given that in women's basketball, as it was played at this time, he had only three offensive players to work with. Mac figured that with Barbara Jeanne in the line-up, most any offensive scheme would prove successful against New Orleans area schools. As she had proven in her sophomore year, Barbara Jeanne Bordelon could score almost at will against any team in the Crescent City.

However, local teams weren't all that good. The New Orleans recreation department offered no basketball program for little girls, so they had scant opportunity for training in the sport as they were growing up. At the junior high level, basketball for women was only played in intramurals, and then, with practically no coaching guidance. Not until high school could a female compete in basketball on an interscholastic level, and even there the absence of a junior varsity program meant that only half as many girls as boys could participate. And even the varsity women's program was woefully inadequate. Mac had been able to arrange a full, thirty-game schedule for his girls, and no city high school team was playing fewer than twenty-four games, but not one of the girls on all of those teams (barring some transfer students Mac was unaware of) had ever played more than twelve games in a single season previously.

In short, in her home town, Barbara Jeanne would not find a single opposing team with the experience necessary to stop her. As long as Barbara Jeanne remained on the Lady Bruins team, Mac could count on a city championship.

In the state playoffs, however, the level of competition would be substantially higher, and victory would be more difficult. People in upstate towns like Jonesboro, Winnfield, Bastrop and Homer had so blessed little to do that they even took their women's high school basketball seriously. Consequently, there were lots of north Louisiana farm girls who had received the years of training that was the only standard ticket to high level athletic achievement. Mac remained confident that there was no single young woman in the state who could pose a threat to Barbara Jeanne, but there very well could be a team of highschoolers somewhere in the state who, in combination, could stop her. Mac's challenge was to build around his star a team that could complement her, and if necessary, could play with patience, discipline and success without her.

To begin that building process, Mac had to overcome an attitude his predecessor, Sally James, had allowed to develop among the members of the team the previous year—an attitude that all they had to do to win was get the ball to B.J. and get out of her way. Otherwise a sweet and kind person who was utterly relieved to have gotten pregnant so she didn't have to teach anymore, Sally James really was an incompetent ninny when it came to basketball. She had been a cheerleader during her own high school years, and with training she could have been a good athlete. But she got no such training, and her cheerleading constituted her only qualification for coaching. Sally had inherited the women's basketball squad because she was the youngest female teacher in the school and had actually taken a college P.E. course. But Sally knew no more about the game of basketball than watermelons know about nuclear physics. She wasn't even clear on all the rules. Still, you had to give her credit. Limited as her strategy was, with Barbara Jeanne in control, the Lady Bruins didn't lose a single game.

Mac knew that to be successful outside New Orleans, however, he was going to have to develop more of a "team" concept. And this meant he had to break the team's total reliance on Barbara Jeanne. The other girls had to be convinced that not only could they contribute to the team's success, but that the prospect of a state championship was possible only if their contributions became substantial. He drilled and drilled the other girls at moving without the basketball and at learning to get position under the basket, and he pushed

Barbara Jeanne to look first to pass to her teammates before trying to score herself. He taught the other girls how to set screens for Barbara Jeanne so she could get free for a jump shot grown deadly from a year's ceaseless practice. He emphasized to the other girls the importance of those screens, the essential role they played in B.J.'s scoring and thus the team's success.

By the time the season was set to open, Mac had his girls trained in the team play necessary to compete with schools from north Louisiana. And he had a full three months of intra-city play to mold a championship attitude. The Lady Bruins' defensive unit was led by Peggy Simons, a string bean center whose job it was to interfere with any shots taken close to the basket. Peggy bore a sad resemblance to Popeye's Olive Oyl. She seemed all rubbery arms and legs, and she had a tiny round head which her long, thin brown hair somehow did nothing to lengthen, especially not when worn, as usual, in pigtails.

But looks have nothing to do with basketball. And under Mac's patient tutoring, Peggy was turning into a bulldog. She was neither quick nor particularly well-coordinated, but she made up in a grim, unsmiling determination what she lacked in natural ability. She was nearly six feet tall, and her long arms and skinny build made her seem even taller. Mac taught her that actually blocking shots was less important than ruining a rival team's shooting percentage by forcing them to alter their shots to avoid having them blocked. He also taught her how to get position for rebounds, to use her bony butt to make contact with her opponents. Peggy never did become a particularly gifted jumper, but she blossomed into a rebounder effective and persistent enough to get dubbed "Windex" by her fellow Lady Bruins because she "wiped the backboard glass clean."

Peggy's two teammates on the starting defensive unit were Tina Wiggins and Debbie Miller. Both were only 5'3", but both had better than average quickness. Mac turned them both into hounding defenders who never gave an opposing forward a moment's rest. He had them dogging the ball from the instant it crossed the mid-court line, reaching, swiping, generally making menaces of themselves. He wanted them to force the ball handlers to drive to the basket where lanky, scowling Peggy Simons waited for them. He never wanted his defense to allow opponents to get into their own offensive passing patterns. The results of Mac's coaching on defense were two-fold. First, he turned a team which only a year earlier had largely relied on Barbara Jeanne to outscore the opposition, into a team that would regularly hold its opponents to under thirty points a game, sometimes to under twenty. On one occasion, Peggy, Debbie and Tina gave up only six points in three full quarters before Mac lifted them for substitutes.

Second, he developed an attitude of pride on the part of the defense. Sally James hadn't understood the finer points of the game well enough to make the defensive players feel that they were really all that important. Part of Mac's strategy in this regard was occasionally to employ Barbara Jeanne in place of either Tina or Debbie on the defensive end of the floor. None of the girls questioned that B.J. was the team's best player. So if she was sometimes used to play it, then defense must be important.

Joining Barbara Jeanne (who had grown in the last year to a rangy 5'9") as regulars on offense were the Laurel and Hardy combination of Mary Masters and Olga Jorgensen. At a skinny 5'6", Mary was the team's resident screw-up. She had the attention span of a housefly, and if she hadn't been so goofily lovable, Mac would have been tempted to throttle her on more than one occasion. She was forever misremembering his instructions or showing up late for practice because she'd forgotten the correct time, or gotten a detention, or had some other muddle-headed mishap. But next to Barbara Jeanne, Mary was the team's best athlete. She was fast, she shot well from close range, and she was a tenacious rebounder. Mac envisioned her as an invaluable weapon for getting loose for easy lay-ups whenever the opposition tried to stop the Bruins by double-teaming Barbara Jeanne.

Invaluable in her own way was slow, overweight Olga. At nearly 6'2" and 225 flabby pounds, Olga was easily the Lady Bruins biggest player. She unquestionably hustled but still huffed her way through most work outs. Although she denied it, Mac suspected that she loaded up on junk food every night just as soon as she could rip the refrigerator door open. And he knew damn well that she packed away whatever eats she could snitch during cooking class in which she was one of his students. Whatever its source, Olga's weight made her a largely incompetent rebounder despite her height advantage. Jumping for Olga meant standing on her toes. But Mac spotted potential in Olga despite her physical liabilities. She lacked speed and agility. But she didn't lack coachability. And this lone quality was enough. She was a kid who desperately wanted to attach some kind of accomplishment to a life that was an almost unbroken string of failure and rejection. And in Mac's scheme for the Lady Bruins that year, there was a very large place for Olga Jorgensen.

Sally James had played Olga on defense, but Mac switched her to offense before the end of the first practice. He recognized in Olga the perfect complement for Barbara Jeanne's shooting ability. Olga, he realized, should be able to set the most devastating picks Louisiana high school women's basketball had ever seen. In many ways, in fact, mammoth-hipped Olga Jorgensen was the key to Mac's simple but consistently effective offensive design.

Basically, that design worked this way: Olga and Mary would establish positions near the basket on opposite sides of the three-second lane as Barbara Jeanne took the pass across the mid-court line. Then, as Barbara Jeanne dribbled a slow jitterbug toward the top of the key, Mary would clear out to a new position about twenty feet from the left side of the hoop and Olga would lumber up the lane to the free-throw line. Barbara Jeanne was then to attempt a drive to the basket, a ploy which resulted frequently in a lay-up and an easy two points. A more skilled defender, though, could be counted on to block such a drive. If so, Barbara Jeanne was to use a reverse dribble, and move to a position directly behind Olga, where, using Olga's protective girth to screen herself away from her defender, she was to go up for her jump shot. On a portable chalk board Mac used as a coaching aid, he diagramed this play for his team. Using their initials to indicate the Lady Bruins, X's to show defenders and P1 and P2 to indicate each player's initial and then subsequent positions, Mac's diagram looked like this·

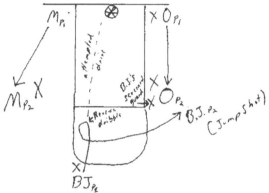

Under the diagram Mac wrote "play number 1."

Obviously, Mac inherited his drawing skills from his mom.

Mac figured that Barbara Jeanne could hit this eighteen-foot jump shot at least sixty-five percent of the time. For those occasions when she would miss, Mac instructed Mary to maneuver into position to snare an offensive rebound just as soon as B.J. had gone into her reverse dribble. With Barbara Jeanne's shooting ability, Mac knew that this play alone would be adequate to demolish most teams on their schedule. But he also knew that somewhere down the line he would meet a coach who would counter the play by having his defensive unit employ a switch.

In a switching tactic, Olga's defender would move quickly around her screen to guard against Barbara Jeanne's jump shot while B.J.'s defender would slide down to guard Olga. The classic basketball response to the switch is the pick and roll, which would send Olga breaking for the basket just as soon as her defender switched to Barbara Jeanne but before B.J.'s defender could switch to her. Had Olga possessed the skills to work the pick and roll, B.J. would then have simply lofted a looping pass to her for an easy lay-up.

But Olga did not possess such skills, of course. She couldn't move with nearly enough quickness. She couldn't have shot the cripple with any accuracy. And she probably couldn't even have caught the necessary pass with consistency.

So to counter the anticipated switching tactic, Mac put in a second play. This was a double pick scheme which allowed the Lady Bruins still to get their mileage out of Olga's heft. It called for Olga to establish her regular position and for Mary to move to a spot right next to her. Again, Barbara Jeanne would attempt a drive. And again, if thwarted she would reverse dribble and screen her guard off on Olga's hips. Olga's guard, in this formation, was prohibited from switching to B.J. because Mary was in the way. So normally Barbara Jeanne could get her jump shot off.

This second offensive design suffered from the sacrifice of Mary's potential as a rebounder for those occasions when B.J. did not score. But it had the advantage of effectively squelching all switching tactics. The only switch which could interfere with Barbara Jeanne's jumper in this second formation was a switch by Mary's guard. And if that tactic were ever employed, *then* the pick and roll *did* come into effect with Mary making an easy lay-up after receiving Barbara Jeanne's sure pass.

Mac also diagramed this play for his team. It looked like this:

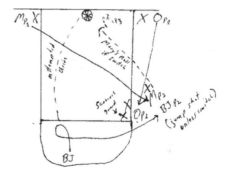

Under this diagram he wrote "play number 2."

Mac had not learned from Sheila the advantage of keeping his drawings simple.

Each day Mac drilled his squad in these two offensive maneuvers. Later he would incorporate several other plays which involved using Olga's Gibraltar screen to free Mary and sometimes even Barbara Jeanne for open passes while cutting to the basket. But basically Mac knew that plays numbered one and two would be the team's bread and butter for the whole season.

But he didn't know that his bland offensive diet would be consumed in such an intensely public arena.

# CHAPTER NINETEEN

As Mac looked to the future of women's basketball at Broussard, he planned for the gradual institution of several changes. First of all, he wanted something approaching equity in the allotment of practice time. He was presently working his girls out for an hour and a half before school each morning. His other options were to practice *after* the boys' teams had left the gym at 5:30, or to use the school's outdoor asphalt courts immediately after school.

Mac rejected the last option for obvious reasons. He didn't want to expose his players to the inevitable torn knees and elbows that the rough exterior courts were sure to inflict if he could get his charges to play the kind of aggressive game he intended. And furthermore, he didn't want to lose valuable practice time whenever the weather was bad.

Mac rejected the 5:30 option for the hardship it would impose on his players and their families. Men's varsity coach Wayne Dawson suggested that the girls could get all their daily homework done in the time after school and before the beginning of their daily late practices. But Mac had no confidence that all his players' parents were committed enough to rearrange their families' supper schedules to accommodate daughters who didn't arrive home until nearly eight o'clock every evening.

That left the before-school practice as the best alternative, though it was hardly one without inherent problems. Female basketball players, for instance, couldn't ride school buses to class because buses didn't arrive an hour and a half early. And probably most troublesome, Mac's players had to go through the school day with either wet or dirty hair, because unlike their male counterparts, once they showered after practice, the whole school day was still in front of them.

The issue of practice-time equity was one Mac had already brought up, and he was well aware of the resentment he'd encountered just from pointing out the discrimination implicit in his women's team's practice schedule. So he was hardly surprised when the Broussard administration rejected the possibility of any adjustment during the current year. And he gave the scantest credence to Arnold Larrett's contention that the matter "was on the board to be looked into for the future."

But Mac figured that with the outstanding success he felt sure the Lady Bruins would achieve, in a year he'd be in a position to let his desire for practice equality stampede from suggestion to request to demand.

A second issue, and one Mac felt perhaps even more strongly about, was the necessity of designing the school's Friday and Saturday night basketball schedules to include men's and women's double-headers. As it was, the men's junior varsity had the opening slot in the standard weekend line-up. The women were scheduled to play their games at four o'clock on Friday afternoons (this gave the visiting teams time to reach game sites after school was over) and ten o'clock Saturday morning (which gave the school's janitorial staff a couple of hours to clean up from the boys' games the nights before).

These times meant, of course, that the women normally played their games in gymnasiums filled only with themselves, a smattering of unusually interested parents, and the echoes of age-old discrimination. The after-school starting time was too late to encourage even the idly curious student to hang around, but too early to allow most parents to attend. The Saturday starting time whispered of vindictiveness.

Mac envisioned a time in the not-so-distant future when his double-header plan was instituted and women regularly played before crowds as large and as enthusiastic as those the men had enjoyed from time immemorial. Unfortunately, there was only so much he could accomplish at once, so for this year Mac prepared to accept a season in which his team might well not attract as many fans as there were games on its schedule. He knew he would miss the excitement that a crowd inevitably generated over a basketball game. But he also knew that his players would miss it far less than he. It's difficult to miss that which one has never had the opportunity to experience.

I encourage you to imagine, then, Mac's surprise that last Friday in November, when he led his Lady Bruins onto the court for their opening game in their thick, constricting, dowdy uniforms—which hadn't been new when Mac himself was in high school—and found a packed gymnasium astir with strong feelings.

# BOOK THREE:

Barbara Jeanne Bordelon's
Junior Season In High School

# CHAPTER TWENTY

Mac was stunned by the size of the crowd waiting to watch his Lady Bruins' first game. He'd expected fewer than ten spectators. Edith would be there, probably with a law book spread open in her lap to be read in snatches during time-outs and half-time. And Sheila would be in the stands next to Edith with a clip-board full of paper on her lap to be used for a shot-chart she'd forget to keep just as soon as some tense series of plays required that she act as cheerleader rather than statistician. In between them would be little Carrie to receive repeated pats of affection from her mother and godmother.

But beyond these four, Mac had not dared hope for even a few students or more than a couple of parents. Stephanie Williams wouldn't be there even though Mac had specifically invited her to come to see the remarkable skills of the remarkably controversial Barbara Jeanne Bordelon. Stephanie had begged off, citing a looming deadline for a graduate seminar paper.

So Mac was speechless when he emerged from the locker room with his team to discover the gym jammed with people waiting to witness the Lady Bruins tangle with the visiting Trojanettes from McDonogh. It was as if he'd stepped out of the Broussard locker room and into another dimension, one Rod Serling would term "not of sight and sound, but of mind." This nightmarish feeling was aggravated by the thin greeting the Lady Bruins received. Usually when a home team took the floor before a crowd of any size, it was rewarded with at least polite applause and, if it had been in the habit of winning, with booming cheers.

But as the Lady Bruins hustled into their warm-up passing drill, only Sheila, Edith, Joan and Carrie rose to clap and shout their encouragement. Everybody else merely sat in a stink of hostility. As Mac began to shoulder his way back into reality, it occurred to him briefly that somehow McDonogh must have developed a loyal following for its women's basketball team. That notion was exploded moments later, however, when the Trojanettes took the court to a silence that was more uniform than the one which met the Lady Bruins. For as Mac was shortly to discover, the crowd in the Broussard gym that Friday afternoon had come to cheer no one. They had come to hiss and boo at Mac McIntire. And they had notified the local press of their intentions.

As Mac walked across the shiny floor to direct his team's pre-game exercises, a female reporter from the *States-Tribune* squatted in front of him, one leg thrown out wide for balance like a runner stretching before a work out. Mac was befuddled by her unexpected appearance, and thus she snapped a photo that captured him in a snarl of surprise. And as if the camera's flashing bulb were the cue, a group in the center-court bleachers stood and unfurled a giant banner that read:

## STAMP OUT SPORTS SEXISM

At one end of the banner they had fashioned a drawing that looked like this:

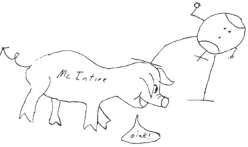

As Mac tried to blink the swimming spots out of eyes, the *States-Tribune* reporter, who had a cassette recorder clipped to her belt said into a tiny black microphone, "Coach McIntire, do you have any comment about today's demonstration?"

"Not really," Mac said. "I would . . ." Mac didn't finish his sentence because the reporter swung abruptly away from him. Mac was going to say that he'd like to know what the demonstration was all about. But in the article which ran the next day, the paper reported, "Coach McIntire refused to comment on the situation."

Mac watched a moment as the reporter rushed to meet a plain young woman who wore her hair pulled back in a severe bun. She was dressed in a peasant blouse and a long, print skirt. The reporter asked her a question, but instead of answering directly she began to read from a prepared statement. The text of this statement, along with the photos of a scowling Mac and the protest banner, constituted the bulk of the next day's article. The statement read:

> The Feminist Organization of Louisiana is dedicated to the pursuit of equality between the sexes. Despite a ruling by the Federal District Court to the contrary, we feel that Broussard High School student Barbara Jeanne Bordelon has been denied equal rights by the action of the Orleans Parish School Board's refusing her a place on the men's basketball team. We furthermore feel that the situation at Broussard has now worsened rather than improved, the rights of all its women students infringed rather than just one. To replace a female coach who did nothing less than guide her women's team to a perfect season, Broussard has appointed no less than Marshall McIntire, the very coach who cut Miss Bordelon from his men's team a year ago. This is not only a sexist attack on the female students at Broussard High, but an insult to women everywhere. We therefore demand McIntire's immediate replacement by a properly qualified woman.

Mac found this article Saturday morning in the Women's Section. In the Sports Section he found not a word about the basketball contest which had been the focus of all this controversial attention. And that was a shame, because the basketball game, at least for Broussard supporters, was truly exciting and carried with it a heady promise of things to come. McDonogh managed to can the opening bucket. But then the Lady Bruins settled down to working their offensive pattern number one. Barbara Jeanne hit two jumpers in a row. She missed on the third try, but Mary followed in her rebound for a six-two lead.

It momentarily looked like McDonogh might make a game of it when they drew a foul from Peggy Simons on the next trip up the floor and converted both free throws. But from that point on, it was a Broussard slaughter. Barbara Jeanne's shooting was as deadly as an academic cocktail party. She nailed four straight jumpers before she missed again and Mary followed home the rebound still once more. Meanwhile, on the other end, Tina Wiggins and Debbie Miller kept snatching Trojanette passes as if they were clover blooms. And any time the Lady Bruin guards got beat, the Trojanette forwards ran smack into grim Peggy Simons who seemed to dare the McDonogh girls to score. The score at the end of the half was 40 to 7. At the end of three quarters, when Mac pulled all his starters, it was 60-13. But not even the final score of 68 to 23 appeared anywhere in the daily paper.

Mac headed off to his ten o'clock game against Nicholls later that morning with understandable trepidation. The protesters had been admirably restrained the day before, but he feared that they would soon feel the need to escalate their display of opposition to him.

He needn't have worried, though. An angry and vigilant Sheila, and equally angry, if legally distracted Edith, an ice-cream-sweet Carrie, a beaming and blithely optimistic Joan and five parents (two of whom were Bordelons) were the only spectators. Mac learned two things from the experience of the game that day which his team won 74 to 31. First, he learned that he had no reason to fear Nicholls during the season's second round, for again, he'd removed his starters long before the game's end.

And second, he learned that radicals are evidently not early risers.

# CHAPTER TWENTY-ONE

When the Nicholls game was played without incident (and once again without so much as an unannotated box score in the local daily), Mac began to harbor the hope that the members of the Feminist Organization of Louisiana had made their statement and would hence forth leave him alone.

But as Sheila chided him, "Get your head out of your butt, son. Radicals may get up late, but they do get up. And they usually get up mean. These women are like John Paul Jones. They've only just begun to shit on you."

As was so frequently the case, Sheila was profanely right.

When Mac led his Lady Bruins onto the floor at Warren Easton the next Friday afternoon, the seats in the gym were packed again, and they were greeted by a mighty cheer. For just the briefest moment Mac found refuge in a sense of deja vu. This was his old high school gym. Not so many years ago he had often come running out of the locker room onto this court to stand before several thousand fans, most of whom had come to cheer him. And so, for a second, it was as if those days had magically returned.

But that second was shattered by an ugly howl of invective. "Sueeeeeeeeeey, Pig!" a hundred voices screamed in unison as others in the crowd realized that Mac was on the floor. Near the top of the bleachers, four women unfurled their banner which showed the angry, personified feminist symbol stamping on a pig labeled "McIntire." Four other women grasped the banner from the bottom to hold it down and all eight raised clenched fists aloft in salutes of belligerent defiance. Below the banner the other members of the Feminist Organization of Louisiana bellowed, "Sueeeeeeeeeey, Pig!" and then with pointed fingers hammering out at Mac they chanted, "You, you, you, you, you."

Even the building's venting system seemed to have taken sides against Mac. As the crowd continued their taunt, "Sueeeeeeeeeey, Pig! You, you, you, you, you," the banner, which stretched nearly the length of the basketball court, bulged in rhythm toward Mac as if it were a vulgar gesture from the skirted lap of some gigantic hostile female enemy.

Shaking his head in dismay, Mac called his players around him to counsel them to ignore the crowd and concentrate on the game. "Remember," he told them, "this really doesn't concern any of you at all. It's me they're mad at, though God only knows why exactly. Y'all are just caught in the middle. So I want y'all to just shut the crowd out and go on about your business." He caught Barbara Jeanne's eye, and the two of them exchanged a tight-lipped, almost imperceptible nod. "Take 'em into lay-up drill, B.J.," he directed, sticking his hand straight into the center of his huddled players to initiate the hand-clasping ritual of team unity.

But before the girls could cry out their usual, "Gooo Bruins," followed by a simultaneous clapping of hands, someone in the gym set off a string of firecrackers. With the nation's history of violence nudging their imaginations, many in the gym that day actually thought what they heard was gunfire and the *States-Tribune* carried an ominous report the next day that guns were spotted in the waistbands of at least a half dozen spectators. Whatever the exact nature of the wave of fear which followed, the shock of the crackling explosions spooked many and set off a panic. The bleachers suddenly looked like a stepped on ant-hill. People screamed and pushed against jammed exit doors. The large pictorial banner denouncing Mac was abandoned by its eight unnerved attendants, but for an incredible moment it refused to settle over the bleachers. Instead, the banner caught the wind of flight and bulged lewdly forward in the middle, that gigantic female lap as if now with unwanted child.

Mac kept his players gathered around him on the court figuring that there they were least likely to get trampled. Somewhere in the Easton school building an alarm went off, nudging the bedlam a decible higher.

Gradually the gym emptied, leaving Mac with his team and the very few others who had kept their heads. Among those remaining were three neatly dressed men who stood together at the foot of the bleachers near the south end backboard. All wearing dark suits and sporting close-cropped haircuts, the three men talked quietly but with evident earnestness. The oldest of the three, a thin and shortish gentleman in his late forties, appeared to be giving directions to his two young associates. All three were carrying books of some sort, but with their free hands each would occasionally gesture toward the bleachers where the feminist banner had finally billowed to the seats. When their conversation ended, the two younger men climbed the bleachers toward the banner.

Mac had idly witnessed their conclave but gave it little thought. He was thinking about the game his Lady Bruins were supposed to play. The Easton coach and the Lady Eagles seemed to have fled along with the frenzied crowd. What course should Mac follow now? Confident that there was no danger from remaining in the gym, Mac told Barbara Jeanne once again to take the team into lay-up drill while he tried to learn whether or not the game would be postponed.

As his team warmed up, Mac set off to find an Easton administrator, coach or athletic official with whom he could discuss plans either to play or reschedule. At the far end of the gym, the two neatly-dressed young men, now back on the floor, began to fold the banner they'd fetched down from the bleachers. It was as if they were soldiers who had just captured an enemy flag.

In the Easton administration offices, Mac found the school's principal, athletic director and women's basketball coach. As Mac walked in, the principal was talking to the police department bomb squad. He had already called the fire department. No one in the room was very happy. And they'd already determined to call the game off, and the Easton athletic director wanted to know if Mac was willing to forfeit, given that the controversy surrounding Barbara Jeanne Bordelon was doubtless the cause of the disturbances. Mac almost suggested that he perform some contortionist's sexual act on himself. He was, after all, his mother's son. But he opted instead for restraint, defended his team's innocence and insisted on a rescheduled game date. The Easton triumvirate finally agreed to a Thursday afternoon time two weeks hence, and Mac returned to the gym to escort his girls back to the team bus.

They were waylaid, however, on the steps of the school. As they came out of the red brick building on Canal Street, they were greeted by a roar almost as loud as that which had welcomed them into the Easton gym a half hour earlier. Only this time the din was not delivered for their benefit but merely coincided with their appearance.

The crowd of perhaps three hundred on the school lawn was divided into two sartorially distinguishable sections. In a largish circle around a smoking, green metal trash barrel were perhaps two hundred conservatively dressed men and women. The men, like those who gathered the banner in the gym, were mostly in suits; the women wore loose-fitting print dresses and many had children balanced in their arms. Most in this group carried Bibles. These were the Soldiers for Jesus, come to voice their support for the decision to place Barbara Jeanne Bordelon on the Broussard women's team and to applaud Mac McIntire's right to coach it. Theirs were the voices who had cheered Mac's appearance on the court. But they had negative views to record as well, and thus they had also come to register their opposition to such groups as the Feminist Organization of Louisiana, groups they considered agents of Beelzebub.

Around the Soldiers for Jesus was a crowd of angry and incredulous women mostly dressed in blue jeans, flannel shirts and soft-soled shoes. They stood together in clumps of twos and threes, muttering indignations and occasionally gesticulating contemptuously toward the circle of their antagonists.

The cheer which had seemed to greet the contingent from Broussard was actually accorded to the oldest of the three men Mac had earlier seen in the Easton gym. At the moment Mac and his Lady Bruins had emerged from the school building, this compact, graying gentleman had stepped into the center of his followers and raised the fallen banner of the Feminist Organization of Louisiana high over his head. Mac and his team members were too far away to hear his remarks, but he was reported in the next morning's paper to have said: "My sisters and brothers in Christ, my compatriots in holy arms, my fellow Soldiers for Jesus, our sacred war for salvation has begun. An opening battle has been fought and the first fruits of victory are ours."

As the Lady Bruins filed onto their bus, however, they could all see what happened next. The speaker brandished the offending banner over his head once more, and then, like Doctor J. swooping in for a dramatic, two-handed stuffer, turned and slam-dunked the folded cloth into the trash barrel that smoldered just behind him. For a second the barrel coughed an objection of gray soot, but after a dormant interval it finally complied with an irising tongue of fire.

Only as their hand-crafted banner gave up its struggle to a flame of bright orange did the members of the Feminist Organization of Louisiana grasp exactly what had taken place. Thus stirred to action, they made one, gallant, incensed rush against their more numerous foes. But the Soldiers for Jesus instantly beat their plowshares into swords, turned on the charging women with a savage fury and drove them mercilessly away, hammered them into humiliated rout with Bibles wielded as cudgels.

Bruised by the Gospel, the women withdrew. They were defeated but they were by no means conquered. And they retreated swearing hot oaths of vengeance.

# CHAPTER TWENTY-TWO

As I presume you have surmised, that banner-jamming Soldier for Jesus spokesman was none other than the Rev. Elmer Kanter himself. But his identity, remember, was not yet known by either Mac or Sheila, neither of whom had had any contact with Elmer for more than two decades. They were, naturally, curious enough about the day's disturbing events that they spent a long night at the Terminal speculating with Edith about the meaning of it all. Neither would ever have guessed the truth, though. Neither was nearly pessimistic enough.

Despite the late hour of their retirement, they all arose early on Saturday as usual. In preparation for her daily routine of endless studying, Edith, dressed in a blue terry bathrobe, was downstairs from her side of the house first. Still addicted to the top-forty programming of WTIX, Edith switched on the kitchen radio as a matter of habit. In deference to anyone not yet wide awake enough for guitar riffs, she kept the volume low enough to annoy only those inside the Terminal.

She made herself come coffee and paged briskly through the paper at the kitchen table. In the article about the affray at Easton, Edith encountered the reference to Elmer, but she lacked the background information to make any connection with her housemates. All Sheila had ever told her about Mac's conception was "Like you, I was an unwed mother. Unlike you, I lacked the fundamental judgment of a gerbil and so insisted on marrying my sperm donor. But after a while I came to my senses and kicked the little putz out of my life."

To which Mac had added at another time, "I don't remember him. But as I understand it, my old man was a shit. This was a condition Mom deeply disapproved of."

But though she lacked a full appreciation of one Elmer Kanter's sudden emergence into their lives, Edith certainly grasped the ominous implications of what she read. As Edith fixed a bowl of cereal to take up to her daughter, Sheila came into the kitchen in her pajamas, bleary-eyed from a poor night's sleep. Mac was right behind her, fully dressed and already exhibiting the nervous energy he could barely contain on game days. Sheila sat almost blankly at the table and began to stir at the paper. But Edith said, swaying with a radio love song on her way to the icebox for milk, "I wouldn't recommend y'all's reading that unless you're planning on Rolaids for breakfast."

Her message was seemingly lost on Sheila who was rubbing at an eye with the back of her wrist and scratching her hair with her other hand. And it was momentarily lost on Mac who couldn't help but notice how luscious Edith looked, especially since she'd showered, perfumed, fixed her hair before coming down to breakfast and tied her bathrobe so that he could see the tops of her breasts every time she twirled about in a dance step. Mac and Sheila and Edith had established a very casual atmosphere in the Terminal. If they felt like it, they would dine or watch television in their underwear in the house's common areas. And though there were separate living quarters on either side of the vast living room, these spaces were not treated as restricted or private. So it was not at all uncommon for them to be in one another's rooms—Mac barging into Edith's study room or even her bedroom with an anecdote about school, Edith bursting into Mac's room to discuss a case she was studying, all three of them after Carrie was asleep lounging at once on Sheila's bed to replay a ball game, plan some bit of strategy or roast some foe. Nudity was not an issue of concern. Living together as they did, they occasionally saw each other naked and thought nothing of it. But sometimes, when Mac saw Edith *partially* dressed, he found himself practically drooling.

And Mac was too natively candid not to have confided this problem to Edith herself. They had discussed it. And Edith had suggested that God should have put men's brains in their dicks as the best way to assure them a permanently adequate supply of blood. Mac had countered that women were instinctive teases who aroused men on purpose, whether they meant to or not. Edith had complimented him on a remarkable logical breakthrough. And Mac had pointed out that it was Edith, not he, who wore bikini underpants.

Despite the repartee, they had reached an understanding. Whenever Edith unconsciously flashed him, Mac would just tell her, and she would stop. He did so this morning in his usual fashion when he said, "Edith, I wish that instead of running around that way with parts of you flopping out and threatening to get all over me, that you'd just get all the way naked so I wouldn't notice."

"Jesus, Mac," Edith said, "it's barely seven o'clock in the morning."

"A man's dick don't wear a watch," Sheila said suddenly, evincing a greater degree of wakefulness than heretofore. "Didn't you know that, Edith?"

"Well, Mac better *watch* his *dick* before it gets him into trouble," Edith said. "One of these days I'm going to lust right back at him, and then he's really going to have problems."

"Promises, promises," Mac replied.

"Trusts, Trusts," Edith said, pointing up to her side of the house and referring to a course she needed to study for.

"If you wanted to go up to my room," Mac suggested, "I'm sure we could find something in the area of Negotiable Instruments to work on."

"I hope you aren't making veiled references to her Security Rights," Sheila said, yawning.

"Not unless he wants to run the risk of Torts," Edith replied as she gathered Carrie's breakfast tray.

"Tarts. Just what I had in mind," Mac said, holding the kitchen door open for her. "Tarts." Like a coach sending a player into the game, he gave her fanny a little swat as she passed. "Tarts," he said. "Study that especially."

"Watch your vowels," Edith said.

"I'd rather watch yours," he said, fluttering his eyebrows.

"Make me some breakfast," Sheila said. "Instead of making me sick."

When Edith was gone, Sheila opened the paper and began to read its account of yesterday's aborted game. Selections from this latest chapter of the Barbara Jeanne Bordelon saga Sheila read aloud to her son as he scrambled eggs and fried bacon.

The paper covered the story of the affair on page one of its second or "City" section, and the article was obviously written against deadline. No attempt, as far as they knew, had even been made to contact Mac for his input. The article contained a straight-forward account of the firecrackers' disruption of the basketball game, a brief recapitulation of the whole controversy surrounding Barbara Jeanne Bordelon, and comments from a selection of people who were in attendance, people evidently still hanging around the Easton school grounds when the reporter showed up. Two young women reported being harassed and even threatened. Peg Manson, identified as the president of the Feminist Organization of Louisiana, blamed what she termed "an explosive atmosphere of violence" on "a bunch of Jesus freaks."

As Sheila read certain passages aloud, she indulged in a little extemporaneous editorializing. The phrase "two members of a local feminist organization," for instance, in Sheila's rendition became "two drowned dips without the daring to be dykes." And the words "Peg Manson" were always spoken as "Peg 'In Another Life, Charles' Manson."

Then Sheila came to the paragraphs that dealt with the Soldiers for Jesus. And suddenly Sheila wasn't reading aloud anymore at all. Aloud she simply said: "The Putz is alive. Death to the Putz."

For only then did Sheila and Mac realize that long lost Elmer had now become a presence in their lives once more. What they both found surprising and finally exasperating were all the nice things Elmer was saying about his boy. Elmer wasn't claiming the blood relationship, you understand. But he sure was singing Mac's praises with a fatherly pride.

Before she managed to finish the article, Sheila threw the paper at the refrigerator. Mac picked it up and read the article with increasing horror.

The paper quoted Elmer saying, "Marshall McIntire's courage and spirit of sacrifice is an example for us all. This young man is like the heroes of old, the kind of men, so rare in today's world, who were willing to lay down their very lives for what they knew was right. Coach McIntire knew a year ago that a young woman had no business in the kind of close association with young men that athletic teams inevitably require. And so he dismissed her from his team and suffered in silence the indignities that this decision brought down upon him. This year, in a show of almost holy charity, he demonstrated that his was decision of principle rather than personality by putting his own career on hold to embrace the obviously unappreciated, even negligible chore of coaching his school's girls' team. This is the kind of action and the kind of man that America must again learn to honor, and by offering him our visible and vocal support, the Soldiers for Jesus hope to enhance his stature before a misinformed and ambivalent public."

His fundamentalist Christian organization, Elmer explained, had decided to interject itself into the Barbara Jeanne Bordelon Affair because its members viewed the situation as "an opportunity to establish a beachhead against our nation's no longer creeping moral decay. The Bible makes indisputably clear that God created woman as man's helpmate. He created her to keep the home fires burning while the man wins the daily bread or provides her the physical protection she cannot conceivably provide herself. The idea that men and women are equal," Elmer went on, "is blasphemous. And the Soldiers for Jesus have dedicated themselves to crushing blasphemy wherever they find it."

Later in his comments to the *States-Tribune* reporter, Elmer offered his opinion that "Barbara Jeanne Bordelon, or at least the radical feminists behind her case, are like termites gnawing at the crucial foundations of our national supremacy. It's no secret that this country is suffering from a crisis of confidence, from a flagging will to be strong and once again a beacon unto all the world. Americans used to be cherished as friends, feared desperately as foes. But now we're sneered at by ally and enemy alike. And it's because we don't have our own house in order and every Russian or Polak or Chinaman knows it. And we don't have our own house in order because groups such as these radical feminists with their lesbianism and their pot smoking and their so-called sexual revolution are confusing our young people as to who they are and who they ought to be. Young men and women on the same athletic teams is an outrage, as coach McIntire has tried to bring so painfully to our attention. How can we teach our young men their proper duty as gentlemen and protectors of the hearth if we're asking them to do battle with the fair sex in the athletic arena? Today Barbara Jeanne Bordelon and her supporters are asking for the right to play basketball with men. How soon will it be before they want women on wrestling teams? How soon will it be that they'll want joint use of shower facilities? And how soon before we will all be forced to use unisex bathrooms in every public building in our land?"

As Sheila had been pointing out for years, just like most Baptist preachers, Elmer suffered from diarrhea of the mouth.

Sheila and Mac feared the worst, some ugly confrontation between the Soliders for Jesus and the Feminist Organization of Louisiana. They feared violence. They feared what Sheila termed "rampant assholery." They feared that because of all the controversy the Orleans Parish chapter of the Louisiana High School Athletic Association was going to force the Lady Bruins to forfeit the rest of the games on their schedule or, worse even, suspend all of women's basketball for the rest of the season.

And their fears were all justified, of course. An odious boil was festering. But it didn't pop open that Saturday morning. Because, it seems, radicals of the religious right are no more early risers than radicals of any other cardinal direction.

So, like the Saturday previous, the Lady Bruins took their home floor against O. Perry Walker High before just a handful of spectators, all but one either parents or friends of the players. The practically empty gym proved no deterrent to Lady Bruin fortunes, though. Frisky with desire to really show their stuff, the Bruins were devastating. Peggy Simons was almost frightening in her determination to keep the Walker girls from scoring. And Barbara Jeanne's expected offensive wizardry was almost matched by Mary Masters who played better than Mac had even suspected she could. It was as if the Lady Bruins were waging a vendetta against the world. Even the subs played with a single-minded tenacity. The score was 65 to 9 midway through the third quarter when Mac pulled all his starters to a delirium of clenched fists and slapped hands. And the backups just kept pouring it on. Every member of the team was able to walk off the floor with some statistical contribution: a goal, an assist, a rebound or a steal. Even erstwhile office worker, drum majorette and rat's ass Judy Trascio whom Mac regarded as the twelfth player on his squad scored her first two goals of the season. And at the end the scoreboard read 89 to 13.

When the *States-Tribune* reporter approached him after the final buzzer, Mac presumed that she was there just to cover the game. It was so patently clear to Mac that his Lady Bruins were a powerhouse that he naturally assumed the local paper would finally want to do a story on a team who were obviously threats to bring New Orleans its first women's state basketball championship.

But he should have known he was wrong. Women didn't write for the Sports Section of the *States-Tribune*.

# CHAPTER TWENTY-THREE

"Can I have a word with you, Mr. McIntire?" the reporter said from behind Mac as he gathered his coaching materials from the bottom row of the wooden bleachers. "I'm Cindy Hiller from the *States-Tribune*."

Elated by his victory, Mac turned with a broad smile and extended his hand toward an attractive brunette about his own age. There was a moment of awkwardness because she was holding a tape recorder microphone in her right hand (the tape recorder itself she was wearing clipped to a cloth belt around her waist) and holding a notebook in her left. But she finally got the mike and notebook clasped firmly enough in her left hand so that she could return Mac's handshake in what he later remembered to be a most distracted way.

"Some game, huh?" Mac said. He noticed that the reporter was scanning her notebook for an opening question. "You never really like beating someone so badly," Mac said to fill the space. "But you can hardly tell your backups not to do their very best."

Cindy Hiller seemed utterly oblivious to the line of discussion Mac had obviously opened for her. Instead of some inquiry about basketball her first question was, "Mr. McIntire, are you a member of an organization calling itself the Soldiers for Jesus?"

Mac was so astonished that he didn't say anything. He just stood there blinking at the young woman until she finally said, "Can I take your refusal to answer this question as an indication of either your membership in the Soldiers for Jesus or at least a sympathy for the support they have expressed for your cause?"

If Sheila had been there she would have responded, "You can take my refusal to answer your question as an invitation to an act of intimacy with your microphone." But Sheila and Edith had accompanied the players into the girls' locker room, and Mac was left to speak for himself.

"Are you a sports reporter?" Mac asked.

"I'm in the news department," she said. She started to ask another question about the events of the night before, but Mac cut her off.

"Do you know what you just witnessed here?" he said.

"Well the people in short pants were girls," Cindy Hiller said, sarcastically. "But I still think it was basketball."

Cindy Hiller meant her observation as black humor. Like too many other successful women of the era, she was an up-and-coming professional who prided herself on their own skills and accomplishments but hadn't yet embraced the cause of all women. She presumed, in fact, that because she'd just witnessed a women's basketball game that she'd attended an event of little significance. Cindy Hiller would, in time, grow out of this self-centered attitude. But since she didn't grow out of it in the five seconds following her last remark, she succeeded not in amusing Mac or ingratiating herself with him, as she intended, but rather in infuriating him.

"Did you come here to talk about today's game," Mac said between lips trembling with anger.

"Actually, we're more interested in the events of last night's game," she said, the "we" meaning she and the city desk editor who had assigned her this story.

"Well," Mac said, "I'm afraid you've wasted an awful lot of time this morning, Miss Hiller. You see, we didn't play last night." Then afraid that he might lapse into the verbal strategy preferred by his mother, Mac stalked quickly away from her and into the girls' P.E. office where the women's athletics files were maintained.

Storming away from Cindy Hiller was a mistake, of course, a big mistake. Cindy may have been immature at that stage of her career. But she was honest and competent enough a reporter to have included Mac's side of the developing controversy if he'd only given it to her. But in his anger and his frustration he didn't. And so, the *States-Tribune* article which ran under Cindy Hiller's by-line on Sunday, included only a recapitulation of Friday night's events at Easton, together with little more than the observation that "confronted directly with his rumored affiliation with the group, Broussard Coach Marshall McIntire refused to deny his membership in the Soldiers for Jesus."

That, of course, transformed the anger of the Feminist Organization of Louisiana from camp fire into forest fire. Edith came home from school on

Monday with the worried news that organizers had been canvassing her campus in an attempt to recruit even more protesters for the Lady Bruins' home game against Fortier that upcoming Friday afternoon.

Mac was distressed enough by this news that he couldn't stay home that night. He was so upset he knew he would upset both his mother and Edith if he were around them. And he particularly didn't want to bother Edith who needed to study. So Mac did what men so often do in times of stress. He sought out sex.

Namely, he paid a visit to Stephanie Williams. Mac and Stephanie still considered themselves an item, still slept together once a week or so even though their relationship had not sustained its summer heat into the cooling of the fall and the clammy nature of Sheila's enthusiasm for their pairing. Once school resumed, both had to battle busy schedules to see each other, of course. That was certainly one of their problems. But another was the insight their current distance gave each of them into the hastiness of their summer's intensity.

Yet, as is so often true when relationships first start to lose their freshness and begin the long drift toward dissolution, neither Mac nor Stephanie admitted the discomfort they too commonly now felt around each other. Incompatibility manifested itself often enough, however, in petty irritation and weak excuses for not getting together. And though Mac had never voiced a single word of complaint, he felt a festering hurt that Stephanie showed no interest in attending one of the Lady Bruin basketball games.

But whatever their recent history of difficulties, this Monday night Mac was sure that Stephanie would perceive his needs and rally to them. He wanted her to listen to his aggravations. He wanted her to fix him a drink and make him comfortable. He wanted her to cuddle him. Then, he wanted her to fuck his brains out.

But as Mick Jagger has observed, you can't always get what you want.

Things started out well enough. Stephanie didn't seem at all annoyed when he showed up at her apartment unannounced. She greeted him with a kiss. But when he tried to run his paw-like hands down her long black hair, which was wet from a recent shower and damp against the gray T-shirt she was wearing tucked into a pair of baggy white gym shorts, she squirmed away and dragged him into the kitchen. She had been working on a seminar paper at the kitchen table, easing the pain of academic drudgery with Tanqueray and tonic. She asked Mac if he'd prefer Scotch or beer, and when he designated the former, she fetched out a bottle, ice and a glass to fix it for him.

She didn't protest when he came to stand beside her at the counter to nuzzle at her, but when he slipped his fingers inside the waistband of her shorts, she slapped his hand and barked at him, "Goddamnit, now, don't do that."

Mac removed his hand immediately, but since he was *always* touching her whenever they were together, he didn't really take her reprimand seriously. Whatever their recent problems, Mac found Stephanie gloriously sexy and couldn't keep his hands off her.

It could sometimes take awhile to get through to Mac.

When Stephanie had stirred the water into Mac's Scotch, she told him to go sit in the living room while she "just jotted down the end to this paragraph." She seated herself back at the kitchen table, but Mac, instead of following her instructions, moved to stand behind her chair where she bent over the disarray of loose-leaf papers. He started to read over her shoulder and gradually stooped until his chin was hooked over her shoulder.

"Don't," Stephanie warned him.

Being stupid, Mac said, praising her prose and thereby paying her the highest possible compliment, "Hey, this is really good. I'd be interested to read all of this, and I don't even know Henry James's last name."

"Goddamnit, I said go away."

Mac was stung by the flash fire of her response but covered himself by backing away on his tiptoes and whispering, "Excuuuuuuuuse me." He retreated into the living room and waited for her to finish. Fidgeting, flipping through magazines, he crossed and uncrossed his legs and sipped at his drink.

When Stephanie finally came in to join him, she seemed penitent. She smiled and patted his knee and flung herself against the far end of the sofa from him with her legs propped apart in a way that he could see she wasn't wearing any underwear. "I'm sorry I'm edgy," she said. "I'm always nervous when I'm writing. And I'm getting my period."

Mac wasn't exactly sure why it was that women could use their menstrual cycles as excuses for moodiness when men were deemed unspeakable chauvinists for doing the same thing. But he knew better than to broach *that* topic. Instead, to initiate what he hoped was the night's main event, he said, "You usually get awfully horny when you get your period too. I hope that's not true tonight. I'm too tired to do it more than twice. Three times at the most."

"What an ass," Stephanie said.

And still basically oblivious to the atmosphere of the evening, Mac said, "If you want it in the ass, twice is absolute tops."

"That's disgusting," Stephanie said.

"Well I'm not the one who brought it up," Mac pointed out and in doing so violated a basic rule of human relationships: no one ever likes a wiseass and especially not when she's already pissed off.

"Don't you ever think about anything other than that piece of meat between your legs?" Stephanie asked with a coolness that would make saliva thick.

"Of course," Mac said. "I think a whole lot about the piece between yours." That's when she threw her gin and tonic at him. Mac reacted with the same calmness he showed in his playing days when he got whistled for a fourth foul. He took the napkin Stephanie had wrapped around his Scotch glass and begin to mop his face. As he did so, she gave him a tight-lipped lecture about how irritating it was to be pawed all the time.

"I don't think you've ever just stood next to me without grabbing my ass," Stephanie asserted, and Mac knew that the accusation was true. He was guilty of having presumed she liked it. And he was confused into silence. When Stephanie finished berating him, and he didn't answer or defend himself, she lit a cigarette and contemplated him through the smoke she exhaled in his direction. Finally she said, "You were joking about not knowing Henry James's last name, weren't you?"

As a matter of fact Mac knew exactly who Henry James was. In one of his college English courses he'd been required to read *The Ambassadors*, a chore that still rated only above Uncle Bob's geography course as among the most torpifying experience of his four years at the University of New Orleans. But instead of admitting it, he said, "Of course, I was. His name was Thoreau. Henry James Thoreau. He wrote a book called *Civil Defense*." He didn't look at Stephanie so as not to give himself away.

It's not clear what Stephanie made of Mac's remark, but she didn't comment and instead got up from the couch announcing her intention to make herself a fresh drink. But while she was in the kitchen, Mac quietly let himself out.

If he'd known what was waiting for him at home, Mac would have stayed at Stephanie's and let her throw liquor at him all night. For while Mac was at Stephanie's, the Terminal had received a phone call from Helen Donalds, Mac's old prom date and now a proud private in the Soldiers for Jesus. Edith had taken the call but quickly turned the phone over to Sheila whom Helen greeted warmly and assured that Reverend Elmer (as she called him) and all the Soldiers for Jesus were working night and day to make certain that Coach Mac (as she referred to our hero) would not be dishonored in his own Broussard gym. Had the caller been anyone other than Helen, Sheila would probably have offered some pungent advice about what the Soldiers for Jesus could do with their crosses. But Sheila could never extinguish the warm spot she had for all her unwed mothers and so let Helen ring off with only the suggestion that Helen and her other Soldiers not trouble themselves on Mac's behalf. At 6'6" and 220 pounds, Sheila reminded Helen, Mac was perfectly capable of taking care of himself.

"I know," Helen responded dreamily. "Coach Mac has always represented the perfection of American manhood to me. And I always say that I want our son to grow up just like him."

Sheila presumed from Helen's reference to "our" son that Helen had found an adoptive father for her child. She would find out sometime later rather differently, however. But for now she was just depressed to learn that Friday's game was already destined to become the venue for, as she put it to Edith when she got off the phone, "a championship farting contest for world class assholes."

As she often did when in the throes of frustration or depression, Sheila turned scathingly poetic. To approximate her reaction to the whirlpool of controversy swirling around her son, she fashioned the following limericked response:

> A group called the Soldiers for Jesus
>
> Of our crises pledged quite soon to ease us.
>
> With a putz for a mouthpiece,
>
> They gave us no surcease.
>
> Their support was the smegma of cheeses.

> Meanwhile the women from F.O.o.L.
>
> Proved pussy no guaranteed jewel.
>
> They thought eggs were for throwin',
>
> Their asses for showin',
>
> Their opinions the absolute rule.

> Both F.O.o.L. and the Soldiers for Jesus
>
> Saw corn-holing the right way to please us.
>
> They just lowered our pants
>
> And rammed in their lance
>
> Without decency enough to grease us.

But cathartic as her rhyming was, Sheila knew the current situation called for action more massive than poetry. And in the time between that black Monday night and the Fortier game that next Friday afternoon, Sheila imagined, designed and executed a strategy of counter attack.

# CHAPTER TWENTY-FOUR

Sheila hardly needed additional incentive to spur on her plans for some sort of response to the members of the Soldiers for Jesus and Feminist Organization of Louisiana. But the *States-Tribune* provided it for her in its Wednesday edition anyway. In a city section story, Cindy Hiller reported on a telephone interview she'd had with "a person claiming to be Broussard High School coed Barbara Jeanne Bordelon."

Hiller spent some paragraphs rehashing Barbara Jeanne's identity, her suit based on sex discrimination, its failure in federal district court and its current status on appeal. Her article also detailed once more the controversial series of protests at Lady Bruin basketball games and the current involvement of both a feminist organization and a religious group. Hiller's story then went on to explain that she'd called the Bordelon home to request an interview, been told that Barbara Jeanne was not home and that about an hour later a young woman "identifying herself as Miss Bordelon" called her number at the *States-Tribune* and agreed to talk for the record.

In the course of her remarks this purported Barbara Jeanne stated that she was embarrassed by support the Feminist Organization of Louisiana had shown her, that she considered Marshall McIntire the best coach that she'd ever played for, that all the reports of his having resisted her promotion to a boys' team were untrue, and that to her knowledge he had nothing whatsoever to do with the Soldiers for Jesus.

The person who talked on the phone to Cindy Hiller really *was* Barbara Jeanne Bordelon. But Miss Hiller, in her wrong-headed version of good reporting, cast considerable doubt on that fact when she ended her article in the following fashion: "When asked to comment on rumors that she'd recently traveled to Houston to terminate an unwanted pregnancy, the purported Miss Bordelon refused to answer and abruptly hung up. Subsequent attempts by the *States-Tribune* to contact Miss Bordelon at her home met only with an unanswered phone."

Thus to her enduring discredit, cub reporter Cindy Hiller managed to communicate to her readers that everything Barbara Jeanne Bordelon really believed was, in fact, the mere fabrication of an impostor trying to protect Mac McIntire, but that the utterly and maliciously fabricated tale of Barbara Jeanne's aborted pregnancy was true.

To all of which Sheila remarked, shortly after having first thrown her Wednesday edition of the *States-Tribune* across the Terminal kitchen and then having set the entire paper ceremoniously afire in the sink: "For certain individuals murder is perfectly justifiable. For those same individuals it's a fate far better than they deserve."

Sheila wasn't really a violent person. But she did fantasize about elaborate acts of homicide wiping out the entire memberships of the Feminist Organization of Louisiana and the Soldiers for Jesus and, for good measure, the staff of the *States-Tribune*, as well.

In lieu of bloodshed, Sheila organized. And on Friday afternoon she showed up at the Broussard gym with a contingent of her own supporters, Edith and Carrie and several dozen pregnant women from the home for unwed mothers. Sheila was pissed. And at her instigation and exhortation, her followers were also pissed.

Craziness reigned beginning that day in the Broussard gym, craziness that would mark Lady Bruin games for the rest of the season. The members of the Feminist Organization of Louisiana, believing that Barbara Jeanne Bordelon was a test case for their most devoted determinations, had come to cheer everything Barbara Jeanne did. They loved B.J. They wanted her to score a thousand points every game. And they didn't believe for a second, probably wouldn't have believed it if she'd broadcast it directly to them over a loudspeaker, that she had no grudge against her nefarious coach. Unintimidated by the loss of their banner a week earlier, they came to the Fortier game with a new banner, this time to honor their heroine.

And when Barbara Jeanne, as Lady Bruin captain, came out to meet with the two referees and the Fortier captain, the members of the Feminist Organization of Louisiana rose to cheer her and to unveil their new banner which looked like this:

In giant letters across the bottom it declared:

## BORDELON SLAM DUNKS MALE CHAUVINISM

Sheila's unwed mothers were ready for the members of the Feminist Organization of Louisiana, however. And when the latter rose to cheer, the former rose to boo. Barbara Jeanne herself knew better, of course, but it looked to the uninformed bystander as if the unwed mothers were joining the Soldiers for Jesus in jeering B.J.

For the Soldiers for Jesus, convinced that B. J. was an apple-chomping siren of darkness, had come to deride her every magnificent exploit. On the other hand, because of their devotion to Coach Mac (as they called him), the Soldiers for Jesus were vocal supporters of the rest of the Lady Bruins. They wanted the Broussard women to sweep to a state title so as to bear out their contention that Mac was a genius. So when Mac and the whole of the Lady Bruin team took the floor, the Soldiers for Jesus rose to cheer them wildly and unfurl a banner of their own. When it was fully stretched out across the bleachers, it looked like this:

Under these drawings were the words:

THE FLAG * * COACH MAC * * THE CROSS

    Sheila and the unwed mothers, of course, felt obliged to register their rejection of any display made by the Soldiers for Jesus as well, so, as the latter cheered Mac and the Lady Bruins, the former jeered. And if Sheila had had her way the unwed mothers would have displayed a banner of their own. She had made one. But Mac had forbade her even to take it out of her sewing room at the Terminal. No thanks to his mother, of course, Mac had a rather substantial concern for propriety, and he didn't want Sheila showing her banner because it looked like this:

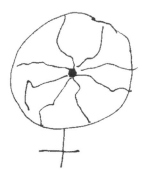

Across the bottom Sheila had stenciled a simple identification:

THE SOLDIERS FOR JESUS

What Mac didn't know was that Sheila had made a second banner too. The second one looked like this:

Across the bottom of this one Sheila had lettered:

THE MEMBERS OF F.O.o.L.

    You can see why Edith and Mac sometimes told Sheila they thought she had an anal fixation.

You can perhaps also see why it appeared that the unwed mothers had come to root for Fortier. Before the game had started, it appeared they had booed first Barbara Jeanne Bordelon, the Broussard captain and star, and then Mac McIntire, the Broussard coach, and then the entire Lady Bruin team.

Imagine Fortier's confusion then, when they knocked the opening tip away from Olga Jorgensen, scored the game's initial bucket and drew a loud cheer. Not from the unwed mothers, of course, but from the members of the Feminist Organization of Louisiana, who, though they were hoping Barbara Jeanne would score a thousand points, were hoping in their hatred for Mac that the Lady Bruins would lose 1000 to 1001, thus proving him an incredibly incompetent coach.

And they were only 1999 total points from their goal when the Lady Bruins got their hands on the ball for the first time and began their overwhelming display of all-court power. The Broussard girls coupled tenacious defense with brilliant offense to crush Fortier 85 to 29 despite the vocal encouragement the Lady Tarpons received from the Feminist Organization of Louisiana, and, at times, it seemed, from the unwed mothers who rose to boo the Feminist Organization of Louisiana every time its members rose to cheer Barbara Jeanne.

But, if anything, this crazy cheering only inspired the Lady Bruins to a better performance. The *way* the crowd cheered made practically no discernable sense. But they were loud and involved, and thus they were infectious. They increased the Lady Bruins' determination for victory.

Fortier was well-coached and rather more talented than many of the teams on Broussard's schedule. They played a switching defense and fairly quickly forced the Lady Bruins out of their number one offense and into the number two double pick alignment. This offensive pattern freed B.J. for the majority of her 45 points, but it also allowed rapidly improving Mary Masters to "shake" loose for 27 points of her own.

I've put quotation marks around the word *shake* in the previous sentence because of a development that took place in the second half. Early in the third quarter, when Barbara Jeanne began a tear of six field goals in a row, the Broussard subs took up the chant of "Cake, Cake, Cake," the nickname B.J. had brought along with her from her softball days in the Ponytail League. Fortier responded to this run by calling a time-out, probably to attack Broussard's number two offense with a double switching strategy. Anticipating this tactic in his own huddle, Mac directed his Lady Bruin offensive trio to "shake Mary loose for crip shots on the pick and roll."

On the next three Lady Bruin possessions, B.J. and Mary worked the passing play perfectly, and the girls on the bench switched from "Cake, Cake, Cake" to "Shake, Shake, Shake," bestowing on Mary a nickname of her own, which she embellished in her endearing hot dog way by gyrating her backside every time she scored. By the end of the starters' time on the floor, the subs had fashioned a nickname for big Olga Jorgensen as well. They called her "Quake," honoring the beating Olga was obliged to take as opponents repeatedly slammed into her in her game-long duty to set screens. By the time Mac called a time-out to give his back-ups their turn on the floor, the Lady Bruins had themselves a cheer: "Cake and Shake and the picks from Quake."

And with that kind of enthusiasm, Mac knew he had a team that was going to be very hard to stop.

To everyone associated with the Lady Bruins of Barbara Jeanne Bordelon's junior year in high school, the Fortier game was a watershed. In attendance for the first time were all three squadrons of spectators who would follow the course of their schedule. And perhaps as a result of the vociferous participation of the crowd, it was against Fortier that the Lady Bruins themselves really came together with the oneness and the wholeness they needed to face the contests ahead.

Sadly, the Fortier game was also the first time Sheila heard the "dyke" rumor. Sitting directly in front of Sheila and her group of unwed mothers were two middle-aged men each wearing a soiled nylon-mesh, baseball-style cap. What these two men were doing at the game Sheila could never determine. They weren't women, so they weren't members of the Feminist Organization of Louisiana. And they were neither neatly and conservatively dressed nor carrying Bibles, so they probably were not Soldiers for Jesus. Possibly, they were fathers of girls on the Fortier team, though they never cheered for the Lady Tarpons. Probably they were just members of the not so idly curious, a couple of guys intrigued by the seemingly ceaseless accounts of the Barbara Jeanne Bordelon Affair they'd seen in the paper. Just a couple of creeps off work early enough that Friday afternoon to crush down a six pack each in a nearby tavern and still have time to catch the neighborhood freak show, which was, after all, free of charge.

"They were asshole scumbags," Sheila declared to Mac and Edith later that night.

We hardly find that judgment from Sheila surprising, but as was usually true of Sheila's earthy proclamations, she was right. They *were* asshole scumbags. I know because Sheila overheard them exchange the following comments:

*Asshole Scum Bag in Dirty Blue Cap (looking at the players moving about the basketball floor): Which one is the Bordelon kid?*

*Asshole Scum Bag in Dirty Red Cap (pointing toward Olga Jorgensen at mid-court): Probably the elephant woman there. She's the biggest one. Looks big enough to play tackle for the Saints.*

*ASBDBC (pulling his jeans to a snugger position at the crotch): You don't know shit.*

*ASBDRC: Shit.*

*ASBDBC: I hear this Barbara Jeanne (he pronounced it the way Mac first had, to rhyme with <u>mean</u>) got herself knocked up. Had to sneak over to Houston to get rid of the little bastard.*

*ASBDRC: Shit. I heard she was a dyke. All these women athuleets is dykes.*

*ASBDBC: Funny goddamn dyke, I'd say. Gettin' herself knocked up.*

*ASBDRC: You don't know shit, man. Don't you know they do it to each other with Turkey basters.*

*ASBDBC: Shit.*

*ASBDRC: Fuck they don't man. Get some French Quarter fairy to beat his meat into a goddamn turkey baster and then squirt it up each other's kazoos.*

*ASBDBC: Fuckin' dykes.*

*ASBDRC: Ain't no wonder they say she's so good is it?*

*ASBDBC: Which one is she anyway?*

*ASBDRC: She's the fuckin dyke, no brains. All the real women athuleets is dykes.*

"I think puttin' one of those trucker caps on your head costs you ten I.Q. points per day," Sheila told Mac and Edith, concluding her story.

But unfortunately for Barbara Jeanne Bordelon and her supporters, morons in mesh caps weren't alone in spreading the word that she was a lesbian. The Soldiers for Jesus soon adopted the allegation and shortly mounted a letter-writing campaign to Broussard principle Samuel P. Riggs to have Barbara Jeanne dismissed from the Lady Bruins because of her "potentially immoral influence on the school's other young women."

To Riggs's credit, he undertook no action on this insane proposal, but he did inform Mac about the pressure he was under.

"What did he want you to do about it?" Sheila asked Mac when he first told her that night about his conversation with Riggs. She was sitting in her old wing-back chair, now located in her sewing room, knitting a cotton sweater for Carrie.

"I think maybe he wanted me to find the letter writers and beat them up or something."

"Either that or at least make sure Barbara Jeanne doesn't get caught eating pussy in the locker room," Sheila said without missing a stitch.

Mac shook his head. "You really have way of getting to the crux of an issue, Mom. Or maybe the crotch."

Sheila smiled. "In either case, the Soldiers for Jesus are behind the letters, aren't they?" She still hadn't looked up from her knitting.

"How'd you know?" Mac asked.

"Because when they go home each day and take off their go-to-church suits and dresses, Elmer requires each one of them to spend at least eight hours wearing a trucker's cap."

# CHAPTER TWENTY-FIVE

I can't exactly say that the Lady Bruins' basketball season settled down after the Fortier game, but events did begin to follow an established, if certainly mad, pattern. The late Friday afternoon games continued to attract full houses and wild behavior wherever in the city of New Orleans they were played. The crazy cheering patterns went on unabated, creating at least a level of noise that the Lady Bruins seemed to find inspiring. Both the Soldiers for Jesus and the Feminist Organization of Louisiana continued to try to use their involvement with Broussard women's basketball as a means of recruiting attention for themselves. But this ploy only partially worked. Since there was no repeat of the firecracker incident, the *States-Tribune* fairly quickly got tired of covering a story not producing new developments.

Meanwhile, the Saturday morning contests continued to draw only Sheila, Edith, Joan Teo and flies. Ironically, Mac noticed that his team played with far less zest on Saturdays than before the packed houses the evenings before. On Fridays they seemed to take the floor breathing fire, as if especially determined to put all the wackos in their places. On Saturdays they were often listless, perhaps wrung out from the emotional displays of the evenings prior.

But whether Friday or Saturday, whether they played especially well or not so well, they continued to win by lopsided margins. With withering accuracy, Barbara Jeanne continued to hit high arching jumpers in Mac's own style from behind her head. She was easily leading the city in scoring. Mary Masters was fourth in that same category. Peggy Simons topped the list of rebounders. And as a team the Lady Bruins led the city both in total points scored and fewest points allowed.

The rumors that Barbara Jeanne was both a lesbian and an aborted unwed mother continued to circulate, though. And Mac could never quite escape the feeling that his Lady Bruins were atop a malignant time-bomb ticking toward an undeserved doom.

Then, in the second week of January, the ticks seem to grow into drum beats. One Friday afternoon, in the interval between the end of the school day and a second round game at home against Easton, Mac was summoned to a meeting with Broussard Principal Sam Riggs and Vice-Principal Arnold Larrett. The ostensible topic was a proposal Mac had made to begin charging a token admission, a buck say, to all the remaining Lady Bruin games. Admission had never been charged in the past because so few people attended games the process wasn't worth it.

This was obviously not the case in Barbara Jeanne Bordelon's junior season, and Mac wanted to capitalize on the attendance (for whatever screwball reasons) to finance new uniforms. His girls were still wearing old-fashioned one-piece uniforms that were frumpy and constricting.

As seems the absolute rule with administrators, however, Riggs and Larrett had arguments for why such a thing just couldn't be done. No other school in the city charged admission for their women's sports, they pointed out. Such policy changes really ought to be made at the beginning of the year, not in mid-season. And even if the Lady Bruins could actually gather enough funds in their few remaining home games to cover the cost of a new set of uniforms, there was a serious question of whether other needs of the athletic budget weren't more pressing.

In other words, no.

Mac felt like Columbus when people kept telling him the world was flat.

But before Mac could excuse himself from Dr. Riggs's office, he felt less like Columbus and more like a character created by Kafka.

Admission charges and new uniforms weren't the real reason Mac had been called in. "We've had some complaints," Larrett said, "that you've gotten a little, shall we say, 'too handy' with some of the girls on your basketball team."

Mac looked at him blankly; not even in the tiniest corner of his mind did he understand what was being said.

"Of course, we're not placing any stock in them," Riggs added, clearing his throat, "what with all the controversy and everything."

"You have complaints that I've been too handy with my team?" Mac said. He looked first at Larrett then at Riggs.

"That you've been grabbing their goddamn little behinds, McIntire," Larrett said.

"I'm sure it's just a playful thing," Riggs added.

"But we've no choice but to investigate, and you're advised to cut it out instantly," Larrett said.

Mac's durable patience was finally stretched thin. "Just who the *fuck* made these complaints," he said, instantly and dangerously angry.

"Watch yourself, McIntire," Larrett advised.

"Yes, please don't get worked up about this," Riggs said.

"I have one thing to say," Mac said so very deliberately that the two men who sat facing him paid the carefulest attention. "If one of the girls on my team lodged a complaint, then I can understand your wanting to take it seriously. But if these complaints have come in anonymous letters or from the Feminist Organization of Louisiana, then I'd hope you'd both have the good sense to place those letters where they belong—right beside any other roll of toilet tissue. Do I make myself clear?" Mac looked at the two of them with such intensity that if he'd been Superman they'd have both melted.

When he moved toward the door of Riggs' office to leave, Riggs said, "Please understand that we aren't making any accusations, Mr. McIntire."

"But please do keep your hands to yourself," Larrett added to Mac's back.

Sheila would have turned back to wish Larrett an intimate experience with Butch the Biker. But Mack maintained his cool and kept on walking.

The scary thing about the latest tempest to blow into Mac's life was that it was true. Or at least it was true in a way that could probably get him convicted by a jury of his peers. Mac *had* gotten "handy" with the members of his team. Like coaches everywhere, Mac had the habit of slapping his girls on their fannies. He might slap a starter's butt to send her out for the start of a game or back onto the floor after a time-out. He might slap a sub's rear as he sent her into the game. When a scintillating series of points by the Lady Bruins caused the opposing coach to call a time-out, he might slap the fanny of every fist-flourishing girl who rushed in triumph to the sidelines.

Mac was an inveterate fanny slapper, and without giving it a single thought he'd committed his sin in front of all the multitudes who had attended the Lady Bruins' games every Friday afternoon since November.

More, Mac was such a physical person that his touching of his girls was hardly limited to their butts. When his girls played well, he threw his arm around them or even wrapped them in bear hugs. When he was talking to them individually, particularly at some noisy point of a game, he had the habit of grasping the player's uniform right about her belly button and squeezing the loose material into his fist so that she couldn't nervously run back onto the court before he was through delivering his instructions.

At one time or another, in fact, Mac had had his hands on *almost* every part of every player on his team, whether from hugging or fanny slapping or taping an ankle or massaging a sore calf or rubbing balm into a strained thigh. But its goes without saying, of course, that absolutely none of such touching was in the vaguest way sexual. The year before Mac had touched his J.V. boys in precisely the same ways.

But Mac understood immediately as he walked toward the gym that Friday afternoon of the second Nicholls game that he'd have to stop touching his players almost entirely. He would have to continue first aid ministrations, he figured. There was no one else to shoulder that essential duty. But all the rest, all the "avoidable" touching would have to end. And he would miss it. The ease with which athletes have always touched each other was a pleasure he'd have to forego. As always a disciplined competitor, Mac was determined not to give his enemies a stick with which to beat him.

Then, that very afternoon and night of the second Nicholls game, Mac had two related experiences that he would remember for a very long time and that were to make life all the more difficult for him.

The first began about twenty minutes or so after Broussard had again crushed the Nicholls women, this time by a score of 88 to 30. The game itself had been an approximate copy of the other Lady Bruin victories this season in every regard but one. And that was the additional floor time Mac provided for his offensive center, Olga Jorgensen.

In part, Mac wanted to give Judy Trascio some game-time experience working behind Olga's mammoth picks. Judy had gradually improved from the Lady Bruin's twelfth player overall to its fourth offensive player, and as the season marched steadily on toward the post-season play-offs and the more strenuous competition awaiting there, Mac wanted this potentially crucial sub to be as well-trained as possible in case, God forbid, something should happen to either Mary or Barbara Jeanne.

Furthermore, Mac needed to improve Olga's conditioning. Come the play-offs, he might well need her to go the entire game instead of just two and a half quarters, and he was by no means certain she yet had the stamina for it. Events following the game proved, among other things, just how much Olga indeed needed the additional work. Mac was in the girls' P.E. office compiling statistics when Judy Trascio suddenly slammed open the door leading to the girls' locker room yelling for Mac to come quickly because Olga had fallen in the shower and was hurt. Mac bolted from his chair and ran after Judy through two sets of doors and into the locker room. At the far end of a long row of lockers, a clump of his players in various stages of dress and undress peered into the beige- and brown-tiled shower room.

Pushing his way through them, Mac found Olga Jorgensen sprawled on the wet floor like the world's largest fetus. Her knees curled up against her sagging belly and her head, locked in pain, tucked down toward her chest. The forgotten shower still beat down on her back. Standing bent over at Olga's head, clad only in a pair of soaked, flowered underpants, tears streaming down her face and a clenched fist beating its frustration against her bare thigh, Mary Masters wiped pointlessly, again and again, at Olga's agony-twisted face. A totally naked Barbara Jeanne Bordelon knelt at Olga's feet, her strong hands kneading insistently at Olga's knotted calves.

Unavoidably positioning himself directly under the shower's spray, Mac moved Mary aside and sat down so that Olga was between his outstretched legs. Grabbing her just underneath her arms, his fingers splayed out across the tops of her huge breasts, Mac pulled his fallen player into a sitting position. "Stretch her legs out straight in front of her," he ordered Barbara Jeanne. Leaning Olga back against his chest, he scooted himself up snug against her, slid his long arms around her body and grabbed her toes, firmly but slowly pulling her feet back toward her head and in the process freeing the knots from her cramped calves. "We're gonna need some ice, kiddo, but before you get it, why don't you turn that shower off?" Mac said to Mary. He smiled at her so she wouldn't feel reprimanded. "I didn't bring a towel," he explained.

As if she'd just awakened from a nightmare, Mary turned the shower off and in the process seemed suddenly to remember that she was topless in front of her coach. She threw her arms across her chest as she ran from the shower room. Neither Barbara Jeanne nor Olga had yet discovered their own nakedness however. "Put your hands on her feet," Mac told B.J. "and keep them pointed back this way." Then, speaking to her for the first time, he quietly asked Olga if she was OK. She nodded meekly that she was, and he stroked gently at her wet cheek with his open palm. "Takes more than leg cramps to stop a quake, huh?"

"Yessir," she whispered.

"Do you think you can stand now?" Mac asked her. "I think if we walk a little before we put the ice on, we can probably reduce the soreness." Olga nodded and Mac and B.J. helped her carefully to her feet. "Stretch out on your toes now," Mac instructed as they assisted her from the shower room. When they had her seated on the wooden bench in front of her locker, someone handed her a towel, and she draped it over the front of her body. Mary, back from her trip to the office refrigerator and now dressed in a T-shirt and some practice shorts, handed Mac two ice bags and the rolls of ace bandages he needed to strap them on.

Olga's injury was not really all that serious, but it was the first one of any consequence any of the Lady Bruins had suffered, and it had obviously scared them all. They had all followed as Mac and Barbara Jeanne walked Olga once around the locker room, and they were now all gathered in the crowded space around her locker. Gradually, though, as Mac wrapped the two blue chemical ice bags to Olga's legs, they returned to their preparations for going home. All except B.J., who continued to sit next to Olga on the bench, holding her teammate's hand and dripping water into a widening pool on the concrete floor at her feet.

When Mac finished taping he asked Olga again if she was OK, and she answered yes with returning confidence and strength. He then stood up and beat his hands on his thighs in a gesture of conclusion. "You're all right, and I'm all wet," he observed.

B.J. then leaped up in front of him and said, "I've got an extra towel you can use, Coach."

This was the exact moment, I think, that Mac stopped being the rescue squad and to his guilty dismay started being a man. Even in the crisis which he'd just attended to, Mac was not blind. He *knew* the girls were naked. But he hadn't *thought* about it. When Barbara Jeanne stood in front of him now, however, her firm little breasts pointing directly out at him like the snow cones of temptation, he did think about it. And as she pivoted to run to her locker for that extra towel, in a move precisely like the one she used repeatedly to make her cut to the basket, he thought about the ripple of muscle in her slender thigh. And as she moved away from him now in long graceful strides, he thought about the firm curve of her nicely rounded little behind.

And even more, after he'd moved over to the next row of lockers and she came back toward him, one arm outstretched with his towel, the other holding her own which covered one breast, Mac thought about the sparse brown patch of pubic hair at the V of her legs. He couldn't help himself. He had looked at her lovely seventeen-year-old body, and he had thought his thoughts, and now as she came so innocently toward him he looked again.

And she caught him.

When Mac raised his eyes to Barbara Jeanne's face to smile his thanks for the towel, he found her eyes already there waiting for him. Her head swivelled almost imperceptibly in recognition. She opened the hand which held her own towel just slightly so that it fell open to cover more of her.

With both hands Mac mopped with his towel at his damp face and dripping hair. "I better get out of here so y'all can get dressed," Mac said with a suddenly hoarse voice as if addressing a group instead of just B.J.

He should have moved off then, but he didn't, and although he lingered less than five seconds, it was long enough for Judy Trascio to turn a corner and find them standing their facing each other, as if frozen in time.

# CHAPTER TWENTY-SIX

The experience in the locker room after the second Nicholls game, stretching out its denouement across the eternity it took Mac to turn away from Barbara Jeanne when Judy happened upon them, taught Mac a lesson he'd denied all his life for lack of conclusive evidence: Sheila and Edith were right. All men *were* assholes. Some might successfully resist their asshole tendencies, but any man, Mac thought in his indignation at his weakness, who looked with lust upon a person as astonishingly wholesome as Barbara Jeanne Bordelon, was an asshole of unspeakable proportions. Mac remembered the countless exchanges he'd had with Edith, particularly during her most mishoministic phase, remembered his litanied rebuttal, "I'm a man too," to her countless generalizations about men. And now in his sudden self-loathing, he recognized the irony of that repeated counter thrust. I am a man, too, he thought. An asshole like all the others.

Mac could really be guilty of overreaction, couldn't he?

Rushing from the girls' locker room that day where he'd been perfectly honorable, he confused impulse with action, temptation with sin. His reddening face and constricting trousers led him to embrace a guilt he hadn't earned, and his unearned guilt led him to refuse himself his usual joy in triumph.

On routine Friday nights at the Terminal, Edith, Sheila and Mac treated themselves to a little celebration commemorating the end of the work week and the Lady Bruins' habitual victory. They'd order a pizza, stock in beer and wine and eat while replaying that afternoon's game, or discussing the issues of some case Edith was studying or the history of some new unfortunate at the home for unwed mothers. They'd get a little drunk, usually, and in the process remind each other how wonderful and secure it felt to be loved.

But this night, Mac felt undeserving of such warm camaraderie. Upon arriving home from school, he just wanted to go directly to bed. He obviously had to explain the circumstances of his drenched clothes, however. So, supplying only the meager details, he related that Olga Jorgensen had fallen in the shower with leg cramps. And because the two experiences were somehow spiritually connected, he also shared with Edith and Sheila the encounter he'd had with Riggs and Larrett. Mac couldn't get into the usually easy flow of the evening. The vision of a naked Barbara Jeanne Bordelon kept rising up behind his eyes like a possession. And sometimes, when he would look at Edith who was, as usual, braless under her Wonder Woman T-shirt, he would see *her* naked, naked except for a pair of tennis shoes and shooting baskets in an empty gymnasium, her long blond hair whipping after her like a kite tail as she ran and dribbled and jumped.

Tortured by such comely demons, Mac claimed an upset stomach, and retired as soon as possible to his room. And psychosomatically he even began to feel sick. Not really sleepy, Mac tossed about in his bed, wetting his sheets with the clammy sweat of self-recrimination. While he brooded there, Edith and Sheila each made visits to inquire about him. Mac was not ordinarily moody. So both presumed him genuinely ill. Edith looked in on him one last time just before midnight. Slightly tipsy from the bottle of wine she'd shared with Sheila, she'd already showered and prepared for bed before she went up to check on him.

As she bent over him to lay her hand on his moist forehead, the top of her bathrobe parted, and he could see her breasts. He squeezed his eyes shut as if they were the clanging gates to the walled city of goodness. But the ghostly breasts had already slipped inside, and in his mind they fell from Edith's robe to rest with a throb against his face.

"You OK?" Edith asked.

"Yeah," Mac said with a chalky tongue.

"You look like you're suffering."

"Some," Mac said.

"Anything I can do for you?"

"No thanks." Mac had still not opened his eyes.

Edith giggled lewdly, the wine making her devilish. "Not *anything*?"

"Good night," Mac said.

"I'm really worried about him," Edith told Sheila back downstairs. "He wasn't even interested when I offered to flash him."

But, of course, Mac was interested, and that was his problem. When he finally slipped into a fitful sleep, all his dreams were vivid and very sexual. Sometimes his partner was Edith Jenkins, sometimes Barbara Jeanne Bordelon, sometimes some third woman who seemed a combination of them both. Sometimes they seemed elusive, teasing him from a distance he could never quite close. Sometimes they allowed him to have sex with the two of them at once. Sometimes Edith lived in Stephanie Williams' apartment and walked about in Stephanie's clothes. Sometimes Barbara Jeanne beckoned to him from the doorway of the girls' shower room. Sometimes Mac would be conducting a Lady Bruin practice session and Barbara Jeanne would be on the floor, naked except for tennis shoes.

But in the most troubling dream of all, troubling because it felt so absolutely real, Mac would whistle his Lady Bruins together, and Barbara Jeanne would rush to stand beside him. And while he was talking, he would circle his arm around Barbara Jeanne and pull her gently against him and bump her hip against his leg. And then he would casually slip his hand inside the elastic of her practice shorts, inside her panties and squeeze contentedly at the swell of her wonderful, muscular behind.

When Mac awoke the next morning shortly after dawn, it was with a feeling of guilt now grown to frightful proportions and with an attendant unspecified sense of dread.

Mac tried to banish his anxiety with a long, hard, pre-breakfast run along the Mississippi River levee from the Terminal at Oak and Leake all the way to the Huey P. Long Bridge and back. He knew it wasn't true, but he could not shake the oppressive feeling that the events in his dream about fondling Barbara Jeanne had actually happened.

Even though the Saturday morning game went off without a hitch, Mac's sense of foreboding plagued him all that weekend. He made sure that he left all the fanny slapping to the Lady Bruins themselves who crushed McDonogh for the second time. The events of the prior day did not seem to have left any feelings of discomfort among his players. As usual, Barbara Jeanne played brilliantly, and the other girls played with energy, enthusiasm and discipline. Mac held Olga out of the game as a precaution, but as expected, an evening of fluids and salt tablets had left her almost totally recovered. Only Judy Trascio, starting her first game in Olga's place, played raggedly.

Mac might have made some connection between his own feeling of impending doom, however, and Judy's nervous play. For it seems Judy had told her mother what she had seen in the Broussard girls' locker room. And first thing Monday morning Mrs. Philby Trascio was planning to report what she'd heard to Samuel Riggs.

# CHAPTER TWENTY-SEVEN

Mac learned of Mrs. Trascio's visit to Dr. Rigg's office even before it took place. Judy told him, fearfully, after their Monday morning practice session.

Mac had kept Monday workouts light, mostly shooting and easy running drills to get his players properly stretched out for the harder work he'd do with them on Tuesday and Wednesday before another light session on Thursday. And because she hadn't worked up too much of a sweat, Judy just toweled herself off and skipped a shower so as to have time to talk to Mac before school started.

Mac gathered two things from that eight a.m. conversation in his home economics room where he'd gone after practice to finish preparations for his day's classes. First, he perceived just where it was that Judy Trascio learned to be a rat's ass. Second, he concluded, that Judy herself didn't want to be a rat's ass anymore.

"I don't know why I told her about it all, Mr. McIntire," Judy explained, so sorry that not once in her confession did she lift her eyes off the floor. "I didn't want to get you in trouble. I know you wouldn't do anything wrong. And I know that you had to help Olga." Judy started to cry then, and Mac told her to go on back to the locker room and try to get a hold of herself before first period.

Mac closed up his teaching notes and considered this latest development. He knew the situation was very serious. But he felt better, actually, than he had since last Friday. Until moments ago he hadn't been sure that his venture into the girls' locker room would really lead to trouble, though he supposed that his sense of sin made him feel that it ought to. Whatever his sense of guilt, he certainly hadn't known what form this crisis was going to take. But with the showdown finally at hand, his spirits quickly improved because now at least he could begin to deal with it. As always Mac was calmer on the court of action than he was on the sidelines waiting for the game to start.

Mac figured correctly that if Dr. Riggs was going to hear that his women's basketball coach had been in the presence of a bunch of naked Broussard coeds, that he'd just as soon hear this news from the coach himself. So Mac headed down to Riggs's office to tell him as much of the story as possible before class started or Mrs. Trascio put in her appearance.

Mac's strategy with Riggs was simple. He told the truth. Nothing but the truth. And if he didn't tell the whole truth, all he left out was the part about inadvertently becoming aroused when he stopped curing Olga Jorgensen's leg cramps and started looking a Barbara Jeanne Bordelon's body parts as something other than the assembled cogs of a basketball scoring machine.

Mac was remorseful. But he wasn't crazy.

Mac also told Dr. Riggs of his understanding that Mrs. Trascio would be stopping into the principal's office that morning and that he was sorry, what with all the other controversy surrounding the Lady Bruins this year that now Dr. Riggs was going to have to deal with this new one as well.

Riggs was not happy with this latest development, but even given the earlier complaints about Mac's "handiness" with his players, a report he actually never put much stock in, he acknowledged that Mac had had no recourse but to respond when he was summoned to Olga Jorgensen's aid. And he told Mrs. Trascio all these things when she came in to see him around 10 a.m. Predictably she wasn't mollified. She just kept repeating over and over again her observation, "But these girls are just children. Babies practically. And Coach McIntire is a grown man."

Riggs told Mrs. Trascio that he shared her concern very gravely, and though he remained utterly confident that Coach McIntire had not done anything wrong, he'd investigate the matter fully and take action to ensure that Coach McIntire was not again put in a position to have to enter the girls' locker room.

And as a matter of fact, that's just the course of action Riggs pursued. He called in the Lady Bruins one at a time all that day and asked them to tell him what had happened after the game on Friday. And one after another they repeated the same story. None of them even bothered to volunteer the information that a number of the girls were undressed when Mac came into the locker room. When he questioned them about it directly, they emphasized only that Olga had started cramping while still in the shower and that a lot of the girls hadn't finished dressing yet when Judy Trascio went to get Mac. Convinced by their testimony that there hadn't been a whiff of wrong doing, Riggs decided first to let the matter drop, hoping it would blow over quietly, and second to devise some kind of adjusted system where such a situation would not arise in the future. Underneath his jaundiced bureaucrat's personality Samuel P. Riggs had a spine after all.

But that's not to say that the solution he concocted to keep Mac out of the girls' locker room didn't cost Mac something. It cost him dearly.

What Riggs did was to appoint world history teacher Joan Teo as Mac's assistant coach. That Joan knew almost nothing about basketball mattered to Riggs not at all. He knew she'd been going to the Lady Bruin games, and he knew she'd take the assignment for the little bit of money he could scrounge out of the budget to pay her.

Round-faced, dimpled and cushiony as the Pillsbury Doughboy, rosy-cheeked and beatific as a Rubens cherub, Joan Teo was one of those boundlessly cheerful women who are in all the clubs in high school, who remain largely dateless and assuredly single through college and go into teaching so they can sponsor all the clubs as an adult. Like many such women, Joan was easy to take advantage of. It wasn't exactly that she lacked a healthy self-concept. It was far more that she simply had too little life apart from school to fill her time. Riggs was always assigning her extra duty because he knew she'd do it without bitching or even sulking.

But Joan's natural sweetness did not save her from being condemned by plumpness to a life of girlish crushes instead of womanly affairs. Mac McIntire was the unfortunate object of Joan's current fantasy. She seemed to have a special smile for him in the halls, and she always made a point of drawing him into conversation in the teacher's lounge. The Monday after the first weekend of Lady Bruin basketball games, she had brought him a batch of homemade cookies and delivered them with a note that said: "Broussard 68 McDonogh 23! Broussard 75 Nicholls 30! Congratulations! And don't let the ghouls from F.O.o.L. get you down!" Joan Teo was a lonely, lovable, hopelessly peppy women with a yen for chocolate and an addiction to exclamation points.

Despite this fact, and despite her suspected romantic fascination with him, Mac anticipated no problems in working with Joan. She was too much of a goodheart for that. But Mac was sad to see her come aboard all the same. Joan's responsibilities, as Riggs explained them to her and Mac that afternoon after school, would be to act as a liaison between Mac and the players. She would not be expected to do any actual coaching, but she was to be constantly available for the girls to talk to should they feel the need. And she would relieve Mac from his duties as a trainer. As soon as she could master the necessary skills, she was to take full responsibility for taping and all other first aid ministrations.

In short, as soon as Joan Teo could learn her way around a roll of adhesive and a jar of Atomic Balm, Mac would be prohibited from touching his girls at all.

What this cost Mac was an intimacy with his players that he thought was basic to coaching, at least at the high school level. He was being forced away from them. Society's obsession with sex was going to rob him of the more personal aspects of his job. He was forced exclusively into the intellectual role of coaching and out of the instinctively emotional and physical aspects of his profession. He wouldn't interact with them as often in casual situations and would no longer be their confidant. There would be fewer opportunities to banter with them about everything from their classes to their home lives to their boyfriends.

Even though he knew Riggs couldn't have given him anyone better to work with than Joan Teo, Mac hated the new arrangement. And with a stabbing irony that Mac was too smart to miss, he hated it for a reason altogether apart from what the new system was going to mean to his coaching. He hated it because it meant that the chances he'd once more get to cast his haunted eyes on Barbara Jeanne Bordelon's naked body were reduced to practically nil.

# CHAPTER TWENTY-EIGHT

While Mac was struggling with the reduced pleasures of his employment as a basketball coach, his chief current adversary, Feminist Organization of Louisiana president Peg "In another life, Charles" Manson, was struggling with problems of her own. In recent weeks, the drive of her organization's involvement in the Barbara Jeanne Bordelon case had clearly slackened. Manson was finding it more and more difficult to turn her members out, more and more difficult to kindle the proper fire of outrage in those who did keep turning out. She even suspected with an incredulous bitterness that some of the members of the Feminist Organization of Louisiana were turning into Lady Bruin fans.

There'd always been confusion about this matter, of course. The official party line was that they were to cheer the exploits of Barbara Jeanne, but root against the team as a whole. At recent games, howeverf, Manson had begun to notice some of her associates applauding when Lady Bruins other than Barbara Jeanne made baskets. When she confronted a group of such backsliders with their apostasy, however, their brazen leader, a jockish redhead named Georgia Franklin, immediately engaged Manson in a doctrinal debate.

"We are *for* Barbara Jeanne," Franklin pointed out. "That's what brought us all into this struggle. But if we're *really* for Barbara Jeanne, then we have to be *for* all aspects of her play, not just *for* her scoring. We have to want Barbara Jeanne to demonstrate her gifts as an all around basketball player. So I think we're obligated to cheer her rebounds and assists as well as her baskets. And obviously Barbara Jeanne can only be credited with an assist when one of her teammates scores."

Peg Manson shook her head. Revisionism terrified her. But she felt incapable of effectively arguing with Franklin, who possessed the unfair advantage of knowing something about basketball.

Imagine Manson's ecstasy, then, when she learned about Mac's ministering to a naked girl in the Lady Bruin locker room. With this knowledge she hoped to drive her straying legions back along the path of orthodoxy. "McIntire * Molester * Monster" brayed the new banners Manson instructed her troops to prepare for the next Lady Bruin game. With this new sortie, Manson hoped, needed media attention would once again return to her cause.

Fortunately for Mac, these new banners never wafted across a gym during a Lady Bruin game or otherwise saw the light of public display. Edith Jenkins, with contacts inside the Feminist Organization of Louisiana, learned of their existence and approached Manson on the evening before they were to be flown. Accompanying Edith on her surgical mission were Sheila McIntire and five pregnant women from the New Orleans home for unwed mothers.

Edith and her entourage met with Peg Manson and several other members of the Feminist Organization of Louisiana at Manson's uptown apartment on Second Street. The meeting had a predictable grim-faced quality. The women had seen each other at enough Friday evening basketball games to know that they were enemies. But to the credit of representatives from both sides, everyone tried to adopt an air of civility. Manson served tea and set out some finger sandwiches. After Sheila ate six or so and helped herself to a second cup of tea, they finally got down to business.

Edith stated the legal case. "If you so much as unfold one corner of any banner that either states or insinuates Mac McIntire has behaved in a sexually impermissible manner, he will slap you with a lawsuit for libel for so much money that the Feminist Organization of Louisiana won't be able to afford spit enough to lick the postage stamps for its bankruptcy papers."

Sheila stated the personal case. "Anybody who unfurls a banner defaming my son, I will beat to death with my own hands."

Sheila didn't really mean this, of course. But Peg Manson and the other members of the Feminist Organization of Louisiana didn't know that. They looked at Sheila with understandable horror. There were streaks of gray in her hair now. But at five eleven and nearly one hundred eighty pounds she was easily the biggest woman in the room. She certainly looked capable of beating up anyone she determined to start pounding on.

But for all of Manson's transgressions, she was no coward. She stared at Sheila cooly and then defiantly shifted her attention to Sheila's right and said to the unwed mother sitting there, "And what are you going to do to us? Miss Jenkins is going to sue us. Miss McIntire is going to batter us . . ."

"We're going to break our water and drown you," the unwed mother said with an absolutely straight face that she held until Sheila and her colleagues collapsed into gales of laughter.

Recognizing the meeting had ended, Edith shepherded her supporters outside. But she paused in the doorway to remark to Manson with great solemnity, "A lot of us would like to put you out of business. If you want to hasten that process, show up tomorrow with libelous banners."

"We know what McIntire did," Manson argued. "You could sue us. But you couldn't win."

Edith's laugh underscored her contempt. "Don't bet on it," she said.

And Manson didn't.

But it was a costly reversal in terms of her leadership of the Feminist Organization of Louisiana. Already under fire from women such as Georgia Franklin who felt that their director's hatred for Mac had led her to shift the proper emphasis of their efforts away from support of Barbara Jeanne, Manson now lost standing among those who had stood steadfastly with her. In the power struggle which followed Manson was ousted and the organization splintered.

Unfortunately for Mac, his days of struggle with the women of the Feminist Organization of Louisiana had not yet ended. But for the rest of Barbara Jeanne Bordelon's junior year in high school, their role in his life was less visible and less important. Some of the diehards continued to attend Lady Bruin games, but their protests were sporadic and disorganized.

The Feminist Organization of Louisiana's great spiritual opponents, the Soldiers for Jesus, meanwhile, also reduced their presence at Lady Bruin games. The Soldiers for Jesus had undergone no comparable doctrinal erosion to sap their commitment. But with the Feminist Organization of Louisiana in retreat, and the victory over Barbara Jeanne seemingly won, the Soldiers for Jesus needed new foes to vanquish.

In the growing quiet at Lady Bruins basketball games, only the voices of the unwed mothers remained strong and true. And as the season wound down toward the playoffs, Barbara Jeanne and all the Lady Bruins gave them plenty to cheer about.

# CHAPTER TWENTY-NINE

As the end of their regular season approached, the Broussard women remained undefeated, their average margin of victory approaching fifty points a game. But despite their unwanted sociological notoriety, their athletic might remained virtually unknown to the general sports-going public. Only late in the season did the *States-Tribune* sports editors finally include a story on a Lady Bruins' victory. No box score accompanied the brief account; no flavor of the contest was even attempted.

If Mac hadn't been the kind of sports page reader who devoured every last word of print in the section, he might easily have missed seeing the story. He spotted it relatively late one Sunday morning at a breakfast table already abandoned by Edith for her ceaseless routine of law-school cramming. The entire article, which appeared in the Prep Parade subsection, read:

> The Broussard High School Lady Bruin basketball squad defeated the Jefferson Davis Devilettes in a game on Friday afternoon by the score of 73 to 29. The Lady Bruins raised their record to a league-leading 26-0 while the Davis girls fell to 13 and 13. Barbara Jeanne Bordelon led Broussard with 32 points, and Mary Masters added 20. Evelyn Smith topped the Davis scoring with 16.

Mac's Biddy League teams had received more coverage when he was in the sixth grade. But ever the optimist, he folded the paper down to the article and handed it across the breakfast dishes toward his mother and said cheerfully, "Hey, look at this." Mac wasn't surprised that Sheila's face creased into a frown as she read. But resolutely upbeat, Mac chided her, "Well, it's not much, but maybe it's a beginning."

"Nonsense," Sheila contended crossly. "It's on page thirteen for Christ's sake."

"Didn't Martin Luther King say you've got to get on the back of the bus before you can have a bus boycott?" Mac asked.

"No," Sheila said.

"I didn't think so," Mac conceded.

"What an asshole," Sheila said.

"Well it's early and I was just trying to be hopeful."

"Hmph," Sheila said. "You know why they ran this piece on us at all?" Mac shrugged. "You know the filler they usually use, the story about the one-legged unicyclist pedaling his way from Kalamazoo to Timbuktu to raise money for one-legged unicyclists with athlete's foot?"

"I think I remember that story," Mac said. He made an exaggerated face of concentrated remembering. He loved to listen to his mother go on like this. It was like listening to Miles Davis blow improvisational riffs on his trumpet.

"Yeah, well, they found out later that the unicyclist was really a sham."

"No!" Mac said in feigned alarm.

"Oh, yes," Sheila said. "They discovered that he used training wheels."

Mac rolled his eyes and snorted.

"And he really didn't have athlete's foot at all."

"Incredible," Mac said.

"Just ingrown toenail."

"Shocking," Mac said.

"But that's not why they didn't run the story on his ride as they usually do on the bottom of page thirteen every Sunday Morning."

"No?" Mac said. "Why didn't they run it then?"

"It was too long to fit."

"So they ran the one on us instead," Mac said.

"Right," Sheila said. "The option was to leave the space blank."

"Why didn't they just do that?"

"Because in the newspaper business any shit is better than no shit."

"No shit," Mac said.

"No." Sheila countered. "Any shit. That's us. On page thirteen."

Even the tiny burst of attention the Lady Bruins received over the Jeff Davis game was not repeated, however. Thus this talented and dedicated group of women was known to the public of New Orleans only as the team with the girl who wanted to play with the boys. To practically no one not directly involved with women's basketball were they known as the co-favorites (with the north Louisiana team from Minden High School) to win the upcoming state playoffs.

But to their immense credit, the Lady Bruins didn't allow any of this to dampen their spirit. They were on their way to a state basketball championship first and foremost for themselves and their coach. If the city finally discovered them as players and not just as curiosities, then fine. They would have been satisfied just to have been discovered by their own classmates at Broussard.

One problem that season of Barbara Jeanne Bordelon's junior year in high school was that the Broussard boys' varsity team was also having a banner season. With the nucleus of players Mac had coached the year before on the J.V., the "Gentlemen" Bruins, as Sheila and Edith always termed them, would also make the state playoffs. And though the boys' team was far from the powerhouse the Lady Bruins were, they nonetheless seemed to swallow up all the attention, prestige and enthusiasm Broussard had to offer for the sport of basketball.

Undeterred by all of this, however, the Lady Bruins took the floor on the last Saturday morning in February for their last game of the regular season against Robert E. Lee with restless determination. They had defeated Lee by 48 points in their first-round game, but the Broussard girls were as keyed up as if only their very best effort could bring them victory.

And the game they played was a fine approximation of their very best effort. Barbara Jeanne and Mary scored at will. A fully recuperated Olga set picks as if she were a lead guard on the vaunted run-to-daylight play of the Vince Lombardi Green Bay Packers. On the defensive end of the floor, Peggy Simons took it as a personal insult every time one of the Lee players managed a basket. Among the subs, Judy Trascio continued to distinguish herself. The game's outcome was assured from the outset. But long after it was an utter rout, Judy played with the intensity she doubtless felt necessary to atone for her earlier treachery. Judy managed 21 points in less than two quarters of play and was instrumental in pushing the Lady Bruins score to ninety-three points, the highest they'd achieved all year. Peggy, Tina, Debbie and the defensive subs, meanwhile, allowed the Lee girls only seventeen.

It was an amazing performance, and Mac was ecstatic because his team was playing so close to its potential. He was bursting with confidence as he began to prepare for the playoffs that were to start the next weekend. The draw was set up regionally, so Mac figured the Lady Bruins for easy victors in the first two rounds of the sixty-four-team tournament. Broussard hadn't played every girls' team in south Louisiana, but Mac had gathered information on every one with any kind of record. Only an unusually big team from Oakdale looked at all troublesome. And though well-enough coached, the Oakdale girls were slow enough afoot that Mac figured Mary and Barbara Jeanne would blow by them as if they were telephone poles.

Once the tournament was cut after the first weekend to the sweet sixteen, Mac knew things could get tougher. The upstate teams were not all likely to roll over to the upstarts from Sin City. But Mac and his players had supreme confidence in themselves. They had not known defeat in two years— for many of them their entire high school careers—and they all knew that they were led by the best female high school basketball player in the state, perhaps in the country.

So imagine their dismay, their almost crippling disorientation, when on the Wednesday before the state playoffs were to begin, just two days before they embarked upon a quest they were determined to make special for the rest of their lives, the Fifth Circuit Court of Appeals handed down its ruling in the case of Barbara Jeanne Bordelon versus Orleans Parish Schools and directed the school board, Broussard Principal Samuel P. Riggs, and head Broussard basketball coach Wayne Dawson to cooperate in promoting Barbara Jeanne to the men's varsity team.

Immediately.

# CHAPTER THIRTY

Barbara Jeanne, as you might well imagine, was placed in a terrible quandary. The appeals judges had made it possible for her dream to come true. But why couldn't they have waited several weeks to hand down their decision?

Of course, the judges didn't tell Barbara Jeanne she *had* to abandon the girls' team for the boys'. But Karen Lutze, and Barbara Jeanne's other attorneys from the firm of Lutze, Piehl, Nord, Schwehn, Uehling and Feaster all agreed that if B.J. attempted to finish out the season with the Lady Bruins, she could end up losing her chance to play on the Bruin varsity as a senior. Prissy Uehling argued the case this way: Barbara Jeanne had the authority of the court behind her now. If she failed to make the move, School Board officials might refuse to let her play the following fall by contending that she'd already been offered such an opportunity and turned it down. She could take the matter back to court at that point, and she might well win again. But the delay and process of appeal might last so long that she'd graduate before the case ever came to a second decision. In sum, if Barbara Jeanne was serious about wanting to play on the Bruin varsity, she better make her move now. Waiting until the fall might mean waiting forever.

Barbara Jeanne was obviously serious about wanting to play on the Bruin varsity, but, she was also a loyal teammate. She loved her fellow Lady Bruins. She had played with them for nearly two full years, and the thought of abandoning them now, the thought of abandoning Mac, when a state championship was dangling at their fingertips, was nigh on to unthinkable.

So what to decide? She was just a girl, but she was made to feel the weight of a whole evolving world. What if Rosa Parks had given up her seat? How long before someone else refused?

The arguments of her lawyers were powerful, and so were the pleas of countless women who called to tell her she owed the move to her gender. But even the appeal to her sense of historic mission was not conclusive. Her dedication to Mac and her teammates was too strong. B.J. discussed the matter at length with her parents, but they were torn too and reluctant to offer advice for fear of swaying her in a direction she ought not go. They really wanted her to choose, and they were ready to rally behind any decision she might make.

Across town that watershed Wednesday, Edith and Mac and Sheila also spent long hours agonizing over the court's ruling. Knowing what kind of person Barbara Jeanne was, they worried about how much she was suffering and tried to predict the consequences of whichever path she chose. Mac's initial reaction was to advise her to stay with the Lady Bruins. He wanted the championship they'd worked so hard for all year. Yes, he wanted it for himself. But he wanted it for Barbara Jeanne too. He knew what it meant to go through one's entire playing career without hoisting a championship trophy, and he knew that championship opportunities seldom knocked twice. Sheila and Edith, however, leaned to the argument that she had to move. Mac argued heatedly when he sensed they were siding against him. "The court says B.J. can play on the varsity. Done. She'll do that next year. You always say you've got to play to win, Mom. B.J.'s got to play to win the state tournament. She's got to go for all of it."

But Edith countered with the murkiness of the legal situation and the possibility that failing to move would be judged foregoing the opportunity to move. The debate among them raged on through the evening. One route was risky, the other painful.

At 10:30 that night, Henry Bordelon met all three of them at his front door and showed them into the den while Marie went upstairs to get their daughter. When B.J. came down in a pair of long flannel pajamas, mother and father sent her in to talk with Mac, Sheila and Edith alone. Mac was so distraught by B.J.'s predicament that he could barely speak, so he let Edith do much of the talking. Their message was that B.J. had to go. "A girl of your talent doesn't come along that often," Edith pointed out quietly. "If you don't make the sacrifice that this requires, God knows how long we'll have to wait until someone like you comes along again. And in the meantime, God knows what little progress talented women with skills less than yours will make because you won't have shown the world what a woman can do. Some girls' team will win the basketball championship this year whether you play in the tournament or not. But no woman will put on a varsity basketball uniform this year and maybe for a whole lot of years to come, unless you do it."

When Edith finished, a silence settled over them like a shroud. After a time Barbara Jeanne looked at Mac who had sat through Edith's speech with his head down. "Coach?" she said, her voice a brittle whisper.

When Mac looked up at her, his brimming eyes spilled over onto his cheeks. "Jesus, kiddo," he said.

And so it was done. Barbara Jeanne was moving on as she had to. And Mac was staying on as he had to, to try to push his Sisyphean rock back up the hill without her.

When Mac and Edith rose to leave, Barbara Jeanne stood up with them. There was an awkward pause, as if none of the three of them knew what to do next. Then Mac opened his arms and Barbara Jeanne fled into them. She clasped him fiercely around his back and squeezed her head against his chest, matching his tears now with her own. Mac cupped the top of B.J.'s head with his massive hands then extended one toward Edith who took it and joined their embrace.

And for an eternally fleeting minute the three of them stood there, together, a universe unto themselves.

# CHAPTER THIRTY-ONE

As one of the corollaries to Murphy's law holds, just when things can't conceivably get worse, they get worse. To wit, Mac discovered the first thing Thursday morning that the Lady Bruins had drawn the aptly named Oakdale Oakettes as their first-round play-off opponents. He had hoped that with a little luck his team might have avoided Oakdale until as late as the round of eight. But luck was smiling in another direction. Mac regarded Oakdale as the strongest team in south Louisisana after Broussard. He'd once figured to neutralize their superior height with Barbara Jeanne's long-range shooting. Now, of course, that weapon was lost to him.

As you can imagine, Mac faced a Herculean task getting the Lady Bruins ready for their state tournament opener. He had only Thursday's practice to try to deal with both the physical and emotional problems caused by Barbara Jeanne's abrupt departure. The physical solution was predictable, if not simple. And it was hardly guaranteed. Mary Masters would take over B.J.'s spot, while Judy Trascio would replace Mary at the off-forward position. The primary problem with this strategy was Mary's jump shooting. She was excellent around the basket, superb at moving without the ball and getting herself open, but now she was going to have play at the point. And though Mary was an adequate outside shooter, she was no Barbara Jeanne.

The emotional situation was even worse, and Mac scheduled a special, after-school classroom session to deal with it. With Barbara Jeanne in the line-up, the Lady Bruins didn't think they could lose; without her, many now thought they couldn't win.

More ominous in the long run, several of the Lady Bruins felt that Barbara Jeanne had sold them out, had thumbed her nose at the spirit of love and camaraderie that Mac had urged on them since the first day of practice in the fall. Judy Trascio was the outspoken leader of this group. "She's a traitor," Mac heard Judy proclaim to the rest of the team just about the time he opened the door to the room where they were to meet. "She's just out for herself."

Mac almost panicked. This was a development he hadn't counted on. He'd hoped, actually, that they'd rally their flagging spirits around a determination to win a championship for their missing teammate. He wished Barbara Jeanne could be there. Her innate goodness was so obvious that Judy could never have made such charges to her face. But Barbara Jeanne couldn't be there, of course, because she was in the gym at the time, practicing with the boys.

To Judy's credit, Mac conceded, she didn't back down when she realized that Mac had overheard her. "She should have stayed with us," Judy said defiantly, as Mac, letting her continue to talk, slid himself atop the desk in the front of the classroom. "We needed her and she screwed us." Mac wondered if Judy was perhaps terrified that she would be found wanting in her new role as a starter, that should the Lady Bruins lose she would be fastened with the blame. And perhaps to honor the beneficence of that judgment, God gave Mac the sudden wisdom of his subsequent remarks.

"If anyone's the traitor," Mac said quietly to all the members of his team, "it's me, not B.J. She didn't want to go over to the boys' team now. She didn't want to leave any of you for anything. She has the opportunity of a lifetime, and she was ready to turn it down to be with you. But I told her that she had to go, for herself, for all of you in a way, certainly for all the young women who'll want to play this game in the future."

"But we can't win without her, Coach," one of the subs said.

"Nonsense," Mac said. "If I didn't think y'all could win without her, then I wouldn't have told her to go." This was a lie, of course. But as Solomon mentions more poetically in Ecclesiastes 3, there's a time for everything. "We've been beating people by fifty points with Barbara Jeanne," Mac pointed out. "Without her it's just going to be a little closer."

Mac knew that such arithmetic was sophistry. But he could tell he was getting through to them and that was the important thing now. It didn't matter how he rekindled their confidence, only that he did. "Barbara Jeanne Bordelon is very possibly the best female high school basketball player in this country. But the Broussard Lady Bruins are more than just Barbara Jeanne Bordelon, and you know that she'd tell you so herself if she were here. What we want to do is go out tomorrow night and start proving that fact to a whole lot of people in this town who don't know it."

The longer they talked, the more Mac could feel their drained well of confidence begin to refill. It was a miracle. And Mac knew it was turned around when Peggy Simons, uncharacteristically, stood up to speak. Her Olive Oyl squeak was gone, and she spoke now with the voice of sudden leadership. "I know Cake, and so do all of you. She's my friend, and she's a friend to everyone in this room. If she did this, then it's right." Peggy's slender hands had squeezed themselves into fists at the end of her long, skinny arms. "And I know something else." Her eyes were blinking and her jaw muscles twitched and Mac realized that, though she was speaking aloud, she was primarily speaking to herself. "If Oakdale is going to beat us then they're going to have to score. And goddamnit, they're not going to score on me."

They were ready.

And they needed to be. Oakdale was big (only Olga and Peggy matched up with them size-wise) and even better than Mac thought. They were very well coached by Joanna Knudsen, a graduate of the prestigious basketball program at Louisiana Tech. Under Knudsen's savvy direction, the Oakettes made up in patience and discipline what they lacked in speed. Mac knew the Lady Bruins were in for a tough, probably low-scoring contest from the opening moments of the game, which was played before a packed house on the campus of the University of Southwestern Louisiana in Lafayette. Sheila and Edith escorted a vocal contingent of unwed mothers, but none of Mac's mad antagonists from the Feminist Organization of Louisiana or unwanted fans from the Soldiers of Jesus put in an appearance. The entire citizenry of Oakdale, on the other hand, seemed to have turned out along with all their relatives from every bayou in south Louisiana.

Oakdale controlled the tipoff and advanced the ball into their offensive end where they played a passing game to determine that Broussard was in a woman-to-woman defense. Then in a beautifully orchestrated clear-out maneuver, their 5'11" center set up in a high post position near the free-throw line drawing Peggy away from the basket to guard her. With Peggy out of the way, one of their two 5'10" forwards, the one Tina at 5'4" was forced to cover, slid down low, just outside the three-second lane and took a lob pass which at 5'5" Debbie could do little to deflect. Using her towering height advantage, Tina's woman just turned and easily put the ball in over her, drawing a slapping foul from Tina in the process. When she made the free throw Oakdale led 3-0.

Mac made a mistake here when he didn't call time out immediately and switch his defense. But he wasn't yet convinced that the Oakdale girls hadn't happened upon the clear-out strategy by accident. He was convinced thirty seconds later, however. On offense the Lady Bruins worked their No.

1 play perfectly with Olga setting a brutal pick. But Mary missed the jumper. Oakdale snatched the rebound, pushed the ball quickly upcourt, ran the clear-out to the opposite side and again scored easily for a 5-0 lead. Mac was off the bench before the ball had settled through the net cords, signaling to his players that he wanted a time-out before the ball was put back into play.

In his huddle, Mac switched Peggy and Debbie and Tina into a triangular zone with Peggy at the point underneath the goal. And the strategy began to pay dividends on Oakdale's very next possession. The Oakettes could no longer manage their virtually uncontested shots close to the goal now, and any time the ball was passed down low, Peggy Simons did everything but climb inside that girl's uniform with her. She was a better jumper than any of the Oakdale girls and with her long arms she began to swat away Oakette shots as if she were hammering volleyball spikes that had been set right to her. Denied their inside game, the Oakettes were forced to shoot from the outside where they were not nearly so effective.

The problem was that Broussard couldn't get much offense going either. Their patterns were working fine. But Mary was having trouble canning her jumpers over the tall Oakdale defenders, and she wasn't getting Judy into the offense much at all. God they needed Barbara Jeanne. Oakdale led 15-6 at the end of the first quarter. Mac directed that they go more frequently to the double pick strategy of their number No. 2 as a way of giving Mary a bigger screen to shoot behind. But Oakdale countered instantly with double switches. The disheartening score at the half was Oakdale 23, Broussard 12.

At half-time Mac made two risky adjustments hoping to find a way to put some points on the board. First, with the tall Oakdale players thwarting Mary's outside shots, he had to find a way to get her inside. So even though she was a considerably better ballhandler than Judy, he had the two interchange positions, Mary going back to her old off-forward spot. Second, he ordered his three offensive players to start pressing the Oakdale girls after every basket.

The second of these two tactics didn't work at all. Capitalizing immediately on Olga's lack of footspeed, Knudsen simply ordered the ball passed to Olga's woman who proceeded to beat her up the floor every time. Realizing that his girls were burning up a lot of energy to no purpose, Mac called the press off. The first tactic had mixed but better success. Nervous about having to handle the ball in such a tense situation, Judy turned it over several times. But when she succeeded in getting it to Mary down low, Mary was frequently able to use her superior body control to work the ball into the basket despite the height disadvantage she suffered. And slowly Mary's scoring began to bring the Lady Bruins back. At the end of the third quarter they had closed 31-24.

And in the fourth quarter, while Peggy and Debbie and Tina summoned almost kamikaze determination and practically shut Oakdale down, Mary went on a tear. Broussard surrendered a basket right after the tip-off, but back-to-back buckets closed the score to 33-28. After Oakdale managed a long range shot, Mary wormed home another pair of goals and it was 35-32. With under a minute left, playing with so much intensity she seemed to be almost breathing fire, Mary took a nice bounce pass from Judy, spun 180 degrees toward the base line, came up inside the tall Oakette guarding her and banked home a leaning five footer. The Lady Bruins trailed only 37-36. Oakdale probably would have benefitted from a time-out at that point. Instead, they inbounded the ball quickly, worked it into the front court and tried to go into a game-saving stall. But Tina Wiggins, moving with the quickness of a sprite, poked away a pass toward Peggy Simons who wrapped it in her licorice-stick arms and screamed for time-out. And when she did so the USL fieldhouse collapsed into bedlam.

Mac could barely make himself heard as he tried to give his Lady Bruins their last instructions. His plan was to go again to what had brought the Lady Bruins back. He wanted Mary working off one of Olga's picks so that Judy could get her the ball down low one more time.

On the other side of the scorer's table Joanna Knudsen delivered her final instructions as well and made her last and best move: Pulling a player off Olga Jorgensen altogether, she double-teamed Mary Masters.

This was not a ploy the Broussard girls expected and for a moment they seemed utterly stymied. Grittily following directions, however, with time elapsing, Judy managed to get the ball to Mary about ten feet out on her favored left side of the basket. On the dribble Mary spun first one way and then the other. But she was so smothered by the two Oakettes draped all over her that she had no choice but to pass the ball away. Judy was well-covered by the third Oakette guard. But Olga Jorgensen, of course, was all alone. Standing short of the free-throw line and slightly to the side, she waved her arms over her head rather like a swimmer crying out in distress. Mary passed her the ball, and when she caught it, she held in her hands a whole season's dreams.

Olga had not scored all night, and though she'd had games with as many as 12 points during the regular season routs, she had never before been called upon to shoot when it mattered. She had no choice now, though. And with the clock ticking down and Mac and the entire Lady Bruin bench on their feet imploring her to shoot, Olga lofted an awkward eleven foot push shot that flew toward the goal with practically no arc at all.

It didn't have prayer.

The ball hit the front of the rim and caromed directly to the floor. The crowd screamed. Olga lumbered madly after it. But a tall Oakette got there first, and surrounded it with her bronzed, country-girl arms as if it were no basketball at all but a lost infant, suddenly found and anxious for the special sweetness of maternal care.

And the Lady Bruins were beaten.

# CHAPTER THIRTY-TWO

Once again, a championship had eluded Mac McIntire. Perhaps, like John Stockton, Ernie Banks and Dan Marino, Mac McIntire just wasn't destined to be a champion. After a series of close calls in high school and college, Mac had figured to be a champion many times over with the Boston Celtics before the ankle injury ended his professional playing career before it ever got started. And he had figured to coach a champion this year. But as had happened before, fate wrote another ending to his story.

A lesser man than Mac might have finally surrendered to bitterness. But God no, he wasn't bitter. He was bursting with pride in his Lady Bruins. Those young women had summoned up the very neutrons of their souls in their first-round loss to the Oakdale Oakettes. They could have quit but they didn't. And the possibility that he had contributed to their undaunted determination provided him more satisfaction than most coaches ever experience.

Mac knew with a certainty far beyond sour grapes that had the contest with Oakdale lasted just two more minutes that the Lady Bruins would have won. And he knew something else: Joanna Knudsen had outcoached him. Capitalizing instantly on her team's superior height, she put five crucial points on the board before Mac made the necessary adjustment. And at the game's pivotal moment she made a move that Mac failed to anticipate, and it was the move that meant the difference.

Mac's appreciation for his opponent's coaching strategy did not mean that Mac blamed himself for the Lady Bruins' defeat. Mac no more blamed himself for the loss than he did Mary's poor shooting in the first half or, God forbid, Olga's errant shot at the end. But he knew that like Mary and Olga he had been less than perfect, and that if imperfection nurtured sin, then in improvement lay redemption.

But most of these conscious reflections were made in the days that followed the Oakdale game, not at the moment of its loss. When that final buzzer sounded and the Oakettes leapt into an elation which carried them all the way to the state championship final, Mac felt only a suffocating sadness. Mary stood under the goal toward which she never got to launch the shot that might have brought the Lady Bruins victory and yanked with both hands at the ends of her sweat-drenched hair. Judy Trascio wandered slowly about the floor in a circle. Olga, having fallen down in her scramble for the last rebound, sat amid the feet of the celebrating Oakettes, her chin on her chest. Peggy and Tina and Debbie stood together at mid-court their eyes fixed heatedly on the score board as if they could will it to show time still remaining.

And his defensive players' frustration with the clock was the key to the winding sheet of regret that enveloped Mac. The Lady Bruins had not a moment's cause for shame over their loss. And it was not the defeat that Mac mourned. Rather, Mac grieved achingly for his players because there were no more games to play. For all of them for this season. For Peggy and Olga and Mary, who were seniors, forever.

As one last time the Lady Bruins finally made their way from the floor—a party of jubilation behind them, a reception of tears in front—Mac took each and every one into his arms.

And damned anyone who dared say he shouldn't.

# BOOK FOUR:

Barbara Jeanne Bordelon's Last
Season In High School

# CHAPTER THIRTY-THREE

Across the state on the night that the Lady Bruins were eliminated from their first state tournament, in the field house on the Hammond campus of Southeastern Louisiana University, the Broussard varsity Bruins departed the men's playoffs with a first-round loss of their own. The next morning's *States-Tribune* article on the game told the story:

> Istrouma High School of Baton Rouge knocked local entry Broussard out of the state basketball tournament last night in an 83-68 blowout at SLU in a game not really as close as the final score. Broussard Coach Wayne Dawson's youthful Bruins managed to stay close to Istrouma's powerful Indians in the first half, which ended with the Baton Rouge school holding a narrow five point lead at 40 to 35.

> Behind its dominating front line of brother forwards Wayne and James Schmitt, both 6'6", and towering center Fred Beasley, 6'10", though, Istrouma pulled steadily away in the second half. The Indians led by 22 early in the fourth quarter before head coach S.M. Whittenberg cleared his bench and saved Broussard from further humiliation.

> "I think Broussard is really a year away at this point," Whittenberg commented after the final buzzer. "They've got four of their five starters returning. Their big guy (Broussard center Donnie Start, 6'9") is only now really beginning to come around. This time next year he could be a significant force. They've got a really slick guard in

(Danny) Waddell. And that (6'5" forward Gary) Cashner sure gave us fits tonight."

Dawson seemed somewhat less optimistic about the Bruins' prospect for next season. He criticized Start's poor rebounding in the second half and answered only with an oath as to why Cashner, who led Broussard with 19 points, made his first appearance in the game only in the second quarter.

In a footnote to the action at the SLU fieldhouse, Friday's playoff game was supposed to have marked the first appearance by a female player in a male varsity sport. Assigned to the Broussard squad by a decision of the Federal Fifth Circuit Court of Appeals, former girls' team standout Barbara Jeanne Bordelon dressed out and warmed up with the Bruins before the game and at half time. Miss Bordelon saw no action, however.

When she'd read this account at the breakfast table the morning after the Oakdale and Istrouma games, Sheila McIntire pronounced her benediction on the season of Barbara Jeanne's junior year. "Sometimes, thank God, not always," she said.

"What's that?" Mac and Edith asked her simultaneously.

"Life sucks," Sheila said.

Barbara Jeanne's last season in high school—calculated as athletes do, not in terms of the calendar, or even of school sessions, but rather of sports seasons —began within days after she rode the bench while her new male teammates lost to Baton Rouge Istrouma in the first round of the state tournament.

It began, perhaps, the day head basketball coach Wayne Dawson informed Broussard principal Sam Riggs that he was resigning. Dawson just didn't feel up to the rigors of handling the Bruins for an entire season with a woman as part of the team, he explained. He was fearful that basketball at Broussard was going to be a circus, not a sport, what with the likely involvement of all the "weirdos" who followed the girls' team this year and who, in small numbers, attended the Istrouma game and chanted from beginning to end "We want Barbara Jeanne."

These, I should say, were the reasons that Dawson gave Riggs. The fact of the matter was, however, that Dawson was a male bigot who wouldn't have conceded the truth of the situation had Wonder Woman joined the NBA and led the league in scoring. And in private Dawson blamed Barbara Jeanne for his team's quick exit before the forces from Istrouma.

"That little bitch Bordelon" was the way he commonly phrased it, "got my boys so screwed around they couldn't have defeated a Biddy League team." But he was wrong, of course. The Bruins had promise, but they needed another year of seasoning before they could beat the team Istrouma put on the floor that night.

If Barbara Jeanne's last year didn't begin the day Dawson resigned, it certainly began a week later when Mac McIntire agreed to take up the reins as varsity coach. I doubt you'll be surprised to learn that Mac was not Riggs's first choice. Riggs had had too many dealings with Mac in the two years he'd been at Broussard, and though Mac was hardly ever the cause of these problems, the words *trouble* and *McIntire* were now rather securely fused in Riggs' administrative mind. But to the principal's dismay, no other coach in the system was remotely interested in coming into the situation at Broussard. So, by default, the job went to Mac.

I should hardly leave the impression that Mac took the job without misgivings, however. On the contrary, the decision was very difficult. Before being offered the varsity men's job, Mac had planned to coach the Lady Bruins for the rest of his career. Had Peggy Simons and Mary Masters not been graduating seniors, he might have turned the men's job down. But as was true in all aspects of his life, Mac was influenced by the attitudes of his mother and Edith Jenkins, and they both thought he should make the move. Essentially they argued that in the upcoming year Barbara Jeanne was going to be making sports history and that only a terribly sympathetic coach could make that process as easy as possible for her. No one used these terms, but Mac had more than a new job to take, he had a call to answer. And so the decision was made.

Mac started the season of Barbara Jeanne's last year in high school immediately. He might never have won a championship, and he might never win one in the future. But every year brought a new championship to pursue. That was the key to it all—not capture, but unflagging pursuit. So as soon as Mac made his decision to direct the Broussard varsity, he was off chasing a state basketball championship that had so narrowly escaped him as a player. He called a meeting of the returning varsity Bruin players, every one of whom he had coached on the junior varsity (except Barbara Jeanne, whom he had also coached, of course) and told them that he wanted them to keep on playing basketball right through the spring and summer. Formal practices were banned at these times of the year by the state high school athletic association, but there's nothing to stop players from practicing on their own and Mac violated no rule by working out with them.

At these sessions through the spring, Mac encouraged his players to concentrate on those particular aspects of their games that needed improving.

Tall, skinny Donnie Start, for instance, worked with weights to improve his upper body strength. Guard Danny Waddell, a superb ball handler, worked on his shooting. And beefy Gary Cashner, an excellent position rebounder and surprisingly accurate shooter, practiced his dribbling. Mac instructed Barbara Jeanne to concentrate on her defense. He knew she had skills as a defender, but he was concerned that because of women's basketball's archaic rules, her good defensive instincts might have eroded. In the two full seasons she starred as a Lady Bruin, she had played less than one full game on defense, and even then only when Mac had employed her out of position as an emblem to her teammates.

Every afternoon, Monday through Thursday until school let out in June, Mac gave his players the kind of individual attention that would be impossible once fall practice started and the emphasis would need to shift to team play. He pumped iron with goofy Donnie Start and played one-on-one with shy Gary Cashner who becomingly hadn't yet realized how close he was to genuine greatness. With Barbara Jeanne, he dribbled round and round the court demanding that she remain down in her defensive crouch until she felt that the muscles in her thighs were going to solidify into permanent iron knots.

Once school was out the work continued. The school gym was closed, but Mac had installed a large, smooth, lighted, concrete half court in his back yard at the Terminal, and he made it plain to his players that they were not only welcome but expected to put in appearances several times a week at his home. Mac stocked in a regular supply of soft drinks and snacks, and any given evening of the summer would find an array of Broussard high schoolers pounding the pavement in pick-up games in the back yard or messing up the kitchen or ruining the furniture in the living room while lounging their sweat-soaked bodies in the air-conditioned cool in front of Mac's TV set.

The Lady Bruins were welcome, too, of course, and many spent a great deal of time at the Terminal that summer, the graduates as well as Tina Wiggins, Debbie Miller, and Judy Trascio who were in Barbara Jeanne's class. The Terminal became such a teen hangout, in fact, that Sheila, who secretly enjoyed having all the kids around immensely, groused about it constantly.

"Fucking brats," she called them behind their backs. "Act like they own the place. Whole house smells like a locker room."

Sheila's determined gender blindness prohibited her at first from identifying the culprits as clearly as she might have. But the problem was mostly with the boys. The varsity Bruins, typical of the majority of boys their age, hadn't yet developed the most acute sense of responsibility. They were polite but they were also seemingly oblivious to everything and everyone around them. The Lady Bruins, on the other hand, were far more reliably responsible and helpful.

Finally, one night Sheila decided that the male Bruins needed some guidance in guesting. So she wrote a triple limerick which she ran off on the ditto machine at the unwed mothers' home and posted at various places around the Terminal. Rather restrained for one of Sheila's poeticizings, it went like this:

> There once was coach name of Mac,
>
> Whose house he reduced to a shack.
>
> The guys from his school,
>
> None being a fool,
>
> Arrived noon and night in a stack.
>
> They ate all the chow they could hold.
>
> They quaffed all the pop that was cold.
>
> Their bodies all soiled,
>
> The sofas they spoiled,
>
> The stuffings soon sprouting with mold.
>
> Coach Mac was one hell of guy.
>
> But Mom was annoyed by the sty.
>
> Her new rule for the Bruins:
>
> The next thing that one ruins
>
> Is the ticket to watch himself die.

Sheila felt certain that the sudden appearance of this poem taped on the mirrors in each of the downstairs bathrooms, on the door from the kitchen to the back yard, and on the refrigerator, would not only catch the eye of every offending Bruin but fairly quickly result in an improved pattern of behavior. As added insurance, however, Sheila saw to it that Mac exerted his powers of influence over the players by sharing with her son a fourth stanza to her poem, one she had not made available to the general public. This last stanza not only elicited the response she wanted from Mac, but also proved, as was probably her intention, that she hadn't begun to lose a single ember of her caustic fire. The final lines of her quadruple limerick went this way:

> The bald truth for the Bruins unfurls.
>
> If they don't soon start acting like pearls,

I'll grab the homewreckers

And wring off their peckers.

Maybe then they'll behave more like girls.

From this last poem Mac got the intended idea that perhaps he ought to establish some clearly stated rules for the Bruins about Terminal behavior. All were free to eat and drink whatever was available, he told them. But they were responsible for cleaning up after themselves. No exceptions and no delay between messing and straightening. Furthermore, they were no longer welcome in the living room with wet clothes. If they wanted to hang around after working out, they were to bring a change of clothes and shower before depositing themselves on a sofa or easy chair. Girls could use the bathrooms in Edith's part of the house. Boys could use the shower facilities on Mac and Sheila's side.

Sheila's crusade produced exactly the effect she desired. The kids kept coming to the Terminal, but they stopped being such pains in the ass. But this was not really a surprising development. For as Sheila herself put it, "The brats may be fucking slobs, but they're still nice kids."

With the matter of Terminal decorum so painlessly solved, Mac and the Bruins were able to turn their full attention to a more lastingly serious matter: basketball. Backyard games of three on three were played for hours on end, through boiling afternoons and into muggy evenings. And without regard for sex. The only rule was that you had to have a least one of each kind on both sides. Whenever the games found themselves gender deficient, one way or another, Mac or Sheila or Edith (less frequently because she was going to summer school and forever obliged to study) was convinced to fill in.

Near the end of the summer when the sun still blistered but the cooling shade promised autumn, the kids convinced Mac to organize a co-rec tournament for three-person teams that would occupy the last couple of weeks before school started. It didn't take Mac long to throw himself into this project with the manic enthusiasm of *Dr. Strangelove's* Buck Turgidson designing a bomber raid over Siberia. He devised a lottery system to select the team memberships. And he drew up a round robin schedule in which the prospective five teams would play each other one time apiece for the sole purpose of seeding a single-elimination tournament to be contested on the last Saturday of August.

As seemed so frequently true in his life, however, Mac's plans went awry from the very first when Peggy Simons slipped Olga Jorgensen's name into the lottery pool and brought her along the day team assignments were made. Early in the summer, Olga had come to the Terminal occasionally but had found herself too slow and clumsy to have all that much fun playing, and so despite the encouragement of her peers she had stopped participating after a while. Thus when Mac designed the tournament he did so with only fifteen players in mind, five Lady Bruins, Barbara Jeanne, and the nine boys who would be returning members of the Broussard varsity. Mac was so delighted to see Olga back among the participants that he didn't realize until a sixteenth name had to be drawn, Barbara Jeanne's as it eventuated, that he had no team on which to put her.

Mac had planned to act as referee and tournament supervisor, but with another player to accommodate, he instantly created a sixth entry with himself and Edith as teammates for Barbara Jeanne. Sheila, he warned the assemblage, when in a spontaneous act of derision it began to boo and complain about the make-up of the last squad, would act as their coach and teach them every dirty trick she knew if the crowd didn't hush its griping. To underscore their fear the teenagers began to hoot and jeer even louder.

The spirited tournament which followed produced two weeks' worth of fun. It also helped immeasurably to cement all the Bruins' affection for and commitment to each other, qualities they would need in the trying year to come. And it produced two remarkable events, the first of which was that a team with Mac McIntire on it finally managed to win a championship.

Or almost, anyway.

Following standard half-court pick-up basketball rules, the games of what was quickly dubbed The First Annual Bruin Invitational were played to 40 points, the winning team being obliged to win by at least four. Players called their own fouls. And no free throws were shot, a practice that succeeded, as was almost always true of playground competition, in making the games rather rougher than "real" basketball.

At times tempers flared and oaths and even pushes were exchanged. But this was not altogether unhealthy, and it was always kept under control. And it was hardly the rule. For the most part, the tournament was contested in an atmosphere of frivolity and good fellowship with the desire for victory taking second place to the purer joy of participating.

Enthusiasm was so high that the three-person teams, with the exception of Mac and Edith and B.J., soon adopted names for themselves. The unfortunate squad of Tina Miller, Debbie Wiggins and Cooke Malmgren, at 5'9" the shortest of the varsity Bruins, for instance, quickly dubbed themselves Short Stuff. The powerful threesome of Danny Waddell, Gary Cashner and Peggy Simons answered to the acronymic monicker WaCS and punctuated their moments of triumph with salutes that everyone found utterly obnoxious and thoroughly enjoyed.

In addition to all the fun, however, the Bruins learned something about their coach's sense of competition. Playing namelessly, Mac and Edith and Barbara Jeanne quickly established themselves as tournament favorites. Mac was so much bigger and stronger and more skilled than anyone else playing, and Barbara Jeanne, of course, was a very capable teammate. Working behind Mac's aircraft carrier screens, she proved predictably deadly with her high arching jump shot which seemed a Xerox of Mac's own. Both Mac and B.J. were careful, of course, to get Edith fully involved in their string of victories. And this was hardly a difficult proposition since Edith was a good athlete and in top condition. But on those crucial occasions when his team just had to have a bucket, Mac would go after it himself. For as always, for love of the game and out of respect for his opponents, Mac McIntire played to win.

In the round robin competition, Mac and Edith and B.J. had problems only with the WaCS whom they squeaked by 40 to 34. As the tournament went along, those latter three began to generate more and more enthusiasm among their peers as the only team that might stand a chance to defeat the favorites. And by the last week of the round robin Danny and Gary and Peggy had developed so much mini-team spirit that they'd even taken to wearing "uniforms": white T-shirts with the letters from their own names that together spelled their team.

Late on that hot Saturday afternoon when the finals were to be played, Danny and Gary and Peggy stood together on the concrete with their arms around each other so that their entire team name was spelled out for the other Broussard teenagers who had come to watch the game that would mark the end of the summer. As they waited for their favored opponents to appear, they leg-kicked like can-can dancers and led cheers for themselves.

Not to be out-done, however, Mac and Edith and Barbara Jeanne took the court in team T-shirts of their own, handmade for them by the unwed mothers in coach Sheila's sewing classes. Each of them had a handsome number neatly sewn on the back—Mac his life-long 34, Edith a 37 (which she told everyone was either her chest measurement or, if added together, her ability as a basketball player on a scale of 1-10), and Barbara Jeanne an elegant number one. Across the front of their jerseys Sheila had designed an electric name:

## Terminal Cases

Except for those fond of slaughters, the championship contest lacked much to recommend it. Despite a relentless effort by Gary Cashner to stop him, Mac scored the first time Terminal Cases had the ball. The next three times he set picks for Barbara Jeanne who squared up instantly for her jumper.

Due to some tenacious defense by Danny Waddell, however, B.J. was able to can only one, and Mac realized he was going to have to carry the offensive load himself.

Because they defended so well, the game would have been tolerable for the WaCS, had Terminal Cases not just completely shut down their offense. Mac and his teammates played as if it mattered, which was the only way they knew.

The glinting sun popped gallons of sweat onto furrowed brows and frayed normally long tempers to the nub. Terminal Cases kept adding to its lead, and the WaCS could not find a way to score. Gary Cashner worked like a mule for a position close to the basket, but when he put the ball up, Mac batted it away. Edith, playing like a terrier, simply denied Peggy the chance to become a factor on offense. And B.J. hounded Danny into missing shot after shot by sticking a hand in his face every time he tried to shoot.

The second and more genuinely remarkable incident of the summer occurred just after Terminal Cases had pushed its lead to 38 to 0. In a commendable display of team unity and determination, the WaCS, refusing to surrender, called time-out and pledged to one another their commitment to getting at least one bucket before the end of the game. With grim faces and set jaws they came back on the court. Peggy in-bounded the ball to Danny, and Gary moved into position to screen him open for another of the attempted jumpers that he'd been missing all afternoon long. But as Danny, who prided himself on his ballhandling, went into his dribble, Barbara Jeanne darted out a freckled arm and stole the ball. In the process she raked her fingernails across his hand, with force enough, perhaps, to be guilty of a foul.

But it was Danny's pride, not his hand, that was really hurt. And in his frustration, as B.J. rose up from her defensive squat with the ball squeezed in both arms against her chest, his hands flashed out at her undefended shoulders and pushed her abruptly to the ground. Her soaking gym shorts were clinging to her body and had ridden up so high on her legs that, as she slid to the rough concrete in a sitting position, the vulnerable skin was unprotected and the asphalt ripped open two strawberry red wounds just under the curved swell of her buttocks.

The ball was flung aside and Barbara Jeanne was on her feet in an instant, her face flushed and fists raised. But there was no way, of course, that their playing companions or any of the spectators would let B.J. get at Danny. Mac and Peggy flashed between them. Edith put B.J. in a bear hug from behind. And Gary cooled Danny down in a moment with strong fingers pressed into the soft flesh on top of Danny's shoulder blades and a glare at once reproachful and mournful.

What followed next was of such powerful significance that the game was left forever uncompleted. All the kids who had frequented the Terminal that summer were on the court now, in a tight circle around those who had been playing. A babble of discussion argued Danny's offense and whether or not Barbara Jeanne had fouled him.

Over that buzz, looking down into his teammate's face, Gary Cashner could be heard to say, "You shouldn't have pushed her, Dan."

"I know," Danny agreed remorsefully. "I'm sorry, Cake," he called out to B.J.

That apology sufficed for Barbara Jeanne, who had already dropped her fists and become passive in Edith's arms. But from flinty Judy Trascio, forgiveness was not so quickly forthcoming. Flourishing the banner of her gender she declared, "You shouldn't pick on a woman, you asshole."

Dropping his hands from Danny's shoulders, Gary turned to stand beside his teammate and to address Judy who had been behind him. "He shouldn't push her," he said quietly. "But not because she's a woman." A breath of invigorating fall freshness seemed suddenly to waft into the humid summer evening.

"I shouldn't push her," Danny explained to Judy, "because she's my teammate."

# CHAPTER THIRTY-FOUR

As we have discovered repeatedly, there seemed always to be storm clouds on Mac McIntire's horizon. And as the sunny afternoon of the First Annual Bruin Invitational gave way to a late summer night, thunderheads gathered anew. By 9 p.m., perhaps a half hour after all the highschoolers except for Barbara Jeanne had finally drifted out of the Terminal full of soft drinks and sandwiches, the heavens were heavy and dark, and the occasional lightning bolt flashed across the Southern sky.

The victorious Terminal Cases, their comrades departed, had adjourned to opposite sides of the house to take their showers, Mac to his quarters and Barbara Jeanne with Edith to hers. If there is one area where men and women really aren't equal, it's in the speed with which they shower. Probably long before the first bead of water had fallen on the shoulders of either of the women, Mac had already soaped himself clean, dressed, and gone back downstairs. He had opened a Dixie beer and almost finished helping Sheila with a last bit of straightening up in the kitchen when the phone rang and Marie Bordelon asked for Barbara Jeanne. A house the size of the Terminal certainly needed some sort of intercom system, but it was an appliance that had not even occurred to Mac when he had renovated the old railroad station. Mac walked through the dining room and out into the living room to call up to B.J., but she couldn't hear him over the omni-present rock music of WTIX that blared from Edith's room upstairs. So, muttering a gripe about the inconvenience, he trudged up the stairs to summon Barbara Jeanne to the phone.

When he stuck his head into Edith's room, however, he was greeted by a sight that momentarily stunned him into silence. The women hadn't gotten themselves dressed yet. Edith had slipped on her blue terry bathrobe but hadn't pulled it together in the front. Barbara Jeanne had on a T-shirt but was naked from the waist down.

But it was less their nudity than their mutual posture that shocked Mac and stamped itself on his tortured memory. Barbara Jeanne was lying on her back in the middle of Edith's bed, her spread legs pulled back to her shoulders. Edith was sitting at the foot of the bed, her face above B.J.'s crotch, one hand swirling between B.J.'s legs.

Mac had uttered only the words "Phone, B.J." when he was struck speechless. He was also struck momentarily motionless. And rather than retreating from the room, he just stared wide-eyed and slack-jawed at the two lovely young women who remained, he thought, incredibly unperturbed by his abrupt intrusion. Barbara Jeanne shifted a pillow over hips to cover herself, and Edith gathered her robe together with her left hand and turned her face Mac. But Edith's right hand kept up its slow, circular movement between Barbara Jeanne's legs.

"What'd ya say, Coach," B.J. asked.

"Gettin' an eyeful, Mac?" Edith said. "We normally charge admission for people to watch us do this." Turning back to B.J. she asked, "How does that feel?"

"It stings a little," Barbara Jeanne said.

"It stings a little?" Mac croaked in a voice that broke twice in four words.

Edith removed her hand from B.J.'s thigh, picked up a little tube of ointment and squeezed a nurdle onto her fingers before reaching to smear it onto the abrasion on Barbara Jeanne's other leg.

"It actually stings like hell," B.J. said to Mac. "My ass is so sore I'm gonna have to stand up in all my classes next week."

So you see, those of you with dirty minds like mine, our two heroines were not engaged in sexual contact after all, though, of course, that's exactly what Mac thought when he burst in on them.

"You enjoying this, McIntire?" Edith asked Mac who continued to stand in the door as if he'd been nailed there. "Are there any special positions you'd like us to get into for you?"

Mac cleared his throat. "Sorry. Right," he said. "Your mom's on the phone, B.J." he repeated and finally fled, pulling the door closed behind him as gently as if he were trying to avoid waking a sleeping baby.

The two women giggled together when Mac was gone. Finished with her nursing, Edith whacked Barbara Jeanne on her flank and told her she could get dressed. As B.J. stepped into her panties, Edith moved to her dresser for underwear of her own and said, "I think old Coach Mac could do with more sex than he's getting. Sometimes I catch him staring at me like a starving man might at a mountain of ice cream."

"Me too," Barbara Jeanne said.

Edith had pulled out the dresser's bottom drawer, but she stood back up without selecting either a pair of underpants or a T-shirt folded there in neat stacks. "What do you mean, you too?"

"I've caught him looking at me, too," B.J. said. "Just now." Barbara Jeanne paused a little as if savoring her memory a moment before sharing it. "And other times."

Edith had let her robe fall open as she prepared to get dressed. But now, she pinched it back together in front of her as if she felt a sudden chill. "What other times?"

Barbara Jeanne told her about the day Olga Jorgensen had cramped up in the shower and she had gotten Mac a spare towel.

"How did you feel about that?" Edith asked.

"I don't know," B.J. said. "I wasn't mad at him. I guess I felt nice."

Edith pursed her lips and distractedly brushed a damp strand of blond hair off her face.

"Nobody except Coach, maybe, ever really thinks about me as a, as a . . ." she hesitated, "you know, as a woman."

Edith shook her head, in part at her young friend's fetching innocence, but in part too, at a moment in her own life now long and forever gone, but one she could nonetheless remember with the immediacy of the fragranced ointment residue that clung to her fingertips no matter how many times she wiped them on the rough stubble of her bathrobe. Oblivious to B.J.'s presence in the room, Edith shook her head again. And then again.

About fifteen minutes later, after Barbara Jeanne had heeded her mom's request to come straight home, Edith marched into Mac's room and shook her finger in his face. She was still dressed only in her blue bathrobe. "You horny bastard," she said. "Haven't you learned anything from your mother all these years?"

Mac sat up in the bed and started to apologize for bursting into her room before she and B.J. were dressed, but Edith cut him off.

"Why is it that a man always prioritizes his organs with his brain ranking somewhere behind his dick?"

"Goddamnit, Edith," Mac said. "I didn't know y'all were in there beating each other off." Mac knew this wasn't true but he somehow couldn't shake the memory of his first reaction.

Edith took a short step forward and slapped his face. The blow didn't hurt any more than a clapped hand, but it reverberated in his high-ceilinged bedroom like a firecracker. His left hand rubbing in surprised shame at his reddened cheek, Mac hung his head. "I deserved that."

"Yes, you did," she said. She spun away from him as if she were going to leave the room. But after a couple of steps, she stopped, turned back and said, "I was just putting xylocaine on the abrasions on her behind."

"I know," Mac said quietly. Edith stared at him a long second, as if undecided about what to do next. Finally she retreated to a reading chair against the far wall and flung herself in it with such sudden exhaustion that she didn't notice that her robe separated below the knotted terry belt, leaving her legs naked all the way to where they joined.

Mac, of course couldn't help but see this, but he was blessed with a spasm of wisdom and deliberately averted his eyes.

Edith took a deep breath and let it out and then another one before she finally asked him, "If you knew, then why did you say it?"

"I don't know," Mac said truthfully.

"You're not ever going to let me forget my experience with Dot Brodie, are you?"

Mac looked up at her face. "Do you want to forget it?"

Edith sighed. "Not really," she said. "But it's such an awful memory, finally." Edith lay her head against the chair back and stared at the ceiling. "That was a special time. I've never been so excited," she said slowly, recalling with the sweet ache of nostalgia. "Every day seemed to bear with it some special revelation, some new understanding of the world. Everything was all wrapped up with ideas that were so new and urgent. And then there was Dottie. She really loved me, I think, but I discarded her and her lesbianism like something I'd tried on at a clothing store that didn't quite fit."

"I'm sorry, Edith," Mac said.

"Sorry that I have to live with having hurt someone I cared about? Or sorry that you were an asshole?"

"Both."

Edith smiled and sat forward a little in the chair. "Mac, don't you know that even if I were gay I wouldn't mess around with a high school girl."

Mac shrugged and allowed himself a quick peek between Edith's legs. Wisdom is such a fickle attribute.

She caught him. Shaking her head she only slowly covered herself and laughed at Mac as she repeated again her earlier observation, "You really are a sad horny bastard, aren't you?"

Mac didn't reply. It was as if he'd been slapped again.

"Whatever happened to that Stephanie Whats-her-pussy you were screwin' for a while?" Edith asked.

"I think she decided I was just a sad horny bastard," Mac said ruefully.

Edith got up from her chair and came to sit next to Mac on the bed. She put her arm around his waist and a hand on his massive thigh. "You've got to watch it with B.J.," she told him gently.

"What are you talking about?" Mac said.

"She knows you've got the hots for her, and she's just a kid."

"She's eighteen," Mac said. "But just like you, I hope you know that I'd never do anything improper with one of my students."

"Of course, I do," she said, patting his leg and laying her face against his shoulder. "You're my dearest friend, Mac McIntire, and I know what a good man you are. Still, you are a man." She paused and twisted her head to look up at him. "I want you to know that you can count on me the way I've always been able to count on you."

"What are you talking about?" Mac said.

Edith laughed and kissed the cheek that she'd slapped a short while earlier. She reached across his body, grasped his long arm by the wrist and slipped his hand inside her robe. Just before he turned to kiss her mouth, she said to him in a thin, strained whisper, "B.J. thinks you regard her as a woman, Mac, and that no one else ever has. You need to let her have that without letting it get you in trouble."

And we know, of course, that Mac did think of Barbara Jeanne as a woman, a woman whose lissome and graceful young body, whose plain, earnest, honest face and whose generous but determined and courageous spirit he found as arousing as anyone's he had ever met.

With the sole exception of Edith Jenkins.

In his dreams that night, with Edith curled in the warm crook of his arm, Edith and Barbara Jeanne, his fellow Terminal Cases, swirled together in his consciousness and became one.

# CHAPTER THIRTY-FIVE

However much his fantasy life may have trekked elsewhere, in his waking hours, Mac thought of Barbara Jeanne Bordelon, not as a woman, but as a ballplayer, a ballplayer like the eighteen others who tried out with her for the Broussard basketball varsity that fall.

Having run an endless gauntlet of negative publicity the year before, Mac was determined to make Barbara Jeanne's last year as smooth as possible. He hoped that by courting the press he could foster an atmosphere of cooperation and amiability. Mac's problems a year ago, he'd decided, had stemmed from lack of preparation born of his attitude that a male coaching the Broussard women was not really newsworthy. On the other hand, he really did feel that Barbara Jeanne's participation on the male varsity was a genuinely historic event. So, certain that the press would cover the story anyway, he invited them to the first day of practice in October, and they showed up in large numbers. The *States-Tribune* was there, of course. And so were representatives of New Orleans' three network television stations.

Mac presumed that they'd primarily want to talk to B.J., so he had a meeting with her ahead of time to tell her to prepare the things she wanted to say. She asked Mac what *he* wanted her to say, and he answered truthfully when he told her that he wanted her to say whatever was true. His confidence in Barbara Jeanne was unquestioned. She was a team player, and he was sure she would keep that first and foremost in her mind. The only ground rules Mac laid down for this pre-practice press conference were that all the media conduct their interviews simultaneously and for a period of only fifteen minutes. The

Bruins did have the important responsibility of practice, after all. Once the group interview was completed, the news organizations were invited to stay around for photos and video taping just so long as they didn't interfere with the workout.

B.J.'s interview went pretty well. She was self-effacing, as Mac knew she would be, emphasized the importance of the team first. When asked what her personal goals for the season were, she stressed that "We've got nineteen awfully good basketball players out for this squad, and Coach can only carry twelve. So first of all I just want to make the team." This observation was greeted with condescending laughter from almost all in the gathering, their reaction mistaking genuine modesty for insincere strategy.

And it was this presumption that started all the trouble anew. The press corps insisted on a follow-up interview with Mac after their fifteen minutes with Barbara Jeanne. Mac had not foreseen the need for this. And he wished he didn't have to do it. But he guessed that, as the coach of the first young woman to compete with men, he was a bit historic himself. So he called Gary Cashner over and told him to get the Bruins started in the first stages of their drills and agreed to match B.J.'s time with a quarter-hour interview of his own.

One of the first things they wanted to know was Mac's assessment of B.J.'s goal "just to make the team."

"I think Barbara Jeanne Bordelon is a sensible, mature, modest young woman. I admire her very much," Mac said. "As a basketball player. And as a person."

"What are your views of Miss Bordelon's chances of making your team?" the reporter from Channel Six TV asked. "Especially since she seems to think her inclusion as a varsity player is not already settled?"

"This is just the first day of practice," Mac pointed out with a smile.

"Yes, but you're well-acquainted with most of the players who are trying out, are you not?" the Channel Four reporter interjected. "And after all, Miss Bordelon played an entire year for you with the Lady Bruins."

"I'd be lying to you," Mac conceded, "if I tried to tell you that I don't come to this season with some established notions about the potentials of my team and the abilities of many of the ball players who will be on that team. At the same time, I'd be doing every kid who's on the floor right now a disservice if I were to state who had the team made and who didn't." Mac looked from the print reporters who were scribbling in their notebooks to the TV people who were shifting under the weight of all their equipment. "Kids grow a lot over the summer, height-wise, weight-wise, and talent-wise. Don't forget that a player like Bob Petit seemed an almost over-night sensation. Maybe there's some future Bob Petit just waiting for an honest evaluation out there right now." Mac hooked his thumb over his shoulder to indicate all the would-be Bruins going through their paces.

The reporter from Channel Eight said, "Coach McIntire, are you trying to tell us that Barbara Jeanne Bordelon doesn't have this team made?"

Mac smiled and shook his head. "I'm trying to tell you that no one has this team made, and it's my job to select the twelve best basketball players to represent our school this year. I think I know who a number of those players will be, but I may well be wrong."

"Do you *think* Miss Bordelon will be among your final twelve," the reporter from Six asked.

"I don't think it at all fair to comment on predispositions toward any player at this time." Mac smiled broadly again, hoping to communicate that his reluctance to answer derived in no way from any hostility toward either the question or the asker.

When time was up, Mac was so foolish that he thought the interview had gone well. No one seemed angry, and he'd been given the opportunity to say what he meant and explain himself in detail. Imagine his dismay, then, as he watched the ten o'clock news that night and heard the Channel Six sports anchor announce near the end of his sports report: "In prep news, Broussard High School basketball coach Marshall McIntire, under a court order to include the state's first woman player among the tryouts for his varsity Bruins squad, refused today to confirm that Barbara Jeanne Bordelon would be accorded one of the team's twelve positions."

What followed was video footage of Mac declaring that no one had the team made and then refusing to comment on the direct question about B.J. The reporting was not distorted exactly. But the story left the slight impression that Mac was resistant to Barbara Jeanne's membership on the team, which, as we all know, was the farthest thing from the case.

When Mac got up the next morning the *States-Tribune* had managed to make matters worse. Their headline on the story ran: "High School Coach Says Woman May Not Play With Men."

The repercussions began even before Mac could dress and get to school. He got a phone call from Stephanie Williams, his old flame, who told him before slamming her receiver down so loudly his ear rang for minutes afterwards that she'd suspected he was a sexist asshole all along.

It was going to be a long season.

# CHAPTER THIRTY-SIX

And it was going to be particularly long for Barbara Jeanne Bordelon. As she had learned long since, despite the beneficence of her spirit and the magnificence of her talent, for her, as for the rest of us, reader and narrator alike, nothing ever comes easy.

She too read the *States-Tribune* story which insinuated that Mac didn't want her as a member of the varsity Bruins that year, and she instantly recognized the kinds of reaction the story might well generate. Because she was at the center of this controversy, Barbara Jeanne felt it her responsibility to devise action to spare her coach and teammates whatever problems she could. Ever the team player, B.J. even went so far as to contemplate withdrawing from the squad altogether. She knew that the Bruins were going to be very good that year, that they were legitimate contenders for the state championship, and the last thing she wanted was to allow her presence on the team to disrupt her teammates' chances of realizing their fullest potential.

But B.J. was too *much* a team player, finally, to opt for resignation. In the first place, she believed, along with Sheila and Mac, that you always played to win and that you could never win by quitting. In the second place, she felt the Bruins needed her talents as a player. No matter what she said to the press, she believed she'd still be on the team when the final cuts were made. Furthermore, she thought she'd play. And when she played, she felt she'd contribute. Given her convictions about her worth to the team as a player, her immediate duty was to take the heat off Mac and her teammates so they could maintain the proper levels of concentration during the crucial pre-season practices.

Thus, without even informing Mac, Barbara Jeanne called a special press conference, and, to demonstrate her utter independence from both her coach and other officials at Broussard High, scheduled the interview not at school but at home. When the several newspaper and TV reporters had gathered in the Bordelon living room two days later, B.J. launched a concerted defense of Mac McIntire and his approach to coaching basketball. As a teacher and as a leader, she argued, he was without peer in her experience.

The reporters asked if she had called this press conference at the suggestion of her coach. And when she told them no, they asked if she felt pressure from any quarter to speak out in Mac's behalf. When she again replied no, they asked about her reaction to Mac's statement that she might not make the team, especially in light of a court-order to include her. That's when Barbara Jeanne gave them a lesson in the law. "The Fifth Circuit's decision," she said (only barely resisting the temptation to add "if you'd ever bothered to read it"), "doesn't guarantee me a place on the team. It did that last year, but only at the season's end and only because it was obviously too late at that point for me to try out. Beginning this year, the court's decision guarantees only my right to compete for a position on the team."

"And you're content with that," the Channel Four reporter inquired.

"Given that Mac McIntire is my coach, I'm content with that," B.J. replied.

"Are you worried about Coach McIntire's statement that you haven't got the team made yet?" the representative from Channel Six asked.

B.J. grinned a little and shook her head. "I'd be worried if he said anything else. Coach McIntire wants to field the best possible team he can, so he wants to pick the twelve best players for his team. I want to be included on that team because I'm one of the twelve best players, male or female, at Broussard High School. Coach McIntire would be doing a disservice to his profession if he behaved any other way. And I'd be satisfied with meaningless reverse discrimination if I wanted to be included on the basis of my sex rather than my ability."

The reporters tried to push B.J. into saying something critical about Mac or anything otherwise controversial. But she steadfastly refused. So, after a while, they packed up their notebooks, video equipment and disappointment and went home.

The TV stations didn't know what to do with a story like the one Barbara Jeanne had given them. To them it was a non-story, a piece about something, sexist discrimination in this case, that might have been happening, but wasn't. So the news directors at two of the stations put the taped material on hold until further developments. Channel Four did make mention of B.J.'s second interview at the end of its five o'clock sportscast, but only in copy read by the sports anchor and without accompanying video footage. The entire story was handled in less than twenty seconds.

To its credit the *States-Tribune* did run a fairly substantial feature on the story under the headline "Girl Roundballer Defends Coach," but the primary impact of the piece seemed to be the appearance two days later of a headlined letter to the sports editor, which read in part, "Coach McIntire's statements that Miss Bordelon does not yet have his Broussard High School basketball team made represent an insult, not only to Miss Bordelon's transcendent athletic abilities, but to the aspirations of women everywhere. In reality, they constitute contempt of court as well. The intimidation Coach McIntire has obviously exerted over Miss Bordelon to ensure her defense of his sexist attitudes is absolutely intolerable and ought to cost him his job." The letter was signed The Feminist Organization of Louisiana, Stephanie Williams, Pres.

"Jesus Christ," Mac said when he read the sports pages that morning.

"I told you that bitch was a cunt," Sheila declared.

But Mac and Barbara Jeanne and the Bruins managed to weather this first squall in a season-long storm. At the end of the second week of practice, genuinely saddened for those he had to dismiss, Mac performed the most odious chore of his coaching duties, and cut his team to the twelve players who would play for the Broussard varsity Bruins that year. And, as he virtually knew would be the case all along, Barbara Jeanne Bordelon was among the number he retained.

But from the very start of pre-season practice, Barbara Jeanne suffered an isolation that she somehow hadn't quite anticipated. Namely, because of her gender, she'd had to confine herself to her own locker room. Like most high schools built in the sixties, Broussard had a special, marginally more luxurious locker room especially reserved for its varsity male athletes. Outfitted with a training table and a whirlpool and a space with benches and a blackboard for pre-home-game meetings, the Bruin room conferred automatic status on even the lowliest sub who was allowed to stow his gear there. Having to dress and undress apart from her teammates robbed Barbara Jeanne, not only of earned, if ephemeral, prestige, but of the more important elements of team camaraderie.

Sensitive to this problem instantly, Mac sought permission from the Broussard administration to erect a temporary partition in the Bruin room so that Barbara Jeanne would have a tiny locker area and access to a privatized end of the shower.

Samuel Riggs and Arnold Larrett thought Mac had lost his mind. He tried to explain to them how important he thought it was to minimize B.J.'s segregation from her teammates. But they responded by arguing that no such "intersexual team facilities" would be available for road games and that Barbara Jeanne might as well learn the necessity of her being apart at her home school. Mac pointed out that the Bruins would play away from home exactly fifteen times, but that counting home games and daily practice they'd be in the Bruin Room on over a hundred occasions. But Larrett summarized and settled the case against him when he reminded Mac "there is no way, Mr. McIntire, that the Bruin Room could be redesigned so that Miss Bordelon would not have to pass through an area equipped with urinals. And though I am sure you'd contend that your male players would consent to use other facilities, and though I'm sure Miss Bordelon would remind me that she has two younger brothers, I will not stand for one of our female students being daily in the presence of, of, of, a *place* where men perform their excretory activities."

"Why is Arnold so obsessed with excretory activities," Edith asked that night at the Terminal when Mac had related Larrett's speech.

"Arnold Larrett *is* an excretory activity," Sheila said.

But all the profane metaphorizing on earth was not going to gain Barbara Jeanne access to the Bruin Room. And thus she was condemned to spend her senior season dressing on the other side of gym from her teammates, getting her ankles wrapped and having her other minor aches and pains attended to by Joan Teo who carried the title of "assistant coach" but who functioned really as Mac's liaison with his one female player.

At least Barbara Jeanne's experiences in the girls' locker room at Broussard were uneventful and merely lonely. For when the Bruins played away games, administrators at opposing schools never remembered to close the girls' locker room for Barbara Jeanne's use, and so she was inevitably harassed by some antagonistic coed who had come in only to fix her lipstick, but who, upon discovering B.J., would hang around to inquire if it were true she was a dyke. Worse, some schools lacked a varsity team room, and their own players dressed in the regular boys' locker room. When Broussard played those schools, the Bruins were assigned the girls' locker room, and Barbara Jeanne was shunted off to change in a women's bathroom where her encounters with hasslers were more frequent and more vicious. In the public restrooms she was repeatedly asked how often she gave blowjobs to her Bruin teammates.

Maybe Arnold Larrett was right after all that excretory activities brought out the worst in people.

# CHAPTER THIRTY-SEVEN

Mac sought his refuge from this simmering lunacy on the basketball court. His kids were good and Mac was feverish with anticipation for what they might accomplish. To start with, the Bruins had size. At 6'9", Donnie Start wasn't as strong as Mac might wish, and wasn't quite the force on the boards he might have been, but he had developed both a power hook and a feathery touch on his jumper. Start was definitely going to give teams fits. Also bigger and better was Whitt McSeveney, who, at 6'6", gave the Bruins a forward who could run, rebound and be counted on to avoid mistakes. Six-foot guard Danny Waddell was as skilled a ball handler as any highschooler in New Orleans. And newcomer Preston Whisenhunt, a 6'3" guard who had transferred from Houston, gave the Bruins a capable all-around ball player Mac hadn't even anticipated.

Best of all, 6'5" Gary Cashner was the kind of player every coach dreams of having. Gary was big—broad-shouldered, big-assed, shovel-handed, boat-footed. He looked slow, and worse, he looked awkward. He possessed less natural grace than any of his teammates who would see a lot of playing time. But he had a heart as big as a truck and a will to succeed that was both awesome and contagious. He wasn't a screamer. But he was a leader. He was the kind of kid who got a look in his eyes that was frightening and who was capable of quietly pushing his teammates to be better even than they were.

When you added to this nucleus 6'6" Painton Richard, who had started and played quite well as a sophomore on Mac's junior varsity team, and who could spell any of the men across the Bruins' front line, and Lyndon Schock,

6'2", and a solid sub at guard, you had a team with size, speed, strength and depth.

And then, of course, the Bruins also had Barbara Jeanne Bordelon. Gifted, spunky, courageous Barbara Jeanne Bordelon. By the fall of her senior year, B.J. had grown to 5'9" and 130 pounds. But in those statistics lay Barbara Jeanne's handicap and Mac's secret agony. In men's basketball terms, B.J. was a pipsqueak. Size, of course, is by no means everything. And B.J.'s basketball talent ran deep. She had terrific endurance and excellent quickness. She handled the ball well. She wasn't quite Danny's equal as a dribbler, but she could match him in terms of court vision and passing. And, of course, B.J. was a superb shooter, in pure terms the Bruins' very best.

But despite her abilities, Mac couldn't start her. For though size wasn't everything, in B.J.'s case, given the other varsity Bruins her senior year in high school, size was crucial, especially because her vertical leap was the weakest on the squad. In sum, though in sundry ways, Barbara Jeanne was a superb player, others on the squad were better. And Mac was a coach who played his best because, his mother's son, he played to win.

It was a matter of team needs. Obviously Barbara Jeanne could not play in the front court. Against forwards and centers she was like a sapling in a redwood forest. On the other hand, in the back court she couldn't dislodge Danny because he was more effective than she was with the ball in his hands. And she couldn't beat out Preston Whisenhunt, even though she was a better pure shooter than he was, because basketball games aren't played in a "pure" environment, but rather in a defensive thicket of waving arms. Whereas Preston was only a good shooter, and B.J. a legitimately excellent one, Mac knew that under game conditions Preston's additional six inches of height would make him more effective, even considering the naturally high arch B.J. got from her Mac-like, behind-the-head release.

Mac regretted making this judgment. He loved Barbara Jeanne and he would much have preferred to see her capable of what she just slightly wasn't. But as much as he suffered the truth of his judgment, he never really considered doing what he might have, namely, starting B.J. in Preston's place out of his personal loyalty to her. That would have violated everything he held holy about coaching the game of basketball.

Mac was at least partially consoled about his decision because he knew that Barbara Jeanne could take it. She, after all, had been on the floor for all the practices that Mac had merely watched. And she knew, that however tight the race was, she was a runner-up. Mac was further consoled because the fact that B.J. would not start did not at all mean she wouldn't play. She was a very good spread court player, filling lanes well on the fast break, keeping the ball moving in a delay game. She was the team's best free-throw shooter, a skill whose importance was inevitably magnified at the end of close games where teams foul as a strategy for stopping the clock. And, despite her lack of size, she was a tenacious defender. Her quick hands made driving against her perilous and her determination to deflect a pass or make a steal was so intense that Mac sometimes worried she'd push herself to the verge of oxygen debt.

All this meant that B.J. would see a lot of action in crucial situations— when the Bruins had to protect a narrow lead and needed a squad of ballhandlers and foul-shooters on the floor, or, more important, when the Bruins had to score quickly and had to play a pressing defense designed to produce turnovers. To capitalize on Barbara Jeanne's abilities in these game-deciding regards, Mac installed both a "four corners" stall and a zone press.

In this day, before the shot clock, the "four corners" employed, centrally, the dribbling ability of Danny Waddell. It spread the court with other good ballhandlers clearing themselves to the perimeters of the floor so that Danny could work his bouncing, weaving magic in the center, passing off to his teammates only when double-teamed. Preston Whisenhunt, B.J., Lyndon Schock, and Gary Cashner were the other Bruins in this alignment designed to keep the ball out of their opponents' hands while the game's ending seconds ticked harmlessly away. Their job was to set a series of picks for each other and repeatedly cut for the basket hoping for an uncontested, easy basket.

Important as her involvement in the "four corners" delay was, though, B.J.'s position in the zone press was even more critical. The zone press was Mac's weapon for catching up as quickly as possible. A relatively high risk defense because it spread the Bruins all over the court and made them vulnerable to the easy lay-up, the strategy, when thrown against a team not expecting it, or one which was tired or undisciplined, could nonetheless frequently produce a series of quick buckets and sometimes spread panic through an opposing team like measles through a first-grade classroom.

In Mac's one-one-two-one zone press, two positions were slightly more important than the others—the front position whose player was obligated to pick up the ball after it was inbounded and initiate the pressure, and the rear position whose player was the last line of defense and was charged with denying the easy basket. In the zone press that Mac designed, Barbara Jeanne was to play the crucial front point and Gary Cashner the rear. All B.J.'s job required were quick feet, a kamikaze's will and asbestos lungs. When she picked up the opponent with the ball, she was obliged to drive him by the shortest possible route toward the sidelines, if possible to deny him the pass, but at all costs to deny him access to the middle of the floor. The second one, of the one-one-two-one, was to pick up the inbounder. The responsibility of each of the two wing-men was to combine with Barbara Jeanne in a double-team trap when she had maneuvered the dribbler against the side-lines. The wing-man on the opposite side was obliged to retreat to center court to defend against the cross-court pass. And Gary, of course, was charged to make up for it all whenever the plan broke down and no steal or ten-second violation resulted.

With every passing week of pre-season practice, Mac felt his insides draw still one notch tighter with sweet anticipation. It was an edgy, vaguely uncomfortable feeling, but one Mac nonetheless enjoyed in the same way he savored the ache of tired muscles after a strenuous workout. He could hardly predict what lay ahead for his team. But all his feelings were good. Workouts were crisp. His players believed they could win. This might finally be the year, Mac thought, he brought home the championship that had eluded him all his life.

The day of the first game, Mac was so nervous that he misdirected his fourth period cooking class on instructions about baking a concoction called Grape Nut Bread. As a result, much to the delight of five of his players who were among his students, they ended up with a cereal brick instead of a moist breakfast cake. But underneath the external and laughable evidence of tension, Mac was really a boulder of confidence. Their first opponent, to be played at home, was McDonogh, a school returning the basic team the Bruins had defeated by fifteen the year before.

Furthermore, once the knowledge had spread that Barbara Jeanne had made the varsity squad, much of the controversy surrounding her seemed to dry up like last year's fruitcake. Edith even reported that the Feminist Organization of Louisiana was claiming victory and was encouraging its reorganized membership to attend the opening game and root for Broussard.

Mac's only genuine concern lay in the fact that due to the presence of those offending urinals, Arnold Larrett wouldn't even allow Mac to ask Barbara Jeanne into the Bruin room for a pre-game skull session and pep talk. It was obviously impossible to hold such a meeting with a team member excluded. So, once all the male players were dressed, and Joan Teo had fetched Barbara Jeanne from the girls' locker room, Mac found himself in a corner of the gymnasium, squatting over a portable blackboard with his team huddled around him to close out the surprisingly high level of crowd noise. At least, Mac thought, as he scribbled out his reminders, Larrett had not yet complained about B.J.'s teammates putting their arms around her as they all hunched toward their coach for their final instructions.

As he rubbed at a painful knee, strained by his uncomfortable position, Mac reflected, that in Arnold Larrett's world common sense and convenience were decidedly secondary to safe distances from the sites of excretory activities.

Unfortunately, Mac and the Bruins were not at a safe distance from the execrable activities of a group of religious fanatics who, at that very moment, had stationed themselves on the steps of the Broussard gym and were informing every fan who tried to make his way inside that Mac McIntire was guilty of "taunting God's laws" by allowing the "promiscuous intermixing of males and females in athletics."

Yes, those same Soldiers for Jesus, who only one year earlier had promoted Mac McIntire as their disciple, were now denouncing him as the "agent of Satan." Mac had been "corrupted by the evils of flesh" they trumpeted. He had "sold out to the indecent urges of a decadent society."

"Turn away from sin," they preached to those who had come to the game as they begged donations and pressed mad pamphlets into the reluctant hands of anyone foolish enough to pause even a second to listen.

"At least root for Broussard to lose," they urged upon those who rejected their guidance and headed on inside.

And off to the side, in a droning voice that failed to muster the appropriate outrage, Private for Jesus Helen Donalds proclaimed that the seven-year-old child she gripped by the wrist was the namesake son Mac McIntire had too long refused to acknowledge.

# CHAPTER THIRTY-EIGHT

But Mac did not know until after the game about the lunacy being practiced on the steps to the Broussard gym. As he huddled with his team during the waning minutes of the Lady Bruins' game, which he had insisted become the opener for a season-long series of Broussard men's/women's double-headers, he rode the wave of enthusiasm in the cheers and applause all around him, toward an unwarranted hope that Barbara Jeanne Bordelon's last year in high school would be eventful only in developments on the court.

And then, only minutes later, he had to deal with the lunacy that erupted *inside* the gym.

Fan spirit remained high through the varsity warm-ups. Many in the crowd called out Barbara Jeanne's name or some slogan involving her. A group of Barbara Jeanne's friends started the chant "Cake, Cake, Cake," which attracted other participants before gradually dying out. As a result, those in attendance that night could almost feel the electricity of excitement as the warning buzzer sounded and the two teams joined their coaches benchside.

Underneath the ripple of polite applause that greeted the announcement of the McDonogh starting line-up was a murmur of anticipation. The crowd was well aware that they were about to witness an historic occasion, the first female to play in a men's varsity sport. Then the announcer's voice blared through the P.A. system, "Starting for the Broussard Bruins" and was drowned out before the names of the players could be heard as they trotted out to center court to face the crowd. First Don Start, then Whitt McSeveney, then Preston Whisenhunt, then Danny Waddell. But then a most outrageous thing happened;

as Gary Cashner jogged out to meet his teammates in the ritual handclasp of unity, and the non-students in the crowd realized that Barbara Jeanne was remaining on the bench, they greeted the Bruin captain with a chorus of boos and catcalls that made it seem he was the least popular man in New Orleans since the Reconstruction carpetbaggers were driven out of town.

But the crowd wasn't really mad at Gary Cashner, of course. Those who were booing didn't know who Gary Cashner was and couldn't have cared less. They were mad at Mac McIntire because it had finally dawned on the members of the Feminist Organization of Louisiana that just because Barbara Jeanne had made the team did not necessarily mean that she had made the starting line-up.

When the Bruin coach was introduced a few seconds later, they made it a whole lot clearer about whom they were really mad at. They booed even louder and a strike-throwing radical feminist, who should have been trying out for a baseball team somewhere, caught Mac with a wadded paper cup right smack in the back of the head. They were quieted when the Broussard band broke into the "Star Spangled Banner," but just as soon as the last notes ebbed away and the teams were taking their positions on the floor for the tip-off, an incensed young woman in the bleachers directly across from the Bruin bench stood up and shrieked, "McIntire, is a pig" and then led a chant of "We Want Bordelon" that continued for most of the first quarter.

Fortunately, it didn't have to continue beyond that. Broussard could have beaten McDonogh with its second team. Don Start knocked the opening tip to Gary Cashner who hit Danny Waddell cutting to the basket, and the Bruins took an instant lead that grew for the rest of the game. With a minute and a half left in the opening period, the starters were up 20 to 7, and Mac demolished the "We Want Bordelon" chant into an earthquake of applause by sending Barbara Jeanne into the game along with Painton Richard and Lyndon Schock.

Barbara Jeanne played the next six minutes before giving way to the third-teamers who finished out the half with the Bruins in front 40 to 20. And she played exceptionally well. In her limited amount of time on the floor, she collected two field goals, one a beautiful, behind-her-head jumper, the other a break-away lay-up off a nifty steal, and two-free throws. She held her man scoreless and also contributed an assist.

The second half was more of the same. Boos again greeted the Broussard line-up, but the jeers had lost their edge now that it was clear Mac was going to let B.J. play. And in her second-half floor time she again sparkled, picking up three more points all from the foul line, notching another steal and two more assists as the Bruins cruised home 74 to 48. The only blot on Barbara Jeanne's evening of work was a missed second-half free throw.

211

Mac was so pleased by his team's performance he practically forgot about the nonsense over whether or not Barbara Jeanne had started the game. He rushed among his players in the Bruins Room, whopping them all on the butt and between the shoulder blades, praising each one for his accomplishments. And after he'd spoken with each one individually, he went over to the girls' locker room where he'd stationed his mom and Edith, kissed the former and wrapped the latter in a bear hug before sending her in to B.J. with appropriate encomiums and the teasing message that he wanted that to be the last free-throw she missed all year.

"Hot damn!" Mac said to his mom while waiting for Edith. He squeezed his fists together and pummeled the air with sweet victory. Mac felt again that special elation that comes from athletic triumph, a high the likes of which no drug on earth can approximate. This narcotic euphoria accounts, at least in part, for why grown men like Mac spend their lives in the pursuit of perfect games and perfect seasons and for why champions pour champagne over one another's heads rather than drinking it.

Sadly, the glow of the year's first victory, which should have shined all the way to the next night's game, was tarnished within the hour. Mac basked in the win until he'd seen all his players dressed and on their ways home. But as he was leaving the gym with Edith and Sheila, he was confronted by an angry platoon of Soldiers for Jesus who spit out at him as he tried to brush past them, "The wages of sin are death, Mac McIntire. The wages of sin are death."

"I've got to talk to these people a moment," Sheila said. And though Mac and Edith tried to dissuade her, she went back up the steps to address the group's spokesman. "You know you've got that quote wrong, don't you?" she told him. "What Jesus actually said was 'the dearth of wages is a sin.' He had this thing for the poor, you remember." All the Soldiers for Jesus just stared at her blankly until she turned away from them. But when Mac looked back at them as he walked away, they were gesticulating among themselves and the spokesman was frantically paging through his Bible.

Mac laughed. "I think you actually buffaloed 'em with that bullshit, mom," he said. "Maybe you should have told 'em what translation of the Bible you were quoting from."

"Wouldn't have mattered," Sheila said. "People who spout off about the Bible the most also read it the least. How can you expect them to understand the fine distinctions between the King James and the Revised Sheila versions."

Sheila's excellent lesson in Biblical errancy didn't sustain Mac's flagging spirits over the realization that the Soldiers for Jesus were once again blackheads in the complexion of his life. He didn't even perk up much when he received an at least marginally conciliatory phone call from Stephanie Williams. Stephanie was frosty throughout the brief conversation which interrupted Mac's celebratory meal of pizza and Dixie, and she made it clear that the Feminist Organization of Louisiana still maintained that Barbara Jeanne ought, as she put it, "to be among the first group of players in the game." Still, she commended Mac for according Barbara Jeanne "a fair share of the playing time."

"I don't think Stephanie understands much about basketball," Mac told Edith and Sheila when he sat back down with them.

"That's because there's so little fucking in basketball," Sheila replied.

And there wasn't much Stephanie Williams in basketball either for the next little while. Perhaps she thought her service in the Barbara Jeanne Bordelon Affair was ended and her call to Mac the benediction. Some of the F.O.o.L. members continued to come to the games. They still booed a little at the Bruin starting line-up and occasionally chanted "We want Bordelon." But basically they came because they were genuine fans. They enjoyed the games and were downright ecstatic when Barbara Jeanne played and did well.

Unfortunately, B.J. didn't dazzle them quite as much in the next couple of games as she did in the opener. The Bruins thoroughly dominated both games against teams almost as weak as McDonogh, and Barbara Jeanne logged approximately the same amount of floor time. Against the Robert E. Lee Generals, she played well enough, even though her statistics didn't show it. She got only one bucket, on a lay-up, didn't go to the line, make a steal or an assist. She held her man scoreless again, though, and didn't make any mistakes. A week later against John F. Kennedy, she managed four points, both baskets on sweet jumpers. But she also made her first errors of the season, throwing away passes on two consecutive trips down the floor. She missed another free-throw too, this time the front end of a one-and-one, and Mac worried a little that she was pressing.

The Bruins' fourth game of the season, at Warren Easton, was their first big test of the year. The Eagles had good size and had lost only one starter from a squad that had split with Broussard the year before. It also turned out to be Barbara Jeanne's first big test as well, and in two ways. When B.J. went into the girls' locker room to dress for the game, she found some pranksters had left a little message for her. Propped in the corner of the room was large piece of white cardboard onto which someone had nailed both a bra and a jockstrap. Underneath the two garments was scrawled, "Which one of these do you wear, Barbara Jeanne? You can't wear them both."

Not remarkably, Barbara Jeanne felt invaded by the poster. She knew the Easton School officials would never have allowed such an item to be placed in the men's locker room, and, though she didn't really suspect the Easton administrators of complicity with the gag, she took offense nonetheless at their carelessness about her membership on the team. She was still chafing from the slight when she took the floor for warm-ups, and Mac made a point of saying to her, "I want you to be ready tonight, B.J. If things get tight, we'll press."

Mac's motive, of course, was to emphasize to Barbara Jeanne how valuable he thought her in big games. But perhaps he shouldn't have said this. For the game *was* tight and Mac didn't go to the press or to Barbara Jeanne. The problem was that the Bruins moved out to a quick 4-0 and then Easton went to a slow down. They didn't stall—they were still trying to score—but they played very deliberately, working for a high percentage shot every time down the floor. The game was low-scoring and remained close, but because the Bruins always held on to their lead, Mac felt it safer to avoid the risks of the press. And so Barbara Jeanne stayed on the bench through the first half which ended with Broussard ahead 20 to16.

Trouble appeared in the middle of the fourth quarter. The Bruins were up 34-29 when Preston Whisenhunt committed his fourth foul as a driving Eagle guard connected on a lay-up. When he also canned the free-throw, the Bruin lead was cut to two. Mac called time out and sent in Barbara Jeanne for Preston. It was a move the Eagle coach must have been waiting for all week. Don Start tried to build the lead back up all by himself and threw up a leaner that touched nothing but the eager fingers of the Eagle center. And then on their offensive end, B.J.'s man, at 6'3" a full half-foot taller than she, posted B.J. down low and banked home an easy five-footer over her for a tie game. When Whitt McSeveney missed a jumper, the Eagles came right back with the same play again. Again the big Easton guard exploited his height advantage to score over B.J., and the Bruins were behind for the first time all year.

Mac called time and sent in Lyndon Schock for Barbara Jeanne who had played less than two minutes. Fortunately, for the team as a whole, the substitution worked. Gary Cashner took over the last three minutes of the game as if he were personally insulted by having been behind. He blocked the next two shots the Eagles attempted, canned two jumpers from his high-post position at the top of the lane and hit Whitt with a gorgeous bounce pass on the backdoor play for the bucket that sealed the game.

But for Barbara Jeanne, her brief and ineffective appearance against Easton was a sad harbinger of things to come. The next two games were again easy victories, and B.J. saw plenty of action. But she played not so well in either contest. She was hesitant and she seemed uncomfortable. Passes sometimes just slipped through her fingers and once she dribbled the ball off her foot, a not uncommon basketball occurrence, but one of which Mac had never before known her to be guilty.

Things turned around a bit in Broussard's seventh game, at home against John Curtis. The Patriots put up quite a struggle and were still only seven back with two minutes left when Mac sent in his ballhandlers to run the four corners. Barbara Jeanne played without error under pressure in this one as the Bruins ran out the clock to remain undefeated, Mac made a big deal of it afterwards. But B.J. had turned down a wide open drive to the basket for an easy layup, and he remained concerned that B.J. was losing her confidence.

That night at the Terminal, over their standard fare of Luigi's pizza and beer, Mac sought Sheila's and Edith's advice on what to do about Barbara Jeanne. But the two women were at a loss for ideas. "Just keep encouraging her," they told Mac. "She's got the ability, and sooner or later she'll snap out of it."

But she didn't snap out of it. Not even when Mac threw his zone press against underdog opponents in the two opening rounds of the Crescent City Christmas tournament and thereby increased her playing time. Mac wasn't ecstatic about pressing teams that had little chance against him. It smacked of an attempt to run up the score and rub an opponent's face in his inferiority. But Mac invoked the strategy anyway. They were going to be forced to press at some point in the season and needed to practice it under game conditions. In addition, of course, Mac wanted to get Barbara Jeanne into some games in situations where she'd feel comfortable.

But the ploy didn't really work. The Bruins won both games in walkovers while B.J. did nothing so egregious in her time on the floor that would require pulling her. But it was clear she was hesitant and playing without the looseness a ballplayer needs to be at her best. Mac didn't risk going with a practice press against the tough Rummel Raiders in the Christmas Tourney semi-final. And Barbara Jeanne saw no action until the final minute when he called for the four corners to protect a five-point lead.

In the finals Broussard went up against Jesuit, the pre-season co-favorite to capture the city crown. The game was hard fought from the opening tip-off. Gary Cashner, who was always intense on a basketball court, seemed to find new resources inside himself against threatening opponents. He seemed unstoppable, scoring as if at will with an array of almost arcless jump shots, drives and soft hooks. The Blue Jays responded, however, by practically shutting the other Bruin starters down. Don Start was particularly ineffective, and Mac sent Painton Richard into the game early for more rebounding strength. Barbara Jeanne also saw first-half action, spelling both Danny and Preston. But she was no more successful than they and left the floor with no stats to her credit.

Gary's performance was so overwhelming, though, that the Bruins maintained small leads until late in the fourth quarter when Jesuit tied it up.

But with just under a minute left, Gary put back an errant Waddell jumper, drew a foul, canned the free-throw and staked his team again to a three-point advantage. Jesuit called time to make its final plans, which Mac countered by sending in his four-corners unit. He should have waited. Jesuit cleared out for B.J.'s man who scored over her easily, cutting the lead to one. Down on the offensive end, the Bruins worked the ball around for thirty seconds. But then with only fifteen seconds remaining, Barbara Jeanne threw an errant pass into the ecstatic mitts of a gambling Blue Jay defender who drove the length of the floor for an uncontested lay-up to drop the Bruins' record to 10-1.

The whole Broussard team was in a daze after the game. Mac made his usual rounds, this time trying to offer consolation instead of congratulations. Barbara Jeanne was in despair, and on the school bus ride across town to Broussard, she insisted on apologizing to her teammates. With a throat so tight she could barely speak, she stood up in her swaying seat and said, "You guys are the best team in this state. I'm the one who cost y'all the game tonight."

Mac started to stand up and admonish her, but before he could move, Don Start said, "Shit, B.J., how can you say *you* lost it when I'm averaging sixteen and didn't score a goddamn point?"

"Cashner's the one that lost it," Danny Waddell said. "S.O.B. may have gotten thirty-one tonight, but he missed a shot in the second quarter. He makes that and we're still undefeated."

When the team returned to practice after the Christmas holidays, all but Barbara Jeanne seemed to have put their tournament defeat behind them. Before their first workout, B.J. again attempted to shoulder the blame for their loss to Jesuit. But Whitt interrupted her. "You talk like you weren't a member of this team, Cake. Please stop that shit. We all win. We all lose. It's never just one of us in any case."

Mac couldn't have been prouder of the way his Bruins handled their defeat and Barbara Jeanne's attempt to blame herself for it. But despite her teammates support, she continued to play poorly into January. Late in the month, in a tough contest at De La Salle, when Preston again got into foul trouble, Mac sent Shock in to replace him as the Bruins struggled to a 69-64 win.

It was the first game all season in which Barbara Jeanne did not play.

# CHAPTER THIRTY-NINE

Mac was delighted by his team's fine record, of course. Broussard was 20-1 as the season entered February. But he remained concerned that another game was coming, like the one against Jesuit in the Christmas Tournament, when a Bruins victory might require a performance from Barbara Jeanne at the very top of her skills. Thus, as the season ebbed through its final third toward the playoffs, Mac cast about urgently for some way to pull B.J. out of her slump.

No one suspected that B.J.'s parents were in any way behind the pressure she was putting on herself, but Edith thought a sharp change of routine might help B.J. screw her head back on straight. So Edith invited her young friend to spend some time with her at the Terminal. Mac and Sheila both commended Edith for her selfless gesture.

But Edith protested, "Don't give me credit I'm not due. I may seem altruistic, but really I'm as self-interested as the next guy. I haven't spent all these years in law school for nothing."

"Yeah," Mac said. "What's in this for you besides an unfortunately second set of ears to soak up some of the decibels that rampage out of your radio all the goddamn time."

"Why honey," Edith Scarlett-drawled. "If I can get Barbara Jeanne Sugar Tits to hang around, I can keep you from ogling *me* all the live-long day."

But this was foolishness, of course, and not just because Mac wasn't about to stop undressing Edith with his eyes whenever she was in eyesight. Mac and Sheila were happy about the invitation and happy to have Barbara Jeanne around. Still, it was after another lackluster personal performance in another easy Bruin victory that she accompanied them back to the Terminal for some post-game pizza and fellowship. For the night, at least, in the high spirits of affectionate teasing, B.J. seemed to relax and blossom in this reunion of the Terminal Cases. The next night Barbara Jeanne played her best game in weeks. And Mac was so encouraged he inquired if Edith would allow B.J. to move in for an extended stay.

But when Edith conveyed the idea to B.J., the latter demurred, confessing in an unguarded explanation that she really shouldn't be away from Laura. Edith pressed to understand that remark, and, after a little prodding, Barbara Jeanne related the entire horror story of her rape, pregnancy and subsequent life at home with a daughter for a sister.

I would have hoped that sharing this misfortune would have lightened the load of pressure that B.J. was putting on herself. But perhaps because Edith's invitation forced her to face in a new way her self-imposed obligations at home, her confession seemed to have the opposite impact. The next weekend B.J. played her worst games of the year, missing six straight free throws over two nights and committing turnovers that ran the gamut from bad passes to traveling to a three-second-lane violation. B.J.'s aggravating underachievement was almost unbearable for Mac. Given the ironic circumstances of his pride and excitement about the success of his team as a whole, Mac suspected he couldn't feel worse. But he was wrong.

Mid-week after Barbara Jeanne's back-to-back disasters, Mac opened the sports section to find a letter to the editor that made him chase his breakfast coffee with a handful of Rolaids.

"Miss Bordelon's season-long performance," the letter went in part, "demonstrates our fundamental contention that she has no business competing against men. The morality of the issue aside, it appears conclusive now that girls just lack the necessary ability to compete with the stronger sex.

"We hope that Coach McIntire's decision to hold Miss Bordelon out of a recent contest against De La Salle High School," the letter continued, "indicates that he has finally seen the light and come back to his senses. His Bruins this year are obviously a fine group of players, and it would be a terrible shame for their potential to be squandered on a disastrous and wrong-headed social experiment."

The letter ended: "We call for all right-minded residents of our city to join us in our continuing struggle to keep the sexes in the places God designed for them." It was signed "Rev. Elmer Kanter, Commander-in-Chief, Soldiers for Jesus."

"Jesus," Mac sighed after reading the letter aloud to his mother and Edith.

"No way Elmer has anything to do with Jesus," Sheila said. "Elmer and his band of assholes rank right in there with Scribes and Pharisees on Jesus' social register."

"What are we gonna do about these jerks?" Edith asked.

"Maybe we could slip some speed into their holy water and they'd all pray themselves to death," Sheila suggested.

"I'm gonna call him up," Mac said.

"I'd rather you string him up," Sheila said.

"No, I'm gonna call him up and ask him to stop it. The man's my father for Chrissake. I'm going to appeal to him as a son."

Well, neither Sheila nor Edith was wild about this idea, but Mac went through with it. And though he was unable to speak with Elmer on the phone, he was told that Elmer would very much like to visit with him in person, that very night in fact, at the unaffiliated Baptist church Elmer pastored in Metairie.

At the appointed hour of seven o'clock, with Edith and Sheila by his side, Mac knocked on the door of Elmer's church office. A middle-aged woman with a bouffant hair-do opened the door, stepped into the hall and then turned and locked the door behind her.

"The church office is closed," she explained.

"Excuse me, ma'am," Mac said to her. "We, or actually I, have an appointment with the Reverend Kanter."

The woman looked confusedly at Mac and then at Edith and Sheila. "Now?" she said.

"Yes," Mac said. "I called and made an appointment this morning."

"Oh," the church secretary said. "Yes. I remember your call now. Rev. Kanter said he'd be happy to visit with you tonight at the church."

"We thought this was the church," Sheila said rudely. "But given that Elmer works here..."

The woman looked at Sheila quizzically, then turned and said to Mac, "I'm sure he meant you could see him at services. Mid-week prayer meeting," she explained. "That's where I'm going now. I just stopped in the office to pick up my Bible. Y'all can follow me to the sanctuary if you'd like. I do hope y'all want to attend. If you aren't born again, Rev. Kanter can show you the way to the Lord."

"Got any holy water?" Sheila asked.

"No, ma'am. Baptists don't drink holy water. But the Rev. Kanter can fill your soul with the water of eternal life."

"My soul's kinda bloated right at the moment," Sheila said. "I was more in the market for a spiritual diuretic tonight."

The woman wrinkled her brow in confusion, then said, "Y'all just follow me. I'll gladly show the way."

"You go on ahead," Mac said.

"Yeah," Sheila said. "We forgot something in the car."

"Our Bibles," Mac interjected.

"And our holy water," Sheila called after the woman's retreated back.

"Mom!" Mac chided. "It's Elmer Kanter we need to get to. I can't see any reason for taking it out on his secretary."

"Yeah, well, knowin' Elmer, he's puttin' it *in* his secretary," Sheila responded.

"What's *that* supposed to mean, Mom?" Mac asked, flashing a glance of conspiratorial exasperation toward Edith.

"Among other things it's supposed to mean that you gotta have a flock before you can have a shepherd."

Mac nodded his head. "Right, Mom. What say we just can the philosophical chit-chat and go to Elmer's prayer meeting."

"You two go ahead," Sheila said. "I've got something I need to do more urgently."

"What's that?" Edith asked, hoping she might use the same excuse.

"Sit down in front of a bus," Sheila said.

So they all went over to the sanctuary and slipped into the back of the prayer meeting, planning to give Elmer an incredulous listen and then try to talk to him once the service was concluded.

"The road to hell is paved with good intentions," Elmer thundered as they entered. He was addressing his faithful on the very issue of Barbara Jeanne Bordelon's basketball career. Out of the pulpit and wandering the aisles of his congregation like an evangelical Phil Donahue, he thrusted his phallic-shaped microphone toward mesmerized parishioners for their antiphonal ejaculations of "Amen!" "God bless you brother," and "Blessed be the name of Jesus."

The point that the charitable Rev. Elmer was making at the time Mac and Sheila and Edith came in was that he didn't doubt the good intentions of those who encouraged Barbara Jeanne to mix her sweat with that of the opposite sex. But that was not God's way. And thus such was the road to hell.

It's not clear when Elmer recognized the three interlopers in the back pew. Perhaps he had even set the whole thing up. Perhaps the confusion about the meeting time was deliberately orchestrated by Elmer to get Mac into one of his meetings. Perhaps Elmer was angling for some hot publicity to help launch a viewership for his "Old Time Wednesday Hour of Prayer" that was set to make its syndicated debut on independent TV stations across the land in only two weeks' time. Whatever is true, Elmer suddenly began to proclaim. "But God works in mysterious ways. As the experience of Job has shown us, sometimes God visits us with suffering as a challenge to our faith. We live in a diseased society. Nakedness and wantonness greet us at every turn—in the pages of Godless magazines, through the blasphemous electronics of television. And now educators are destroying the identification of our children with their God-given maleness or femaleness. This is perfidy."

"Amen!" someone called out.

"God bless you, Brother Kanter," another voice called.

"Blessed be the name of Jesus," a third suggested.

"Blessed be the name of Jesus," Elmer agreed. "God works in mysterious ways. And tonight he has sent into our midst Barbara Jeanne Bordelon's coach." The congregation gasped and spun about as if Elmer had employed the world's most multi-pronged cattle prod to suddenly goose them all. Elmer strode briskly to the rear of the church and said down at Mac who had turned the color of cooked beets, "Do you come to taunt us with your sin, Coach McIntire? Or, praise be to God, do you come to confess before us, to repent and then to join us?" He lowered the microphone toward Mac's lips.

"I came to ask you to leave Barbara Jeanne alone."

"Sin!" a parishioner called out.

"Desecration!" another cried.

"Bless the sinners," Elmer spoke into the microphone, "for they know not what they do."

"We know goddamn well what we're doing," Sheila said, standing up and pulling Mac and Edith to their feet as well. Elmer thrust the mike past Mac and toward her. "We're leaving this Godforsaken place before lightning reduces it to splinters."

"Tarry a moment with us, sister," Elmer said, blocking their exit out into the aisle. "And we will let Coach McIntire appeal to all the Soldiers for Jesus gathered here." He cocked the microphone toward Mac again.

And Mac, falling into Elmer's trap, spoke from his heart to the congregation about doing the right thing. "You are all Christians," he counseled. "Don't needlessly hurt people. Practice your faith and try to help someone."

As Elmer swung away to address the gathering himself, Mac and Sheila stepped into the aisle behind him, intending to leave until they heard him say: "Help someone, Coach McIntire, like you have helped your illegitimate son?"

In an extreme corner of the church, against an outside aisle, in a pew near the front, Helen Donalds rose and pointed hysterically at Mac. "He's the father of my child."

A sudden menace seized Mac with the ferocity of a steam shovel biting into the side of a building. His disgust at how Elmer had manipulated poor

Helen was more infuriating than the outrageousness of the charge itself. Mac turned back toward the congregation with the intention of snapping Elmer in two like he might a potato chip. But Sheila wisely stepped between them and screened Mac away from her wicked ex-husband like Bill Walton blocking out for a rebound.

"I have something to say," Sheila announced in a voice loud enough that it didn't need artificial enhancement.

"And what is that?" Elmer asked, extending the microphone toward her as she neatly glided this way and that, protecting him from her outraged son.

But as the mike loomed up toward her on the end of Elmer's extended right arm, she took a sharp step away from Mac's mammoth body and delivered an overhand right punch to Elmer's jaw that knocked him flat on the church's flecked terrazzo floor. She bent briefly over his prone body, and, before the stunned Soldiers for Jesus could stir from their pews, spoke into the microphone which Elmer still held clutched in his fist.

In a tone that rang through the church like the voice of God, Sheila said, "You're Out!" Then she slugged him again.

# CHAPTER FORTY

But Elmer wasn't out, of course. He was momentarily out of his senses, and he was arguably out of his mind. In dealing with the likes of Sheila, he was certainly out of his league. But he was by no means yet out of Mac's and Sheila's lives.

It is perhaps miraculous, then, that our three heroes escaped Elmer's Baptist church unharmed that night. For though the Soldiers for Jesus regarded themselves Christians, they were pretty much an eye-for-an-eye kind of people. They believed in right to life and capital punishment. They believed that vengeance belonged to the Lord. And they believed that they were the Lord's agents and thus should hasten His vengeance on anyone who disagreed with them. Since they considered forthrightly sinful the smiting of their leader, they lusted to lay hands of virtuous retribution on Mac and Edith and Sheila.

But even Elmer was right about some things. And he was certainly right that God works in mysterious ways. For as your narrator is obliged to report here and elsewhere, miracles do occur. And one occurred, if you'll indulge my statement of outright judgment, right there in that place of blasphemous worship. All of Elmer's parishioners were so astonished that he'd been cold cocked by a *woman* that they were slackjawed and frozen in their insidious pews long enough for Mac to snatch his mother up from Elmer's unconscious form and steer her, sputtering incendiary oaths, toward the sanctuary which lay not inside that seething church building but rather outside in the bracing air of the late winter's night.

The Soldiers for Jesus remained committed to a squaring of scores for some time afterwards, of course. But there was little doubt that this round and this bout had gone to Sheila.

In the aftermath of her outburst, Sheila was regretful. Her outrage at Elmer and all his parroty minions lessened not one whit. But she was wise enough in the ways of provocation to realize that her moment of impulsive violence could spawn responsive violence that might very quickly rage out of control. So she took the precaution to arrive at the Broussard games that weekend with a protective phalange of unwed mothers surrounding her at all times.

Marvelously, the games gave respite to Sheila's worry. The Soldiers for Jesus kept their sour distance. And the Bruins looked unbeatable. They played both nights with an intensity and confidence that represented everything Mac could hope to develop in a team. Best of all, in terms of the looming state playoffs, Barbara Jeanne suddenly snapped out of her slump. When Preston picked up three first-quarter fouls on Friday, Mac sent her in, and she played with distinction the rest of the half. She filled the lane on the fast break, avoided the floor mistakes that had been plaguing her for weeks, and shut her man down on defense. When Preston was whistled for his fourth foul in the first minute of the third quarter, B.J. went back on the court for what would turn into her longest floor time of the season. Granted, the Bonnabel team the Bruins dispatched that night were hardly a testing opponent, but B.J.'s ten points, three assists and two rebounds were a commendable effort no matter what the opposition. It was her best game all year. Only two missed free throws and a slip of the lip marred an otherwise perfect effort.

B.J. missed the free throws in the fourth quarter when she was tired and her concentration had lapsed a little, but the game was well in hand by that time and her missing them did no harm. The slip of the lip came at the game's end and seemed to spark nothing but laughs.

Relieved and pleased by her performance, Barbara Jeanne consented to chat with one of the sports reporters who had taken to following all of Broussard's games now. She answered questions about her defense and her shooting, about how she fit into Mac's overall strategy, about whether tonight's performance indicated she'd be seeing more floor time in upcoming games. She confided her frustration at the large number of free throws she'd missed this year and her seeming inability to translate good practice form into a regular rhythm under game conditions. Then, just as the interview was drawing to a close, three-year-old Laura Bordelon squirmed from the clutches of Marie and Henry who were watching their daughter's interview from the bleachers and went dashing across the floor calling out "B.J., B.J., B.J." and leapt into Barbara Jeanne's arms with a squeal.

The reporter warmly asked the little girl's identity and B.J. smiled and wiped at a smudge on the youngster's face and said, "This is my daughter, Laura."

"Your *daughter*?" the reporter said in understandable confusion.

"My *sister*," Barbara Jeanne said quickly, giggling nervously, hoping the blush she felt rush to her cheeks wouldn't be noticed in her still slightly perspiring condition from the game's exercise. "I have to babysit for her so much," B.J. added sucking in a sharp breath, "That I feel as much like a parent as an older sister. That's what I tell Mom and Dad all the time and whenever she's bad they say maybe I can just have her."

"I'm not bad," Laura said, flouncing her brown curls. Barbara Jeanne and the reporter both laughed, and the incident was presumably forgotten. And for a time it was. By everyone other than Judy Trascio who sat nearby while the interview took place and heard the whole thing. Long after B.J. had returned Laura to her parents and headed for the locker room to shower, long after the reporter had closed up his notebook and headed home, Judy Trascio continued to sit as if nailed to her seat in the bleachers. Alone in a darkened gym she sat, knitted her brows and chewed at her lower lip.

But whatever Judy may have made of Barbara Jeanne's strange statement, she kept her peace, and the next night saw B.J. duplicate her Bonnabel efforts against an even weaker squad from Walker. Preston stayed out of foul trouble, so Barbara Jeanne didn't log as many minutes on the court. But again she looked sharp, contributing hard-nosed defense, lung-blistering hustle, five points and two steals. The only blot on the whole weekend's developments, as far as Mac could detect, was Preston's sub-par play. Otherwise, as the season rushed toward its conclusion, the Bruins seemed to be matching the peak of their potential with performance.

Lady Luck, though, as I may have noted earlier, is notoriously fickle. And by the middle of the next week she was smiling once more upon the non-Bruins of this world. It was as if the games against Bonnabel and Walker were but lulls in an unspent storm.

Mac had recruited most of his senior ballplayers (other than Barbara Jeanne whose P.E. requirement necessitated that she take her home ec second hour) into his fourth-period cooking class. There, as was his characteristic wont, he emphasized the proper organization and preparation of traditional fare far more than he did specialty cuisine. But the students in his class had successfully pressured him for the opportunity to practice something exotic, "Something," they insisted, "that will seem fancy enough to be impressive if we ever cook for somebody other than ourselves."

So Mac had designed a project on the preparation of a labor-intensive Cajun delicacy called crawfish bisque. Monday after the Bonnabel and Walker games was devoted to boiling the famous Louisiana "mudbugs" and the subsequent tedious process of peeling the tails. Tuesday was spent cleaning and preparing the heads. On Wednesday the class ground the peeled tails up with breadcrumbs, onions and celery and various seasonings, sauteed the lot in butter and then stuffed the spicy crawfish paste back into the cleaned heads. On Thursday the class simmered the stuffed heads in a rich brown gravy and served it to themselves over white rice. And on Thursday afternoon, Mac had to reorganize his practice because so many of his team members had come down with food poisoning.

What went wrong no one was ever able to determine. The best guess was that the crawfish were tainted with pesticide before ever arriving at Broussard. But other possibilities, of course, abounded. The food could have spoiled during its period of refrigeration. Or the giant pot in which it was cooked could have been poorly cleaned or perhaps improperly rinsed of detergent at some prior time. Sheila, predictably, had other ideas.

"Elmer," she stated that Thursday night over dinner at the Terminal.

"What?" Mac said.

"Sabotage," Sheila averred. "The Soldiers for Jesus are really the Saboteurs for Jerboa." Sheila nodded at Mac and Edith sagely over her post-meal cup of coffee. "Small rodents who spoil your food and make you sick to your stomach. I think we should make inquiries about renting a food taster."

Mac rolled his eyes, and Edith shook her head, and Sheila told them both to commit sexual acts with luxury automobiles. They never really pursued the food taster gambit, of course, and the incident of food poisoning never recurred. But Sheila never wavered in her conviction that Elmer's henchman had somehow managed to contaminate Mac's crawfish bisque. And nothing ever came to light to prove her wrong.

Whatever the cause of the digestive distress which flattened the Bruins that Thursday night, its immediate results were painfully apparent. The only good news imaginable was that Broussard was scheduled to play only one game that weekend. The double-barrelled bad news was that the game was against the tough Easton Eagles and that it was scheduled for Friday. On Friday Don Start, Whitt McSeveney, Danny Waddell and Painton Richard were all still so sick that there was no question about their playing. Gary Cashner was in slightly better shape, thank God, due to the fact that, a dedicated weight watcher, he'd restricted his ingestion of the bisque to a few sample tastes.

Thus when the Bruins took the floor at Easton's Canal Street gym, Mac had to resort to a line-up that had never even practiced together as a unit heretofore. Gary was determined to play even though Mac could tell from his chalky complexion that he was shaky. With Don out, Mac had no choice but to start Gary in the pivot. Lyndon Schock had been absent the day the class had "dined on death" as Sheila put it, and so was healthy but had to play out of position at forward. Mac had to shift Preston Whisenhunt, who was a junior and therefore not in the senior home ec class, from guard to forward too. Preston's spot at wing guard was filled by another junior, diminutive Cooke Malmgren.

And Barbara Jeanne, of course, filled in for Danny at the point. Plucky, brave Barbara Jeanne who on that night of her first starting assignment, hardly buoyed by her maniacal supporters from the Feminist Organization of Louisiana, had to put up with the insane jeers of the relentless Soldiers for Jesus. As the game announcer called her name and she joined her fellow starters for the ritual handclasp at mid-court, the Soldiers for Jesus followed their obligatory boos with such homiletic taunts as "A woman's place is in the home, not the gym."

It was thus a short and understandably nervous squad of Bruins who faced Easton that night. Broussard had turned the Eagles back in a tight contest earlier in the year when the Easton coach had driven Barbara Jeanne back to the bench by repeatedly posting her low. Mac suspected from the outset that he was in for a long evening. And he was right, even though he put his team in a 2-1-2 zone to diminish Easton's distinct height advantage. The Eagles jumped to an early 6-0 lead and despite typically dogged play by Gary Cashner stretched their edge to ten points by half-time.

In the second half, Mac countered with his zone press which gradually paid dividends. Early on Broussard gave up some cheap baskets. But even with three second teamers in the game, the press began to take its toll on an Easton squad longer on muscle than finesse. The hustling Bruins cut the margin back to three by the middle of the fourth quarter. Late in the game, with Easton ahead 64-61 Barbara Jeanne, still in a brutal slump at the free-throw line, missed the front end of a one-and-one. But with twenty seconds left, Gary Cashner rammed home one of his line-drive jumpers to cut it to one. As Mac had come to understand with a fierce certainty, where there was Gary Cashner, there was a way.

Easton called time out, doubtless to put in some kind of delay game in hopes of running out the remaining time. Mac responded by ordering his players to foul immediately on the in-bounds pass. But Barbara Jeanne went her coach one better. Intending to follow directions she knifed in front of the Eagle player she was guarding, but instead of grabbing his arm, snatched away the pass which was headed toward him and then whirled instantly into a pounding drive toward the game-winning basket.

And dribbled the ball off her foot.

A look of profound despair spread across B.J.'s face like the shadow of a solar eclipse. Even in the time-out huddle Mac called to try to rally his troops once more, B.J. stood with her head hung. She was not alone, though. Of her teammates around her, only Gary Cashner would meet Mac's gaze as the coach gathered them together for a final set of instructions. Along with Barbara Jeanne the other emotionally and physically drained Bruins wore the cowed faces of whipped dogs. Mac couldn't stand it. Like any coach who thrives on his work, he believed beyond rationality in his team's ability to pull games out of the fire. He spoke to them sharply in hopes of kindling their wills to match Gary's and his own. He balled his fists in the fronts of their soaking jerseys and screamed his instructions into their faces above the din of the crowd. He reached out with that mammoth, precipitous paw of his toward Barbara Jeanne's face to pull her wilted gaze to his. And he jarred her with all the passion of his love for the game of basketball when he bellowed "Goddamn it, B.J. you didn't lose this game. It's not even lost yet. There are fifteen seconds left, and I still want an immediate foul on the in-bounds pass. Now you do it."

Barbara Jeanne went back on the floor with pursed lips and gritted teeth. And attempting the needed steal, she committed the required foul.

But when the Eagle shooter canned both ends, the gamble failed. Gary's jumper at the other end shaved the margin again to a single point. But time expired before they could get the ball back another time. In the only game Barbara Jeanne Bordelon would ever start for the Broussard varsity, the Bruins had fallen to 25-2.

# CHAPTER FORTY-ONE

You'd have thought the world had ended. Voices were raised against Mac and his Bruins from every quarter.

The sports editor of the *States-Tribune*, for instance, wondered in his column on the Monday morning after Broussard's defeat by Easton ". . . whether the Bruins, as we've been led to believe, really represent all that great a threat in this year's state high school basketball tournament. Their defeat last Friday raises serious questions about both the strength of Broussard's bench and about Coach Mac McIntire's continuing commitment to extensive floor time for Barbara Jeanne Bordelon, the nation's only varsity female."

Later in his article, the columnist wrote, "Furthermore, McIntire's whole career to this point has been marked by a series of coaching gaffes. There's no doubt that he's fashioned a fine won-lost record. But that's perhaps due to the luck of superior material. At any rate, it's already arguable that he can't win the big one."

The sports editor also contended that "In the last twelve months McIntire was outcoached by Oakdale's Joanna Knudsen when his Lady Bruin squad made a quick exit in its maiden appearance in the state girls' championship. Then his overuse of Miss Bordelon likely cost Broussard a defeat at the hands of Jesuit in the Crescent City Christmas Classic. Easton's Rick Franson has bested McIntire twice. Hampered only by inferior material, Leake almost pulled an upset with some sharp matchups (again involving Miss Bordelon) earlier this season, and last Friday his eagles thumped a group of Bruins clearly searching for leadership at this late stage of the season. Leake victimized McIntire's devoted deployment of the weaker sex when his Eagles forced crucial mistakes from Miss Bordelon at gut-check time."

The sports editor concluded Monday's column with this observation: "Most important, perhaps, Broussard's loss at Easton raises grave questions about McIntire as a floor strategist. As the Bruins were falling almost out of the ball game in the first half, where was the press that almost saved them in second?"

Nowhere in his column did the sports editor mention that Broussard played Easton without three of its starters. Nowhere did he mention that despite a couple of critical mistakes at the end Barbara Jeanne had acquitted herself quite well against Easton, contributing nine points and leading her team in both assists and steals.

"Why doesn't that son of a bitch write the whole truth," Edith asked no one in particular as she and Mac and Sheila sat glum-faced over the ashes of a Monday morning breakfast at the Terminal.

"That bastard doesn't write at all," Sheila observed as Edith and Mac girded themselves for the anticipated onslaught of coarseness. "He just wipes his ass on a typewriter once a day."

"Thank you for that little metaphor, Mom," Mac said without breaking a smile.

"Things go better with gross," Edith said, allowing her mouth to crinkle just a fraction at the corners. When Mac's funk refused to crack even in the slightest, she urged him, "Come on Mac. Things could be worse."

Mac shook his head. He looked sour-faced at Edith and said, "Yeah Counsellor, just how could they be worse?"

"You could have to live your whole controversial misunderstood life without me and Edith to cheer you up," Sheila said. She stuck out her long arms across the table toward her two loved ones and took their hands into hers.

Mac was so touched by his mother's uncharacteristic gesture of sentiment that he felt ashamed of having let something so insignificant as a basketball game cause him such heartache. "Y'all are right," he said. "I'm sorry." He reached and took Edith's free hand in his and completed their triangle of joined arms and interlaced fingers. "I don't know what I'd do without y'all."

"I know you don't, honey," Sheila said, freeing herself from her son's grasp and rubbing maternally on his wrist and forearm, "so just remember it, OK. Edith and I will always be here. As long as you don't fuck up anymore."

That wrenched the desired laughter from Mac's recalcitrant depression, and he made his way to school that morning in better spirits.

And things got worse anyway.

At school, Arnold Larrett wanted a meeting with Mac about his alleged carelessness in the previous week's food poisoning incident. Larrett didn't *really* believe that Mac was culpable in any way. He was just, as I'm sure you've long since concluded, one of those butt-headed administrators who constantly had to make things difficult for his subordinates for no other reason than the affirmation of his authority. To bastardize Descartes, Arnold Larrett's strategy for self-ascertainment, like that of a lot of self-important journalists, ran: "I kink; therefore I am." So on the Monday after the home ec food poisoning episode, he presented Mac a hand-written reprimand long enough to thoroughly convince himself anew that he really was the vice-principal whereas upstart Mac McIntire was just a teacher and coach.

And when the tempest in that particular teapot had blown itself into oblivion, things got worse still.

As if the Arnold Larretts of this world needed any more weapons in their anti-Mac arsenal, Stephanie Williams showed up at school late in the day with a F.O.o.L. petition bearing 500 signatures calling for Mac's dismissal on the grounds of psychological and physical abuse of his basketball players. The document to which all these names were affixed read:

> Last Friday night in the Warren Easton High School gym at a varsity basketball game contested between Easton and Broussard High Schools, Broussard head coach Marshall McCall McIntire was guilty of conduct demeaning to the school he serves and the pupils for whom he is responsible. Coach McIntire was observed repeatedly to raise his voice to the members of his team and to intimidate them with coarse language. Worse, he was witnessed laying rough hands upon several of his players. Easily worst of all, he was seen to have struck in the face his lone female squad member, Miss Barbara Jeanne Bordelon. Mr. McIntire's sway over Miss Bordelon approaches the level of brainwashing. So we fully expect her to support Mr. McIntire's predictable denials and excuses. Regardless of whatever statements Miss Bordelon may choose to make, the undersigned call for an immediate suspension of Mr. McIntire's coaching duties pending a thorough investigation of these charges by Broussard principal Samuel Riggs and appropriate authorities of the Orleans Parish School Board.

Thank God Sam Riggs had seen enough of the members of the Feminist Organization of Louisiana by now to have concluded that they were raving lunatics. He was guilty of generalization, of course. The members of F.O.o.L were, for the most part, bright, energetic women, understandably frustrated by a sexist society that thwarted their ambitions and talents at every turn. They were hopelessly twisted in their assessment of Mac McIntire, though. And in their determination to do him harm they frequently behaved like raving lunatics, which gave plenty of weight to Sam Riggs' assessment.

Let me not overpraise distinguished-looking old Sam, however. I naturally applaud his developing support for Mac. I readily defend the accuracy of his memory and his judgment that Mac cared deeply for the welfare of his players. I further affirm his presence in the stands at the Easton game and his certainty that Mac had most definitely not slapped Barbara Jeanne's face. But I would be sloth in my duties as a narrator not to make clear that the thought of removing Mac from his team right now gave Sam Riggs heart palpitations. Broussard had never been a state basketball power before, and Riggs liked the prospect of being principal at a school that was a power in anything. He didn't know enough about basketball to be sure that Mac was the best possible coach for his school. But he was easily savvy enough to know that the team's considerable post-season hopes this year would go right up in smoke if Mac should be removed.

In other words, thank God Arnold Larrett wasn't principal at Broussard. For whereas Riggs took seriously that he looked like Robert E. Lee and therefore just presumed the rectitude of his authority, Larrett was a petty tyrant too obsessed with his need to intimidate his underlings to give a shit about how he might appear to the outside world. Had Larrett been principal, Mac would have been relegated to being merely the largest home ec teacher in New Orleans. Larrett resented everything he knew about Mac. Mac was kind and gentle and sensitive and popular with students and co-workers. He was hardworking and honest. He was as big as a bear and as strong as an ox. In short, he was totally intolerable. But Arnold Larrett wasn't principal, so he couldn't do a blasted thing about it.

The Orleans Parish School Board might have been able to do something about it. They were damned sick and tired of all the negative publicity that Mac was attracting. But coincidentally, the Board was hardly anxious to do anything that might bring the court system back down on them again in what they too had taken to calling the Barbara Jeanne Bordelon Affair. So they bided their time.

Frustrated, Stephanie Williams took her case to the public. And, always on the lookout for a juicy story, the *States-Tribune* printed the text of her demented petition in its Wednesday editions.

So things got worse yet.

Oddly invigorated by the renewed opposition of the Feminist Organization of Louisiana, Elmer Kanter invited representatives of the local media to attend the debut of his "Old Time Wednesday Hour of Prayer" where he told fundamentalist videophiles across the nation that it was time "for God's anointed to join with groups of whatever persuasion and orientation who share our concerns and who will march with us, the Soldiers for Jesus, into holy combat."

Elmer stared directly into the camera, which was also providing a taped feed to the three local TV stations for use on their ten o'clock news shows. He was moist of brow with the ecstasy of moral self-righteousness as he announced that, "Here in our hometown of New Orleans, we've long been fighting a serious case of Biblically condemned sinfulness. Many of you across our great land know of New Orleans and its reputation for infamy along the slime-infested sidewalks of Bourbon Street. But many of you might not yet know that iniquity has spread to our schools. We join all of you in our national quest to bring God back to the schoolhouse in the form of daily prayer. And we pray for support from all of you in our sanctified determination to make our schools once again places where little boys grow up in the images of their fathers and little girls in the images of their mothers."

Elmer then went on and filled in the country's ignorant masses on the details of the Barbara Jeanne Bordelon Affair, begging them to send him large quantities of money to help him get Barbara Jeanne out of her boys' basketball uniform and back into dresses and thereafter proper sexual subordination. Then, as he was wrapping up, Elmer returned to the radical point of his message: "To facilitate our victory over Satan in this current battle, the Soldiers for Jesus stand ready to embrace any and all who will march with us. Our city has a group of young women calling themselves the Feminist Organization of Louisiana. We know little about them." Elmer brandished at his camera a clipping from that day's *States Tribune* which recounted F.O.o.L.'s most recent sortie that contained the text of its most recent petition. "But in today's paper they make clear that on the issue of Barbara Jeanne Bordelon and her demonic coach, they stand with us. And so we say unto them, come forth, be with us, join hands. On other days, on other issues we may choose opposing sides, but for today let us unite. For in unity victory will be ours."

Mac shook his head at it all when he and Edith and Sheila learned of these latest developments while watching the ten o'clock news that night. He felt thoroughly exhausted by it all. "They've finally found the strategy for getting us, I think," he confided in a despairing tone. "I've been victimized by the double team all my life, it seems. And I haven't yet figured out how to beat it."

Edith moved from a wing-back chair to sit on the living room sofa where Mac was sprawled in dejection. She put her arm around her friend to comfort him. Across the room Sheila seemed to be staring into space. She had been quilting as she watched TV with her loved ones and now sat with a piece of material tented over her left hand and a threaded needle poised aloft in her right. After a long moment in this pensive attitude, she looked at Mac and Edith, plunged the needle down into the quilt and announced:

> Without proof no one would believe us
>
> That F.O.o.L. and the Soldiers for Jesus
>
> Have joined their forces,
>
> Ignored their divorces
>
> In hopes they can rend us to pieces.
>
> In the age of the Second World War,
>
> An occurrence almost as bizarre
>
> Wed Stalin to Hitler
>
> Lake Batman to Riddler
>
> And reduced hapless Poland to char.
>
> That earlier non-aggression pact
>
> Holds lessons for this one, in fact.
>
> For Deutschland turned Eastward
>
> And Russia lend-leaseward,
>
> And cities in either got sacked.
>
> So get this you unholy alliance.
>
> Look elsewhere for submissive clients.
>
> The one that survives
>
> Won't mess with our lives'
>
> Fearsome existential defiance.

Mac and Edith were stunned. "Mom," Mac pointed out, "you're losing your touch. There wasn't a thing in that quadruple limerick that made me want to gag."

> "Sometimes my verse makes you shudder," Sheila said.
>
> "At best my rhymes make you mutter.
>
> But when they resume,

You shouldn't presume

That my mind's always in the gutter."

"Now I'm gonna gag," Mac said, laughing.

Edith rubbed her hand affectionately on his broad thigh, "You're a lucky fella, Mac McIntire, you know, to get to have Sheila for a mom."

"Hmph," Sheila observed. "He's a lucky fella to have me for a dad."

But despite the Terminal's warm and nurturing familial camaraderie, things got worse still.

That very night under the cover of an overcast winter sky, camouflaged by the rustle of the wind along the levee, by the fog horns of boats on the river, by the clanging bells of passing streetcars, vandals stole upon the opposing sides of Mac McIntire's home and left him twin messages. Whether the messages were left by a single group working in concert or by separate groups ignorant even of one another's presence was never determined. It was presumably the angriest members of F.O.o.L. who attacked the left wall of the Terminal and defaced its light blue paint with smashed eggs and a spray-painted message that looked like this:

And it was presumably the Soldiers for Jesus who assaulted the right-side wall with a blow-torched cross and the following quotation from Revelation 15:8:

Power Was Given Unto Him to Scorch Men With Fire

In the days that followed, as a result of these attacks, Sheila and Edith insisted on an immediate increase in security. And the very next day at the unwed mothers' home, Sheila recruited and organized a contingent of residents who undertook a twenty-four-hour surveillance of the Terminal beginning that same night. But the graffiti's threat, of course, announced on the walls of his home, was aimed at Mac's person. And so to provide him what protection they could, four unwed mothers began to accompany him whenever he ventured into any public place. Like some Arabian prince or ancient Mormon, Mac seemed to trail pregnant women in the wake of his every step.

But the defacing of the Terminal was not the worst event in our heroes' recent streak of bad luck. The worst was Barbara Jeanne Bordelon's confrontation with *States-Tribune* reporter Cindy Hiller Thursday night after basketball practice.

Devoted to a principle that fresh legs make better ballplayers, Mac habitually kept Thursday sessions light when his team had to play on Friday, as was true this week. And so most of the Bruins had already showered and left for home by the time the reporter arrived at the Broussard gym. Mac was in his office going over statistics and scouting notes on their weekend's opponents. Only Gary Cashner and Barbara Jeanne were still on the floor. Gary had already completed his obsessive weight-battling post-practice routine of 200 sit-ups and was rebounding shots for B.J. who was practicing free thows in a determined effort to break out of her slump at the foul line.

Hiller walked in just about the time Barbara Jeanne canned her tenth shot in a row. As you may remember from Barbara Jeanne's junior season in high school, Cindy Hiller was not a member of the *States-Tribune* sports department. She was a news reporter and feature writer, and she was currently working on a story of "grave local and national concern." Whether Barbara Jeanne was relevant to her story or not, Ms. Hiller did not know. But in all the whirlwind of B.J.'s notoriety, Hiller had heard certain rumors, and as a good reporter, she felt bound to check them out. So she marched into the gym, politely asked permission for a brief interview and when it was granted inquired if it was true that, like a frightening minority of her age group, Barbara Jeanne Bordelon was an unwed mother.

# CHAPTER FORTY-TWO

Barbara Jeanne Bordelon had stood up with consistent courage and determination to a lot of hardship in her short life, but Cindy Hiller's question had finally probed B.J.'s most vulnerable spot. And like a boulder that has withstood repeated smashing by a sledge hammer, she suddenly cracked when Hiller pounded her from just the right angle. Bouncing the ball absently against the floor, Barbara Jeanne looked at the reporter, then, without offering an answer to Hiller's question, shifted her gaze to Gary who recognized her distress without fully understanding it. Her lip trembled, and he took an instinctive, protective step toward her. All at once her handsome, freckled face exploded into a mask of tears and she went running from the gym into the girls' locker room.

As Gary watched B.J. dash from the basketball court, he shook his head in profound dismay. When the doors of the locker room swung closed behind her, he turned back toward Cindy Hiller and moved toward her with a gait of unmistakable menace. The lazer intensity of his wide-eyed gaze would have melted concrete. Hiller retreated before him. "Why don't y'all leave her alone?" he demanded.

"I just asked a question," Hiller pleaded. "It's my job."

"Yeah?" Gary said, still closing in on her as she back-pedaled. "Well, I'm tired of what's going on here. I'm tired of what it's doing to our team, and I'm real tired of what it's doing to B.J. So from now on, I think I'm gonna make it my job to kick the shit out of anybody who thinks it's their job to pick on her."

"Stay away from me," Cindy Hiller ordered as the two of them continued their stiff tango across the Broussard gym. "You, you wouldn't hit a woman."

Gary bore steadily down upon her as she backed toward the exterior doors. "I look at you," he said. "I don't see your sex. I see a first-class louse. And I'd sure like to crush all the lice in Cake's life." He extended his long arms slowly toward her. "Just like that," he said, snapping his fingers in her face.

Hiller hit the crash bar to the gym foyer with the small of her back and even though her momentum forced the door open a crack, she stopped and cowered as if trapped. Gary moved up so close to her she could feel his body heat. He stooped down so that his face was thrust into hers. A drop of sweat dripped off his forehead onto her cheek. She thought he was going to spit on her or maybe even bite her. But instead, in a hoarse whisper he merely said, "Get out of my school." And then he smashed the door open so that she stumbled into the hall before she regained her balance and fled.

Gary went back to the doors of the girls' locker room and called out to ask Barbara Jeanne if she was OK. When he got no answer he summoned Mac and reported the entire incident to him. Mac told Gary to get his shower before he contracted a chill and walked immediately to the girls' dressing area. B.J. didn't answer when Mac called out to her either. He stuck his head inside and called again, and she still didn't answer.

Panic flashed through Mac's insides as if a mortar shell had ripped through his chest. She'd done something awful to herself, slashed the veins in her wrists or wrapped a cord around her throat. Mac burst into the girls' locker room like a thoroughbred escaping from the starting gate at the Kentucky Derby.

But no, thank God, distraught and tempted by resignation though she was, Barbara Jeanne had not done herself harm. She'd retreated to the locker room and pulled herself together long enough to strip out of her practice uniform. But before she made it to the shower, she'd surrendered to a wave of distress. Mac found her slumped on the blond wooden bench in front of her locker, her forehead wedged into supporting palms, her chin down on her naked chest, her breasts wet with tears of fatigued despair.

"Jesus, B.J.," he said. "Why didn't you answer me?" He was out of breath with anxiety. "I thought something terrible must have happened."

Barbara Jeanne turned her red-streaked face toward him. "Coach," she said. "I'm so tired."

Mac moved to sit beside her. He put his arm around her and pulled her head against his chest. And they sat a while together before she began to cry again. And when he shifted his hand from its grip on her shoulder to caress her sobbing face, she spun against him, buried her face in his shirt front, squeezed both of her arms around his waist. And that's the way Gary Cashner discovered them when he entered the girls' locker room to check on them.

Mac turned when he heard Gary's footsteps. Their eyes met and Mac made the situation clear without moving the first muscle in his face. He petted his hand through Barbara Jeanne's damp brown hair. Gary nodded his head slightly and silently made his way back to the gym. It never occurred to him for a fleeting instant that there was anything improper about Mac's holding a naked Barbara Jeanne in his arms.

Mac and Barbara Jeanne sat that way for a long time that Thursday night and gradually, when B.J. was ready, they began to talk. The problem was less the threat that B.J.'s unwed motherhood might be made public than the way in which the threat forced Barbara Jeanne to confront her growing unease at having to deny that for which she was not responsible. She didn't choose to bear a rapist's child before her fifteenth birthday. But she had, and she was exhausted now from the pretense that she hadn't. And so, holding on to each other in a bond that transcended anything corporeal, Mac and Barbara Jeanne decided that the benefits of deceit were no longer worth the emotional strain. Barbara Jeanne *was* Laura Bordelon's mother, and she wanted to embrace that fact in every meaningful way. If Cindy Hiller wanted to make the relationship public in her *States-Tribune* article, then so be it.

Ironically, across town that night, Cindy Hiller jettisoned any plans to print such allegations. For despite occasional pushiness, Ms. Hiller was too good a journalist to print rumors substantiated only by an anonymous source. Now perhaps you're suspicious that Ms. Hiller was motivated more by a fear of lawsuit than by journalistic ethics. Or perhaps you wonder if Gary Cashner succeeded in scaring her away from B.J.'s story. Well, I can assure you, Gary's dramatically demonstrated annoyance did have an impact. But he didn't scare her off the story. Once she realized that he never intended to harm her, Hiller grasped how special Barbara Jeanne's relationship with her teammates must be. And thus Barbara Jeanne stopped being just a "story" for Cindy Hiller and became for the first time a person. For the rest of her life Hiller regarded this abrupt awakening the blinding light on her personal road to Damascus. The event changed her career; it made her a different and better person. Up until that point in her young career she'd been a writer hustling to forge a name for herself. Henceforth she became a writer far more sensitive to her subject and the overall best interests of her readers.

So Cindy Hiller would never have published the details of Barbara Jeanne Bordelon's unwed motherhood had not B.J., accompanied by Edith Jenkins, approached her at the *States-Tribune* office the very next afternoon and asked her to.

The decision Mac and B.J. had reached in the dankness of the Broussard girls' locker room the night before was to say aloud what had heretofore been whispered, to surrender the flimsy armor of denial and cling to the stronger shield of truth. Cindy Hiller was so moved by B.J.'s story that she decided to hold it back from the broader piece she was working on immediately and make the story a separate feature the following week.

Leaving the newspaper offices after the conversation with Hiller, B.J. confided to Edith that she felt better than she had in a year. The weight that had been lifted from her was spiritual, of course, but to Barbara Jeanne it seemed physical as well. She felt lighter and quicker, stronger and sharper; she felt reborn. The emotional exhaustion she had experienced the evening before had evanesced, and she was ready to take on the world. And she started to do so that very Friday night in Broussard's game against Chalmette, the first of only three games remaining on the Bruins' regular season schedule.

Mac had only scant opportunity to talk with B.J. after her meeting with Cindy Hiller. But he could sense she had a special intensity during warmups. She seemed to move with a zip he hadn't seen for a very long time. She seemed to be getting up higher on her jumper. And she punctuated every made basket with a clenched fist.

Barbara Jeanne couldn't have experienced her rejuvenation at a better time. Chalmette's Owls were among the toughest foes Broussard had to face all year. They were 21-5 with two of the losses at the hands of Jesuit and the other a narrow defeat by the Bruins before Christmas. To make matters worse, aside from an electric Barbara Jeanne, and solid-as-always Gary Cashner, the rest of the Bruins seemed sluggish, not fully recovered from last week's bout of food poisoning. Worst of all, Preston Whisenhunt had lapsed even deeper into the slump that had been plaguing him the last several games.

After moving out to an early 4-0 lead, Broussard suddenly found itself trailing 16-6 after Preston threw a bad pass that Chalmette turned in to a lay-up, missed a wide-open shot and then followed with a silly foul of frustration. Mac called time-out and replaced Preston with Barbara Jeanne. And B.J. proceeded to light up the Chalmette gym as if she were a human Roman candle.

Mac had watched Barbara Jeanne put on some amazing displays of basketball fundamentals in his nearly three-year association with her. But he had never seen her play like this before. It was as if she were back on the Lady Bruins again, firing that flawless, behind-the-head jumper from the protection of Olga Jorgensen's earthquake screens. Only these weren't spottily coached women she was playing against. These were the 21-5 Chalmette Owls. But it didn't matter because Barbara Jeanne Bordelon was somewhere outside that school gymnasium in suburban St. Bernard Parish. She was in a territory athletes know as the zone, the zone where talent marries will to self-confidence and a player can do no wrong. For a basketball player the zone is the perfect rhythm, the certain feeling, the blessed surety that every shot is going in. Everything B.J. put up that night drew nothing but net, and she knew it every time from the second the spinning ball left her outstretched finger tips.

Indeed the game came to B.J. just as if she was playing again for the Lady Bruins. Only the picks were set by Gary Cashner, and the opponents she humiliated were male instead of female. With B.J. bombing holes in the Chalmette defense from the outside, or wrapping tricky bounce passes into Gary whenever the Owls tried to jump switch on her, the Bruins turned a tight first-quarter game into a rout. Barbara Jeanne finished the night eight of nine from the field, three of four from the line, with nineteen points, her career high as a varsity player. And the Broussard fans at the game saluted her with a standing ovation when Mac took her out in the fourth quarter, the crowd joining her teammates in a frenzied, astonished chant of "Cake, Cake, Cake."

# CHAPTER FORTY-THREE

That night at the Terminal, with the joyous echoes of "Cake, Cake Cake," still ringing in all their ears, Mac and Edith and Sheila replayed Barbara Jeanne's marvelous performance and the Bruins' surprisingly easy victory over Chalmette. First around the kitchen table over their celebratory pizza and beer, and afterwards, as was their custom, slouched onto shifting thirds of Sheila's king-sized bed, they recounted for each other, late into the night, every shot and rebound, every intercepted pass, assist and instance of good defense, every seized opportunity and every missed one too.

Mac had simply never been more satisfied, more confident in his choice of professions. He still didn't know everything there was to know about coaching, he realized—there were still coaching strategies to master, still mentors to study and emulate—but at the very least, B.J.'s play that night was a vindication of his judgment of her talent, an affirmation of his decision to include her as a member of his team.

Mac was so wound up in the thrill of victory, in fact, that after Sheila had finally kicked them out of her bed, he insisted that he and Edith share one last beer. And then, as if sweet triumph were not elixir enough, Edith propositioned him.

Mac's grin was as wide as a Wyoming sky. He leaned across the kitchen table where they had adjourned when Sheila went to sleep and laid his hand on his friend's wrist and rubbed with his fingertips at her forearm. "Has it occurred to you yet that you've had too much to drink," he said. "Or could I get you a quick shot of whiskey before you sober up?"

"Maybe I'm just drunk with the sight of you," she said, lifting her hand and placing it on top of his.

"Now I know you're drunk," Mac smiled. "No one could conceivably talk to me like that while in possession of her senses."

Edith moved her hand from Mac's to the can of Dixie which sat between them. "Oh, I'm in my very rightest senses," she said.

"I see," Mac bantered. "In deciding on the glories of having sex with me, you've finally *come* to your senses."

"Something like that," Edith said, licking her tongue slowly around her lips in exaggerated seductiveness. "You see, I've been thinking. You seem to have had such an amazing impact on Barbara Jeanne last night, I figured that maybe if I'd get naked and let you hug me a lot between now and my final exams that I'd get hired as a clerk for the Supreme Court."

Mac pursed his lips to hide a flicker of embarrassment. He'd thought Edith really wanted to make love. Because of her frequently expressed determination to avoid "getting serious" until sometime after she'd gotten established in her law career, Mac would never proposition her, but he was always available, as she well knew. Mac stashed his disappointment inside a riposte: "If it's a Supreme Court clerkship you're after, you're best advised to focus your naked hugging on a Supreme Court judge."

She raised and finger to his lips and said, "Ssshhh." She picked up the beer can and drained it in one long swallow. Then she stood, dragged Mac to his feet and led him by the hand upstairs to his bedroom. There she shrugged off her robe and the thin cotton pajama top that she slept in and stood in all her wonderful blond nakedness before him. Mac was aroused instantly. But the gesture with which he quickly clothed her in his arms was almost paternal.

In the special, tender lovemaking that followed, Edith would brook no conversation, blunting even Mac's whispered endearments with an insistent, "Ssshhh." And in the midst she made a point of pausing a moment to switch on the beside lamp. Afterwards, as they lay twined in each other's arms, Mac asked her why she'd done so.

"I just wanted to make sure you didn't forget it was me," Edith said, her eyes away from him.

Mac laughed. "You must still be drunk."

"No," she contended, "but I think maybe you are." Mac snorted at that notion, but Edith continued, "I think maybe you're drunk with the memory of mesmerizing Miss Barbara Jeanne Bordelon, salty with sweat and sticky with tears and naked in your protective embrace."

"What does all that mean?" Mac said, trying to twist himself around so that he could see Edith's face.

But she kept her eyes diverted and replied, "It means I'm bringing up this whole business of your sitting around for two hours last night all folded about B.J.'s supple and notably unclothed body."

Mac sat up now and cupped Edith's face in his hands so that she had to look at him. "You understand that none of what happened was in the vaguest way sexual."

"Of course I do," Edith said. "But do you think that would matter a rat's ass to Arnold Larrett if he found out? He'd move heaven and earth to fire you anyway."

Mac shrugged with more apparent nonchalance than he felt. "It was the right thing to have done. I've never seen her so upset. I'd have sent Joan in, of course, but she'd already gone home."

"I know you would have, Mac, but . . ."

"But what?"

"But you must be aware that B.J. is in love with you."

Mac's hands dropped away from Edith's cheeks as if pulled down by an anchor. He collapsed back into a prone position with a sigh. He guessed he did know that Barbara Jeanne was in love with him. But it was such an insensible notion. He felt embarrassed that Edith would force the whole issue out into the open.

Edith sat up now to face him. "And you know what's more, Mac McIntire? I think you're in love with her too."

Mac looked up at Edith with desperate eyes. This was something he had not admitted to himself, something he felt would be shameful to acknowledge. But forced to now, he guessed it was true. He felt nothing for Barbara Jeanne Bordelon that he didn't feel for Edith Jenkins but for both of them he felt a depth of concern and obligation that was heightened by a tenderness so powerful he sometimes thought it would reduce him to tears. And all these feelings were mixed up by a sexual attraction for both. "I'm not sure I even know what love is," Mac said, reaching out to stroke his hand through Edith's hair.

"Oh yes you do," Edith said, her green eyes shining. "You know better than most people on this earth."

Mac smiled and rolled his eyes. "Let's see, as best I can remember, paging mentally through the Gospel According to Sheila: 'Love sucks.'"

Edith laughed and laid her hand on his chest where a tuft of hair sprouted from the taut skin over his breast bone. "You know better than that because you grew up in a home with more love than most people would experience in five lifetimes. That's why you know that love doesn't have anything to do with sex, and that sex has very little to do with love. And that's why you could sit with a strong beautiful young girl like Barbara Jeanne in your arms for hours and probably not even get aroused."

"But I did get aroused," Mac admitted.

Now Edith laughed loudly. "You bastard," she said. "You've probably got a boner right now just remembering her firm tits and sleek muscular bottom."

"You're half right," Mac said.

"Half right?"

"I do have a boner. But it's not Barbara Jeanne's firm tits and sleek muscular bottom I'm remembering."

Edith slipped her hands down his chest and under the sheet which covered him to the waist. She smiled and clucked her tongue as she touched him. "Whatever you say, I know my duty in this situation and I'm equal to it. In a better world you could have both me and Barbara Jeanne if that's what you wanted and that's what we wanted. But now you have to think of your job and your team and B.J.'s age and vulnerable reputation. And I," she paused to smile at him, "and I have to think of you and help you concentrate on thinking of me." Her hand at work, Edith laid her head on Mac's chest and kissed his nipples.

Mac stroked her hair again and bent his neck to kiss her on the top of her head. "So what's all this Edith's duty business mean?" he asked.

She kissed the softer flesh of his chest just below his sternum and then his navel, and then twisting herself completely over him said, "It means practicing and practicing, over and over again, and then some more if necessary, until fatigue works its wonders on libido."

"Practicing?" he said, nibbling at her thigh. "Practicing what?"

"Practicing," she giggled against him, "The Gospel According to Sheila."

# CHAPTER FORTY-FOUR

When Barbara Jeanne followed her nineteen-point effort against Chalmette with a fifteen-point performance the next night in the Bruins' victory over East Jefferson, Mac was ready to promote her to a starting position. He could always counter any attempts to take advantage of her lack of height by shifting to a zone defense. At the moment she was playing substantially better than slumping Preston Whisenhunt. Against East Jeff, Preston played so badly that he missed a breakaway layup and even threw a pass directly to an opposing player.

But wiser heads prevailed against the strategy of inserting B.J. into the starting line-up. Superstitious Sheila opposed it on the grounds that what was working ought not be tampered with. Edith argued the same point in a slightly more sophisticated way, maintaining that the team had achieved a certain rhythm that involved its expectations about the starting line-up. With the playoffs little more than a week away, Mac ought to avoid upsetting that rhythm. If he needed Barbara Jeanne in the game, he could get her in just as early as required. For illustration, Edith pointed to Mac's hallowed Boston Celtics who had won more championships than any team in history while always employing some sixth man at least as important as the starters.

What clinched the decision to leave Barbara Jeanne as a substitute, though, was Barbara Jeanne herself. She rejected out of hand any plans for her to start. "Preston is struggling now," she explained. "If he loses his spot as a starter, it's going to get worse before it gets better. And we're gonna need him before the state tournament is over. I'm comfortable coming off the bench. I've been doing it all season, and he hasn't. I think things are best the way they are."

And so as he'd done all his life, Mac McIntire listened to the women in his life. And things were best the way they were.

Or at least they were best during three whole weeks of spirited practice sessions, school-wide enthusiasm and generally rising hopes as Broussard destroyed Earl K. Long in its regular season finale, marched through the first two games of the state tournament with easy victories over Istrouma of Baton Rouge and Bolton of Alexandria, snuck past Jesuit in the third round on the shoulders of Donnie Start's best game of the season and almost errorless performances from everyone else, and then set up a state championship match against Mac's old nemeses from Bunkie with a lopsided semi-final win over Shreveport Byrd.

Madness at all these games was now predictable. Mac continued to arrive surrounded by his honor guard of unwed mothers, who then proceeded to occupy the entire row of bleachers directly behind the team bench so as to shield him from lunatics with the bulges of their maternal bellies. Members of the Feminist Organization of Louisiana continued to boo Mac's every gesture and chant for Barbara Jeanne's early participation. But she was playing so well and so much now that a definite edge to the F.O.o. L. protest had been lost. Only the antagonism of the Soldiers for Jesus remained undiluted.

In tribute to Barbara Jeanne's nascent coaching instincts, Preston settled down and contributed a series of performances solid enough to restrict B.J.'s number of minutes in each game. But even with reduced floor time, B.J. continued to ride her hot streak. She played well in every outing with especially fine efforts against Istrouma where she shot six for seven and collected thirteen points in barely two full quarters and in the crucial contest against Jesuit where she found Donnie and Gary with bounce passes underneath all night on her way to thirteen assists, a team high for the season.

So things were best the way they were. The Bruins were slight favorites as they headed into their championship meeting with Bunkie. They were playing their best ball of the year, bolstering God-given talent with hard-won self-confidence. Springtime sprung forth across the South. And as if in the Bruins' honor, the Crescent City burst into a bouquet of redolent bloom. Azaleas and oleanders and sweet olives lit the city with their reds and pinks and soft whites.

But as any good Louisianian knows, spring is also the season most prone to flash floods. And for Mac McIntire, a man born in the eye of a storm, things never seemed to remain placid for long. Dark thunderclouds began to gather on the Sunday following Broussard's semi-final win over Byrd. That's when Cindy Hiller published her feature on Barbara Jeanne in the Weekend

Magazine section of the *States-Tribune*. With Edith there as counsel, B.J. had confided to Ms. Hiller the entire story of her rape, unwanted conception, and lonely pregnancy, and the agonizing subsequent story of her years as loving sister to her daughter. And Hiller had written that story as a profile in courage, Barbara Jeanne's and the whole Bordelon family's. In Hiller's rendition of this tale, the Bordelons fought long odds to provide their child as normal an adolescence as possible. As a result of their loyalty, reluctance to surrender to the temptation of self-pity and consequent willingness to embrace sacrifice, they had emerged as one of the happiest, most emotionally healthy and united families Hiller had ever encountered.

B.J. and her family couldn't have hoped for better treatment than the piece's tone of frank admiration. But the article caused problems for Barbara Jeanne all the same. For the obvious fact that Barbara Jeanne Bordelon was a victim was lost on the Soldiers for Jesus who seemed agitated to unprecedented levels of viciousness by the revelation that B.J., like so many of the women in Mac McIntire's life, was an unwed mother. On his "Old Time Wednesday Hour of Prayer" that week, Elmer Kanter called for all his viewers to join him in repudiating "the decaying morals of a society which would allow an unwed mother to attend public high school classes with those of our children still pure of heart and mind and body." He urged his supporters to write Broussard High School principal Samuel Riggs to express their concern. He implored the faithful to support the labors of the Soldiers for Jesus with a check to be mailed that very night. And he encouraged all who possibly could to journey to Baton Rouge's Assembly Center that very Friday to register their outrage that "an unclean young woman was being allowed to mingle her impure flesh with beardless boys still years from the flower of their manhood."

Elmer's persistent opposition had resulted in at least one remarkable development. Mac, Edith, Sheila, the Bordelon family and the members of the Bruins basketball team were all regular viewers of "The Old Time Wednesday Hour of Prayer." And when they all witnessed Elmer's most recent attempt to deny Barbara Jeanne's participation on the Broussard basketball team, they responded with anger and defiance.

Sheila spat out her summary of Elmer's broadcast thusly: "That putz hasn't been laid in so long he thinks everybody in the world has got sex on the brain."

"We catch passes from her, not make passes at her," Donnie Start assured his parents.

"I've been shaving since I was fourteen," Lyndon Schock warned his snickering younger brother.

Not all the Bruins reacted so blithely, however. And "The Old Time

Wednesday Hour of Prayer" had hardly blinked off the Terminal television when Mac answered the phone and heard Barbara Jeanne offer to sit out the championship game "for the good of the team." Mac replied, of course, that such a proposal was colossal nonsense, but in his anger, fatigue and frustration, he gave it a moment's satanic consideration. He wanted that championship badly. And his wanting gave nurture to vile temptation. Preston seemed to have shaken his slump. Maybe defusing the disruptive impact of the Soldiers for Jesus was worth losing B.J. Of course, Mac cast these blasphemous ruminations away from himself in horror. But yielding to her insistence, he agreed to let Barbara Jeanne make her offer to the whole team. And therein itself, he sinned.

Before practice the next afternoon, on the wrestling mat in the gym's corner which, because of Arnold Larrett's obsession with urinals, had served them all year in place of the Bruin room, Barbara Jeanne suggested sacrificing herself for her teammates. Even as she spoke, Mac wanted to hush her and tell his players, "The best way to make clear one's opposition to the bigots of this world is never to walk away from their attacks, but rather to offer defiance in face of their threats. Our best response to the Soldiers for Jesus is to beat the hell out of Bunkie and in so doing demonstrate that the Broussard Bruins are a team, a team on which every player's contribution counts, a team with one player who happens to be a woman, but first and last, win or lose, a team that stands together, cares for one another and will spare no effort in its pursuit of becoming the very best it can." But instead of interrupting, Mac sat silent. And when B.J. had finished making her offer, and Painton Richard immediately asked what Mac wanted them to do, Mac responded as he'd promised B.J. he would. "Three years ago when I first worked with most of y'all on the junior varsity, I emphasized that the coach is part of the team, too. I'll cast one vote just like each of you."

I can tell you for certain, Mac was courting pandemonium, dangling by the gossamer strands of faith. A moment's temptation now threatened damnation. But his faith was strong and well placed and the Bruins saved his soul.

Danny Waddell spoke up first. "I said it last summer, and she's proved it all year. Cake's one of us. And no one on this team is gonna let a bunch of Jesus freaks turn us against her."

"If B.J. doesn't play, none of us play," Whitt McSeveney said.

Murmurs from the rest of the players echoed John's sentiments. But the crucial comment was offered by Preston who said, "If anyone had a reason to wish B.J. off the team, it'd have to be me because it's me she's coming in for most of the time now. But if anyone ought to resign now, I ought to. Cake's been playing better than me for over a month. And if she weren't a girl and a bunch of assholes hadn't made such a big deal about her, she might be starting right now. All I know is that more than anything in my life I want us to win that state championship, and it helps me a lot to know that if I screw up, we've got B.J. ready to help bail us out."

Preston looked around the mat at his teammates sitting slouched back against the concrete block wall or leaning forward, cross-legged, palms cupped around chins, elbows supported by knees. He was a junior on a team heavy with seniors. He was a newcomer to Broussard who had had the ability to be a starter and the misfortune to go into a late-season slump. He had never tried to take a role of leadership before, and it felt awkward to him that he did so now. He looked down at the soiled mat between his feet and studied the years of sweat encrusted there for some key to all the emotion that swirled inside him, the potent mix of embarrassment at having spoken out in front of his teammates, fierce pride in being a member of a team only one victory from recognition as the state's best and a simmering fear that one night hence his team would be found wanting and he would be the cause.

Then Gary Cashner said to no one in particular, "There aren't nearly enough Soldiers for Jesus or women from F.O.o.L. to stop us. And there certainly aren't enough buttheads from Bunkie."

Gary's remark was greeted with the splash of laughter the stocky Bruin forward expected. But as Mac studied the eyes behind the smiles, he saw the commitment there that was his redemption. As he had concluded about his Lady Bruins a year earlier, he judged about his coed varsity Bruins now: They were ready.

And they needed to be. For in the fresh spring night outside the Broussard gym, it had started, already, to rain.

# CHAPTER FORTY-FIVE

It was still raining the next afternoon when the Bruins boarded their bus for the two-hour ride to Baton Rouge. And it was raining even harder when they arrived amid the madness that was raging all around the LSU Assembly Center.

Was it raining as a sign of God's mysterious determination to frustrate the championship dreams of Mac McIntire once more? Or contrarily, was it raining as a sign of God's displeasure with those who, like Elmer Kanter, dared to speak blasphemy in God's own name? Or was it raining merely because a cool Canadian high-pressure system had collided with a warm moist low-pressure system out of the Gulf?

Whatever the cause, it was raining a steady downpour on those who had gathered outside the Assembly Center to hail the competing teams' arrivals. The majority of those gathered there were either Soldiers for Jesus or their fellow travellers, misguided religious fanatics of one sort or another whom Elmer had managed to stimulate to Bible-thumping activism through his "Old Time Wednesday Hour of Prayer." But a significant number in the crowd were members of the Feminist Organization of Louisiana. And as much as the two sides were gathered to voice opinions about the outcome of the game between Broussard and Bunkie, by the time the Bruins arrived, the two groups had turned much of their sopping sloganeering on each other.

Elmer's group got things going when they momentarily shifted the focus of their campaigning from the Bruins to the group of disapproving women in their midst. It's always been my contention that religious fanatics and other right wingers prefer the violent sport of football to the grace and finesse of basketball, and some evidence of that can be found, I contend, in the inappropriate threat that the Soldiers for Jesus announced to the Feminist Organization of Louisiana when they began to proclaim in unison:

HUT ONE, HUT TWO, HUT THREE, HIKE

LET'S RUN OFF TACKLE AT SOME FEMINIST DYKES.

Not for a solitary instant intimidated by this inept rhyme, the members of F.O.o.L. came right back with:

IF THERE'S AN ACTION THAT WE DESPISE,

IT'S A KNOW-NOTHING'S EFFORT TO PROSELYTIZE.

So Sheila was right after all. The unholy pact could no more survive than the one between Hitler and Stalin. For like Stalin to the massive warehouse of the west, F.O.o.L. had converted to the allied cause. On another day and in another situation they might again deem themselves enemies, but for the day of the state championship basketball game in Barbara Jeanne Bordelon's senior year in high school, the Feminist Organization of Louisiana had marshalled all its forces in support of Broussard and even coach Mac McIntire.

In a situation of soggy contrition, F.O.o.L. president Stephanie Williams explained her organization's turnabout. South Louisiana rainwater dripping from the end of her flawless nose and sputtering with each word from her tastefully tinted lips, she stood on the steps of the Assembly Center in the ceaseless deluge and detailed for New Orleans media representatives the change of heart Cindy Hiller's article had effected on the membership of F.O.o.L.

"We do not think that the whole story has yet surfaced," Stephanie emphasized, making room for whatever retreat she might later deem expeditious, "and we most certainly do not think that Coach McIntire's every decision has been made in the best interests of Louisiana's young female athletes. Yet at the same time, we have been moved to an attitude of support for such efforts as he has made on behalf of Miss Barbara Jeanne Bordelon. And so we've come today to voice that support and to display our opposition to those reactionary groups who have gathered here in the name of sexual discrimination."

Asked what that meant in terms of today's championship game, Stephanie wiped a wet hand across an equally wet forehead, smiled brilliantly and said to the cheers of her soaking supporters: "Go Bruins."

Fredrick Barton

Of course, Stephanie and the members of F.O.o.L. were far outnumbered that dreary evening by the Soldiers for Jesus and other running dog disciples of decorum who took offense at a young woman's sweating in the same vicinity where young men were themselves sweating. And these drenched hundreds of platitude mutterers and standard maintainers were screaming themselves hoarse with such alliterative chants as:

BRUINS BORDELON BROUSSARD BORDELLO

and

MONSTROUS MALEVOLENT MCINTIRE MOLESTER.

This last was the cheer that the Bible pounders offered for Mac's ears as he stepped off the Broussard team bus just behind his honor guard of pregnant women and just ahead of Edith and Sheila, the latter of whom commented, "Who's taking bets on how many of these assholes can spell *malevolent.*"

When the members of the Feminist Organization of Louisiana recognized the contingent from Broussard, they rallied with a cheer of their own, which just for a moment managed to penetrate the din from the Soldiers for Jesus. It went:

GARY AND DANNY, WHILTMAN, AND DON

PRESTON AND BARBARA JEANNE BORDELON

BRUINS OF BROUSSARD YOU'RE ON FIRE

YOU GOT THE COACH NAMED MCINTIRE.

Will wonders never cease?

We'll see. Meanwhile, it's also important to remember that the state championship was to be decided in basketball not cheerleading.

Winning the state championship in basketball indeed required turning deaf ears to all the vicious nonsense which the Soldiers for Jesus concocted to disrupt the Broussard squad. Fortunately, Mac's Bruins were more than equal to that task, their powers of concentration honed season long by the absurd maelstrom which had swirled around them since their first day of practice back in October. By the time the Bruins had hustled through their warm-up drills and the horn to start the contest had blown, the Bruins had put the nonbasketball aspects of the year-long controversy out of their minds save in one symbolic way. And that one way was manifested when the game announcer read off the roster of Broussard's starters. First Preston Whisenhunt, then Danny Waddell, then Donnie Start, and then Whitt McSeveney trotted out to center court. Each raised a clenched fist toward the Broussard fans and shared a series of clasped hands with one another.

But when captain Gary Cashner's name blared out over the public address system, he didn't immediately jog out to take his place among the others. Instead, he reached a massive right hand around the wrist of Barbara Jeanne Bordelon and, just about the time the announcer declared "Head coach of the Broussard Bruins, Marshall 'Mac' McIntire," Gary dragged B.J. toward center court and into the spotlight along with him. And though the announcer was oblivious to her presence there and never called her name, many in the Broussard crowd were sensitive to her electric appearance and responded with a cheer of "Cake, Cake, Cake."

But winning the state basketball championship required more than special concentration, more even than throat-lumping loyalty to a courageous teammate. Foremost, the last night of Barbara Jeanne Bordelon's senior basketball season in high school, it required defeating a team from Bible-belt Bunkie that was supremely well prepared by "old double teamin', simian semen, Jimmie Beamon."

Bunkie's Buccaneers lacked the size to match up well with the Bruin front line. At 6'6", their tallest starter was four full inches shorter than Donnie Start. Their two forwards, both 6'4", gave away an inch or so to Gary and Whitt McSeveney. But anything the Buccaneers lacked in height they made up in bulk, muscle and grit. They had a quicksilver point guard, and his backcourt running mate, 6'2" Billy Jim Smith, was the leading scorer in the state, possessor of a long-range jump shot so deadly that he sometimes seemed to beat opponents all by himself. Mac's strategy for the title, then, was to utilize his height advantage on offense by getting the ball down low, particularly to Donnie. On defense, he'd schooled the Bruins on the need to keep Smith from getting his hands on the basketball. "If he doesn't have it, he can't shoot it," Mac recommended to them. "And if Billy Jim Smith doesn't shoot it, to beat us Bunkie is gonna have to exhibit some offense they've been hiding all year long."

Danny Waddell drew the unenviable assignment of guarding Billy Jim. "You want me to pick him up at mid-court?" Danny had asked Mac.

"I want you to pick him up when he leaves the bench," Mac advised. "And I want you to stay with him until he gets on the bus to go back home."

Mac's game plan was exactly the kind of approach most coaches with his line-up would have employed against Bunkie. But it was a plan with problems caused by two developments Mac couldn't have anticipated: that Smith was going to maneuver Danny into three quick fouls, and that Jimmie Beamon was going to squeeze the high-powered Bruin offense with a defensive strategy that hyperbolically compared to mere double teaming as an atomic bomb compares to a sling shot.

# CHAPTER FORTY-SIX

The tone for the game and the Bruins' instant difficulty was established immediately after Broussard nabbed a 2-0 lead when Donnie tipped off to Whitt who hit Gary on the right side who found Preston all alone underneath for a cripple. Bunkie's howl of unearthly tenacity was sounded by Billy Jim Smith. Billy Jim, Mac noticed, bore an uncanny resemblance to Barbara Jeanne Bordelon. They had similar coloration and the same angular features. But the resemblance resided more in the way they moved than in their facial characteristics. Both were blessed with a special athlete's fluid physical grace. In a disturbing way, though, Billy Jim seemed Barbara Jeanne's reflection from the dark side, less her male self than her evil counterpart. He characteristically held his head cocked downwards so that his face was partially hidden in shadow. And his wolfish jaw and darting, predator's eyes collaborated in a leer of ugly smugness that Mac had never seen on Barbara Jeanne's shining face, forever aglow with modesty and generosity.

After Preston's opening basket, Bunkie came down the floor with Danny on Billy Jim like snow on the South Pole. Only the intensity backfired, and Danny quickly picked up a foul when Billy Jim scraped him into a pick from one of the Buccaneer forwards. Lupine Billy Jim made the jumper in the process and the free throw which followed. And then Bunkie fell back into the defense that Jimmie Beamon had designed especially for Broussard. It was a triangle and two, a derivation of the famous box and chaser which has been thrown at star offensive players for years. The purpose of this mixed man-to-man and zone defense was both to put maximum pressure on the best Bruin players and to neutralize Broussard's power inside. Thus Gary Cashner drew man-to-man coverage wherever he went, and so did Donnie Start. Furthermore, with the one-high, two-low design of the Buccaneer players in the zone, Donnie found himself effectively double teamed whenever he set up in his customary low post. The first time down the floor Beamon's design so disconcerted Donnie that he traveled when Danny got the ball to him on a nice bounce pass.

And so the struggle began, Bunkie moved out to 5-2 and then 7-2 after Preston had a pass snatched away when he tried to force the ball down low. Mac called time and sketched what Bunkie was doing on the portable slate he kept by his side at all games. He pointed out to his players that the weakness in Beamon's design was at the perimeter. The Bruin guards should be able to get wide open shots, Mac told them. The problem, though, as Bunkie built its lead to 14-6 and then 20-10, was that Danny had never been that great a jump shooter and Preston's late-season slump returned as quickly as it had temporarily disappeared. Only four baskets by Gary kept the game from turning into a farce by the end of the first quarter. Donnie was 0 for 3, Whitt 0 for 2. Danny was 0 for 3 and committed his third foul just before the horn sounded ending the first quarter, and Preston's opening lay-up was his only basket in four attempts.

Mac had no choice but to go to Barbara Jeanne. So seemingly desperate were Broussard circumstances, though, that the Bruin crowd, instead of displaying its usual enthusiasm, barely acknowledged B.J.'s early appearance. The Bunkie supporters took notice, however. And as B.J. ran out to start the second quarter some loud mouth in the stands stood up and foghorned: "I thought Broussard just played like a bunch of pussies. My God, some of them *are* pussies."

The coarseness of that taunt lit a fire under the Bruins and got the shocked Broussard rooters back into the game. But fevered play and more vocal support could not instantly overcome a ten-point deficit, especially not against a team prepared by Jimmie Beamon, who seemed to be waiting for Barbara Jeanne's entry into the game the way Babe Ruth waited for a fast ball right down the pike. The Bruins again controlled the tip and converted it into a basket. But when Bunkie came down on their offensive end, it was with B.J., in the game for Danny, guarding Billy Jim Smith. Smith stutter dribbled Barbara Jeanne lower and lower on the right side. She hounded him like a sheepdog nipping at the heels of her herd's waywards. But he kept himself between her and the ball, and when he'd worked himself within five feet of the basket, Billy Jim sprung his height advantage on her, turned and banked the ball in over her. This strategy was the one the Easton Eagles had used on Barbara Jeanne so successfully early in the season. Billy Jim's ball control had worked the clock to under six minutes, and just as surely rebuilt Bunkie's lead to ten.

Generally speaking, Mac's strength as a coach resided in a set of characteristics that included unusual patience. Because he didn't try to intimidate his players, because he instructed them with positive reinforcement rather than negative, because he didn't employ the quick hook that punished a mistake with a trip to the bench, Mac got far more out of his material than did most coaches. On rare occasions, in game situations, though, that great patience could switch from advantage to drawback. Mac sometimes waited a beat too long to change a tactic that was being exploited by an opponent. He was not guilty, however, of such a failing today. Billy Jim's shot had barely settled into the net when Mac was on his feet signaling for time. In the huddle he ordered the Bruins out of their person-to-person defense and into a two-three zone on Bunkie's next possession. He also reminded them that the Bunkie defense should lead to open jumpers at the 15-18 foot range. The warning buzzer sounded, and the Bruins thrust their hands together as always. Just before they broke back to the floor, Preston looked around at the players about to return to the court. "Let's get it to B.J.," he said. "You light 'em up, Cake, one candle at a time."

They did get it to Barbara Jeanne, and she proved that the hot streak she'd been riding was no fluke. She started lighting them up, one candle at a time. And when she missed, Gary Cashner, effective double team or no, was like a man possessed underneath. Together they gradually brought the Bruins back.

Those in the crowd who had not seen Barbara Jeanne play before were agog that she was so good, those that were there to cheer the Bruins were in a frenzy that she might show the way to athletic salvation. But despite a night by B.J. that any player dreams of, when the confidence on every shot starts at the heart, flows through the fingertips and feels the ball all the way to the basket, Bunkie was too good for B.J. just to outscore all by herself. And she carried defensive liabilities that offset, at least partially, her offensive assets. With Beamon's determination to post her low if ever she had to pay defense one-on-one, the Bruins were confined to a zone. And a jump shooter like Billy Jim Smith yearns for nothing in the whole world more than a zone to shoot over and bunch of selfless teammates to feed him the ball. And he didn't fail them. The Bruins had stopped the onslaught and battled their way into the game. But Bunkie clung to its lead. The score at half was 32-24. At the end of three quarters the Bruins had crept closer but still trailed 43-37.

As the final period began, Mac made a crucial move. He put Danny in for Whitt and switched the Bruins into a box and one. With the other Bruins in a rectangular zone, Danny's job was to chase Billy Jim from locker room to parking lot. The strategy paid instant dividends. Three straight times Danny either denied Smith the ball or harried him into a poor shot. On the other end, B.J. catapulted home one of her patented behind-the-head jumpers, found Gary underneath when a Bunkie forward tried to jump out on her next time down and watched Preston get into the act with a nineteen footer of his own to knot the score at 43 all with four minutes remaining.

Beamon frantically demanded time. And the LSU Assembly Center leapt headlong into bedlam. The thundercrack of emotion inside the athletic complex was matched by the raging storm that hammered down upon it outside. Conjuring black magic amid the tornado of noise, Jimmie Beamon was a demonic Prospero diverting the tempest to his own designs. The taunts started as soon as the teams returned to the floor. Game-long, as was the usual practice, the competing players had said little or nothing to each other. But as he moved by her to take up his position for the inbounds pass, Billy Jim Smith said to Barbara Jeanne, "I heard you had a kid." Billy Jim's face registered no precisely describable emotion. He didn't give himself away with a smirk. But his demeanor was undeniably satanic all the same.

Barbara Jeanne made no reply, but Danny Waddell, who overheard the comment, told the Buccaneer guard to shut his face and play basketball. Positioning himself for a break to the ball, Billy Jim backed his way up against Barbara Jeanne until his butt was against her hip. In the box and one Danny was right in Billy Jim's face. And thus it was to Danny rather than B.J. that Billy Jim said in his hill country drawl, "But what I caint figger, see, is how some dyke got her knocked up."

The heels of Danny's hands shot into Billy Jim's chest and sent him sprawling over backwards with such force that B.J. was knocked down too and trapped underneath the flailing Bunkie star whose rampaging elbow bruised a breast and puffed her cheek. The other Bunkie players immediately surrounded Danny, but Gary Cashner jumped into their midst and gave them pause to ponder the disadvantages of violence. But Danny and the Bruins were hurt anyway, however, when the referees, ignorant of the provocation, whistled him for a personal foul and two technical fouls and kicked him out of the game.

With the consciencelessness of Mephistopheles, Billy Jim Smith climbed off Barbara Jeanne and converted on all four free throws. Broussard trailed 47-43 and was back in deep trouble. The situation worsened moments later when the Bruins advanced the ball over mid-court and found Bunkie in a new defense. Finally convinced that his triangle and two was unworkable with Barbara Jeanne hitting the easy shots that setup provided her, Beamon had switched the Buccaneers into a sagging man-to-man with which he hoped to get a hand in B.J.'s face and still pressure Broussard's inside game. Determined not to panic, the Bruins worked the ball around carefully until they sprung

Whitt McSeveney for an open twelve footer. But Whitt, who'd just come in for Danny, was cold. He missed. And before the Bruins got settled into their 2-3 zone, Billy Jim Smith had rammed in still another long-range jumper. The Bruins were down by six with under three minutes to play.

Mac called time out for what he figured might be the last team huddle of Barbara Jeanne Bordelon's senior season. If the Bruins didn't score on their upcoming possession, Bunkie was sure to go into a delay game, and Broussard might never get the ball back. Mac sent Painton Richard in for Donnie, trading Painton's quickness and defensive mobility for Donnie's size. Screaming to be heard over the crowd, Mac ordered his offense to set picks for Barbara Jeanne and for B.J. to look inside for Gary. On defense, the Bruins were to go back to the box and one. Preston was going to have to replace Danny on Billy Jim. And after every Broussard basket Mac wanted the zone press, again with Preston taking Danny's spot behind Barbara Jeanne. The horn sounded, the Bruins joined their hands with Mac's and went back on the floor to discover their destiny.

Painton inbounded the ball to B.J. who brought it up. Across mid-court she hit Preston out top on the left side. He worked the ball down low to Whitt who kicked it right back out. Starting from the low post, Gary came out to seventeen feet on the right side and set his pick as Painton rolled under. Preston gave the ball back to Barbara Jeanne, and she dribbled her man toward Gary's screen. The scrape worked, but Bunkie had become convinced B.J. could shoot and switched. And Gary rolled. And B.J. found him. And the margin was cut back to four. There were two minutes fifteen seconds to play.

The Broussard press did not produce a steal and the Bruins fell back into the box and one, Preston draped all over Billy Jim like chocolate sauce on ice cream. But Bunkie wasn't looking to shoot, and they were in no hurry not to do it. They ran off twenty seconds then thirty. In no mood to let the game wither away, Gary fouled intentionally. The Bunkie player hit the front end of the one and one but missed the second. Whitt rebounded. There was 1:20 to play when the Bruins got into their offensive set. They were down five. Again they worked the pick and roll. B.J. curled in the bounce pass and Gary jammed it. 50-47. Fifty-five seconds left.

Bunkie inbounded and again broke the Bruin press. Playing kamikaze defense, Preston fouled Billy Jim the first time he touched the ball. There were forty seconds remaining, and the state's best shooter was at the line. Broussard's fortunes seemed about as dark as the raging night outside. Billy Jim sank the first foul shot to push Bunkie's lead back to four and then the second to make the margin a seemingly insurmountable 52-47. The Bruins hustled the ball up court and tried to work the pick and roll a third straight time, but this time

Bunkie shut down the passing lane. B.J. went up for her jumper with Billy Jim Smith's hand jabbing like a Nazi salute toward her swollen face. Had she employed a conventional release, Billy Jim would have blocked her shot and in the process broken the back of the Bruin rally and thereby the hearts of Broussard fans everywhere. But like her mentor's, Barbara Jeanne's release came from behind her head, beyond the reach of Billy Jim's thrusting arm. The ball spun off her finger tips into a perfect arc and through the nylon cord of the goal. There were only twenty seconds left but the Bruins were back within three, 52-49. The Assembly Center rocked with a delirious tidal wave of sound.

Freelancing a wrinkle of his own to Mac's zone press, Preston picked up Billy Jim immediately after the basket, and his double team with Barbara Jeanne almost prevented Bunkie from getting the ball into play. A Bunkie forward saved a five-second violation, however, by hustling back to receive the inbounds pass. With Painton swarming all over him, he gave it instantly back to the inbounding point guard who was Preston's responsibility. But Preston had worked himself out of position doubling on Billy Jim, and Barbara Jeanne was a step late covering for him. The clock had ticked down to twelve as the Bunkie point guard began his drive, to ten as he crossed mid-court with B.J. still chasing him. A step inside the mid-court line, as the clocked blinked to 00:09, Barbara Jeanne, oblivious to skinned elbows and knees, launched herself in a dive. She got only a fingertip on it but pushed it from the Bunkie player's control and into the hands of Gary Cashner. Gary took two left-handed dribbles to clear himself and then found Whitt open on the left side short of mid-court. 00:07. B.J. was back on her feet, the energy of the screaming crowd in her very soul. Whitt hit Painton on the break right at center court. B.J. was flying in the lane on the right side, Gary pounding down on the left. Waiting for them at the free-throw line was Billy Jim Smith, all-state in basketball, arrogance and sexism and just about to make the most incredible mistake of his life. The clock said 00:05. Painton hit Gary. Gary touch passed it directly back. Top of the key. 00:04. Painton hit B.J. slicing for the basket. And Billy Jim, confident he could block her shot picked her up. One dribble. She left her feet. She soared. She pumped. She sailed under the goal for a reverse layup that caught Billy by surprise. The ball caromed high off the glass and fell through the basket. And Billy Jim Smith, who should have just left her alone, was whistled for a foul that was to send Barbara Jeanne Bordelon to the free throw line with a chance to tie the score. The game clock read 00:02.

Jimmie Beamon called time to give B.J. a concentration-shattering minute to think about what faced her. But there was no doubt in a single mind in that arena that Barbara Jeanne would make good. She was the invincible devil incarnate to her astounded enemies. And she was an invincible Saint Joan to her legions of fans who stood now as she came to the sidelines and hailed her as if with one voice, "Cake, Cake, Cake." Students and parents and teachers, Broussard Principal Samuel Riggs who didn't even know why, unwed mothers and members of the F.O.o.L., teammates, Edith Jenkins and Sheila McIntire, and across the way, squeezed to the fringes of the contingent of Soldiers for Jesus, even a porcine Helen Donalds raised her contrite contralto to join all the others in the thunder that rumbled, "Cake, Cake, Cake."

"Cake, Cake, Cake. Cake, Cake, Cake."

# CHAPTER FORTY-SEVEN

Through the entire time-out the crowd continued to chant, "Cake, Cake, Cake," in a tumultuous serenade to Barbara Jeanne. Mac was so hoarse by now that he could barely make himself heard. But it didn't really matter much. If B.J. made the free throw, the game would go into overtime with the momentum all on Broussard's side. If she missed, Mac McIntire would be a bridesmaid once again, and all his players would graduate without experiencing the indelible thrill of a championship.

Still, Mac continued to coach to the end. He substituted Donnie for Painton to increase his rebounding strength. Then he pulled his team into a tight circle around him and strained to make himself heard. He reminded the Bruins that there were still two seconds on the clock, that Gary and Donnie should concentrate on getting good position once B.J. released the ball because even if she missed, the game could still be won if one of them could rebound and quickly follow it home.

The warning buzzer sounded. Mac stuck his hand into the center of the circle of his players, and all the Bruins thrust theirs on top. And the din in the Assembly Center actually intensified.

As the players began to make their way toward the deciding free throw line, Mac pulled Barbara Jeanne to him, his arm about her shoulders, his face up against hers to whisper a last piece of advice. Across the court, dirty-minded members of the Soldiers for Jesus declared he was kissing her. "Take a deep breath and relax, kid," he said. "'Cause in the grand scheme of things, it doesn't matter a lick whether you make this shot or not."

B.J. smiled and turned her own lips to Mac's ear, a hand laid flat against his opposite cheek. "Coach," she said, "if I never make another shot as long as I live, I want to make this one. For you." Then, as if in slow motion, she turned away from Mac to join her teammates on the court. And he reached out, as he had not in over a year, and swatted her on the fanny.

And the crowd continued to demand, "Cake, Cake, Cake."

Everyone in the arena was standing, the fans, the players, the coaches, the trainers, the statisticians from both schools, even the radio announcers. Edith Jenkins and Sheila McIntire climbed from the stands behind Mac and came to stand beside him, one on either side, their arms intertwined around his waist. On the court, one Bruin after another stepped up to Barbara Jeanne, who waited for the ball inside the foul circle, and clasped both of her hands in his.

When the players had all returned to their positions and set their feet along the black lines which separated the golden varnished floor from the purple paint of the lane, one of the referees blew his whistle, spun the ball backwards into the air, and let it bounce twice against the floor before he flipped it to B.J. She caught it in both her hands, let it fall to the floor and dribbled it once with her right. She slid her right foot forward, the toe of her sneaker an inch behind the foul stripe. The dull orange ball dangling loosely in splayed fingers, she took two deep breaths, the second stretching her lungs till they seemed to press into the hollow at the base of her neck. Again she dribbled quickly, once, twice, three times. She raised the ball to her lips like a chalice. And then in one practiced motion she lifted the ball for her shot, first chest high; then, rocking her weight in smooth rhythm from the toe of her right foot, to its heel, to the outside of her balancing left foot, she swung the ball over her head, above it, behind it and slightly below.

As her arm began its move forward, thousands of Broussard rooters seemed to catch their collective breath all at once, and despite the continued screaming of the Bunkie fans, the arena was plunged into an instant of comparative quiet so remarkable that afterwards some of those in attendance claimed to remember the rain pounding on the Assembly Center roof and a crack of thunder at the very moment the ball spun from Barbara Jeanne's fingertips. But others maintained that detecting any such noise from inside that structure was unlikely, that instead what people heard was a sudden explosion of sound from the momentarily silent Broussard crowd, who realized that the stroke of reckoning had arrived.

The release was smooth, the ball rising from off the insides of B.J.'s index and middle fingers into an arching parabola with just a touch of controlling backspin. But, dear God, perhaps indeed there had been a distracting jolt of thunder, and perhaps Barbara Jeanne had been among those who heard it and had flinched ever so slightly. An eerie piercing whistle seemed to sound, as if from heaven, a keening sign of divine regret. The ball settled toward the goal on perfect line. But it was a tad short. It hit the front rim, bounded to the back rim, up against the glass, and to the front rim again. And fell away into pandemonium.

The clock was an instant late starting, jarred into motion by the roar that filled the Assembly Center, a roar which was less like a cacophony of human sound than one created by a horrible force of nature, a hurricane's tidal wave slamming a shoreline, tossing trees and cars and dwellings about like so many stirred motes in a shaft of sunlight. Oblivious to that wrenching, crashing, wailing sound, Mac's Bruins were a blur of motion. His coaching, even at the end, had not gone for naught. Gary Cashner knifed to the basket for the rebound, only partially screened away by the Bunkie forward whose sluggish movement into the lane suggested the daze of unsuspected and unearned reprieve. With his right hand sweeping around his opponent, Gary swiped at the ball, knocking it high against the glass and into a carom far to the left of the goal. The Bunkie forward's late-starting momentum carried him a step farther to the right side of the lane, and Gary slid left behind him for one last tip. He went up in gut-constricting panic that the clock would deny him, and thus didn't dare the time to cradle the ball but rather slapped it with a straining left hand back toward the basket. The fateful horn sounded its requiem. The ball bounced once more against the glass and on the far side of the rim.

And fell into the irrelevant hands of Donnie Start who waited there for a chance that came too late.

At the Bruin bench Mac stood with his arms raised in disbelief. A stride inside the faithless foul line, Barbara Jeanne knelt one knee on the purple paint of the lane and cupped her hands around her forehead, her fingers twined into the wet curls of her brown hair. Along with Gary and Edith and Sheila and thousands of others, Mac and B.J. stared for a moment of frozen eternity at a scoreboard which read Bunkie 52 Broussard 51.

And at a clock that said 00:00.

EPILOGUE

# CHAPTER FORTY-EIGHT

Now I'm fully well aware that the events I have just narrated were not at all what you wanted to discover was the end of Barbara Jeanne Bordelon's career as a high school basketball player. I know because I identify completely with your dismay.

In some future, more reflective mood, it may matter what happened to Barbara Jeanne and Mac and all the others in the aftermath of B.J.'s missed free throw at the end of Broussard's championship game against Bunkie. But at the moment it makes no difference that in the long run Barbara Jeanne and everything she stood for were vindicated. It makes no difference that she had actually broken the sex barrier, had actually competed an entire season as a varsity basketball player, had competed, I must emphasize, with distinction.

No, to you, I'm sure, as to me, for this moment at least, it seems not to matter that Mac would recover from Barbara Jeanne's last game and would go on to establish an exemplary record as a high school basketball coach, ecstatic to live in a world in which there is always a next game even if it didn't come until next year, because that next game, whoever the opponent, always provided a next challenge, to win with pride or to lose with dignity, but most of all an opportunity to prepare with diligence and play with joy.

Yes, these ashes in our collective mouths keep us, now, from tasting what was the undeniable victory of Barbara Jeanne Bordelon's high school basketball career. The prohibition against women competing against men was gradually lifted in sport after sport, and with time, more and more got the training they needed in their youth, both the coaching guidance and the drill, and more and more stepped lively along the rocky trail of intergender competition that Barbara Jeanne, the Jackie Robinson of her sex, had blazed.

It even makes little difference to us at this moment that Barbara Jeanne's athletic example led to a boom of popular interest in women's sports where silly, discriminatory rules like those for six-woman, half-court basketball that Barbara Jeanne had labored under as a sophomore and junior, or best-of-three-set instead of best-of-five-set tennis matches, or marathonless women's track meets, eventually atrophied in shame and finally disappeared from our midst to the same curio shelf of history where black people were obligated to drink from separate water fountains and ride only in the rear of public conveyances.

We acknowledge the significance of all these things, of course. But we are comforted by them only intellectually. And the intellect can contribute little balm for our emotional distress at how often right does not prevail. As Donnie Start repeatedly spun an obsolescent shot off the backboard and through a belatedly receptive nylon webbing, the jubilation of our opponents scored us too deeply. In the stands, the Soldiers for Jesus, their hands thrust heavenward in triumph, have jitterbugged their delirium at our defeat. Worse, we have heard Billy Jim Smith bellow with glee to a gesticulating Jimmie Beamon, "I knew that bull dyke bitch would blow it, Coach."

Worse still, we have seen odious Elmer Kanter lick his smug lips and announce to a sycophantic follower with sebaceous self-righteousness, "Our job now will be to speak for the healing of wounds. The merciless will gorge themselves upon the young woman's failure. But her inability to respond adequately to the situation in which she was placed was not of her own making. As God so ordained, so still it remains: the female of the flesh is the weaker vessel."

I know you join me in fantasies of leveling the son of a bitch with a sucker punch square in the center of his supercilious face.

And don't we wish the same for Arnold Larrett when he turned to an intimidated Broussard teacher and remarked with a flicking tongue of superior disgust, "I just knew that impertinent little cunt would choke."

But such reveries of violence lack all capacity to address the last instance of our dismay when we heard that perfidous teacher, who only an instant earlier had lent his voice to the throng chanting, "Cake, Cake, Cake," respond with a backsliding heart, "I guess you're right, Arnold. Unlike a man, a woman just can't handle prime-time pressure. Damn you, Barbara Jeanne Bordelon. Damn you. You just cost us the fucking state championship."

Yes, the ache of that missed free throw and Gary Cashner's heartbreakingly failed effort to control the rebound and alchemize our astonished despair into precipitous rapture is too great, for now, to be eased by the possession of mere information about existential perseverance and future sociological progress. For the heart craves victory, not solace in defeat.

My reaction to this story is analogous to the way I would feel if I knew for certain that late in the twenty-first century, in the lifetimes of my very own grandchildren, selfishness, ruthlessness and exploitation would disappear from the American workplace. I love my offspring and would naturally be pleased that sometime after my own unavoidable demise they would be spared a condition of employment that plagues those who must labor in our own age. But such cosmic reassurance would provide me little solace that this day and the next and for my foreseeable future, I must earn my living in the employ of people who abuse my talents, conspire to frustrate my ambitions and derive perverted delight that they wield the power to subject me to purposeless humiliation. For the characters in this narrative, as in my own life, I yearn for justice. And in that yearning I am confident you join me.

I hope you'll believe me, then, when I confide, that as your narrator, I would not have ended Barbara Jeanne Bordelon's story this way. But a narrator's job is to tell the story as he or she knows it. The narrator relates, but an author translates and only God creates. And the author's translation of *Courting Pandemonium* embraces Aristotle's constraint to make his art imitate life. In the life our author knows, the fate of all men is ultimate oblivion. And in such a world, he sadly submits, the heart is inevitably denied and there can be no such things as happy endings.

# CHAPTER FORTY-NINE

But as Blanche DuBois, another Southern loser once said, "Sometimes—there's God—so quickly."

And in the world of *Courting Pandemonium* just as in the world in which you and I live, miracles do occur. God prescribes them; authors transcribe them; narrators dutifully describe them.

Those of you with particularly acute hearing may remember a whistle which seemed to sound in the space of time between the release of Barbara Jeanne's errant free throw and Gary Cashner's frenzied attempts to save the game with a tipped rebound. Well that whistle did sound. And it came not from heaven—at least not directly—but rather from the instrument in the lips of a referee. The cyclone's roar of the crowd prohibited any of the players on the court and most of the people in the stands from realizing that the referee had spotted a violation and was trying to stop play. Thus Gary attempted his heroics thinking they would have counted had he managed them. But they wouldn't have. For the referee had spotted Billy Jim Smith with his right sneaker trespassing on the black stripe of the three-second lane. Desperate to make up for the arrogant idiocy of his needless foul, Billy Jim was determined to put himself between Barbara Jeanne and the goal, so that should she miss, she'd come nowhere near any long rebound that might bounce in her direction. But in his single-minded concentration on blocking B.J. out, Billy Jim slid his foot across the line an instant before Barbara Jeanne released the ball. And that required that the clock be reset to 00:02 and that Barbara Jeanne be awarded another chance to tie the score.

Well, you can imagine the incredible confusion that ensued as the referee attempted to communicate his call to game officials, to the opposing coaches and players, and to the crowd. Since the noise in the Assembly Center had precluded any of those from hearing his whistled decision at the time he made it, all presumed that the game was over and that the Buccaneers of Bunkie had thieved victory. The Bunkie players and fans had already gone into gyrations of celebration. Mac and the Bruins and Broussard's supporters had already collapsed into depression. Thus both sides had to be jerked back from their emotional extremities to a renewed state of mere anxious agitation.

But the referee had made his call, and despite the near violent incredulity of the Bunkie backers, he stuck by it. The Bruins fans were so thunderstruck by the divine intercession of a second chance that their voices were temporarily stolen away, and they sat like mutes while the Bunkie fans railed at Barbara Jeanne as she was marched again to the line and again yoked with the burden of an entire season's and even an entire gender's dreams.

And this time launched her gently rotating foul shot into the wonder of redemption.

The game was only tied, of course, but the apocalyptic eruption of reborn voices from the Broussard faithful was to Mac and Sheila and Edith and Barbara Jeanne and Gary and all the other Bruins like a canticle from a celestial choir. And as if directed by the guiding breath of angels, the game, in the three-minute overtime, was no contest. Damnation and election had been determined elsewhere. The force of the tempest had been turned, and it blew now away from the footsteps of iniquity and toward the paths of true righteousness. The Bruins' press blew Bunkie down like a prairie tornado obliterates a shanty town brothel.

Donnie knocked the opening tip to Gary who whipped it to B.J. who flicked it to Preston for a layup and the lead. Barbara Jeanne deflected the pursuant inbounds pass which was chased down by Painton near mid-court. Preston got it to Whitt on the left side who found B.J. right of the key who fed Gary thundering home on a trailer. The big Bruin captain left his feet one step inside the free-throw line and went up for a slammer that seemed to start at his ankles and scrape the Assembly Center rafters before exploding through the net like one of the bolts of burning sulfur that atomized Gomorrah.

And so it went. Bunkie scored not a solitary point in the overtime, while the Bruins, in a display of otherworldly shooting, canned eight straight shots.

The response of the Broussard crowd was almost religious. And through it all, until the scoreboard carved Broussard 68, Bunkie 52 into history, the fans in the Assembly Center sang a seraphic anthem of atonement whose syncopated chorus forever echoed, "Cake, Cake, Cake." To a person, those rooting for the Bruins experienced a sensation akin to conversion. And their sinful despair was vaporized into the unfathomable grace of salvation.

# CHAPTER FIFTY

So as you can see, there are two endings to the story of *Courting Pandemonium*, the latter decidedly more mystical and satisfying than the former. What Aristotle might have remarked about an art that imitates not life, but afterlife, I cannot say.

In fact, *Courting Pandemonium* has more than two endings. There are countless endings, a minimum of one for every character who appears in these pages. But no human storyteller, save perhaps Tom Stoppard, knows most of those endings, certainly neither your narrator nor your author.

But I have been apprised of the following:

Bunkie basketball coach Jimmie Beamon never again led a team into the state playoffs.

Star Bunkie player Billy Jim Smith was arrested in a point-shaving scandal while in college. He did five years at Angola State Prison and was never heard of again.

One-time *States Tribune* report Cindy Hiller became an editor for *Ms. Magazine*.

In her mid-fifties, Barbara Jeanne Bordelon's discrimination-suit attorney, Karen Lutze, was appointed by a Democratic president to the United States Supreme Court. In a sort of reversal of the Earl Warren Rule, by which a Republican appointee came to head our nation's most liberal court, Lutze voted as a consistent conservative on all the major issues of her day.

Helen Donalds, Mac McIntire's infamous high school prom date, continued her life-long ideological wavering. For a while she was a Moonie, a while longer a Hare Krishna. Later she joined a fictive radical feminist group called the Ellen Jamesians who protested the continued presence of rape in the world by chopping off their tongues. Sometime later still, she joined an idealistic corp of volunteers who disbursed the food purchased by international rock musicians for third-world famine victims. In addition to their allotment of canned rations, Helen frequently pressed into the hands of her emaciated clients, impassioned hand-written notes begging forgiveness for once having claimed that her only son was fathered by a New Orleans high school basketball coach.

Arnold Larrett retired from public education in a snit when he was passed over for promotion to succeed Sam Riggs as Broussard principal when the latter retired. He went into private business where he found great difficulty getting people to work for him.

Joan Teo was awarded the post Larrett coveted so dearly and helped turn Broussard into one of the finest high schools in the nation, its students regularly recruited by such universities as Harvard, Yale and Princeton.

Stephanie Williams was impregnated by a rich corporate lawyer, who reluctantly agreed to marry her. She never finished her Ph.D. and, as a matter of fact, never held a full-time job. In her late thirties, however, she wrote an autobiographical novel which not only garnered nice reviews but also, after a handsome sale of the film rights, provided her enough financial independence that she divorced her husband, moved to Paris, and was occasionally mentioned in *People* magazine as having attended the same party as Mick Jagger or Jacqueline Kennedy Onassis.

Mary Masters recorded two gold records including a re-release of "Shake, Rattle 'n' Roll."

Olga Jorgensen became a New Orleans celebrity as host of a local TV cooking show.

Peggy Simons took to wearing her hair long and blousie and turned her lean leggy frame into hundred thousand dollar annual salaries as a New York fashion model.

Gary Cashner won a basketball scholarship to U.C.L.A. where he helped revive a program that had lapsed into decay after the retirement of John Wooden. He was signed out of college by the Boston Celtics and joined Larry Byrd and Kevin McHale in leading that franchise to several championships. When his playing days ended, Gary became a liberal United States senator. At the time of his death, in his early eighties, he had earned the highest life-time rating from the Americans for Democratic Action.

Elmer Kanter was arrested for fraud in connection with misappropriation of funds contributed to his Soldiers for Jesus. In prison he wrote *Souls on Heist*, an expose of his TV ministry he hoped would make him rich by the time he finished he sentence. He was never able to find a publisher and was subsequently converted to orthodox Islam by a black prison evangelist. When he got out of prison, he emigrated to Afghanistan.

Eventually and sadly, the New Orleans home for unwed mothers was closed due to a municipal budget crunch. In the aftermath of its demise, however, unwed mothers found refuge and succor at a private residence on the river-side corner of Oak and Leake, where Sheila had knitted them a black-humored banner of greeting that affirmed:

UNLIKE OTHER WORLDS

WHERE THE CONDITION APPLIES TO ALL

IN THE WORLD OF UNWED MOTHERS

ONLY THE BEST OF US

ARE TERMINAL CASES

Until the day it closed its doors, Sheila McIntire continued to work at the home for unwed mothers, as a sewing instructor and later as home administrator. After the home shut down, her life remained precisely the same except that for the first time in some years her residence was once again the place of her employment. Until the day of her death at the ripe age of ninety, Sheila continued to contend that she had more sex than anyone she knew. She never confided, even to her closest loved ones, the identity of her partner or partners. All I can tell you is that she wasn't lying.

Edith Jenkins, as I revealed pages ago, became New Orleans' first female City Councilperson. Her first two sallies on the office of mayor were aborted by her association with the controversial characters and events who gravitated to Sheila and Mac McIntire. Eventually, though, she did become the city's first female chief executive, and she did so without ever, before or after, altering her official residence. When she died, at a very old age, she stipulated in her will that she be buried in a T-shirt that read:

ANOTHER TERMINAL CASE OF UNWED MOTHERHOOD

Shortly after her graduation from high school, Barbara Jeanne Bordelon began to list the Terminal as her life-long residence too. She went on to star at UNO as a Lady Privateer basketballer and, though she never again formally competed against men, she was the leading scorer on America's Olympic basketball team which captured the gold medal against a squad of Russians many suspected were frightfully short in the category of female genes. After a spectacular career in high school coaching, when Barbara Jeanne gave a deathbed interview to a reporter seventy years her junior, she claimed that the most exciting sporting events she'd ever participated in, were those staged on a blacktop half court in the rear of the renovated old railroad station where she'd lived the great majority of her life.

And Mac McIntire, of course, lived happily ever after. Surrounded by the women he loved, he continued to believe in perseverance and miracle. Because he never married, and because neither Edith Jenkins nor Barbara Jeanne Bordelon ever married either, people in New Orleans always gossiped about the nature of their relationships. About this there is much that I might say. But I am directed to concede the last words to our hero's mom. "Like the Creator who made him," Sheila observed cryptically, "Mac has managed to have his Cake and Edith, too."